Love Thy Sister...
Watch Thy Back

Love Thy Sister, Watch Thy Back

Denise Campbell

ISBN # 0-9742269-1-2
Published by Universal Write Publications
PO Box 1432
Valley Stream, N.Y. 11582
212-592-4523
www.UniversalWritePublications.com

Type setting and the cover jacket of
this book was designed by
Jiggly House Of Design.
To find out how we can help you
promote your product please visit us
on the web at
www.JigglyHouseOfDesign.com
or call us at
718-421-6262

Cover photographs and book promotion materials by:
Derrick Slack of www.Dslack.com
Email Derrick@Dslack.com
&
Calvin Grace of www.CGMediaPublications.com
Email: CGMediaPub@aol.com

OTHER BOOKS BY THE AUTHOR

Spanish Eyes

A full length novel available at Barnes & Noble,
Amazon.com and everywhere fine books are sold
www.UniversalWrite.com

Ebony Passion
Spoken Word

A collection of poetry
ISBN: 0-9742269-0-4
www.UniversalWrite.com

Acknowledgements

Working on this book has been one of the most rewarding experiences of my life. It has helped me to make contacts, strengthen and build friendships and relationships that I will forever be thankful for and consider lifelong foundations in my life.

First, as always I would like to count my blessings and humble myself before my God. Walking by faith gave me the strength to press forward. I will always get on my knees in awesome reminder of God's glory and thank him for counting me among his greatest creations.

I would also like to thank Dexter Brathwaite of Black Print Publishing for believing in me and for opening the doors of opportunity to help make my dreams into reality.

My Team, Charles Perkins Webmaster (www.Graphic-Effects.com), Calvin Grace Publicist (www.CGMediaPublications.com) and Johnny Etienne Graphic Designer (www.JigglyHouseOfDesign.com). You are the ones who really did the hard work to get me out there. Your help, support and friendship mean the world to me. Your footprints have been crystallized in my heart forever.

Special thanks To Tee C Royal founder of RAW Sistaz Book club. Your help and support came though right on time. You added glitter to my star so it shone a little brighter. Thanks again from the bottom of my heart.

Table Of Content

Prologue

"Help!" She screamed hoping someone would rush to her aide.

"Help! You mother fuckers come get me out of this shit you son-of-a-bitches." She demanded again as she struggled to break herself loose from the restraints that held her firmly to the hospital bed.

She yelled and screamed and no one would come to her rescue. She worked herself into frenzy until fatigue overcame her. She still struggled lightly, talking to herself.

"These people are aliens, and they have kidnapped me. Yeah! I know, they want to study me like those science shows. No! No! Please leave my vagina, I need that to have kids…Get AWAY from me!" she screamed again as the vision of knives and needles approached her.

"What are you doing to me?" she asked the blank faces that were only a hallucinated figment blurred into her imagination.

"What do I mean to you?" she mumbled again, drool running from her mouth and occasionally she would choke on the clustered foam that would form in her throat making her gag.

"Ah ah! Gotcha!" she shouted again with renewed vigor. "Thought you would get away that easily?" she bragged, as she tasted the blood in her mouth from the alien's finger she had just dismembered…

They watched her as she tried to struggle loose from the straight jacket, and marveled at the strength of this small frail woman. She kept on talking to herself and they took notes of her progress, or lack of as the days and weeks passed by. "Does she still have any cocaine in her body?" The specialist asked the attending physician.

"No. We have replaced the drugs with methadone to help her wean off, but she doesn't show any signs of improvement and as of now we are worried about the child she carries."

"Child? What child? I was not told that this patient was pregnant!" He exclaimed in shock. "You must take her off methadone immediately; this patient is going to have to quit cold turkey. The child is already in danger having been conceived by a crack addict. Its life is already in jeopardy and we must do all we can to see if we can save them both." He stammered adamantly.

"I thought this patient was brought in due to a drug over-dose which was assessed as attempted suicide?" The specialist questioned as they walked out of the earshot of those they did not wish to be privy to their conversation.

"Yes she was," Returned David who had watched this patient go from bad to worse since the day she was admitted to their emergency ward. "But as we ran tests, the pregnancy showed up. It was an unexpected turn of events that made the circumstances worse." He explained.

"Have we identified who she is yet? A name? A relative?" He asked with subsequent concern. But David just shook his head, "no there was no one, she is still Jane Doe."

"You bastard!" The hails came suddenly and everyone within hearing distance jumped. "Leave me alone you losers. You think you can hold this bitch down, you think you can take over my body? Hey daddy, you like my twat? Yeah work it." She rambled on. "Turn up the music big daddy," she commanded to the figment in her imagination; "I am going to put on a show for you tonight." She snickered as she slowly attempted to gyrate her loins to meet the thrusts of the stranger in her mind.

Some of the nurses and orderlies started to laugh because they couldn't understand it. This patient had been there for more than two months and she had shown no signs of improvement. It's almost as if she was holding onto something, holding onto the pain and the drugs. It's like she didn't want to come back to reality.

She gained an audience and a following as she continued to drool and gyrate with herself. Her mouth spat foam and venom as she spoke obscenities into the sterile psychiatric hospital. She would come in and out of consciousness and cry at the memories that would haunt her. Most of the time she wasn't sure where she was or how she had gotten there, she just knew that she was tied down and unable to move. Whenever she started to remember anything, she would act out of control so they would come and administer more drugs to her. She didn't care what kind of drugs just as long as they gave her something to make her forget. The tears would come streaming down when she thought about being in the middle of nowhere, with no one to love her, support her or even visit her. She could feel the life growing inside of her and there was nothing she could do about it. With the drugs and the growing fetus in her she wasn't sure which made her more nauseous and cursed the child that she carried.

David shook his head as he and the visiting specialist walked back to the office. He listened intently to the recovery method that his superior wanted him to administer to Jane Doe in hopes of saving her life. But he couldn't help but wonder what he could do personally to help this young woman. She couldn't be more than twenty years old. There was no one to contact; no friends, and no family. She had no identification on her. It was as though she or someone didn't want anyone to find her. This was one of the reasons that they calculated into their prediction that her drug overdose must have been attempted suicide.

As the months went on, she slowly became independent of drugs. Though she was still in the psychiatric hospital she was moved to the maternity ward where she could carry out her pregnancy and come into full health.

It was there in the maternity unit that she befriended Justin, a young doctor who was only a year out of his internship. He took a liking to her immediately and tended to her with regular visitations and delicious treats, as a woman who is with child should be pampered. She had no one and he feared for her. So Justin decided to take it upon himself to help her out.

As the weeks rolled by, she started to show and the shame and sadness she felt became overwhelming. She felt that she had lost all the pride and dignity her grandmother had instilled in her. She was embarrassed that the lessons that were taught to her about strength and family seemed to have been lost in her mind and her behavior. Whatever happened to all the values and virtue that she had? When did she go wrong? She was resolved not to let anyone know who she was. She couldn't allow anyone to remember her by name when she was ready to leave that horrible place.

She could only imagine the snickers and the laughter behind her back. Some of the patients would taunt her about her behavior while she was under the influence of the drugs. Her decision was made. She wanted them to keep referring to her as Jane Doe and she would keep pretending she didn't remember who she was, or where she was from. The determination that once drove her kicked in. This would be just a minor setback; she would have the baby and give it away. She would move on with her life and make her family proud. She would not allow those who thought she was Panamanian trash the satisfaction of thinking they were right. She had a purpose and now she was on a mission. This was not going to be her downfall.

Six months pregnant and the small roundness of her tummy helped to give her radiance. As her baby grew, her body filled out and the needs of the baby helped to make her look healthy again.

Justin was proud of her progress. Every day on his way to work he would pick up fruit bowls and chocolate for her to snack on. She would complain about how horrible the food was and he would sneak her slices of pizza and watch as her maternal instincts kicked in.

On this day, Justin did not feel the usual jubilance he would experience right before he went to work. He felt weak and tired. She consumed him the entire night. He was restless and did not sleep. He had vivid sexual thoughts of her and felt it was wrong. When he awoke his thick shoulder length dread locks was heavy with sweat. His body ached with fatigue and yearnings. He wasn't sure what was different about today than all the other days. The connection he felt toward this patient was undeniable; he was falling in love with her. But how could that be? He didn't even know her name. It was as if she didn't exist before she came to the hospital. She had no records, no past. She refused to be fingerprinted, and would become hysterical if anyone tried to force her. The concern for her baby would send them into retreat and leave them still to wonder who she was.

Justin knew that his feelings for her could be coming from his own pain and loss of self-esteem when the woman he loved and decided he wanted to marry left him. He still couldn't believe that she just got up one day and left. He hated and resented her, not knowing if he would ever see her again, or if that pain would stay with him forever. But the reality of it still taunted him, the idea that he was not enough, though he gave her everything.

His pain and anger toward not just her, but women in general grew with each day after her sudden disappearance. Now here he was, finding himself caught in another uncertain situation. He couldn't help caring about this woman, maybe out of pity, but with emotions he thought he no longer had. Emotions he thought had died when Kay vanished from his life.

Slowly, Justin climbed out of bed and shook his locs until they fell peacefully to his shoulders. He hauled his naked, long, lean frame up and stood there gazing off at the vision of his beloved sitting in her caged room. It had a window, but was barred just in case she tried to kill herself again. It pained him to think of her constantly watched by leery eyes who thought she might hang herself with her bed sheets. They had everything nailed to a solid surface where she couldn't move anything. What could he do? He couldn't tell her how he felt. In a few months she would give birth and if her psychological evaluation panned out, she would be released. If she still refused to be identified, she would become lost to him forever.

He pulled himself together and marveled at the will of the woman. She was so young, so stubborn, and so full of passion. He grabbed his towel and headed toward the shower. On his way to the bathroom he happened to glance at the cuckoo clock on the wall and realized he was already an hour late for work. He jumped into the cold water and it made him shiver causing goose bumps all over his body. He needed to wash away the heat that had found its way between his thighs for her. As the cool water washed the evidence from the night before off him, his mind stayed there, lingering in the amazing dream he had about his Jane Doe rocking her baby to sleep then making love to him under the moonlight until the crying baby would send them rushing to its aide. He tried to shake his feelings and wipe them off as the towel sucked the water dry from his body, but to no avail.

He threw sweatpants over his legs without putting on underwear. Pulling a tee shirt over his head, he dabbed on a little of his **Givenchy** cologne and ran toward the door grabbing a light jacket on the way out.

As he walked through the hallway of the vast University of Rochester Hospital and passed through the lobby he saw a vendor selling fresh-cut flowers and roses. He knew he couldn't see her without something to present to her. He also knew she looked forward to his visits, as he was her only personal visitor as well as her doctor. It was almost lunchtime, so he stopped in the cafeteria and picked her up some meat loaf and mashed potatoes. The food in the doctors' cafeteria was far superior to what they served the patients.

With his hands full, he rushed to the elevator and across the other side of the building to the psychiatric maternity ward. As he approached her door *"lucky number seven,"* he slowed his pace and held his breath to the vision he was about to behold. She was breathtaking. It was as though her pregnancy gave her new life. He wished she would consider keeping the baby. Today was the day she was to sign the papers of adoption over to the hospital. Maybe he could still change her mind.

Turning to see where the faint knocking was coming from, she saw Justin standing at the door. Her eyes lit up in anticipation of seeing him again and she got up from where she sat at the window and moved as hurriedly as she could towards the door to greet him.

"Doctor," she squealed, "how good to see you again!" She told him openly. They had been sharing moments and visits since they brought her over to the maternity ward almost three months ago. She couldn't imagine what her days would be like without Justin and wasn't ashamed to let him know that she relished the affection he adorned her with.

"Hey Nubian Princess." He greeted her as casually as possible. He couldn't allow his visits to be construed as fraternization to his colleagues or he could be removed from caring for her. "So how are we feeling today?" He quizzed as he walked over to her small table and emptied his hands. Then walking toward the vase he had brought filled with flowers for Valentine's Day only a month before, he emptied it of last week's dead roses and replaced it with the fresh ones he carried.

"We are doing well," she told him, "I am so happy there are only three months left to go and then I can finally go home." She rambled and bent slightly to smell the fresh scent of the flowers. Justin turned to look at her but she didn't notice as she admired the way he so delicately arranged the flowers and thought about how he would phrase his next words.

"So, where *is* home?" he asked, but not wanting to seem too interested or to send her clamming up again, he walked toward her charts to see what her progress was and what had been administered to her for the day as well as who her attendees were. Justin was all too aware of how sensitive she was to being quizzed and he didn't want her to shut him out.

She retuned to the window where she previously sat and Justin pulled up a chair next to her. As they sat there, he pulled out his stethoscope and began checking her breathing and her heart rate. He then decided to take her blood pressure. Seeing her hesitation in responding he decided to change the subject. He didn't want any abnormal readings.

"So, are you excited about signing the papers today?"

"Of course I am. You know that!" She told him jubilantly. "This will be the first step in the rest of my life. This will be the beginning of my starting over." She said this without a hint of regret or remorse for the decision she was making or for the child she was making permanent plans to part with. Justin's heart fell. He wasn't sure what to feel or how to react. He didn't have a right to intervene in anyway and he had already broken the sacred bond between a doctor and his patient by getting emotionally involved with her. It's one of the biggest follies of doctors, an act that was warned against time and time again in their bedside manner courses, and one year out of his internship, he had already fallen victim.

He listened as she babbled on about how her new life would be, how she would go to college and maybe become a lawyer. He fought the tears because she seemed so oblivious to how he felt for her, and he knew that one day soon she would walk right out of his life the same way she came in, like a phantom, filled with mystery and as elusive as a dream.

As their time together ended, he gave her his usual speech, "now, take your vitamins, your iron pills, and don't forget that if you get heartburn just ask the nurse for some Tums. That should clear it right up." He cautioned with a smile, and then resisting the urge to kiss her, he held onto her wrist a little longer than necessary and then exited.

Justin did his rounds that day without incident. The days, weeks and months passed and he waited anxiously for the moment they would page him to bring Jane Doe's child into the world. She had gained some popularity at the university hospital during her stay. The doctors and nurses spoke of her often, and more often than not, they spoke fondly of her. They wondered what her future held, what her life would be like, where she would go. But she did not hold those concerns. She had it all planned out: the university she would attend, the city, and back to her family and her treasured girlfriends. She knew they must be worried sick about her, wondering where she was. She missed their little group, people she shared everything with, but this she would keep to herself. She wouldn't dare tell them where she'd been, what she was about to do, because it was all about survival and if this is what it took for her to survive, then this is what she planned to do.

"Push!" Yelled Dr. David who was there to make sure she had mental support and emotional stability. It was going to be a difficult transition handing over that child to its adoptive parents who were there in the delivery room, cheering on the entry of their new son into the world.

"Wait, I can see the head. Don't push anymore yet, let me adjust the baby. This is going to be the hardest part, the baby's shoulder. After you get that out it's down easy street from there," Justin encouraged.

He fought the emotions that threatened to overtake him in order to adequately perform his duty. The nurses who assisted him knew how fond he was of this patient and felt sadness for him.

"Okay. Now! Push Jane, push!"

Hearing the urgency in his voice, she looked past the fatigue and pain that consumed her and focused on the light at the end of the tunnel. Soon the worse would be over.

"That's it, that's it," He coached.

"It's out."

"Yeah!" Squealed its adoptive mother.

"Can I cut the umbilical cord?" asked the adoptive father. But Jane Doe didn't care. She turned away from the cries that would be etched into her memories forever, and didn't see as her son's new mother took him into her arms to offer him the comfort she refused to give. Minutes later, she passed out.

Chapter 1

Sandra was celebrating her twenty-second birthday with the freshman hunk that everyone wanted. College was working out well for her. She had no obligations, no responsibilities, nothing to hold her back from doing anything she wanted. She sat in one of the dimly lit private booths with mutual friends and watched Brian bump and grind with all the girls. She didn't feel jealous or threatened. He was hers and hers alone.

Sandra paid no attention to the extra queasiness she felt and the nausea that overwhelmed her every time she smelled someone's cologne or fried foods. She just thought it was just one of those days. She had her period regularly and was not concerned about pregnancy. She sat and sipped a Bloody Mary and joined in on the games and laughter, and reminisced fondly on that day when she became the luckiest girl on campus.

She remembered when Brian walked into her physics class last semester. She had no clue what was going on and he seemed to have all the answers. Brian Arnold, she had sighed as he raised his muscular deep chocolate arms over and over again in response to the professor's questions. "So who can tell me the answer?" The professor would ask, and his arms would go flying up like a skyscraper. Sandra was not the only one who noticed Mr. Universe. He had the attention of every woman in the

large auditorium classroom, so much so that one day the professor made a joke and said, "Hey Arnold, maybe you should teach
the class since you seem to have the female attendees under a
fixated spell." Everyone had laughed, but Sandra thought it was
a great idea.

She didn't think she had a chance in hell with Brian
Arnold. He was smart, handsome, played running back and was
Captain of the school's division one football team, and he had the
pick of all the most beautiful women on campus, freshmen and
seniors alike. He had it all.

One day after class Sandra dragged herself to the water
fountain in the hallway depressed that this was their third quiz
and she had again gotten a big fat "F" that blared at her in neon
red that the evil professor must have enjoyed writing diagonally
across her paper. She slouched in a corner on the hallway floor
and buried her face in her hands as tears streamed down her
face. She couldn't flunk out of school. This was her first semester of her second year, one semester down and she would be
able to start taking classes in her major and she wouldn't have to
deal with those classes that she didn't like anymore. But she had
to make it through Physics first. All she needed was a passing
grade, a "D" would suffice, but even that grade seemed unattain-
able.

Brian walked by and saw her sitting there. She had
caught his eyes from the first day he walked in. She was the reason his hands would shoot up to answer a question. He wanted
her to notice him, but he just couldn't seem to get her attention.
He got the attention of all the bimbos and football groupies. All
the fake blondes, fake boobs, fake fingernail wearing hair heads
seemed to be drawn to him and he couldn't shake them. This
was his opportunity to approach her.

"Hey, you okay?" he asked tentatively, hoping she would-
n't do or say something to embarrass him. He had eyes on him

everywhere he went and an embarrassing moment would follow him through the rest of his college career.

"Yes! I am fine thank you." Sandra said without raising her head. She didn't want this stranger to see her crying. She didn't want him to see how much more ugly she was with her eyes puffy and red.

Brian ached to reach out and touch the thick soft curls of her naturally auburn hair. He had never seen anything like it on such a dark skinned complexioned woman. Her hair was thick and curly as though she was of both black and white heritage and hung in a huge mass over her shoulders. The curls danced playfully as Sandra shook her head up and down in response to his question.

"Are you sure you are okay? Is there anything I could do to help you?" he insisted, not wanting to leave without her so much as noticing that he was the one who was talking to her. He wanted her to at least remember him, see his face and realize that he wanted to help her.

"Trust me; there is nothing you can do." She sobbed.

"Well, you really don't know that until you tell me what the problem is, do you?" he continued in a more jovial tone, hoping she would shake out of it a bit.

"Yes I do. Nobody can help me!"

"Maybe I could if you just gave me a chance." He pleaded hoping to get her attention. Wiping the tears and drool from her face, she took her hand and brushed the chaotic mass of color from over her face. She was almost stupefied to see that the voice that spoke to her so kindly was none other than Mr. Universe himself. She stared at him in shock and he smiled at her as sweetly as he could. Then wiping her face again to make sure she didn't look like a complete mess, she hung her head and lowered her voice.

"I guess you're right." She told him, embarrassed that she

didn't even recognize his voice. "It's just that I need to pass this class and I have failed my third quiz." She confessed. "I guess you got an "A" eh?" She asked already knowing the answer to her question and not really wanting him to answer.

"Well actually,"

"No don't answer. I already know that you passed with flying colors." She stated before he could finish his statement.

"If you had allowed me to finish, you would have been delighted to know that I got only a "B+" on this quiz." He teased, and they both laughed.

"How about I help you off the floor and we can set up a kind of study date to see if we can both do better on the next exam?" He suggested, and Sandra happily obliged him.

This was the beginning for them. They became inseparable and she was the envy of every woman on and off campus. She was happy and nothing could come between them. Now they were celebrating her birthday together. It had been three months since that first day when he rescued her. That very night, as they tried to study and keep their eyes and hands off each other, they did the deed. He claimed it was his first time and she said it was hers. She was so tight that he couldn't use a condom, it would break and it was uncomfortable for both of them. So deciding that they were both virgins they decided to have unprotected sex. Sandra could not forget how experienced he seemed. After tearing off her bra, he fondled and nibbled at her breast until it hurt. She didn't want to seem too weak and frail so she allowed him to do it. She closed her eyes and allowed the memory to flood her brain.

Brian moved swift and with expertise. He spun her around on the barely carpeted floor and pushed her into the floor. He used his teeth to bite her all over until she squirmed in pain. He didn't bother to undress her further, he just unzipped his pants and without warning just jabbed his dick inside of her. He got more and more excited at her screams and penetrated her even harder. Feeling his orgasm building and not ready for it to end yet he stopped and Sandra remembered just laying there wondering if that was the same man who was just being so gentle as he instructed her in her studies.

When he returned he had a lit candle and had honey in his hand. Using his teeth he ripped at her panties until they tore on one side and hung loosely revealing her closely shaved twat. He buried his face between her legs until he could taste her juices flowing. Taking the candle he would drip the hot wax all over her vagina until she screamed in pain, then he would smother the honey all over the hot areas and lick it off of her. He spread her legs wide and stuck his tongue inside her heated vagina. She was wet and excited, yet the pain from the candle wax remained. He took his tongue and soothed her. Gently nibbling at her outer vaginal lips and sucking tenderly at her clitoris, he took the honey and poured it over her clit allowing it to run down towards her opening. He used his fingers and inserted them inside of her. With the taste of honey and candle wax mixing, he could feel his dick harden with excitement from seeing her squirm in pain and pleasure. He felt her muscles tightening and he knew she wanted to cum, so he stopped and disappeared into the kitchen.

This time he had pieces of ropes in his hands and tied her arms behind her back and then brought her up on her knees with her face pressing into the floor. With her bare ass sticking out and her pussy fully exposed, he penetrated her. With hard deep strokes he pressed himself into her holding her thighs and pulling her ass toward his groin meeting each thrust. With each plunge, she screamed out in pain. Her body was exhilarated and excited, yet burning with anguish. With each scream his excitement grew until he exploded into Sandra, not caring that he did not have on a condom. Not caring that she may get pregnant. Just raw unprotected sex.

That night started it all. And the extent of the kind of freaky sex they had was indescribable and they did it whenever and wherever they could. Even though Sandra didn't like it, she had no other experience to measure this kind of torture by, so she went along with it because she loved him, because she didn't want to lose him.

Sandra retuned to the party from her mental time travel back into the past and saw that Brian was still having the time of his life. As the night drew into the 3am hour Sandra decided she was ready to go home, but Brian wasn't ready. He was having too much fun dancing. She insisted, but the blaring music, the smell of weed in the air and the fact that he was intoxicated from all the drinks he had must have clouded his judgment and he turned around raising his skyscraper arms and sent Sandra flying across the floor. She grabbed her coat and ran out into the chill of the oncoming spring air. She didn't stop until she reached her dorm apartment, and spent the rest of the morning with her face buried in her toilet bowl.

The next day in class Brian was no where to be found...

Matter of fact, Brian Arnold disappeared that night and was never to be seen again. He didn't show up for classes, for study groups or for football practice. He just disappeared "poof," just like that.

Sandra found herself getting weaker, more fatigued and sicker by the day. Her only friend Sasha Henderson, which she had met during their summer orientation and had remained close with throughout their freshman year, had also disappeared. Nothing remained but a note saying she was taking some time off from school and no one had heard from her since. Sandra had no one else to turn to for help so she decided to visit her campus health center for some answers.

"Don't worry," the work-study student had told her, "it's

going to be fine. Really." She assured the worried Sandra, who sat there wondering why they wanted her to stay and take some tests.

"Sandra?" The nurse had called her privately to a small room filled with brochures and paperwork about sexually transmitted diseases, safe sex and contraceptives. She walked in and the nurse closed the door behind her.

"I understand you were not feeling well and that you were concerned you had the flu bug?" She asked calmly.

"Yes. I wasn't sure what else to do. I have been feeling like this for a few days, but I thought it was because I was drinking and stuff at my birthday party this past weekend." She told the kind white-haired woman sheepishly. She watched as the woman slowly placed the clipboard with her questionnaire and other paper work about her on the small night stand next to her. Sandra thought how comfortable the room would seem if the walls weren't so white and bare except for the posters on the wall about warts, and the light above them wasn't blaring so brightly. She was seated on a cozy sofa and the lady who introduced herself as Ms. Smith, sat on a loveseat.

"Sandra, the reason I wanted to talk to you is because I believe you need to consider the possibility that you may be pregnant.

"What do you mean pregnant?" Sandra asked, alarm sounding in her voice.

"Well, the symptoms you describe are those very much like morning sickness. I thought you would want to be safe than sorry, and if worse comes to worse you can consider your options and plan around this so you can continue on to having a successful future." She encouraged.

Sandra cried as she walked into the little white bathroom and peed into the plastic cup the lady had handed her. Sandra could not contain herself when she found out she was pregnant, but she decided she was strong, and that she could have the baby even without Brian.

Five months into her pregnancy and almost at the end of her sophomore year during some routine blood tests, Sandra found out that she was HIV positive. Soon she found herself on rigid medication regiments to help her immune system so that she could successfully bring her baby to full term. The pills made her weak and too tired to study or even get up for classes. That summer Sandra gave birth to a son who was not born with the deadly virus his mother carried. She applied for Section 8 housing and it was there that she settled and made her life in the projects of Brooklyn and got on welfare. Needless to say, she didn't return to college in the fall.

Chapter 2

Dear Diary. It's me again, Kayla. I have been sitting here thinking about the occurrences that took place in my life and the lives of my friends as I have watched things happen, and I think I have finally come to realize that life is really a bitch. Before my epiphany, my metamorphosis, my growth, that I can now look back upon and hang my head in shame at my scarlet memories, I was a bad person. I know that right now a lot of what I am saying does not add up, but that's because I am really confused myself about some of the things I have done and what my friends have done that brought us to the places we found ourselves in our lives. I for one, have been told on countless occasions of how spoiled and selfish I was, but I just didn't see it. I have been told that I had too many choices, and that I did not know what it was like to have been said no to. But the truth is not that I have never been said "no" to, it's just that I never listened. I referred to my scarlet memories fondly then, because my misguided escape of a broken heart and emotional mind games made me who I am. It gave me the power most women only dream of, power that has kept me hostage from true love, love I now long for, even today, though I have long put those days behind me, and I think that this must have been the same disease Sasha suffered from. I got the picture eventually, but I think that she is just too stubborn and too conceited to learn her lesson.. . .

*Looking back now, if I was to analyze myself as an objec-
tive bystander, I would not know whether to love or hate me. I
have been cruel and kind, cold and loving, giving and selfish. I
have been a total contradiction that would blow a deconstruction-
ist mind. Maybe this is why I tolerate Sasha, because I understand her, because I see myself in her. Maybe the girls can see
themselves in her too. I have to laugh when I think about her, but
I know I can only now speak for myself and I offer myself now as
the sacrificial lamb, to be stoned, put on the butchers' block, or to
be pardoned. I'm probably well deserving of the disaster that
now follows my path, and have been deeply humbled by the irony
of life. There is just no way I could have known. As a matter of
fact, there is no way Sasha, Sandra, Karen, or Charmaine could
have known either. So whoever said that experience teaches the
best school, they weren't kidding. It's just one of those things you
have to experience. How else could we have known that what
we didn't know really could hurt us? How else could we have
learned that mistakes are a hard pill to swallow and that when
you hurt the people you love, you lose and sometimes though
you may try to mend it, you just don't get that back, or a second
chance. This is Kayla stepping off of my soapbox, and this is how
I see it.*

Kayla

It was a warm early Saturday afternoon. One of those
long lounging lazy days in the middle of the summer, the kind that
just takes you to places in your mind where only you can go. It
was supposed to be cool, or according to the weatherman it was
cool, but the heat inside overwhelmed me and I felt like I was on
fire. Thank God for ice water. I felt so hot, especially since I was
battling with a bit of the sniffles that precede some sort of cold.

July is one of the hottest months of summer, and I felt the effects ten-fold.

I sat staring out the window of my Starrett City apartment, watching how easily and effortlessly they designed and built the new plaza that was so desperately needed in the area. This plaza would definitely help out with jobs; the new BJ's, Circuit City and Old Navy are really going to bring shoppers to their area.

I couldn't help thinking that life would really be good if I could ever find true happiness so I could stop daydreaming of how much life has changed and truly begin to live the life I am living right now. No one could have told me five years ago that life would turn out this way for me. I have long fallen short of my dreams and capabilities, and everyone who knew me well enough would confirm that. I am disappointed in myself, but I must say that I am luckier than most and luckier even, than I deserve.

I was jolted from my thoughts by the telephone ringing and wondered if I should answer or let the answering machine pick it up. I decided on the latter, and listened patiently to who the caller might be just in case it was someone I might actually want to talk to. I dropped the journal that I was jotting down my thoughts in and jumped to grab the phone as the familiar female voice reverberated through the house.

"Hey woman. Hey! If you can hear me woman you better answer the phone!" she demanded before I could pick up.

"What is your problem?" I asked her and waited for the sound of her laughter that usually followed. She seemed to get pleasure from the sound of annoyance in the tone of my voice when she called and acted like this on my answering machine.

"I don't have a problem. I am just bugging you 'cause you bug me by screening your calls all the time." She said again with a chuckle. "So what's going on girlfriend? Can you hang out today or are you on lockdown with your good girl routine?" She quizzed.

"I don't know. Since you know so much 'Miss Thang' why don't you tell me?" She ignored my question and continued as though she hadn't heard me.

"Girl, do I have a piece of news for you. But I can't tell you until you come over. You have got to come over and hear this one face to face."

****

Sasha was crazy and excitable. Every little thing was news for her and she just had to share it. It always gets me how this child's attitude was always bigger than her size and God knows she has a big attitude. Standing only five foot five inches, Sasha is a dark skinned sista' from Panamanian decent. Her long jet-black hair hangs below her shoulders and over her slender shoulder blades.

As I listened to her trying to convince me to drop everything and rush to hear her precious news, I think back to when Sasha and I first met only a little over three years ago. It happened purely by coincidence. I had a girlfriend named Taisha who I hadn't seen in a few years since college, and when I ran into her, she was with Sasha and introduced us.

We met up again several times and I began liking Sasha's extravagant personality and excitable disposition and became very good friends with her. At that time Sasha was just in her first year of law school. I don't know what Sasha did, but Taisha's man musta looked at Sasha too hard and she got jealous. Knowing Sasha, she probably flirted a little because from my understanding she and Taisha were not very close either. So when Taisha told me she and Sasha were no longer friends and that she would appreciate it if I would stop communicating with her too, I wasn't having it. I liked Sasha too much and Taisha was just an acquaintance from school and we never really hung out much. The problem was that Taisha was close with some of my other close friends and that's what caused the drama.

It was rough for a while with the gossiping and the back-stabbing because if I remember correctly, everyone was against our friendship and as Sasha would put it, 'the sources of evil, the devil himself was working against us, but God was just not having it'. "Kayla, are you listening to me woman?" she intruded on my thoughts.

"Yeah, I'm here. Why can't you just tell me over the phone? It's not like anybody else can hear you!"

"You see, there you go again. You just don't understand the delicate nature of these things. Who told you no one is listening? You never read the book "Big brother is watching"? The government taping your conversations and shit?" She rambled on and on.

Here she goes again, I thought. This woman is ridiculous and I knew that once she got started she would not stop. So I just let her play herself out. I zoned back in and she was still rambling, "why don't you just come over, it's not like you have anything better to do anyway. It's Saturday, and that man of yours is still going to be there when you get back." She insisted. She was right. Even though I do love Michael, it's not like I am one of those whooped sistas or anything, just sitting around the house waiting for her man. I loved the way he walked through the door, his long graceful muscular legs making the entrance first. I loved the way he loved me so much, and thinking about it, I know it is really that love that has kept us together for the past five years.

"Alright," I gave in, now starting to feel the excitement creeping in to rescue me from an uneventful Saturday, "but you better have food, cuz I ain't driving all that way for nuthin."

"Yeah, yeah, yeah, ah uh, whatever. Just get your ass over here already," she said and before I could respond, she hung up. I got up from the comfort of my old brown stained recliner that I know Michael loved because of its comfort and roominess. And I loved it because it smelled like Michael. I couldn't help sinking myself back into it one more time before replacing the handset back in its cradle, just to savor that old musky smell of his cologne combined with sweat or whatever else that comes off of him. He sat in that chair after a basketball game or while waiting for me to get ready when we are going out. His essence is so powerful and so sweet; I just cannot get enough.

I was not even about to take another shower as hot as it felt outside, because I am sure crazy Sasha is about to drag me somewhere where I am about to get all funky anyway. As I grabbed a tank top and pulled the small denim cargo shorts over my long caramel legs, the phone began to ring again. I picked up the journal that was still like new, I barely ever wrote in that thing, I chuckled to myself and cocked my ear to listen to who was leaving a message. I was not about to pick it up because I know that its gotta be Sasha again calling to tell me something she forgot, so I let the answering machine pick up again.

"Hi, you've reached Michael and Kayla. When you hear the beep you know what to do Ciao." At the end of the long beep signaling that I have message waiting that I haven't checked in awhile, Karen's voice came flooding through.

"Kay! Kayla are you there? Please pick up the phone." She pleaded. I always like the way Karen's voice sounded. It was sweet like she was licking the words off of a softie ice-cream cone, and had a singsong quality to it that made you want to run to her rescue. The fact that she is a petite five foot two does not help. Though Karen Grace is athletic from running years of track and field from when we were back in high school together, she still seemed vulnerable and meek. Karen's mom and my mom where best friends from way back then and still are, so Karen and I are close and I had to spend most of my time defending her honor because people either thought she was a slut or gay. My mother isn't gay, but Karen's is and we had both suffered for that growing up.

"Kayla, com'on. You can't be gone already! Sasha just talked to you." She sounded desperate just as I picked up the receiver.

"Why do you always sound like you are begging like a puppy dog?" I joked.

"This is not funny. Why must you always screen your calls?"

"Because that is how I am and y'all know that so quit complaining."

"I know but doesn't it ever get tired?"

"No. Besides, did you call to grill me about me screening my calls or was there something else?" I interrupted, changing the line of conversation I am all too familiar with, and that gets tired.

"Yeah, crazy woman just called me saying she had some piece of news she can't share over the phone. That we just have to rush over to her house that you know is an hour and thirty minutes drive for me."

"So I wanted to call and find out if you were going because I just don't want to waste my time. Remember what happened with her last big news?"

"I remember," I reassured Karen with a chuckle as the memory of Sasha telling off her neighbor rushed back to my mind. Her neighbor owned a big piece of land across from her and ran a nudist colony out of it. You could see everybody's whats-it-nots hanging out and they were proud even though most of them had nothing to be proud of or to show off.

"That girl had me drive all that way to show us that she was not just complaining about telling those poor people off. Now was it any of our business what they do? The county said it was okay, so what's her problem anyway?"

"I'll tell you what her problem is, she just thinks that since she is a lawyer she can throw her weight around and everybody is just going to cower at her powerful presence, that's her problem." Karen remarked somewhat amused and somewhat annoyed.

"You know that's how she is. Besides, I have nothing better to do today. Michael is out playing ball at some new park. He and his boys, or whoever he is hooking up with and I am left here hanging by myself and lonely. I know he isn't getting back here anytime soon so I think I can manage to put up with some of Sasha's antics. Besides, I am starved and maybe I can convince her to go to that restaurant down the street from her. Did you see that hottie that started working there as a chef?"

"You are just as crazy as she is. Do you hear yourself?"

"Just put some clothes on and come join us. If you don't want to drive I'll pick you up."

"I can't. Shawn is coming over."

"Shawn is constantly coming over, doesn't he have a life?" I hissed, "Whatever you guys have to do can wait until dark. I will be there to pick you up in fifteen minutes so be ready." I told her and hung up the phone. Sometimes she just makes me so mad. She and Shawn have been on this on and off binge for years and the bum is not going anywhere with his life. He is just a washed up *has been*, living in the past reminiscing on his class clown day title, like he is not a grown man and out of high school. I thought about Karen and Shawn as I brushed my teeth, pulled and yanked on my short tresses until I looked half decent. Then I grabbed my keys. Just as I was about to walk out the door, I heard the phone ring and ignored it.

"I am not answering the phone again."

I told myself as the answering machine picked up. I was tempted to listen a bit longer and find out whom it was that was calling this time, but passed. Looks like Sasha outdid herself this time and called the whole Klan. This one must be big.

Chapter 3

Sandra ran from her crowded balcony to the living room that was separated into a living room, slash playroom, slash dining room and also a partial bedroom for her eldest child Anthony who was pushing six years old. She rummaged through his toys, blankets, and empty food plates that he had left lying on the floor after he was finished eating, looking for the telephone.

The phone kept ringing and ringing and she still couldn't find it and she had to run back to her now wailing six month old she left on the balcony halfway through her feeding. Suzette was usually a good baby, but she did not play when it came to her food. Sandra knew if she didn't get back to her soon, she was going to have a cranky baby on her hands the rest of the evening and that would not be good. Running back to the balcony she snatched up the frantic child and returned to again attempt to find the phone that had stopped ringing and suddenly started ringing again. It sounded like the phone was screaming at her. Ringing unusually loud and harsh, but she knew it was the irritation she felt from the baby crying and not being able to find the phone.

Sandra was usually a very calm even-tempered person. She had some trouble early in life with her family that was not very supportive or loving. She left St. Martin ten years ago to come to the states and live with her aunt and common law uncle. She had to drop out of college after her second year because her virgin boyfriend gave her HIV and a baby, then he disappeared.

It was like whenever she turned around something bad was happening to her. The father of both of her children was either a deadbeat dad or nonexistent.

A few years back she ran into someone she knew from school while sitting in downtown Brooklyn's welfare office with her son Anthony waiting to get her benefits. This was before she had even met Seth and way before Suzette was a possibility. A mutual friend of both her and Brian, apparently another victim he also infected with HIV, told her that Brian died of AIDS only a few months back.

The girl explained to Sandra how he had lost weight and broken out into dark blotches and purple sores all over his body. She mentioned how no one would visit him; his friends and family abandoning him in his final days. Sandra didn't have tears to cry. She was filled with anger and hatred for the life he left her to lead. The pain and regret that she woke up to face everyday was all Brian's fault. She felt that he had gotten off easy with death. She felt that God had done him a favor because if she had found him first, his death would have been prolonged by sadistic pain. It had been years since she was out of school and years still since the night Brian disappeared out of her life. She couldn't believe he was living in Brownsville, not far from her all that time.

"Well, we can't cry over spilled milk," she had told the girl whose name she didn't remember and didn't care to ask. The social worker had called her name in that instance and she said goodbye. That was the last she saw of the girl or heard of Brian again.

****

She heard the beginning of a ring coming as clear as day from underneath a pile of clothes on the floor and grabbed it before it could ring again.

"Hello," she panted, waiting for a response.

"Yello girl, what'cha doing?" came Sasha's excited voice over the telephone.

"Was that you calling here non stop for the past ten minutes?" Sandra quizzed almost irritably.

"Yeah. I was trying to reach you to tell you something very important. The phone was just ringing so I thought you might be on the other line or in the shower or something." Sasha justified her persistence. Sandra hated this about Sasha; she was persistent and neurotic to irrational standards. No wonder Kayla always screened her calls. She would never admit it, but it was because of Sasha and people like her. It is at times like these that made her want to do the same thing but the screening would eventually get on her nerves. Truthfully, she wasn't sure how Kayla did it so naturally.

Sandra brushed some dirty clothes off the love seat squeezed tightly in the corner of what was supposed to be the living room and stuffed her right nipple back into the irritated baby's mouth. She put the phone to her left ear while she cradled and soothed the baby.

"Okay, so now you've got me, what is the big fuss about this time troublemaker?" Sandra hissed the irritation still very evident in her voice. "You know you almost gave me a heart attack calling like somebody was dying and you know I got two kids to take care of up in here!"

"It is not even like that."

"It doesn't matter. I should be used to this by now anyway. Well, like I said, everything is under control now so spill it. I know in your eyes it's gotta be some kind of close call crisis for you to be so unbearably persistent." Sandra commented half joking and half-serious. She and Sasha were once close when they had first met in college before her disappearing act. After Sandra dropped out of school, word in the grapevine was that Sasha was dancing at the Hot Chili Pepper gentleman's club in Manhattan and that she was queen of the pack for bachelor and orgy parties.

Sandra reconciled her friendship with Sasha Henderson through Karen Grace, who went to high school with Sandra. Karen met Sasha through Kayla who was the daughter of Karen's mother's best friend. She never told anyone what she heard about Sasha, but they were never able to rebuild the close bond they once shared, and being that she had kids and HIV that kept her busy, she never usually got the chance to hang out with the girls as she would like; let alone gossip about people's past. Sometimes she felt so much older than twenty-eight years old, but what could she do? This was her life, struggling in the projects of Brooklyn like every other welfare single mother, dreaming of making it out. She felt happy and grateful for the friendships she had forged and could depend on for a shoulder, a listening ear and from time to time some much needed cash they may dispense her way for the kids birthday or just because.

"Well, if you are done telling me off let me tell your sorry ass why I was calling yah." Sasha began with an attitude that was all too familiar to Sandra; "I was going to ask you if you wanted to come over this afternoon and hang out with us girls for a change. You are always so busy and we never see you. I just thought it would be nice to ask."

"Now how do you expect me to come by? Are the kids invited too?" Sandra spat in annoyance.

"Well, can't you have Seth look after them for a few hours? Isn't he home?"

"No he is not home, this is not his home and he does not live here. Come on Sasha, how can you make such a presumption when you know my situation as well as anyone else? You know I cannot depend on Seth even if he is Suzette's father. He only comes here when he wants some punani and this is not one of those times. Besides, you know I don't have the time or the resources to just drop whatever I'm doing at a whim and just take off. I am not some big lawyer with some hot career making how much grand a year. I don't have the privilege of meeting rich men and I am not some single woman with no kids or responsibilities that I can just throw my time away at whoever demands it whenever they feel like." Sandra could feel her blood boiling and the frustration building as Suzette yanked at her nipple to drain the milk from it. She didn't know why she was so angry with Sasha or why she was taking her frustrations out on her.

All she knew was that it was always about Sasha. Sasha was a fiend for attention and she did whatever she could, whenever she could, to get as much of it as she could. That's all she ever did, even from back in college.

"You know what? I don't have time to listen to some hard up bitch tell me off because she is pissed off about her life and jealous of mine." Sasha screamed through the telephone receiver, startling Sandra who had started to daydream about the Sasha she once knew. Sandra didn't expect the outburst but she also forgot whom she was talking to. This was not diplomatic Kayla, or soft-spoken Karen. This was Sasha, miss tell it like it is, and tell it as she feels like.

"And next time I have the nerve to even invite your tired ass some place, please slam the phone down in my fucking ears before I can say hello." Sasha continued before Sandra could get a word in edgewise to even try to apologize or defend her position.

****

When Sasha got off the phone, her feathers were ruffled

and her mood for the afternoon was just about ruined. She was already on pins and needles and Sandra was making her situation more difficult. She wanted to be as calm and as composed as possible when everyone got to the house, and she already felt like she was losing her grip. She hated to feel vulnerable. It was a sign of weakness and she had been put in compromising positions once too many times. This time she was going to take care of it all once and for all.

She walked over to the bar where she kept her stash and poured herself a glass of champagne. As she indulged in the cool fizzle that crept down her throat, she walked toward the balcony and took in the breath taking sight of the hills and well-manicured trees and grass that caved in, hovering over and covering her beautiful West Hampton home.

"I cannot believe that woman." Sasha mumbled to herself as she let her fingers slide over the long thin stem of the champagne glass.

"Like I told her to go pick up that worthless ass white man who does nothing for her or gives her nothing but a headache." She realized she was getting even angrier and decided to finish her champagne and allow the beautiful view of her home to soothe her like it usually did. Only this time it wasn't working.

The smell of the trees and freshly cut grass did not help her to feel better. She was worried and it wasn't just because of Sandra. What was she going to do? She knew she was playing it off like this was just another one of those times, pretending that what she had to say to the women she had known since they were just on the verge of beginning their lives, wasn't about to change all their lives. How was she going to tell them the mess she'd gotten herself into this time, how would she explain that she needed them?

Sasha paced up and down her balcony, fondling the glass until her palms had sweated the cool out of the drink. She tried to remember why she bought this house in the first place, why she went through all the bullshit she had to go through fighting all those racist neighbors who didn't want her in their neighborhood.

"It didn't matter that I am a lawyer," she thought.

"You would think that my beautiful long hair would make me kinda pass, but hell no!" she discussed with herself cynically.

"I am just too dark. They would much rather a light skinned nappy haired sistah like Kayla with her skinny anorexic ass than me." She spoke viciously of her friend who had been one of her biggest and long-time supporters. But that did not cross Sasha's mind. This was her life that was falling apart and all is fair in love and war.

She had always wanted to live out in the Hampton since she was a little girl. The Hampton gave her the luxury of the sub-urbs and the high-class life she created for herself. It was out in Long Island so she wasn't too far from Manhattan where she worked or from her friends in the city.

Coming from a broken home, she was raised by her grandmother who was the Matriarch of her family and the pillar of strength that Sasha always leaned on when life got too hard. Her mother was nonexistent in her life and she did not know her father. She often wondered if that was the reason why she was always attracted to the wrong kind of man.

From time to time she would drift back to the nice doctor she had met when she was in drug rehabilitation. A time no one knew about and she did everything she could for it to stay that way. She thought back to how it broke his heart to see her give up her son. She had pretended not to notice how he felt about her, just as he tried to hide his feelings for her.

Maybe she should have given him a chance. She knew he loved her, but she had to get away from there before anyone figured out whom she was. She needed to start over and he was too close to that time in her life; a time she wanted to forget, but now it was all coming back to haunt her. The past she tried and worked so hard to get away from had now returned and she must face it or risk losing everything.

She wished she was not so attracted to the lover boy types. The three hundred-dollar shoe wearing, Armani suit types, the broke ass niggahs looking for a sugar mammy or borrowing money from their mammy types. She loved those tall dark and handsome muscular types that had no problems getting her panties wet, and maybe that was her problem, her pussyplayplay instead of a brother who was making his way. Sasha giggled softly as she remembered why she was calling that heffah Sandra in the first place. She had enough on her mind, enough to concentrate on knowing the other girls were on their way, and she was not about to make Sandra a priority right now. She would deal with her later.

Chapter 4

Beep... beep, came the noise from outside Sasha's expensive neighborhood. She could just hear the whispers from her white neighbors calling her ghetto, paranoia setting into her mind again. But this time she didn't care. Right now she couldn't afford to care.

"What? Hold up guys, I'm coming," she shouted from her balcony excitedly. She was happy to see them all, all except Karen. "That worthless bitch," she hissed under her breath as she hugged Charmaine.

"Well excuse the hell outa me!" Charmaine hissed. "I know you didn't call and invite me, but it was assumed that I was also invited to this here shindig since I usually am." She bellowed. "And if you didn't want me here, there was no reason for you to say that shit. You could have just asked me to leave. I just happened to stop by Kayla's and she was on her way out to go and pick up Karen, so I left my car at her place and decided to tag along." She almost slipped when she continued. "...And it's a good thing too, because we got there just in time." As the last statement left her mouth she turned to see Karen and Kayla looking at her. "We got there just in time to pick up Karen, so we could come to your sorry over exaggerated promise of a good time." She embellished and walked past Sasha.

Sasha didn't even notice the slight remains of blood on

Karen's forehead, or the blister on her semi-swollen lips. She just kept on talking about herself and remained focused on her own problems.

"I wasn't talking about you girlfriend. I was just thinking about some bitch that just pissed me off on the phone." She told her omitting whom it was that she was talking about.

"Besides, I called your black flat behind and got your mom. She said you left like an hour ago to the dentist or whatever, so I told her to tell you to drop by my crib if you came back in time." Sasha defended and gave Charmaine another hug when she saw that, "oh you love me?" and a smile creep across her face.

"Oh guys I am so glad you are here." Sasha swallowed hard. She didn't know if she should cry or laugh or just come right out and say what she had to say. But she found herself stalling and somewhat speechless which wasn't at all like her. "All my closet friends together, under one roof, to share one momentous moment. I am touched." She said dramatically, putting one hand to her heart and the back of her left hand to her forehead in fake exasperation. Everyone burst out laughing, then stopped to look at Charmaine who was laughing so hard she snorted and that started another fit of laughter. They stood outside Sasha's elaborate home like that for a few minutes before Sasha gathered herself like a good host and broke up the laughter.

"Okay ladies; let's get inside before these people decide to call the police on our rowdy butts." She hushed and they all ran inside like anxious kids about to dive into a bowl of candy. When they got inside everyone was in awe.

"Sasha girl, no matter how many times I come to this place I am always dazzled. This place just seems to get more and more beautiful everyday." I chimed as Sasha took bows like a famous actress who just stepped out of her limousine on a red carpet in front of her adoring fans.

"She is just so humble isn't she?" Karen whispered to Kayla loud enough for Sasha to hear and they laughed when she turned to them and frowned.

"Okay, I'm hungry," I moaned. "And I done told your sorry behinds that I am not coming here unless I get food." I reminded Sasha and turned to the girls for some backup and everyone started mumbling their agreement, rubbing their tummies and grimaced.

"Yeah girl, if you gonna entertain, do it right. And we all know a party ain't a party without some grub." Charmaine egged on. They kept mumbling to themselves unaware of the turmoil inside of Sasha, unaware of the anxiety she was feeling and bewilderment of trying to figure out how to tell her friends, the closest she had to friendship that she was in trouble. That all the money and fancy house in the world couldn't fill the void that she had built for years, the emptiness that she never seemed to be able to close up.

"Well, well, well, looky here. I didn't know that her skinny behind could eat and she's
actually complaining about food." Sasha spat. "Well, not to worry. I am a lady and a good host so I will be feeding you poor hungry people before the day is over. As a matter of fact," Sasha continued swallowing the lump that was swelling in her throat and kept up her act, "I will call and order some pizza and Chinese food. I've got liquor for those who would like, so I don't want to hear another word about it."

Sasha spun around and the short summer dress she wore rose in a twirl showing a glimpse of her perfectly formed ass. Sasha liked any opportunity to show off her body. She is a work out freak and takes pride in the result. Just as she walked away Charmaine made an about twirl to imitate Sasha and switched her ass from side to side to emphasize the walk.

****

Karen wanted to go with the girls and decided that she would, even though she didn't want to upset Shawn. She did everything for Shawn. She ate, slept and drank Shawn. He was her everything. He had specifically called her and told her to be home because he was coming over to get some tonight, so she knew he was ready for "his" as dependable as she was when it came to sex.

She slowly got dressed and waited outside her Bed Sty apartment for Kayla to come pick her up. She fidgeted nervously, because she knew if Shawn came home before Kayla was able to come and pick her up, there was going to be drama. So she just sat there quietly, wondering why Sasha wanted everyone to be there and what the big news could possibly be.

As she waited she saw the tall light skinned man walk towards her building. She knew that it was Shawn. After all those years of either being desperately in love with him or being completely terrified of him, she could pick him out of a crowd. He was really a beautiful man in his own right. Wasn't exactly what you might call a looker, but back then he had personality to make up for it. He had a great smile and beautiful even white teeth. His head might be a little too big for his body and his ears too small, and extended like Dumbo, but she loved him nonetheless. He had basically controlled her life from the get go. No matter how much she tried to get away from him she couldn't. If she left him he would come begging for forgiveness and saying all the things he knew she wanted to hear. But as soon as she took him back, he would forget all about his promises. Never mind all the crying, she'd been a fool to allow him to take her for granted that way, but she didn't know how to stop loving him.

As he walked closer and started to approach her, she cringed. She knew the situation was about to be intensified and become explosive. She was going to have to be very careful about what she said to keep his temper at a minimum.

"Hey princess," He greeted her excitedly. He was looking forward to a piece of her.

"You sitting out here waiting for your man baby?" He asked her as he gently moved up close to slipping his hands under her halter top and gently pressing his fingers into her spine. He pulled her close to him so she could feel his erection growing in his pants.

"Hey baby," she responded with a casual uninterested smile, trying to figure out how she was going to get him off of her back.

"You're early, what happened?" She asked. Just her bad luck. As he pressed closer into her 5'2" petite frame, she could smell his breath as he bent his knees so he could feel her better. She could smell that he was drinking, an early celebration no doubt to begin his little freaky deeky party.

"Shawn, have you been drinking sweetie?" She asked finding and using the smell of liquor on his breath to put distance between them. He didn't answer; he took her resistance as a queue and started to slobber wet kisses all over her. She could feel his penis growing to its max, but she had no concerns about it being openly visible to strangers in his baggy pants. His penis was not that big.

"Shawn listen, I can't stay today and entertain your desires today. Something has happened to Sasha and we are all going over to her house to see her." She explained slowly, anticipating the rage that usually comes after he is unable to have his way with her.

"What do you mean you are going to see Sasha? I thought we had plans?" He quizzed, trying not to get her too upset. He knew this was a sure way of really not getting any of her sweet stuff and he didn't want to take that chance.

"Baby, I came all the way over here to see you. I thought you were waiting for me looking all sleek and sexy, sitting on the building stoop like a sixteen year old horny babe waiting to get laid." He joked, but he could tell that Karen wasn't having it. It was like she had already made up her mind and he didn't have a chance in hell of changing it.

"Listen Shawn, you are welcome to stay if you want. You have a key so it shouldn't be a problem for you to come or go if you like." She told him, building up the courage to sound more adamant, and more determined.

Shawn stared at her, his nose flaring and his eyes squinting, already blurry from the alcohol that was taking effect in his system. Karen knew this was her chance to step out of the way of oncoming danger, but he still held tightly onto her, staring down at her with his mouth half opened and drool building up at the corners of his mouth.

"You cannot do this to me. What's the deal with those bitches anyway? Are you fucking them too? Turning into a lesbo whore like your mother?"

Karen didn't know where she got the strength or the nerve. All she felt was her hand stinging from the slap she had just planted on Shawn's face. That slap caused him to loosen his grip and release her. Karen stepped back and the tears ran down her face. She was shaking. She didn't know what was going to happen next, but she knew Shawn would retaliate. She stepped back to brace herself for the blows that would come and didn't see the growing crowd of spectators gather around them. She didn't hear her neighbor Carla from upstairs, who saw and was into everybody's business, yelling to her from the third floor.

"Hey Karen! Karen! Run you idiot. Don't you see he's about to slap you back into your mama's womb?" She warned.

"What's happening?" Another bystander asked. But no one responded everyone was trying to get a better look as the crowd thickened.

"Hey you no good worthless excuse for a man! Leave her alone." Came another female voice from the distance. But her cries went unheeded, because Shawn's hand rose as high as a flag and came crashing down on Karen's fragile body. Her screams echoed throughout the neighborhood and Kayla sped up when they turned the corner and saw the crowd in front of Karen's apartment.

Kayla jumped out of her small 1989 Volkswagen Jetta with Charmaine on her tail. They ran towards the wails that were clearly Karen and pushed themselves through the crowd to get to where they could truly see the viciousness that was taking place.

Kayla walked up behind Shawn and pushed him from behind. He didn't know who it was but he turned around swinging to hit anyone in the line of fire, but Kayla ducked.

"What the hell do you think you are doing hitting on someone like her?" I screamed at him pointing at Karen lying helplessly on the ground. Charmaine ran to her aide to find that her mouth was swollen and bleeding and she had hit her head on the concrete sidewalk causing it to bleed slightly as well. Charmaine couldn't contain her anger; she ran at Shawn with all the fierceness, jumped in his arms and wrapped her legs around his waist. Before he knew it, she was hitting and punching him, her arms flying all over the place and she scratched him across his face just before releasing him from the grip of her thighs and backing away before he could do her any harm.

"You no good sucka," she yelled at the top of her lungs breathing hard and panting from her contact with him.

"How dare you lay one of your no good filthy hands on my friend?" She asked and made at him again. Shawn rose up to retaliate before she could get close to him again this time, but a group of men grabbed him from behind.

"Whoa, whoa boy. Didn't your mama ever tell you not to

hit a woman?" The older of the gentlemen asked as Shawn struggled to free himself.

"Yeah brotha', you should be ashamed of yourself, hitting on that there little filly. You need to pick on somebody your own size." The tall skinny stranger told him in a high-pitched squeaky voice, just as they turned and pushed him towards the crowd and away from the three girls.

"You want us to call the police Karen?" Charmaine asked, ready to hang a black man. She despised this most about men. Some of them just liked to show their colors by hitting on women smaller and more vulnerable then they were. Karen nodded no and sent Charmaine into a screaming frenzy.

"What do you mean no? How long has he been doing this to you without you telling us, telling somebody?" She asked Karen harshly.

"Come on Charmaine, take it easy. Can't you see she is in a tough situation? Go easy eh?" I pleaded, hoping that Charmaine would see the hurt and embarrassment that Karen had already endured and just let it go, but she didn't seem to get it.

"Take it easy? Take it easy? Do you have any idea what he might have done to her if we hadn't come by?" Her nose flared and her fists were clenched. "None of these people would have done anything to help her. Look at them." She admonished Kayla to look around her, and as she did she saw the group of spectators whither away, hanging their heads in guilty shame.

"It's okay Karen, com'on? Let's take you to the hospital." I placed my arm gently under Karen's and helped her to her feet. I was so embarrassed, for myself and for Karen. I just wanted to get out of there. It's bad enough that this is where Karen lives and she will have to come back here when this is all over.

"I think we should call the police and have his no job, worthless, squandering ass thrown in jail." She said again, intent on seeing Shawn pay for his behavior. She turned to look at the crowd that was slowly drifting away, and then she turned to look at her friends. I tried to beg Charmaine for tact. I met her eyes and pleaded with her to let it go. Then she looked at Karen whose face was drenched in tears. Her heart softened and she walked over to me and helped me to get Karen into the back seat of the car. We drove together in silence. I wasn't sure what to do since Karen didn't say a word the whole time. So I decided to drive to the hospital. As I pulled up in front of Mercy Hospital, I could see the fear that plastered itself across Karen's face. When Karen saw where we were she started to cry again.

"Why don't you want to go in?" Charmaine asked her painfully. "Why are you protecting someone who would hurt you without a second thought?" She asked again, but still no answer from Karen.

"Do you still want to go to Sasha's Karen?" I asked her. I saw her gentle request as she nodded yes. I looked at Charmaine and saw the anger on her face but this was not her fight and it was not her call. It's Karen's and what Karen wants, Karen gets.

As we approached Sasha's house, Karen slowly spoke up.

"Can we please not talk about this? I mean, can you please not tell Sasha or anyone else about what just happened." The fire in Charmaine's eyes could have burnt through Karen.

"No, absolutely not. We have to talk about this in the open and decide what to do about Shawn." Charmaine told them.

"Charmaine, I know you care about me and I know you want to help, but I will let you know when I need you okay? Please, just let us go enjoy ourselves and find out what Sasha as to tell us. I am okay, honest."

Reluctantly, I saw Charmaine submit and I gave my word that what happened would be kept strictly between us.

Chapter 5

Sasha went into her kitchen, while Charmaine, Kayla, and Karen surveyed the high cathedral ceiling, marble floors, eccentric art décor, and spiral stairways that seemed to climb to the heavens. Sasha was glad for the moment to exhale, and to compose herself. She knew she shouldn't drag it out, that she should just tell them and get it out of her system. She knew she was probably kidding herself that they would even understand, but they were all she had. As she poured herself a glass of wine she leaned against the refrigerator door and took a deep breath. She raised her eyes to the ceiling as if in prayer then lifted her glass as if to say *'Cheers'* to the Lord, then finished the glass in one swift gulp and prepared to make her entrance.

When Sasha came out she saw Karen curled up on her velour sectional sofa with her dirty smelly socks and she almost shrieked. Everyone had gotten comfortable, the music was blaring from the entertainment center. I had the remote control to her *Bose* music system, and with the little tiny speakers surrounding us in every which direction, it sounded as though I was floating in the music. Charmaine hadn't been to Sasha's place since she renovated, so she hadn't seen the new sixty-inch flat screen hung elegantly on Sasha's wall. First chance she got, she grabbed the remote and started flipping through the channels and marveled at the clarity of the picture. Charmaine wanted the remote control for the Bose radio so that she could tune it in to the television to add the audio surround sound effect, but since I didn't want to give it up so easily, we kind of playfully went at it wrestling and rolling on the plush carpet to see if she could take it away from me.

We honestly didn't see Sasha walk in and was surprised at her reaction. We knew she called us there to tell us some big story, but this is Sasha's wolf cry and we didn't take it too much to heart. So when she came out and started acting up I was taken totally by surprise.

"What are your feet doing on my sofa?" She asked, her question directed at Karen. I noticed that she was acting a little standoffish with Karen, but I couldn't figure out why, and now suddenly she was acting as though we have never put our feet on her sofa before. Karen being caught off guard just like the rest of us jumped to her feet and turned to look at everyone for support.

Poor Karen. It's like she was batting a thousand today. First Shawn and now Sasha. Poor thing didn't know what to do, and Sasha still didn't notice that something was wrong with Karen. Didn't even see how emotionally fragile Karen was behaving. I saw how hard she tried to hide the pain of what happened to her earlier, but Sasha was not making it easy. The look that was on her face was one of embarrassment, anger, confusion and pain. I wanted to reach out to her. But I didn't know how without giving away the fact that something was wrong. Then she turned to look at a fuming Sasha, but didn't say a word.

"I just had that upholstered and I don't want it getting dirty." Sasha realized her reaction. She didn't want to nor did she have the time to deal with Karen right now, after all, it wasn't Karen who rejected her. As a matter of fact, as far as she knew, Karen didn't even know about the relationship between her and Shawn.

Shawn was a dog anyway, so she didn't feel exactly guilty about sleeping with him. He was fine and she heard he had a big dick he was willing to share, so why not. No! She wasn't mad at Karen, she was mad at Shawn. However Shawn wasn't there, but the woman he supposedly cut her off for was, and she couldn't see what Karen had over her. She couldn't understand why she was still upset. The rumor about his big penis was all a lie, but he knew how to use what he had. She was more upset that he turned her down this morning when she called him to her service. Apparently he was going to be getting some from somewhere else.

"Sasha calm down," I said gently tapping her on her shoulder. "We were all just sitting here waiting for you to come back out and started goofing around like we usually do. We didn't mean to get you upset." I told her almost in a whisper.

"I know. I am sorry. I am just a little on edge." She said hanging her head and getting everyone's attention.

"Damn, this must be serious." Charmaine commented getting up and walking over to where I stood with Sasha.

"Come over here Kayla," Karen asked, patting on the seat next to her tenderly as though the seat wouldn't break but more afraid to make too much of a sudden movement in fear that Sasha might break out on her again. Charmaine and I took hold of each of Sasha's arm as she hung her head in a whimper. Her tenacity and her composure lost, at least for the moment. So she allowed them to lead her towards the sofa. Karen took the remote control and turned off the television. She got up and walked towards the Bose system that was surrounded by a vast collection of CD's. She checked to see if there was something already in the CD compartment and seeing that there was, she pressed play and listened to some smooth jazz so that the silence wouldn't suffocate them.

They all sat there for a few minutes quietly. Each contemplating what the situation could be. They had never seen Sasha this unraveled. What was going on? So Charmaine, Karen, Sasha and myself sat there waiting for Sasha to feel comfortable enough to speak what was on her mind. And so we waited and waied. I am not sure if everyone else realized that we sat there quietly for more than half an hour. I was starving and I wanted her to hurry up already, so I decided to break the silence in five minutes if Sasha did not open up her usually big mouth and cheer up so we could all laugh at whatever the damn situation or problem could be and move on.

"I cannot believe I am breaking down like some vulnerable weak woman. I didn't realize that this had already gotten to me so much. I know I have to tell somebody, and I have to tell my friends because sooner or later this thing might come out and I don't want to have to deal with this all alone." Sasha didn't move she stood there in the same position thinking to herself, trying to figure out how to begin and still feeling a little tongue-tied and hoping someone might break the silence.

Eventually I got tired of waiting and her five minutes were up so I had to say something to get this party going.

"So Sasha, why are you so upset? Does this have anything to do with what you wanted to tell us, because you didn't make it seem like your news was anything bad?" I asked as calmly as I could. We all looked at her, waiting for an answer and were held captivated as her head moved up and down in an everlasting yes.

"So what is it Sasha? We can't exactly help you if you don't talk to us." Charmaine chirped in.

"And we can't exactly read minds either" Karen added boldly.

I was wondering where she just got that piece of nerve from to say that out loud. Just as the words left Karen's lips and the thought crossed my mind, Sasha gave Karen one of those looks that could turn someone to stone, but again tapered herself and her attitude to focus on the issue at hand.

Karen didn't do anything to me, Sasha kept telling herself. *I would be doing her a big favor just to tell her I was getting my groove on with her so-called man.* She thought maliciously.

"I am sorry guys," I didn't mean to take things out on you. I am just so scared and worried. I am not sure what I am going to do. I don't know how this happened, and I don't know where to start. I hope you guys' won't think badly of me, you're all my friends and I need you right now. Please understand my situation. I need you." Sasha rambled leaving a puzzled look on everyone's faces. They couldn't understand what she was talking about or why she went on and on like that. But now they were curious as to what this big story was that Sasha had to tell them, and as Miles Davis blew his heart out with his trumpet and the music reverberated through the house, Sasha began to speak.

"Guys, I am very sorry. I just don't know where to start." She sighed

"Its okay Sasha, it really doesn't matter what it is, we are here for you. You can talk to us." Karen chimed in sweetly. She wanted to focus on somebody else but herself. She wanted Sasha to know that there were no hard feelings about the way she had treated her. That's just like Karen, the doormat. Forgiving everyone and everything and not letting it get to her. Always being reasonable and understanding to everyone.

I thought it was nice of Karen to comfort Sasha after that killer look she just gave her. I couldn't believe Sasha of all people was acting like this. Sasha, the one who had it together, the one who was on top of her game, the one who didn't need anyone and everyone could use a little of what she got. Sitting closest to Sasha, Karen rested her head on her shoulder and wrapped her arms adoringly through Sasha's arm. Sasha began to cry.

"Oh no! What did I say? Is it something I said," Karen asked feeling guilty. She thought her comments were helping but here she was making Sasha cry.

The water works opened up and Sasha released a fresh burst of tears.

"No it's not you Karen," she started, knowing full well that the reason for her tears was not even that her life could potentially be in ruins. Not even for the fact that she had a lot at stake for the news she was about to break, but because suddenly she felt a kinship towards Karen. Suddenly she felt somewhat sorry for her.

"Then what is it?" I asked, my patience running thin with this drama.

"Well then, can you tell us what the problem is? Stalling is not helping the situation." I told her impatiently, but the tears just kept on coming.

"Please Sasha, just tell us how can we help you and we will do our best. We are here for you?" I asked again more softly taking the edge out of my voice.

"It is something really bad, really, really bad." She started. "I need your help because this thing is about to break loose and I don't want you guys to be the last to know. I don't want you to be surprised. I know you might be disappointed but this happened a long time ago and this is not what or who I am now. I worked really hard and don't think it is fair what is happening, but I want you guys to promise to try and understand before you judge me or the situation. You are my best friends, we have known each other for a long time and I don't want to lose you." She finished, taking a deep breath.

Charmaine, who was sitting across from Sasha, got up and went and squeezed her way in between Sasha and Karen.

"Listen girl, I have known you since high school, and we

have been through some tough shit. We still here aren't we?" She asked grabbing a hold of Sasha's shoulders and turning her to face her. She looked deep within Sasha's eyes, and Sasha turned away in shame.

"You mean I got into some shit and you either took the rap or got me out of it."

"No, it was nothing like that and you know it. Don't I have secrets that only you know that you've kept?" Charmaine almost whispered. "Didn't I get myself into some terrible situations that I really could not have made it out of without you?" Charmaine began to tear up. She was scared for Sasha, she didn't know what on earth could have this diva so riled up.

"Okay, you're right," Sasha admitted, "but this is nothing like those little petty high school things, this is worse." She almost chuckled.

"Okay Sasha, but you called us here for a reason. Obviously by now you realize you can trust us. Now whatever this dilemma is we will get through it and we will get through it together. Okay?" I said, once again hoping that this time she would just come out and spill her damn guts so we could rest our minds.

"Okay guys, it's obvious that Sasha is not comfortable enough and is not ready to talk about whatever it is that is bothering her. So why don't we just relax and play our favorite game the worst experience until she is ready." Karen suggested. Charmaine thought it was a great idea and rallied everyone to join in.

"Yeah come on guys. Remember how this game always made us feel better?" the last time we played that game you all had me rolling. It was too funny!" I recalled the last time we hung out. After the whole restaurant scene with the new waiter that Sasha just had to show off.

"Remember that guy that Sandra told us about? The one

that hopped like a bullfrog during sex and swore he had it going on? I added, trying to get Sasha to laugh. The first time we heard it she laughed so hard that she almost peed on herself. I knew I wouldn't exactly get that effect, but if she would at least laugh, that would lighten the mood a bit and maybe calm her down.

"I knew this guy once," Karen piped in, "he was cute, he dressed nice and suave. Rumor had it that he had a big penis and that no one ever walked away unsatisfied."

"What?" Charmaine jumped in, "there is no such thing as the man that always satisfied every woman. Do you know how different and unique each woman is, with her desires and needs? I don't think so." She hissed and cut her eyes.

"This is my story isn't it?"

"Whatever!" Charmaine rebutted.

"Anyway, tell the story Karen, you know Charmaine is a bit of a feminist anyway." I encouraged. I liked these stories, and no one can tell it like these girlfriends of mine.

"Anyway, as I was saying, this guy was supposed to be God in pants. So when he came on to me, I decided to give him a test run."

Sasha smiled coyly and coughed, "you, giving someone a test run? Excuse me. I didn't know you had it like that."

"Anyway, I didn't want to just do it like that. I wanted candles, and romance and for him to earn me a little."

"Does Shawn know about this so called God in pants?" Sasha asked again in a small meek voice, trying not to sound too much like the devil's advocate that she really is.

"This was during one of those times when Shawn and I were on the outs, okay? So this doesn't have anything to do with him. Now can I finish telling my story?" Karen asked a bit perturbed, but even when she raises her voice she sounds like a pleading little girl.

"Go ahead gurl, finish your story." I jumped to the rescue.

I didn't want to see Karen getting all flustered and turning red. Every time she gets embarrassed or upset, she would turn red all over her face and she would break out into what would seem like heat rash all over her light skin. So even though she may sound vulnerable, one look at her can tell you if Karen was playing or if she was really upset about something.

"So we got together and everything was going okay, next thing I know he is turning out all the lights and blowing out the candles. So I asked him what was up."

"Awe nothing girl, I just want to be able to completely feel you and immerse myself into you so that we are dealing totally with the sense of touch. When we shut out the other senses, your sense of touch is heightened" he said.

"And it made perfect sense so I went along with it. Brother started with the tongue action and wouldn't let me touch his thing."

I busted out laughing, "his *thing* Karen?"

"Well you know what I mean."

"Yeah but we all grown women here, you can say it. Go on, try it." I implored, "Say dick. Day dong, penis, shaft, woody, or whatever else they call it." Sasha was laughing now, and Charmaine couldn't contain herself.

"Okay, okay. Let me finish." Karen begged. "So when it was all said and done, come to find out that home boy didn't have a big thingy, as rumored. He had a big tongue, which was fine by me. And he had only one ball and he was ashamed, thus his whole shutting out the lights thing."

"Oh no, oh no!" Charmaine blurted out. "You've got to be fucking kidding me. Men cannot usually do shit for a sista to begin with, now homeboy had a pencil dick and one ball?" She was on the floor now, rolling around on the carpet like she had a bellyache. "This is too much, it don't even sound like something that really happened." She continued rolling and laughing so hard it became contagious and we all blurted out into a fit of laughter.

"Wait that's not even the end of the story," Karen interrupted under a fresh burst of laughter that brought tears to her eyes. "He was begging and sometimes even paying off women who he made it with to spread this rumor. Now that is sad." Karen said, and suddenly she really felt sad. My goodness, I wonder what happened to him? She thought to herself and wiped away the tears before anyone would notice it was real.

"I've got one." I jumped in like a schoolgirl waiting for the teacher to pick on me. "Now this was before Michael and I got together so don't go getting any ideas." I said clearing the air. Yeah, yeah whatever Sasha thought. Before, after, what difference does it make? You are not giving him what he needs at home so he eating out anyway. She thought maliciously. Sasha couldn't take it that these women, her friends, were so content with their relationships. They didn't even stop to think if their boys were creeping, and here they are laughing and carrying on like they got it like that.

"This dude was from out of town. I met him at a party with some girls I was hanging out with after this movie we went to see. They knew and swore that he and I would like each other right away. So we hooked up, met up at some café in downtown Memphis where he lived and chatted a bit. It was kind of awkward because girlfriend who introduced us wouldn't leave. So we decided we would hook up privately the next time. He seemed to have had it going on. He seemed educated, seemed classy and was trying very hard to act like he was all that with his short self." I told them, remembering that weekend when we went down to Tennessee for this grand book expo/carnival type thing.

"Was it those same girls that we hooked up with in Atlanta for the Playas' Ball like four years ago?" Charmaine asked

"You remember that?" I said excitedly.

"I remember that your chickenshit ass backed out on me

cause you didn't like your costume and had me go alone, a freaking dominatrix without a trick. That's what I remember."

"Okay let's not go there." I tried to end it. Charmaine never got over that damn thing. It was so long ago now. I just didn't want to go to that ball, not after hearing all the freaky stuff that goes on there.

"Yeah you better end it, before I start on you Kayla." Charmaine spat.

"As I was saying; So Kenton played himself well enough to make me drive down to freaking Memphis the following week. I really didn't want to sleep with him, because I thought he was really nice and I wanted to get to know him. But I noticed during the whole week we spoke on the phone before we got together, all niggah wanted to talk about was sex, how he like sex like he like food. I told him that I preferred the oral thing myself and he didn't have anything to say about that so that was strike two for sex."

"Can you get to the point already? You are losing me." Charmaine commented. I decided to ignore miss thing.

"Once I was there, it was hard as hell to hook up with this niggah. Always talking about he got called in for work or he has to talk to his mother or whatever. So by Sunday I decided I didn't want shit to do with this dude. I called up the girls and hung out all that Saturday and was going to drive back to the city on Sunday. Would you know that one o'clock in the morning he was calling my cell. I didn't really like him by then but I decided that I was kinda in a dry spell and niggah done boasted about how he can tease and please and all kinds of shit. So I went over. He wanted the lights off."

"Lights off means trouble, you can't see what you're getting and he can't see what you offering. Most of the times he might have sores and or other things they don't want you to see." Karen said.

"Yeah well when the lights came on with this one, what he had was a ugly nasty black birthmark on his back that looked like some nasty hairy insect attached itself to him. He had some skinny legs that were just not attractive, and the worse part is that he couldn't even fuck."

"Now you see that? That's why I don't let these no good; don't know how to fuck niggahs experiment with my pussy. That is not why God gave it to me and I am certainly not going to misuse it." Charmaine instructed.

"Man I was pissed." I told them, "He was on top of me, huffing and puffing like he was the wolf that was going to blow the little piggy house down. Sweating and shit! He had a big dick all right, and kept saying 'my little thing' so I could say something about his dick. I felt like a nail, like he was trying to hammer me into the freaking floor. He didn't know what the hell he was doing. I wasn't turned on. He kept saying, "come for me baby, you want a man to fuck you right, the way you want, to make you feel like a woman." I thought, *yeah and you better get your ass off of me so I can go find him.*

He was not appealing, and didn't even know what foreplay was. He just grabbed a condom and went at it. I kept moaning because my pussy was dry and it hurt. I wanted him to stop, but he thought that meant to go up and down on me harder. Eventually I had to tell niggah to get up off me. I could tell he was trying to play it off like his feelings weren't hurt."

"What happened? My little thing doing damage?" I wanted to laugh so loud, but I contained myself.

"I refused to let him come and get satisfied and leave me all hung up, so I told him that this just was not the right night. I haven't heard from him since and I didn't call."

Sasha was laughing. She was laughing hard but I didn't even realize it until I was done telling the story. I was so immersed in that very painful memory. I hate that guy. I regret fucking this guy. Not just to regret it, but because it was a complete and utter waste of time for me. He wasn't worth the twelve dollars I paid for the cab to go to his house. He wasn't worth my time. He wasn't worth me getting out of bed. As a matter of fact, he was so bad that he made me miss my dry spell, made me not want any more sex.

"Okay, okay I get it," Sasha surrendered, "we have shared some really weird times and God knows we have been through a lot." She continued more solemnly. "I have a problem. Not just any problem, but my life could be on the line here."

"Holy shit, this is big, ain't it girlfriend?" Charmaine chirped in, "no wonder you're so fucked up, but it's okay. Just remember if you want me to mess somebody up for you, I know who to call." She reassured.

"Naw, it ain't nothing like that. This is bigger than us now." She said and sighed deeply.

"Okay," I said, "maybe it's time for you to just tell us and let us be the judge of that. Let us help you. After all, this is why you called us here right? So it's time." I sighed; finally glad to have gotten it off my chest, glad to say it.

Charmaine was sitting closer to Sasha now, hugging her securely in her long arms. Karen sat there on the opposite side meekly, almost afraid to hear what Sasha had to say. I just sat there, trying not to explode and say, bitch you called us here and whatever shit you got yourself into just spill it already God dammit. But instead I smiled softly and crossed my fingers.

"Okay, it's something at work. Well it is more than just something at work, it is something that happened years ago that is trying to come back and bite me in the ass." Sasha began. I heard Karen take a deep sigh and close her eyes.

"Go on Sasha girl, go on." Charmaine encouraged her.

"Charmaine, remember back when I started college? Remember how grandmamma was? It was hard being the oldest in our Panamanian immigrant home. It was as though everyone expected that I would graduate from high school and get a job, stay home and help grandmamma with the younger ones." She snickered softly.

"Yeah Sasha, I remember." Charmaine collected her thoughts and tried to follow where Sasha was going with this.

"Now do you remember drunk uncle Sadi that used to come stay with us for months at a time? He had all those women and kids and it was disgusting. I hated him. He would steal from grandmamma's purse and everyone would blame me. No one gave me the benefit of the doubt. I didn't want to be around him or the sluts he would bring in when everyone was sleeping. I hated him for beating on me every time he got home drunk or one of his bitches didn't give him any pussy that night. I really wanted to go to college; I had to get away from him, grandmamma and that bad neighborhood."

"Okay you are losing me Sasha. Does the problem have to do with work or home?"

"I knew I had what it took. I got good grades in school, good grades on my SAT's; I just couldn't understand why she or the rest of them would want to hold me back. I couldn't understand why she didn't see what he was doing." Sasha continued as though she didn't hear Charmaine's question as to why she was dredging up the past. She was way past that and had accomplished a lot.

"I don't understand. That was a long time ago girl. You made it out of that now. You don't talk to your uncle or any of your other family members any more so he is not a part of your life. What does that have to do with what is bothering you now?" Charmaine asked again, hoping Sasha would answer her this time.

"I am getting to that," Sasha said softly and breathed lightly before continuing.

"It's not that I am trying to blame them for my actions or what happened and is happening to me now. I know that though their behavior played a part in my decision to do what I did, it was still ultimately my choice, and I made that choice. I am still angry with them for that. Angry that I had never met my father, angry that my own mother just disowned me and went on with her life as though I didn't exist." Her voice raised and the tears started welling in her eyes. But this time she brushed them away. She already started and she had to get it out now before she lost her nerve.

Chapter 6

Charmaine sat there listening to Sasha break down. She remembered when she first met this girl in school. As an only child she had no friends. As a little girl she and her mom packed up and left dead boring Albany, Georgia and moved to New York to make a better life for themselves. So Charmaine had no family to turn to and learned to survive and defend herself. Elma Fibinezer and Charmaine Fibinezer moved to Brooklyn where Charmaine attended school and still lived with her mother in the same apartment they moved to more than ten years ago.

Her mother told her as the years went by that her daddy was no good that's why she left him back in Georgia. She told Charmaine horrible stories about how her father was a weed head who would have kids with anything that had a pussy between their legs. How all the girls in their neighborhood would laugh at her and disrespect her because she was the only one who didn't realize he was a dog until it was too late. She told Charmaine that he did nothing but treat her like a slut and acted as though Charmaine was not his child. He was light skinned and told Charmaine's mother that his child wouldn't come out looking like burnt charcoal. And since Charmaine was dark, there were no more discussions.

These were the stories that Charmaine grew up with. So as her mother worked at McDonalds and Burger King to make ends meet, Charmaine went to school and decided she hated men and that no man would treat her the way her father treated her mother. As the years went on she found herself finding the female body attractive. Her own lean, narrow body did not sport the curves on her hips or the roundness of her bosom the way it did most other girls her age. It took her breath away.

When she met Sasha in high school, she was a trouble-maker. She found herself sexually drawn to Sasha but was afraid to say anything. Sasha was a transfer student and didn't know the rumors of Charmaine being a lesbian. She sat next to Charmaine in her math class and Charmaine was the first to befriend her when all the other girls were jealous of her good looks.

One day as they left math class only a couple weeks after Sasha transferred to her school, someone threw a sandwich and hit Charmaine in her head, laughing and running while scream-ing, "I got her, I got the lesbo straight in the head."

Sasha had turned to look at her with bewilderment in her eyes, wondering what was happening. But before she could ask, two guys brushed up against her hard and yelled, "fag hag," as they walked by.

Charmaine's embarrassment was insurmountable and she felt then for sure that Sasha would no longer want to be friends with her. Why would anyone want to get called names and abused and become unpopular by being friends with the worst person in school she had thought to herself. Just at that moment three girls from the girls wrestling team confronted them.

"Hey lesbo, see you found yourself a new friend," one of them addressed her.

"Yeah, didn't nobody wanna be friends with you so you went and picked on the new girl that don't know no betta, eh?" The second girl asked with a shove of Charmaine's shoulders.

"Why don't you all just leave her out of this," Charmaine

had mumbled under her breath.

"What? You said something fish eater?" The first girl confronted her, stepping up closer and in her face.

"I bet if I come any closer I would smell pussy on your breath?" She snickered. The three girls were getting heated and a crowd of students surrounded them chanting, "fight, fight, fight, fight."

"Just wait one second. If you hate fish eaters that much why the hell you getting in her face?" Sasha jumped at Charmaine's defense. "Oh wait," she said before they could respond, and putting her index finger to her forehead as though she just had an epiphany, "you want to taste some of the pussy on her mouth that's why you getting ready to kiss her." The crowd broke out into a "whoooooo, haaaaaaaaa" just as the offended girl jumped to Sasha with her balled fist to defend her honor. But Sasha didn't back down. She stepped back at the girl and stood face to face with her, their noses practically touching.

"Do you know who you messing with newbie?"

"Nobody important. Obviously." She responded drawing out the word obviously slowly as if to make sure they understood her. The growing crowd roared again in response to Sasha's witty comeback. Words and anger flared and Charmaine decided to put a stop to it. Just as the girl was about to take Sasha, Charmaine pushed the girl out of Sasha's face.

"Listen, get the hell away from her okay?"

"Bitch..." was all she heard right before one of the girls punched her in her temple.

"Break it up, break it up. Classes have already started and everyone here is going to get a late slip and get sent to the dean's office," came the voice of relief. Two security guards walked up and broke up the crowd, but Charmaine and Sasha still stood unrelenting face to face with the three girls. The security guards took them to the principal's office and they all got suspended for a week. That's when Charmaine decided that she was going to be Sasha's friend for life, her first true friend and first crush.

Sasha's voice again invaded Charmaine's thoughts, and she turned to look at the group of girls surrounding her friend. Her eyes got misty just thinking about the pain that Sasha must be enduring to call them together like this, breaking down the way she was.

Sasha tried to compose herself in order to continue. She had to finish her story before she broke down again and loose her nerve.

"I don't know if you remember Kayla, but you and Charmaine were worried about me one time during my sophomore year in college. Remember when you guys couldn't reach me no matter what. I was constantly tired and at one time you even thought I should go to the doctor because I looked anorexic? I had denied it then. I denied it until I started failing classes and was being threatened that I was going to get kicked out of school. Well you were right." She paused. The tears silently running down her face and she swallowed hard to stop the lump in her throat from suffocating her.

"You mean you needed us and you lied? Sasha my goodness, shit. Why did you do that?"

"Please Kayla, let me finish."

"Give her a break will ya. This is past tense. She needs to tell us what the problem is now, she has obviously gotten through the worst.

The tears came faster now, and Sasha sniffled and swallowed again to clear her throat.

"I was on drugs." She cried out now unable to control herself.

"I started dancing at strip clubs to get money for school.

I was doing really well saving money for school. Then I met this guy who started paying me for nude pictures for a porno site on the net. It was good money so I took it. During that time we became lovers and he introduced me to coke."

"Wait. Take your time and breathe girl. Take your time." Charmaine soothed. She didn't even seem shocked by the news, but I was stunned. My mouth hung open and Karen had started to cry for Sasha.

"No I'm okay. I need to say this." Sasha said, pushing away Charmaine's hands as though she needed to feel isolated and alone. Even from Charmaine who had stood by her side in every way she could.

"Things got so bad that I was really going to get kicked out of school because I was blowing the money I saved on drugs. So I took time off and committed myself in a detox center. That is when I told you guys I was going out of town on a school study program. That's why you guys didn't hear from me for over a year. Anyway, when I came back I went straight. I used the rest of the money and finished school. I was so happy when I got the grant for law school that I didn't know what to do with myself."

"I remember that. I remember you saying how hard it had been for you, how no one would believe what you went through to get your law degree. But I had no idea to the extent of what you meant." I said.

I remember Sandra saying something about that once. That you acted so much like a bitch because you had to work so hard to get where you are so you don't think you should have to do shit for anybody." Every one looked at Karen.

"Those were her words." She screeched. "I didn't say it, I am just repeating what I heard." Karen blurted out hoping Sasha wouldn't attack her again.

Here we go again, that heffa Sandra. I can't stand her knocked up ghetto fabulous ass. Sasha thought, and had to check herself. Why did Sandra bother her so much? But she shook it off and continued.

"When I started working for Branson and Brendan law firm I was happy, until about four months into my employment there. One day Mr. Brendan, one of the partners called me into his office to tell me what a good job I was doing and offered to give me more responsibilities and an actual case that might go to court. This is what I needed, a case that would get me exposure and into the courtroom to give me experience. So I jumped at it. The trick was that I would be working closely with him. Anyway one thing led to another and I found myself in bed with him. It became a frequent thing, but secret. About eight months ago I tried to break it off with him. It got ugly. When I wouldn't change my mind he got a hold of those pictures and dug up my past and started blackmailing me with it."

She had to stop. Everyone was stunned. They were so quiet that you could hear a pin drop. The music had faded and stopped. The CD had played itself out a long time ago but no one even noticed. Sasha was afraid to raise her face or make eye contact with her friends. She felt it was better to hold her head down so she wouldn't lose her nerve. She was angry now. The tears still came but there were no apologies in her voice. She did what she had to do to get where she wanted to be. There was no one to help her. Her mother was barely making it in the projects. She hadn't seen or spoken to her since she dropped her and her baby brother off at her fathers' door so many years ago.

"Anyway that's my problem. I am tired of sleeping with him. Faking it, being on call and at his whim whenever he wanted to because he had something over my head. Holding me hostage like a fucking sex slave with my past. I decided a week ago I wouldn't do it anymore. So he threatened my job, and when that didn't do it, he threatened to leak it to the press. Tell everyone; ruin my life and my career, not to mention my chances of getting into another firm.

    I have busted my butt at Branson and Brendan for four years. I am one of their best litigation attorneys, I am feared and I have made a name for myself. Me sleeping with one of the partners did not get me where I am, I worked hard damn it, and now they are trying to take that away from me." Her head fell in her hands and her body shuddered. She cried now, openly. Not holding back, and waited for what her friends would say.

    I couldn't believe my ears. I lay back into the plush softness and comfort of the huge sectional sofa and took a deep breath. Karen still cried silent tears streamed down the side of her face and into her soft curly hair. Her light skin now seemed red. Charmaine hovered over Sasha. Holding her. She took her hand and soothingly ran it over Sashas' back. We were all quiet and shocked. No one knew what to do or say. All we could do was just stand there and allow Sasha to cry as we absorbed the information that had our heads whirling. The look on everyone's face was one of disbelief and discomfort, we didn't know how to handle this bomb she dropped on us and who's to tell if there was more to this story.

Chapter 7

Back at home I didn't know what to think or what to do. I thought to call Charmaine but with her revelation that she is a lesbian in the midst of all this had gotten me confused. What are we supposed to do now? What did she expect us to do that would help her.

"Good morning baby." Mikey announced turning to me with a delicious morning breath kiss. His morning breath is not like most stinky morning breaths. It is like he got up in the morning and brushed his teeth and then came back and lay in bed before I wake up just to tell me good morning. I know it's far fetched. But that's what it seems like.

"How was your girl's day out yesterday?" He continued in a sleepy raspy voice that is so sexy it just makes me want to jump his bones.

"What was that?" I asked pretending not to have heard.

"I said how…" and before he could continue I was all over him. I couldn't help myself. I rolled over from my spot on the bed right on top of his muscular frame. I gently stuck my tongue all the way in his mouth to absorb all that morning breath sweetness and felt his body come alive under me. His hands grabbed my posterior and I attempted to take him with us both still wearing our underwear. I wanted him so bad I didn't have time to take off something as unimportant as underwear. But before I could really show him how much I appreciated his full attention he was pushing me away. I couldn't believe it and I was about to cry. My body was all tingly and I could feel the throbbing in my loins. I don't think I could take being rejected by Mikey today. He used to love me waking him up like this in the morning, but I don't know what's been going on with him lately.

Michael could see her anger and thought he better moved fast before what he wanted to do got blown out of the water. He wanted to do something special for her. Something she loved him to do and what always drove her crazy. But he could see that she was thinking he was stopping for some other reason. He wanted her. All day yesterday he had to focus real hard to not get a hard on around the guys during their basketball game. He couldn't stop daydreaming about her long legs wrapped around his midsection totally controlling him. He ached waiting for her to return home and finally fell asleep with a huge erection. He knew he could have called someone else like he usually did if things got a little slow with Kayla, but this day he wanted her and only her. So he flipped her over gently on the bed laying her semi naked body on her back. Crawling up towards her face he kissed her hard, sucking her face and pulling on her tongue until he felt her body relax and started moving into him.

"I love you." She whispered.

"Don't talk." He hushed and as she whimpered and shivered beneath him as he slowly moved his tongue downward, nibbling on her breast and licking her torso. He kissed her until her body quivered uncontrollably under him. He slowly parted her legs and moved her down so he could position himself between them. He allowed her to savor the feel of the tip of his erect penis and then pull out, causing her to moan softly.

Slowly he slid down between her legs and buried his face in her moistness. He sniffed her and sighed at the sweet smell of her juices then tauntingly and gently licked the exterior of her flesh. He tasted and relished her like he was having the best ice cream he had ever tasted and was in no rush to hurry and finish.

I sighed deeply and thrust my thighs into his face. He grabbed a hold of my buttocks and shifted me so he could fully thrust his tongue deep within my pussy that was boiling with desire for him. I loved that and he wanted to drive me wild. It's been a long time since he has taken this kind of time and care in making love to me and I wanted to savor each touch, moan and sigh.

He wanted her to want him as much as he wanted her today and the day had just begun.

I grabbed a hold of Michael's head and gyrated my hips into his face and he did not resist or protest. He shifted and allowed me to lead him into what felt good to me and he kissed me wherever I itched. Using his tongue he explored my flowing rivers and got more and more excited with every moan, sigh and throb that let him know I was on the verge of implosion.

He didn't want her to stop until she was completely drained, completely satisfied and he resisted the urge to plunge himself within her.

I pushed Michael's head deeper between my legs and felt the burning sensation build between my thighs spreading like wild fire through my entire body. I tried to restrain myself but I couldn't help letting out the most pleasurable scream so he would know just how much he was tuning me on. Totally blowing my mind to nowhere land. Before I could stop my quiver Michael slowly inch by inch lowered himself into me causing a new rush of orgasm and scream to tremor through my palpitating body.

The heat from her was too much and the throbbing moistness of her muscles overwhelmed Michael. He couldn't harness his desire anymore and he buried his face into her shoulder and enjoyed the pulsing release that rushed from his body and into hers.

Completely satisfied and relaxed I turned and kissed Michael passionately in a silent thank you. It's been awhile since I have felt this loved by him, this connected and intertwined with him. As we lay there breathless I watched his magnificent chest heave with every breath he took and sighed a grateful sigh that I was not in Sasha's shoes today. Suddenly I remembered Sasha and what happened the day before. I had to and needed to share it with somebody and why not Michael?

"Darling?" I began slowly. "I have to tell you something that happened yesterday."

"What is it Kay?" He asked turning towards me, the sweat from our lovemaking only a few moments before still glistening on his body.

"Sasha revealed something to us last night. She is going through a tough situation that can ruin her career and I don't know what she expects us to do to help her." I uttered slowly and solemnly. When I was finished telling Michael all that had transpired the day before he was speechless. I could see concern written all over his face and I was reminded of how lucky I was that he stayed with me through our difficult times. We lay beside each other in quiet contemplation and lost in our own thoughts. While I thought long and hard about what would become of Sasha, Michael seemed to be immersed with his own concerns.

"Did she say anything else about other men she's been seeing?" He asked her, wondering just how much Kayla knew and if she was just biting her time to pull him out of his foxhole.

"Naw, why would you ask that?" I turned to look at Mike but he kept his cool. Though it seemed like Kayla could see right through him he didn't want to get caught up more than he had to. So he remained quiet.

"I never mentioned anything to you about her seeing any

other men. Why would you think there were others involved?" She asked him, curious as the where he would get his line of questioning.

"Nothing Kay, I was just wondering, since we know how caught up she gets and the character types she usually seemed to be attracted to. I just thought that they might have something to do with it." He told her calmly.

"I guess I understand your point. But she didn't say anything about any other man being involved. Just her boss at the law firm."

"Wow, I feel bad for her. What is she going to do? It seems to me that it's just better if she went along with it. After all, she gave it up to him for free all this time anyway. What's the big deal if she kept doing it? That's all he really wants isn't it?" Michael asked callously hoping this thing stayed quiet and did not blow over. If shit started hitting the fan he wouldn't want his name to get splattered on the ceiling with it.

I decided to get up and stuck my underwear between my legs to stop the drip from our lovemaking from dripping all over the floor and ran to the shower. Unaware of where Michael's concern was coming from I listened to him intently and smirked when he made the comment about her keep giving it up to her boss.

"That's not nice Mikey. After all you've known Sasha and the girls for as long as we've been together so you should really be concerned about what's going on." I shouted above the shower.

"Sorry, I didn't mean anything by it. It's just that you know how Sasha is just as much as I do, and you know she is kind of freaky. Her only prerequisite for getting busy is that you are really cute, have a big dick or loaded." He snickered.

"Why do you have to say it like that? Its not like she's a slut," I said in a sort of matter of fact tone, "she just knows what she likes in a man."

"Well you know what I mean. The girl just does not discriminate on any true value." Michael reiterated.

"That may be true, but she is my friend and after what I have gone through in my life, it is not up to me to judge anyone."

Michael looked at her then, a look of understanding and curiosity as to what particular thing she referred to this time. But he dropped it. Having a conversation with Kayla about her past was something he didn't want to get into at that moment. He just had a nice nut, she got her groove on and for the moment the smell of satisfaction was still in the air. All is well with the world and digging up coffins was not on the agenda for today.

"I understand Kay, and I am behind you one hundred percent. Whatever you want to do I will see what I can do to help. What about Sandra, Karen and Charmaine, what's their take on this drama? How do they feel about the situation?" He asked as he suddenly began to feel naked watching, as Kayla got dressed. So he got up and walked over to the closet and grabbed a pair of Nike basketball shorts and a T-shirt he pulled nonchalantly over his head. Walking to the bathroom to wash his hands, he was unaware and not concerned that his T-shirt was not only on wrong side out, but also the back was in the front and the front was in the back.

"Well your guess is as good as mine Mikey. They seemed as shocked as I am, but I think we have all reached the same consensus. I think we are all going to stand by her and offer whatever help we can."

At that moment I stopped and turned to look at Mikey. He had carelessly thrown some water over his face and was wiping it off with the washcloth when it occurred to me again as it usually did on countless occasions how lucky I am that he stayed with me. Lucky that he had put up with all the crap I had dished out to him on so many occasions, and yet here he is and he still loves me and me alone. I suddenly had this incredible urge to go over and give him a huge hug and that's exactly what I did.

Before he could remove the washcloth from his face Michael felt her warm delicate arms around his waist as she pushed her midsection into his causing a slight sensation of a returned erection.

"Wooooo! What's that for?" He pulled away from her and looked into her beautiful wide hazel eyes and studied her face as she acted coy and her thick eyebrows frowned together as she pouted.

"Nuttin' I just wanted to give my sexy wexy baby a huggy buggy hug." I told him in a puppy sounding silly voice that made him laugh out loud.

He laughed so hard it shook the house and his voice rumbled like thunder. It was one of those rare moments that brought a soulful laughter that came from the depths of his guts and boomed out in uncontrollable mirth.

"You are too much," he told her lifting her to him and feeling the heat that still radiated between her legs as she wrapped them around his waist, "you are just the silliest little thing when you wanna be." He hugged me tight, snuggling into me affectionately and I couldn't help savoring the smell of him, the sheer strength of him.

"I just want you to know that I love you. I am honored and I am thankful." I had to say something; I had to tell him that I knew how lucky I was. I could feel the heat in my back from Michael's stare as I ran to grab the phone before the answering machine picked up. It was rare that I did this, answering the phone before hearing who it was that was calling, but I was expecting a call from Sasha and being that she is going through a tough time I wanted her to know that I am here for her. By answering the phone I am giving her a little special something because I know how much she hated the fact that I screened my phone calls.

"Oh Sandra, what's up?"

"What? Are you disappointed it's me? Is there some kind of conspiracy boycott against me now or something? I just don't understand what's going on." Sandra almost yelled the frustration rising in her voice. She had called Charmaine earlier that morning and felt like she got the brush off and then Karen sounded kind of weird and rushed her off the phone before she could really get into a conversation with her and now Kayla. Sandra had been out of the mix and had not been clued in to all the drama that seemed to be happening in her friends' lives. She just felt like the connection was lost and wasn't sure if they had just decided to not be friends with her anymore just because of Sasha.

"I'm sorry Sandy, its not you. It's just that I was expecting a call from Sasha, she is going through a rough life transition right now and I want to be there for her.

"Sasha? Sasha is going through a tough life. WHAT? She does not know what it is like to go through a tough life transition. She is not dealing with HIV everyday popping drugs like an addict? Is she so tired from the drugs and the sickness that sometimes she forgets to feed, bathe and clothe her own children? Does she live in the projects where right outside her door there are drug dealers and the sound of twelve-year-olds losing their virginity in the hallways? No! So what the hell is everyone fussing over Sasha for? I am going through these things and I could use the help and support but do I get that?" Sandra rambled on. She was angry now and I wasn't sure what to make of her outburst. I guest I had never thought about it like that. She always seems to have it together. She never asked for help or complained.

"Gee, my gosh Sandra, where is all this anger coming from suddenly?" I asked calmly and slowly trying to absorb what just happened and at the same time I kept thinking that Sasha is going to be mad when she tries to call and the line is tied up. "Did

I do something to upset you Sandy? Because all I said was that I was expecting a call from Sasha."

"I am sorry. It must be the drugs talking. I have been so weak I couldn't even get up to go to the bathroom and pooped in my panties before I could make it to the toilet. Suzette has got a cold again and I am sometimes so drained and weak that I can't even lift her up to feed her. I know I am taking a risk breast-feeding her but sometimes that's the only food I have to give her. I swear social service is going to take her from me if they ever find out that I am getting too weak to take care of my kids." And she broke into tears.

I didn't know what to say. I just sat there and let her cry it out. What is going on? When it rains it really pours and if it is not one thing it's something else. I sometimes completely forget that Sandra is sick. We don't really see her that often because she is in an area of Brooklyn where none of us wanted to go. Sasha lived the farthest away in Long Island and Charmaine, Karen and myself all lived in more tolerable places in Brooklyn.

"I am sorry Sandra, is there anything I can do to help you out?" I asked. I felt terrible for Sandra and it was obvious she didn't know the drama that was going on now with Sasha.

"Do you want me to stop by later, hang out some so we can talk?" I asked hoping this would be enough to pacify her and get her off the phone.

"I don't understand Kay, why doesn't anyone want to talk to me? What did I do?" she asked.

"I have no idea what you are talking about Sandra. Why would you think no one wants to talk to you? I love you and I am sure the others care about you as much as I do. No one wants you to be unhappy." I told her calmly but it didn't stop the tears and the sadness in her voice just grew deeper.

"I am so sorry baby girl, but I do have to go. I will stop by and spend some time with you later okay? I promise." I couldn't believe I just left Sandra like that. I could understand why she would think that no one wanted to talk to her. She was in distress and yet Sasha's pain was more important to me, even though Sandra's pain was life threatening and there were children involved. Anthony is my godson. Have I really gotten that cold? These thoughts went through my head, as I waited for her answer that I hoped would quell the guilt that I was feeling.

"Okay." She agreed reluctantly and I listened as the phone slowly clicked disconnecting us from each other.

"What was that about?" Michael asked curiously. While I was on the phone he had decided to take a shower and get ready to go out. He had gotten out and sat quietly behind me on the bed listening to my end of the conversation with Sandra.

"Where are you going? I thought you had today off." I asked ignoring his question. I couldn't believe he had plans.

"Well, I did but since you are going to be preoccupied with girlfriend problems I have decided to go in and make some extra cash. I couldn't help feeling appalled. I thought he was going to stay home and relax.

"Man it's a good thing I am not the jealous type. From the way you are hooking yourself up with the get up, you don't look like a man going to the warehouse to lift and package heavy boxes." I told him half jokingly.

"Well that goes to show you how much you know. A man has to always put his best foot forward. Just because I am only a warehouse worker does not mean I have to look raggedy and torn up." He emphasized with one last squirt of cologne against his temples. Picking up his wallet and sticking it in his back pocket he walked over to me and barely brushed his lips against my own. As he walked out the door I watched in amazement and disbelief that I had just made passionate love to that same guy who just kissed me like I was a distant cousin.

I was jolted from my thoughts by the phone ringing again sounding almost angry and I was forced to take my mind off Michael and on to Sasha as her voice came at me like a boomerang over the telephone.

"Some friend you are. I thought you were supposed to be waiting for my phone call. How many times now I tried to call and all I got was a busy signal. All you had to do was say you didn't want to go with me you know, you don't have to take the phone off the hook to avoid me." She attacked before I could say hello.

"What the hell is going on today? Did every freaking soul wake up on the wrong side of the bed this morning. And what the fuck did I do to be bombarded with everybody's shit. All I am trying to do is be there for everyone and instead everyone is jumping down my damn throat." I yelled back at the silent receiver. For a while I thought she had hung up, but then I heard this squeaky voice come back quietly at me.

"Dag, sorry. I didn't mean to come off like that. I guess with all that I am dealing with I am a little nervous and anxious." She said apologetically.

"No it's okay. It's just that today I feel like I am supposed to be everybody's mother and so many demands are being placed on me."

"I didn't mean to be one of those people Kay, I need you." She begged pathetically and I had to laugh.

"Okay, so what's the deal?" I asked her ready to move on. It was already one in the afternoon and I really wanted to stop by and see Sandra. She sounded as though she was really desperate and in a bad place and I wanted to see if there was anything I could do to help her out. Maybe give her some money or something.

"I wanted to meet up with Charmaine. She had an idea of how to handle *Mr. Brendan*." She accentuated his name with pure sarcasm, disgust in her voice. I can only imagine what devious plans Charmaine is concocting now.

"I am about twenty five minutes away from your house. I am calling you from my cell so could you please be ready and waiting outside so we can just go." She demanded.

"Damn the way you talk and carry on pushing people around you wouldn't think you are the one that is getting screwed right now. *Literally*." I spat. I just cannot believe the gall of this bitch. She is the one with the problem and yet she is acting like she is doing your ass a favor. "Fine, just hurry because I don't have all day to spend with you. Other people have more legitimate problems which are a matter of life and death." I told her and slammed down the phone. I think I must be going crazy. This girl is insufferable and she still does not realize with all the mess that she has gotten herself mixed up in that the world does not revolve around her.

****

As I stood outside my door waiting for Sasha's bright red 2003 convertible Mustang GT to come swerving around the corner, my mind went back to Michael and it suddenly occurred to me how weird he behaved right before he left. It was almost as though he hoped that Sasha wouldn't be able to get out of this. Like he thinks she deserved it. It didn't occur to me then he might be feeling that way because my head was still spinning from that great oral sex he gave me. Man he hadn't licked me like that in a long time. And suddenly a profound sadness engulfed me. What is going on? Is there some kind of evil destructive bug in the air?

I didn't have much time to explore the thought. It appeared as though Ms. Thang sped up as she turned the corner of my block because she was burning rubber and you could hear the revving of the engine. I stood up and met her at the curb and I didn't even bother to say anything about it. She knows it drives me crazy when she does shit like that and she still does it. Before I could close the door, home girl took off like a bat out of hell and I thought to myself that is exactly where she was going. Hell.

Chapter 8

Karen sat at the desk of the temp job she just landed as a Data Entry Clerk of one of New York's major publishing companies only a couple months before and felt overwhelmed by the pressure her boss was putting on her. This Monday morning was not going well at all and the fact that she now knew what Sasha was going through after that heart to heart and blatantly honest discussion that they had only the Saturday before she was happy that her boss was a woman and not a man. Even though she could be a dike from the way she dresses like a man wears her hair shortly chopped in a man's crew style and bosses everyone around. She didn't even sound feminine.

Karen was consumed with how Sasha had been treating her lately. It was like she could do nothing right with her. Even when she tried to talk with her or be a friend to her, she still stepped on Sasha's toe and she was beginning to think that maybe she should back out of Sasha's life for a while and let whatever it was she did to Sasha blow over.

She hadn't seen Shawn since the whole drama about her going over to Sasha's on Saturday either. The bruised marks on her lips and forehead were still visible reminders of what she wanted to forget. Over the years Shawn's abusive behavior had gone from bad to worse. At first he used to just hit her in places that didn't show, and if she had to go to the hospital she could say that she fell or something. The doctors called the police already on a couple of her visits suspecting spousal abuse and she denied it. The other time they investigated and caught Shawn in a lie. She didn't press charges then, but he was faced with several warnings. She was ready to get rid of him but she wasn't sure where to start. One of the nurses on her last visit told her she could contact the shelters or the abuse hotline. Maybe that was the answer. Just as she was dazing off into a world of questions and possible solutions she heard her name being called.

"Karen." She heard her boss's voice and suddenly sat up at her desk from where she previously had her elbow rested and her head in her hands in quiet contemplation. It was only eleven in the morning and the day was just dragging.

"I am here." she replied in her meekest most humble voice and looked up at that moment to see her boss who stood at five foot ten inches tall and one hundred and eighty pounds over her own five feet two and ninety pound frame.

"I was just bringing the last of the project that was required for this afternoon." Karen told her and began shuffling through her desk to gather the files with the last of the project she had completed since nine o'clock that morning. She had tried to make herself busy but it was difficult keeping her mind on work and she had sat at her desk the entire time daydreaming about Shawn and Sasha and the problem she was having with both of them.

"Oh Karen that's not what I want to speak to you about," her boss's voice resounded, softening in a way that gave Karen some relief.

"You can bring that to my office after lunch but I also wanted to let you know that I had something else I wanted to discuss with you so before you go today, please be sure to remind me okay?" She made an attempt at a smile that looked as plastic as her patent leather men's shoes and walked away before Karen could answer.

Karen slouched back into her chair at that time and breathed a sigh of relief that she had left, but had now become filled with a new worry. What did her boss want to talk to her about? Yet she couldn't take her mind off of the two of them. That idiot Shawn was always home, and as much as she loved him she realized that it was time she did some things with her life. She wanted to make some changes including getting rid of him. She was tired and fed up with the fact that he was always in and out of work from week to week and sometimes months at a time. Whenever he found work would be the appropriate time for him to break up with her and take off and guess who he found when a week or a month later he lost his job? Yep. You guessed it. And she was just as much of an idiot to keep taking him back.

"Thank you for calling DMac, Inc. where you write and we do all work. This is Karen speaking, how may I help you?" She answered with that incredible mundane programmed way that everyone in the office was trained to answer.

"Hey Karen, are you busy?" Came Sandra's weak voice over the phone. Out of all five of them, Karen had been the only one to really pay attention to Sandra's needs and seemed to understand the true devastation of the disease and what she had to go through with her kids and trying to keep Social Services out of her home.

"Sandy what's wrong?" Suddenly alert and scared of what she would say next. She knew that Sandra wouldn't call her at work except if it was an emergency, and with her sounding so fatigued and barely audible tears welled in Karen's eyes.

"Sandra is everything okay? Please tell me what's wrong." Karen knew that it wasn't just because of the way that Sandra sounded why she suddenly felt so helpless and instantly struck with grief. It was from everything. From the thoughts she had harbored all day regarding Shawn's position in her life, her friend ship with Sasha that was being tested, and the way her boss approached her all contributed to her distress.

"Karen, I know this is a lot to ask, but can you please come over? I am so weak today from the medication and Suzette has been crying for hours. I don't even know where Anthony is. I know he has to be hungry and I haven't done anything for them all morning. They have been up since seven this morning. I hate to ask you this girl, but...."

"No don't worry about it. I am on my way. I think I am screwed with this job anyway and I need to leave too."

"Okay so I will see you soon, thanks Karen." Sandra sighed, trying to stop the tremor of her hands enough to finish her conversation with Karen.

"Just see what you can do to pacify Suzette and I will be there as soon as I can."
Karen told her and then hung up the phone, wondering how she was going to get out of work for the rest of the day. It really didn't matter anymore because of the tone her boss took with her she had a feeling that something was up anyway. She got on the company internal email network and emailed Terra about her situation and asked if she could leave early. Half an hour later when she got no response she gathered her nerve and walked into Terra's office.

"Terra, I know you wanted to see me before I left for the day, but I have an emergency. A friend of mine is very ill and I was wondering if it would be okay if I took the rest of the day off." She stood shakily at her boss's office door waiting for what she thought was the inevitable. She was going to get fired.

"Do you have the completed file from the project?"

"Yes, I have it all right here." Karen told her and walked timidly toward Terra's desk and placed the file gently in her outstretched hand. She stood there uncomfortably as Terra slowly flipped through the pages of the file in her hands and frowned with a concerned look on her face.

"Is something wrong?" Karen asked.

"No, not at all. Why don't you go on and take the day off. We will talk first thing in the morning." She said in finality and placed the folder neatly in front of her and looked softly at Karen.

"I hope your friend will be okay. Let me know if there is anything I can do." Karen stood there totally flabbergasted at what she just heard, so, not sure if she heard right, she asked again.

"So it's okay if I go?"

"Yes Karen, I just said that. Go! Go on now. Your friend needs you."

Karen took one last look at this woman whom everyone talked about behind her back and called her names. This woman whom she was so afraid of, her boss whom she was sure to give her a hard time, and yet here she was being concerned and supportive. She slowly walked out of the office and once the door was closed behind her she rushed to her desk and grabbed her purse and rushed out the door. It had now been an hour since Sandra called and it would probably take her another hour to get into Brooklyn from Manhattan where she worked. She hoped she would be on time to help out Sandra.

She rushed to the train station in hopes of catching an express number four or five train then she would have to change for the local number three trains to take her into the projects of Brownsville. She hated going into that neighborhood and wished she had money where she could help her friend out of that depressing piss drenched place. If only she had it easy like Sasha. To think Sasha had so much money that she does not know what to do with it, living in that big house by herself and wasting money when she could be helping out others. Even if it was just one person, even if it was just Sandra she helped. For whatever reason she and Sandra were always butting heads and for the life of her she couldn't figure out why, except for the fact that she couldn't push Sandra around, she couldn't understand why someone so powerful could hate someone with so little.

It was only twelve thirty in the afternoon so there were not that many crowded on the train. She sat down and opened her purse and pulled out the now crumbled and brown faded old newspaper clipping from only four years before. Again tears welled in her eyes as she unfolded the article that she had clipped out back in 1998 about that poor girl Chyna who found out she might have AIDS. She remembered that news story when there was a terrible car crash that killed Chyna's lover Miguel just like it was just yesterday. She couldn't stop the tears and she didn't try to hide them when out of the blue this old lady came on the train and sat next to her. She didn't say a word at first; she just gently tapped Karen on her shoulder and smiled when she looked up.

"All things are possible with God," she said softly with a wrinkled smile, "he that believeth in him should not perish but have everlasting life." She continued and sat back to brace herself from the rumble and bumps of the train. Karen turned to look at this wayward stranger. She looked old and weary. Her clothes were ragged and stained. To put it plainly…she stunk. Holding her breath was all Karen could do to stop the stench from making her regurgitate. She leaned on a thick piece of stick that was not polished and you could still see the brittle on it as if it had fallen off a tree and left to rot when the old woman came along and found use for it. She leaned on the makeshift crutch and held her head down in an attempt at slumber. Her dark skin seemed to have hardened from a rough life and its wrinkles seemed to have developed a home for caked dirt, like she hadn't washed in a while. She smelled like a homeless woman, yet here she was being faithful, being supportive, offering advice and encouragement.

At the next stop the woman got off, and before the train pulled away she saw the woman nestle herself in a box in the far corner of the train station.

Karen looked again at the crumpled newspaper article in her hand, one last look at the way Miguel got smashed up. How sad! Then it struck her and made sense what the old lady was saying. All things are possible with God and things could work out just fine. She quickly folded the paper that she had been carrying around for so long, carrying around without knowing why. She just felt sorry for those people and the whole thing touched her.

Finally arriving at her stop, Karen went to the store to pick up some groceries for Sandra. She didn't know if she had anything in her house so she got a variety of food and toiletries. Going into the unsecured building and up the stairs caused her to be nauseated from the stench of human waste and urine in the place. She walked up to the third floor where Sandra lived and went to knock on the door when it pushed open. She walked in and realized the stench was coming from inside the apartment. Suzette had cried herself to sleep on top of Sandra. She was lying down on the floor and Suzette had used the bathroom seems like several times in her unchanged diaper. Her diaper was so full it was leaking over Sandra. She seemed almost lifeless and pale. She didn't see Anthony anywhere in the apartment. So she tip toed back out of the apartment and started looking out in the hallway of the building.

"Anthony," she called out. "Anthony, where are you?" She called out in fear. Fear that he had walked out of the house and into the streets. What if he got kidnapped, raped or even killed. Frantically she called out his name again. "Anthony sweetheart where are you?" she called as loudly as she could and keeping her tone of voice as amicable as possible. She didn't want to anger some drug lord or anything like that.

Suddenly she heard a noise in the stairway and she slowly walked toward it. As she got closer to the stairs she smelled what could be marijuana. She moved closer, slowly and then she could see smoke coming from there. Peering around the corner she saw an older guy from the back. He was tall and going gray. He had a receding hairline at the top of his head and bending over what looked like a child. It seemed as though he was trying to coax the child into smoking and he looked a little touchy feely. His hands were all over the child, caressing his hands and head. He was bent over the child so closely they seemed like they were almost hugging.

"Anthony?" She called again more quietly knowing that both the man and Anthony could now see her. "What are you doing out here sweetheart. Your mother is worried sick about you." She told him calmly while maneuvering her way through them and pulling the boy away.

"Have a good day." She remarked to the gentleman who was clearly pissed off. She knew she was in no position for a confrontation and that she would be in a lose-lose situation to try and get nasty. So she just smiled as sweetly as she could and pretended she didn't realize what was really going on, then quickly rushed Anthony away from the man and into the direction of Sandra's apartment. Once inside she sat down and trembled. She was scared about the possibility of what might have happened to little Tony and wondered how many times he had gotten himself caught up with those junkie makers. She shivered because she knew that as petite as she was, if that man wanted to hurt her, there wouldn't be a darn thing she could do about it. As she calmed herself, she looked around again and the tears welled in her eyes.

"Oh Sandra, how is it that this is happening to you?" She moved towards her still sleeping body and touched her hair.

Slowly, she removed Suzette from on top of her mother and rushed into the one bedroom that was in the apartment. There she changed Suzette. After she washed up the baby, she realized that all of her clothes were dirty and that Suzette didn't have any diapers, so she just wrapped some cloth around her for the time being and pulled one of Sandra's old shirt over the baby's frail little body. Karen couldn't stop the tears as she realized that if this were happening to her, she would want people to care about her. But how did Sandra do it? Karen wondered, mostly so optimistic and positive, yet here she is dying.

She told Anthony to help her by picking up his toys and clearing out the separated area that Sandra had created for his room. He moved slowly but at least he was busy. Karen put Suzette in front of the television and put it on channel thirteen where they had the entire kiddy cartoon shows. Since they did not have cable, there wasn't much for Karen to choose from. Suzette played and giggled happily because she was now clean and fed. Karen wanted to have the place spotless for Sandra before waking her up and asking her to take a bath and giving her something to eat. So she worked fast. She did the dishes in the tiny kitchen sink. There was no stove, just a hotplate with two burners, so she put on a pot of water and made some pasta. On the other burner she simmered some ground beef and spaghetti sauce and veggies until the small apartment started smelling and looking like a home.

Just as she put away the broom and mopping with some pine sole and the place smelled like some place she would actually stay, Sandra turned her head slowly and looked around. She was weak and pale, but she realized that there was something remarkably different about her apartment. She looked toward the balcony and the glass sliding doors looked spotless, she saw the clean curtains on the windows that allowed a fresh burst of sunlight to come streaming through. She looked around and saw

Suzette as content and as quiet as could be shaking her rattle and cooing. Anthony sat quietly beside her. She tried to get up but she couldn't, her head spun and a sharp burst of pain rushed through her. Karen saw this and ran to her. She put a pillow under her head and asked her what she could do.

"Look at this place," Sandra said happily; though her mouth was dry and had white morning stains all around it. Her eyes could barely open, but Karen could still see the gleam of appreciation in them. She started to cough.

"What's wrong Sandra? What can I do?" Karen asked again trying not to sound frantic.

"I need my pills." Sandra muffled. "I had them here before I passed out. Where are they?" she asked. She was getting more and more scared of the pain that was slowly working its way back into her body, that same pain she escaped by passing out. Karen remembered the scattered bottles that were settled around both Suzette and Sandra when she first came in. She didn't realize what they were so she just put them all in a plastic bag and threw them in a corner under the kitchen cupboard.

"Yeah, I know where they are," she said and eased from under Sandra's head leaving the pillow to give her support until she returned. Karen hurried and returned with the plastic bag she had thrown the bottles of medication in and gave it to Sandra.

"Thanks!" Said Sandra, and she slowly raised herself up on her elbows and went through the bag to get the assortment of pills she needed. By the time she was finished, she had consumed about fourteen different pills of a variety of colors, shapes and sizes. Some of them were so huge that Karen didn't understand how she could swallow them whole.

Sandra saw the puzzled look on Karen's face and smiled, "they drain me most of the time, but they make the pain bearable. At least with the pills I can function somewhat and get around." Sandra told her as she slowly recuperated and regained some energy. Soon she was able to get up and give herself a short bath. She couldn't stay wet for too long so she rushed out of the shower. Once she was clean and dressed, Karen presented her with a big bowl of spaghetti and sat Anthony next to her while she held Suzette in her arms and fed her bits and pieces of the food.

As they sat there, Sandra asked Karen if Kayla had called or stopped by.

"No, the phone didn't ring once. Why? Were you expecting Kayla?"

"As a matter of fact yes. I remember I felt really sick and I called her. I asked her if she could come over when she got a chance. She sounded busy and pre-occupied but I was desperate and I begged her. I didn't let on how sick I was but she promised she would come by." Sandra felt angered but more sad and disappointed than anything else. She thought if anything she could depend on Kayla, but she didn't come through for her. Instead she could have died here after asking her for help and she still wouldn't have showed up to help her. The tears flowed freely.

It was dark out when Karen left and Sandra thanked her for her friendship and kindness. Karen felt guilty leaving, but she was happy she was there to help her friend with whatever little she could do. Now it was time for her to help herself.

Chapter 9

Sasha and I drove full speed to Charmaine's house. Charmaine had a plan and Sasha was willing to try anything. She couldn't wait to get to Charmaine's house and the twenty-minute drive only took ten with Sasha behind the wheel. We pulled up to Charmaine's house and parallel parked in a spot across the street from Charmaine's house. She didn't even bother to put her convertible top up or lock up the car even though she was very paranoid in that neighborhood and there was a crowd of guys outside enjoying beer and loud rap music. She was in too much of a hurry to be bothered.

We ran to the elevator and I was getting annoyed and feeling like I was being dragged around. I didn't like the way this felt. Like I was about to get involved in something that I was not going to like. I held my breath and followed suit hesitantly.

"Hello we haven't got all day you know Ms. Thang," Sasha hurried to the door ahead of me as though I was slowing her up and this was a matter of life and death. I guess for her it was. I was tempted to tell her to go screw herself but I bit my tongue and moved faster. I just was not in the mood.

Sasha sashayed and swung her hips back and forth to the entrance. Her sultry hair bouncing on her slender shoulders and her jeans gripping her plump behind, with her high-heeled boots clicking loudly as she ascended.

As we walked into the cramped space of the small town house that Charmaine and her family rented, I could smell incense burning and hear chatter coming from a far off room. The door was open so we went in and decided to call out to see if anyone would come out to greet us. It seemed as though no one heard us so we decided to call out again and this time we did it in unison, "helloooooooo?" We called together and turned to giggle sheepishly as we realized we sounded like two impatient high school girls about to divulge our deepest secrets. But more anxious now than ever, Sasha called out again with tension in her voice.

"Hello Charmaine, we are here and we came as fast as we could." She conversed by herself. We were about to enter the last partitioned barrier when we were greeted by Charmaine's devilishly cunning smile. I could feel there was something going on here that was more than a plan to save Sashas career and I wasn't sure why I felt fear, but that is exactly what I felt. Fear.

Charmaine grabbed Sasha by the shoulders and threw her arms around her, picking her up off the floor and spinning her around. Sasha shrieked gleefully but did not resist her. When she finally put her down she looked at me and winked, grabbing us both by the hand and then stopped to look at us one more time before breaking through the curtains and into the living room where it had suddenly gone quiet.

"Okay, you guys are not going to believe the luck we are in. You are not going to believe whom I met, you are not going to believe how we are going to fry this asshole and you will never have to worry about Mr. Brendan again." Charmaine said in the most serious tone I have ever heard her speak in. She almost sounded tantalized, as though the thought of castrating this man was giving her a hard on.

"Okay already. Enough with the suspense I want to know."

Sasha demanded.

"Brace yourselves ladies and let's make our entrance. Slowly, with both of our hands still held tightly in her grasp, we were led into the room and there on the black and white sofa was a beautiful dark skinned sister that looked as though she could be a relative of Sasha's. Like Sasha she had luscious full black hair that flowed on her shoulders into a breathtaking cascade crowning her face. Like Sasha she was small framed, couldn't be more than about five foot five inches tall. She had her head held down seemingly captivated by the magazine she held on her lap, with her feet elevated on the recliner. Her feet were free of her blue sandals that waited patiently to be greeted by her feet once more and her toenails glistened bright red nail polish. She wore a matching crimson red spaghetti strap top that hugged her small breasts and highlighted her petite torso. Her blue jeans were a snug fit to her full hips that seemed perfectly proportioned to her body. It seemed as though we stood there for a good five minutes without her looking up and before anyone spoke. I was not surprised by whom the silence was broken.

"Listen Charmaine, I am not in the mood for any bullshit on this fine day. What's the deal? Who is this and what is she doing here?" There she goes again thinking about herself and too impatient to wait and figure out what was happening.

"I just hope you are not putting my business out on the streets. This was supposed to be a private thing. If I wanted every, Tonya, Donna and Jane to know I would just let him give his info to the papers." She snapped. I was shocked at her rudeness and was totally embarrassed.

"Why do you always have to act so destructively ignorant at times?" I asked her adamantly, "I swear sometimes you wouldn't know that you were an educated top notch lawyer, the way you lower yourself and undermine your dignity with your hoochie mama attitude." I continued sarcastically.

Sasha opened her mouth to spit out her defense but Charmaine raised her hand, placing her palm so close she could almost touch Sasha's nose with her fingers.

"You know what Sasha, hush. You don't have a clue. So for once why don't you sit down and shut up so I can tell you my brilliant plan that you did not think of and I held it together long enough to figure out." Charmaine lectured without looking at her. Instead, she walked towards the statue of her guest that still did not seem to move and sat next to her. Slowly she raised her head and smiled warmly displaying gorgeous white choppers that seemed to go on forever and eyes that seemed to penetrate you.

"Hi I'm Delia." She said with a sultry greeting as her eyes met Sasha's gaze.

"Hello," responded Sasha in a snobbish tone that made it was obvious she disapproved of Delia's presence. I decided to just ignore her along with everyone else and say hello.

"Sasha did not like the sight of Delia. Charmaine seemed too close to her. She eyed Delia from the moment she got in the room and her disposition was totally rude.

"Hello Delia, it is very nice to meet you." I said as I walked over to her and extended my hand in a warm welcome. I looked at Sasha out of the corner of my eyes as I went and sat juxta-posed to Delia. She seemed nice enough, but it was obvious that Sasha was a little jealous. Delia and her could almost be distant cousins in the way they looked. They both had the same type of long thick sultry hair and chocolate dark smooth skin. You could see in their demeanor that they were both used to getting their way and being in a position of power and if something didn't give, this was not going to be pretty.

"It's really nice to meet you Kayla, Charmaine have told me a lot about you. And you too Sasha," Delia mocked deliber-ately turning her gaze towards Sasha's sourpuss face. "As a matter of fact I have heard the most about you since Charmaine and I met, and you are the reason we are here today, aren't you?" She continued almost provokingly.

"What is that supposed to mean?" Sasha spat.

"You know what Sasha, you are a bitch. And worse than that you are an ungrateful bitch. I am almost tempted to say that you deserve the shit you are in, and even though there are people here trying to help your dumb ass you are still acting like a spoiled little child without a clue. You are disrespecting my guest, a person who is here to help you and if you are not interested in help just leave because you are starting to piss me off." Charmaine fumed and all eyes turned to Sasha to see what her response would be.

Her mouth was pursed in a determined pout but her eyes were true to her real feelings. She was shocked and she felt stupid, but she just sat there and said nothing. Delia decided to kill the issue and went straight to business and opened up the subject of the topic at hand.

"I heard you are a lawyer Sasha? I worked with Branson and Brendan law firm while I was getting my masters here in the United States a few years back. But that was at the Florida location. I was actually surprised to hear that they have expanded and that Brendan has been heading things off here in New York." She began openly.

Delia paused as she silently replayed back those years she endured in her mind. It was a terrible and dark time for her. She was heart broken and almost completely destroyed and she had to pick herself up and put herself back together. It was difficult for her but she did it. Not alone though. She was lucky. She had her closet and most trusted friend Chyna who went through her own thing and all because of a man.

Men seem to be fucking up women's lives all over the damn place and getting away with it. She felt herself getting angry and she clenched her hands together to help to compose herself. She was now stronger and wiser because of what Michael Brendan did to her. But he killed a part of her that she could never get back. She felt herself reach to grab a hold of her abdomen as she recalled the emptiness inside her. She looked up to meet Sasha's inquiring stare.

"Yes." She continued, "I worked with that bastard and I am sure after all this time he thinks that he has gotten away with what he did to me for him to have done this to someone else." Delia fumed.

"What did he do to you?" I asked Delia. Maybe she didn't hear me or just didn't feel like responding. Either way she maintained her focus on Sasha and kept talking to her as though I had not said anything.

"If you would like Sasha," Delia paused and looked up to meet her gaze, "if you would like, we could work together to really fix him. I would like to help you get out of this, I would like to see him finally get what he deserves." She finished and sat silently not moving and waited for Sasha to say something.

"Are you mute all of a sudden?" Charmaine asked, her question oozing sarcasm.

"No, no it's not that. Its just that." Sasha stopped and stood up. She turned and her hair that was pinned in a ponytail at the front and hang loosely around her shoulders moved with her. Sasha's five feet, five-inch frame was aided by high heel red boots, which brought her three inches taller. She walked around to the sofa where Charmaine was sitting and consciously aware of being watched and subtlety admired she turned to accentuate the way her jeans gripped her well defined posterior and her frilly salsa cream top outlined her bust line and perky 36c chest and then folding nicely into her small waistline.

She stood like this for a second longer just to make sure that Delia saw that she was no amateur. She didn't want a competition but she wanted the new comer on the block to know who was boss and as long as that was understood she could move on with the issue at hand.

"It's just that I was a little taken aback. I didn't expect that we would be bringing anybody else in on this. I am having enough trouble as it is keeping things under wraps and this situation is embarrassing enough without telling perfect strangers my business." She retorted and landed her eyes on Delia so she knew whom she referred to as a perfect stranger. "I really mean no offense. But if you went through this as you said you did, I am sure you understand my dilemma and exactly what I have been dealing with. So please forgive my harshness. I really meant no harm." She apologized coldly and in her eyes you could see that there was no meaning behind her words.

I looked at her as she positioned herself once again in a position of power. She wanted to be loved, admired, feared and worshipped. I could see that old diva lashing out of her. It was like a scene out of a well-rehearsed play when Delia stood up. Her disposition a little shorter because she wore sandals and not heels, but she was cool and collected as she gently eased herself from the lazy boy.

"Well." Delia started as she dragged the word out slowly as if uncertain as to whether that was the right word to start with or not. "It seems to me that this bind you got yourself into made you come to your friends for help and they are helping you the best way that they can." Delia paused and went to stand directly in front of Sasha as though to position herself for a fight. Sasha felt the space tighten around her and you could hear her clear her throat.

"You are entering my personal space." She warned and waited standing her ground firmly.

"You see, I am here for one reason and one reason only. My life is established and I have already been through my crap with him. Him seeing me again will be a surprise. My life in

Jamaica is set and I came here on purely a pleasure trip, but now in light of these new circumstances my purposes here has been adjusted somehow. I knew there would be a day when I would hurt that man for what he did to me and this is my chance. So we can work together or apart, but I intend to bring him down and I intend to use whatever information I can to do so." She swallowed after slowly and deliberately spitting her words so they were clearly understood and Sasha stepped back.

"You ARE in my personal space and it wont just be Brendan you are taking on if you come any closer." Sasha fumed

"I see it this way Miss Thang. I don't need you but you need me. You say you don't want people in your shit yet you are putting it out there and it is only about to get worse. Its either you work with me and make me your ally so that you can benefit from what's about to go down, you can be a victim right along with him and go down when I put all this shit on the table for all the flies and scavengers to partake." She calmly finished and was right in Sasha's face at the end of her words. Sasha was stumped by her tenacity and awed that someone had the nerve and the audacity to out step their bounds.

She heard every word Delia said and knew she was right. Right now she didn't have a choice. She didn't want her friends to think she was a total dick and she didn't want to lose Charmaine's friendship. After all, it was Charmaine who brought Delia in on the deal. It was Charmaine who was trying to help her. She was in Charmaine's house where Delia was her guest and not her own and Charmaine, of them all, knew things about her that the others did not know.

Stepping back from Delia Sasha sighed.

"First of all, I don't like to be disrespected. Despite the crap that is filling up over my damn head I am a powerful and respected attorney."

"Well, so am I." Delia interrupted.

"I have worked hard and made many sacrifices to be here despite what is going on now and despite what people may think after the shit has hit the fan. I would first appreciate some respect if we are to be allies and not enemies. I would appreciate you stepping up out of my fucking face before I have to take you out." Sasha firmly stated and under no uncertain terms.

Delia broke out into total laughter. Laughter so sinister and patronizing that it could make a dog put its tail between its legs and walk away in shame. Regaining composure, Delia's face became stern and rigid, her eyes glowed with viciousness and there was no smile on her lips.

"First of all missy, respect is earned, so first you need to stop cursing at me and ask nicely. You have been acting like someone fucked you without your permission since you got in here. I know what your issue is and it is not that someone else knows your business. It is that I am just as and possibly *am* prettier than you, just as and maybe sexier than you. I have a head full of bouncing hair, the long flowing type, so you can't call my hair short and nappy and you are as black as I am so you can't call me a darkie. So if you are that ignorant, that insecure and that hard up to let a little jealously get in the way then that is your problem. But I don't believe you would be that stupid to let this opportunity to fry that lawyer's ass pass you by."

Delia stepped out of her face and went and took her place back on the recliner. She flicked her hair and threw her head back allowing her hair to fall all over her face. Then smiled to let them all know that she knew they were watching. Without turning to look at Sasha, she continued to address her.

"Why not put all that you are feeling towards me, for whatever reason because I did not do anything to you, and put it into the sweet revenge we are going to have on Branson and Brendan Law, Inc. and we can continue this later." She suggested with her back to Sasha and a devious smile crossing her face, putting a sparkle in her eyes.

I couldn't believe what I had just seen and I could tell that Charmaine too was shocked. Sasha had really finally met her match. Someone who would not cower in her presence and who just put her perfectly in her place. I watched her as she walked over and sat beside Charmaine who now was the barrier between the two of them.

"So what happened between you and him if you don't mind me asking?" Sasha asked and as the conversation doors open the words slowly started to flow.

Chapter 10

Kayla felt overwhelmed when she returned back to her apartment. It seemed like they had gotten a lot accomplished. Delia told her story and she was in shock at what she went through with her friend Chyna. She remembered vaguely someone telling her about the story that was on the news back in 1998 with that girl and the AIDs note in that guy's hand. Life is so funny. What goes around really comes around that is really scary. Who would have thought she would meet a real live person associated with that story so long ago. She was really pleased with the way things went down with Sasha too. That girl really needed a reality check.

It was 10pm by the time Kayla and Sasha got back into her red Mustang. They both drove quietly until they were almost back at Kayla's place.

"So what did you think about this girl Delia." Sasha asked not wanting to sound too enthusiastic about the progress they made and the plan that they have devised to finally get Mr. Brendan.

"I like her Sasha. I know you don't but I really like her." I told her as candidly as I could and hoped that she had learned a lesson from her temper tantrum earlier and prayed that she wouldn't throw one now.

"She seems to know what she is doing. She is smart and

she's already been through and survived what you are trying to go through now. She had no help but now you have hers. What she went through was kind of worse than you. She lost her first child and at her own hands because she had no choice. You are lucky in a way." I told her calmly.

"You really cannot compare oranges and apples. Her situation is not worse than mine just because she allowed him to manipulate her, force her out of the country to finish her education and threaten her to have an abortion or he would ruin her. She made the wrong decision, but I am going to put a stop to all this right now." Sasha said smugly.

"You are really cold Sasha. Really cold." I couldn't believe she would talk about someone else's pain like this. Even after what she was going through, even with this person trying to help her. I always knew she was cold and conceited but I didn't realize she would go to this extent.

"Well, the plan is now in effect," I reminded her with a tinge of sadness. I sort of wanted to see Sasha suffer some more for her chilling disregard for others, "I know you will be happy when this is all over." I sighed as she pulled up to my door.

"We're here sweets." Sasha told Kayla now fully ready to get rid of her. She had had enough of high and mighty people who thought that for a second they could possibly be better than her, lecturing her. She was ready to get Kayla out of her sight and it was a relief that the night was over.

"All right then Sis, I will talk to you later. Go home to that big comfy house of yours and give me a call when you feel like talking." I told her and gave her a hug before jumping out of her car. As I walked to the door I could feel her stare in my back and turned around just in time to see her speed off.

It was really quiet inside my apartment and my mind slipped back to Michael and wondered why he really dressed up so nicely to go to work and why he wasn't home yet. I could use his arms wrapped around me right now. I remember a time I did my dirt and I am just lucky I didn't get into the kind of trouble that Delia and Sasha would have to live with. I have had my share of wackos and stalkers and almost destroyed my relationship with the love of my life Michael. But even though I am trying to put things back together, repair the damage, things just didn't seem to be getting better. Trying to fix things with Michael was like a dog chasing its own tail.

I dropped my bag to the ground as I entered the bedroom, took off my shorts underwear and top and spread eagle on the bed. I was exhausted.

****

Sasha was pleasantly surprised when she drove to her big empty house and found a guest waiting for her at the entry of her driveway. She smiled sexily at him and was not angry this time that he had shown up unannounced. Tonight she felt good. The wondering about what to do and the stress of being black-mailed had finally rested to the back of her mind. The game had begun, she had a plan and things would all fall into place now. As she drove up to her garage and watched the door ascend, she felt that familiar twitch between her legs. Just the thought of getting some good loving ignited the fire in her thighs.

She loved the way he always smelled so good and the way his tall muscular frame overpowered her body. Oh she knew this was wrong but what the hell. There was nothing and no perfect being no matter how much Miss Kayla might wish it or try to make it happen. She deserved to be happy and if that meant sampling someone else's man's dick from time to time, that was just fine by her. Sasha got out of her car and walked toward the masculine figure that awaited her. She had to stand on tippy toes just to reach his neck and he bent over to grab her around her waist. She pushed away from him realizing she was still outside. She didn't want her neighbors in her business because once their plan went into effect anything might happen. She didn't want witnesses and any added eyes so she had to be careful.

"Hey gorgeous, let's go inside." She ushered him. She smiled as she turned to lead the way and made sure there was an extra switch in her thighs just to warm him up to the dynamite night he was about to have. She giggled as she thought that he really did not know how lucky he was that he chose this night to drop by. Under other circumstances she might be pissed since he is not her man and she might have had other company, but tonight, the rush from her day had really made her horny and she was ready for a workout.

Sasha quickly opened her door when she felt his bulging erection press into her backside and shrieked happily when he walked in and slammed the door behind them. She turned around and jumped high so she could wrap her legs around his waist. He held her tight and navigated his way through the dark room that he was very well familiar with. He knew his way to her sofa and knew how she felt about dirt or stains on them but he didn't care. He was here to fuck her brains out tonight. It could be the last from what he heard earlier in the day about her blackmail worries so he intended to make the best of it.

Sasha wanted to take her clothes off and take a shower but the heat between them had ignited and she didn't want to stop. She felt like she could go all night though she knew soon he had to be back home to his woman. She wanted him right at that moment so she threw those thoughts from her mind and started taking his clothes off. With her legs wrapped securely around his waist, her hands were free to help him undress. He walked with her that way and sat her down on the sofa so he could rest her body for support while he kneeled in front of her. He helped her to take her boots off and bent down to kiss her feet. He unsnapped her button and helped her out of her restricting jeans as he kissed her midsection that exposed her hairless passion. He stuck his tongue deep between her legs and watched her squirm to open them but couldn't with her jeans still hanging just below her knees. Finally removing the rest of her jeans from her legs and the top she wore, he was free to maneuvere into and through her fluidly, so he followed suit, dropping his pants to the floor and freed himself to partake of her pleasures.

Sensing the urgency she felt, his own needs and desires grew. From the passionate lovemaking experience he had earlier that day with his own woman he didn't think he would be this excited. But there was something about Sasha that drove men wild. An untamed honesty about her sexual needs and the nerve to take what she wanted was a turn on. Anything and anyone she wanted was hers for the taking and that included him, even though he was her best friend's man.

He didn't have to worry about foreplay or hurting her feelings because she was just interested in one thing, his third leg and as far as he was concerned that was fine by him. Afterall, all he wanted from her was what was between her legs that made her different than he was, so the feeling was mutual.

One deep plunge and he was within the depths of her. The excitement she felt sent a rush of explosion and Sasha had her first orgasm that took her by surprise. Feeling her volcano erupting he forced himself deeper inside of her taking strong, deep, long strokes in an attempt to work up his own tidal wave. Feeling his excitement Sasha could tell she was ready. She pushed him off of her and got on her knees while leaving her torso on the sofa to brace her body so he could angle himself behind her. Another immersion into her vagina and he saturated himself inside of her plummeting deeper. He felt the rush of passion surge through him, as his manhood grew and she felt his desire soar and grew wings. Hearing him grunt his satisfaction heightened her excitement and she felt her own body explode into a spasm just before they both passed out and she screamed his name, "Ohhhhh Michael!"

Chapter 11

Charmaine was so excited after Sasha and Kayla left that she started jumping up and down. Charmaine was walking through the supermarket one day earlier that week when she saw this fine ass sister walk by her. Delia's petite frame excited her but she knew that she was not gay. Charmaine had been at this thing now for so long that she could almost smell sexuality. She knew she wanted her from that first moment but she also knew she had to be careful. She had walked up to her and accidentally bumped into her causing her shopping basket to tumble out all that was in it. She was taken by surprise by the jealousy she felt when some tall light skinned sista ran up to help her. She was almost as tall as she was and just as thin, you could tell that she was the model type, flat and small in all the right places with the perfect height. She wore her hair in a short fade cut with curls crowning her face. The tight shorts she wore to help keep her cool were very revealing and her brown tank top left nothing to the imagination.

She had looked up at her then and smiled as Delia tried to tell Charmaine not to worry. "It was just an accident." She had said naively as Chyna grabbed the basket from her hands.

"I am so sorry," Charmaine had apologized and was more embarrassed than anything else to think that maybe she was wrong this time. This one was gay and this was her lover. Delia quickly dispelled that thought from her mind when she introduced herself.

"I am Delia and this is my friend Chyna." At that moment a chocolate, brown sugar coated macadamia nut brother with dread locs walked by. Chyna could not contain her stare, and put her index finger in her mouth while biting down to prevent herself from screaming.

"Damn!" The brother looked to be about five feet, eleven inches, was lean and muscular. His rich dark frame glided gracefully by and he put his wrist to his chin and did a cute wave to them. He smiled as he witnessed the effect he had on them. However, he was used to this kind of attention, almost every day there were women drooling and perusing themselves before him. If he were to pay attention to them, he would become a straight up male whore and a dog. He didn't believe in sleeping around and was a gentleman as his mother taught him to be, so he smiled and just kept walking.

"Did you see that?" She had turned to ask Delia.

"Oh mama!" was all the comment that Delia had and that's when Charmaine relaxed. Okay, she had a chance.

Chyna couldn't stop staring at the brother; she walked away from Delia and Charmaine and followed him from aisle to aisle at the opposite end of the supermarket as not to seem conspicuous. But he was fully aware of his admirer and decided to play along. Eventually Chyna got bored and went back to join her friend as they introduced themselves.

"I am Charmaine," she introduced herself back once the distraction had passed and was certain that Delia and this Chyna chick had not noticed that she showed no interest in the slender dark skinned brother that they were both gawking at.

From their accent she could tell that they hadn't been in the States long. It was fresh and beautiful. She knew they were Jamaicans, because she usually hung out with and around

Jamaicans but this accent was better, stronger, and more defined than the JaMericans.

"You guys visiting the Big Apple?" She fished, while going over ideas in her mind of how she could savor the taste of this fine sister.

"Well actually I am a citizen," Chyna jumped in, "but I have been gone for a few years, back to Jamaica finishing up my studies and once I was done I just decided to stay a little longer."

"I still live in Jamaica but I have travel to the States quite often." Delia contributed. "However," she stated after a brief pause, "this is our first time back in this country 1998 and we are really just here on a little bit of business and a whole lot of pleasure." Delia looked up at Charmaine's charcoal dark skin and smiled. She knew exactly what she was trying to imply to Charmaine and her eyes danced the teasing game as she winked and stated; "you are really pretty."

Charmaine was shocked and pleased. This might not be so hard after all.

"Thanks," she blushed, "you took me by surprise."

"Don't worry about Chyna and don't let her intimidate you Char…"

"Charmaine." Charmaine helped her as she was having problems pronouncing her name.

"Sorry. Charmaine. She is tall but she is a mouse of a lady." At that moment Charmaine knew for sure. This might be it. She could feel herself falling for her.

As they headed to check out their items, Charmaine walked behind them and continued to chit chat about their meeting and their plans to get together. In the aisle next to them was the hot chocolate brother that had Chyna all caught up in a hot frenzy. He was ahead of her in the checkout line and was about to leave when he briefly paused and stepped over to their checkout lane.

Justin couldn't help it. There was something simple and refreshing about Chyna. She made it obvious that she liked him, but she didn't invade his space. He had waited until it was time to leave to see if she would insinuate herself, but she didn't. Her behavior was not that one of the typical American bold type women. Even in her efforts to get his attention she was very feminine. He was curious and wanted to get a chance to know her better, so he stopped.

"Hello, I noticed you checking me out over there and I thought it would be nice to formally introduce myself." He approached her cockily and smirked at the effect he knew he was having on her.

"I cannot stay long, so here is my card. Please, I would love for you to use that number." He continued, and then he winked at her and disappeared out the automatic doors. Chyna couldn't believe her ears or her eyes. It had been a long, long time since a man had caught her attention. Is that brother for real? Damn he is fine. She watched as he walked away, perfectly chiseled tight ass wrapped neatly into a slotted package and immaculate bowed legs stretching from his thighs and melting into his feet. She saw the strength of his flawlessly worked out shoulders and sighed at the thought of what it would feel like to have his arms wrapped around her. She sighed deeply and quickly looked down at the professional business card he handed to her. On it was printed in bold Dr. Justin Etnas. She shrieked. On it was his office number, his pager, his voicemail and his home phone number. She was totally oblivious to her friend and the new girl who was now inserting herself into their lives. Returning to the states might just have some perks in it for her after all.

The next day Charmaine had invited both Delia and Chyna to her place, which was about twenty minutes from the

Radisson Hotel where they were staying until they could find a time-share apartment or rental.

Chyna didn't want to go, she wanted to stay at the hotel to see if she could get in touch with Dr. Etnas, so Delia went alone to Brooklyn with Charmaine. That's when the subject came up. When Delia started talking about being an intern at a prestigious law firm as the only student who was not studying law and how she had returned to Jamaica to complete her Masters when things went wrong at the firm she was working for. Charmaine didn't say anything right away. All she did was ask questions, she asked about the stories she remembered from the news of that event as Delia filled in the gaps. She wanted to know if Chyna was over Miguel, how she took it and why they had decided to run away instead of fight. There were some questions Delia couldn't answer, like the ones regarding Chyna. They had a code of respect that she couldn't violate.

"We were too weak and too young. There was no way we could have taken on a powerful firm such as Branson and Brendan then and now they are larger and more powerful. Chyna was devastated from the shock of everything, she and I both needed to get away, recoup and regroup." Delia explained. "We were not trying to run away." She insisted in a voice that was not very convincing.

Three days after meeting Delia and Chyna in the Plaza supermarket, Charmaine told Delia the dilemma that Sasha was having. It was during this conversation that both Delia and Charmaine thought it would be a great idea for them to work with Sasha to help bring Mr. Michael Brendan down.

Charmaine went and sat as close as she could next to Delia and leaned toward her, "you are brilliant." She whispered emphatically to her. "I have never seen anyone, and I mean anyone, talk to Sasha like that and get away with it." She told her in her childlike jubilance.

"It was nothing Charmaine. I understand how she must feel, having her independence and freedom snatched from under her and have someone else pulling her strings." She stated almost in retrospect.

"Well, she will be okay and your plan is fantastic. The way you want to make him suffer, have him disgraced, and debarred among his peers is perfect. I cannot wait to see his face when he sees you." Charmaine commented more calmly as she absorbed the idea and the true essence of what was about to happen to this man who manipulated and destroyed other people's lives. She thought of what he would have to live with or through once they were done with him. It would not be pretty.

"Would you like some snacks Delia?" Charmaine asked as she stood quickly to head towards the kitchen. She needed to get some air so she could breathe. Delia was suffocating and exciting her with her essence and the way she took control enticed her.

"Oh what's this you're reading?" Charmaine asked taking the chance to grab at the magazine on Delia's thighs and perhaps a chance to have her hands brush up against her. Delia had given her no reason to think she had any interest other than platonic friendship, yet her hopes to have Delia fall into her arms one day persisted.

"Ah, I don't know. Just some magazine to keep my thoughts from wondering." Delia responded and took a hold of Charmaine's hands to brace and pull herself to her feet. The touch of her soft delicate hands on Charmaines sent chills through her and she had to contain herself from wrapping her arms around Delia. They both stood up and though she stood more than a foot above Delia she felt like she was face to face and could almost feel Delia's breath in her face.

They went to the kitchen together and every time

Charmaine had to reach for a cup, or a plate and she had the opportunity to reach above Delia or slip by her brushing against her firm behind or allowing her elbow to sweep against her bosom, she took it and felt herself get moist all over at the thought of maybe one day when Delia might willingly give herself to her.

****

Kayla woke up at almost two in the morning and heard Michael easing himself into the room. It was dark so she didn't move, she just watched as he attempted to quietly remove his clothing and jump into the shower. Of course there was nothing out of the ordinary with that. He went to work, he sweat, now he was home and he needed a shower. No problem. But why is he sneaking in at two in the morning? Why didn't he reach over to kiss her, as he would usually do at times like this when he got in late? He didn't even call her once during the time he was gone. So she watched him. Watched as he hid his dirty clothes at the bottom of the clothes hamper, watched as he jumped in the shower and still she just watched.

****

"Thank you for calling DMac, Inc. Karen speaking how may I help you?" Karen chirped into the phone. It was a new week, a new day and she felt great. When she arrived into the office that morning there was a note on her desk from Terra. She wanted to know how her friend was and if everything turned out okay. She wanted to see her in her office once she got the note and when she knocked on Terra's office door she was greeted warmly. She didn't know why or how or what happened to this lady who had such a reputation for being cruel, but she was happy for whatever it was.

"Hello Karen how was your weekend?"

"It was great thank you. I really wanted to thank you for allowing me to leave last week early. My friend was really in a bad situation and everyone else who could help her seemed to have been indisposed." Karen said uncomfortably still uncertain as to why this meeting first thing Monday morning.

"I looked over the project last week and I really appreciate the time, effort and thought you put into your work Karen. You show real initiative and I would like to offer you a permanent position on our team.

Karen was so overwhelmed that she almost screamed. She placed her hand quickly over her mouth and then just as quickly removed it. "I'm sorry. I just thought. Well, I thought you didn't…"

"It's okay Karen. I know what my reputation is around here and I know what you thought. Not to worry I am use to it by now, the gossip and the whispering when I pass by. It is hard to be in a position like this when you are someone like me." Terra offered and then immediately changed the subject. "So what was wrong with her?" Terra asked with genuine concern in her voice.

"Well, I don't want you to think bad of me because I know that this is a touchy subject for most people. But she has HIV and it is developing into full-blown AIDS. She has a young baby girl and a little boy and no one to help her. Child Protective Services are always waiting in the wings for the chance to take her kids away. We try to help her but its getting worse and I don't know how much more I can do for her." Karen confessed sadly.

"I understand what your friend is going through, if there is anything you need, don't hesitate to ask. Okay?"

Karen could not believe her ears. She felt so good the rest of the day working at her desk. Her job seemed easier and her day went smoother. She didn't have to worry about her temporary Data Entry assignment ending with the agency she got assigned through, because she was offered a permanent position. She could now pay her bills and pick up the slack where her worthless man Shawn wouldn't and couldn't even help her out like a man should be able to. Not that he was doing much of anything to begin with. She had to find a way to get rid of him because he was hindering her and she knew that he was fooling around behind her back. She just didn't know with who and she was not sure if she really cared anymore, even though she still loved his sorry behind. Today nothing was going to bring Karen down; she was going to have a great day.

****

"Hey Kayla, it's me Sandra. Are you there?" Sandra spoke into Kayla's answering machine and sighed disappointedly when there was no answer. Michael sat next to the phone in his favorite chair with a Heineken in one hand and the remote control in the other. When he got up that morning Kayla had already left for work and did not say goodbye to him. He was upset because she had left a note next to his dirty clothes that he had buried at the bottom of the clothes hamper the night before. It read:

Michael I hope you had a good time last night. And by the way Elizabeth Taylor White Diamonds is a good choice. She has taste.

Michael was steaming and the thought of her trying to show him up, after everything he put up with her. All those years he chased after her, forgave her for cheating on him over and over again. All those years he sat quietly in the background and turned a blind eye every time she broke his heart, every time she treated him as though he was disposable. Half the time she didn't even see him, he might as well have been invisible. But he loved her, so he waited while she got it all out of her system. But now he was tired and bored. She had changed and now she had become clingy. How dare she put him on the spot like that.

As the thoughts consumed him he became more and more angry. All the hurt and pain that he endured for her surfaced and he needed to lash out on someone.

"Okay Kayla, I guess you are not home. I am sorry you were not able to make it the other day like you promised you would, but it's..."

"What do you want? Don't you have a life?" Michael asked grabbing the phone before Sandra could finish her thought. Why don't you go find a man to take care of you? All of you always leaning and depending on Kay, don't you realize that she has things to do and that her life does not revolve around the whole set of you?" He screamed into the phone and felt the sting of tears as his eyes became filled with water.

"Exactly who do you think you are talking to?" Sandra asked shocked. She just couldn't believe her luck. Every time she seemed to be reaching out lately someone was lashing out on her. She didn't know what she was doing wrong and her heart sank deep into sadness.

"I was calling for Kayla, not you, so since when do you answer her calls?"

"Listen you little heffa. Know what? Whatever!" And the phone went slam into Sandra's ears. She couldn't help it. A pain went through her and she remembered that she hadn't taken the twelve or so pills that she was supposed to have taken by now. Her head started reeling and she could feel herself pass through a morbid state, light and sound disappearing from her. She heard the thud she made as she fell to the floor and reached for Suzette who crawled up to her and shook her rattle with a jovial giggle. She went blank before her hands touched the baby.

She felt faint and nauseous and dragged herself over to the bathroom and tried to pull herself up to the bathroom sink to reach the medicine cabinet. She was able to reach open and take the pills from two bottles before she felt too weak to hold herself up any longer. So she slumped to the floor and thought back to how Michael had just spoken to her. How he sounded angry. She thought that maybe she had done something wrong for God to be so mad at her and for causing her so much pain and loneliness. Just as the tears ran down her dark brown cheeks and the pain cramped her stomach from a broken heart, she felt herself get dazed and then she passed out.

****

Karen was so excited after talking to her boss and getting a permanent job that she couldn't contain herself at the end of the day. She had to tell somebody but who? Sasha behaved as though just the sight of her and knowing she was alive annoyed her, Kayla seemed as though she only had time for Sasha. She knew that Charmaine's true love and support was reserved only for Sasha since they were friends before either she, Kayla, or Sandra came into the picture. So the only person who she could count on to be happy for her was Shawn and Sandra. She didn't feel like calling Shawn, though she knew he was lounging around in her house, eating her food, and not even trying to work, or out doing whatever it was that he did best. The only other person she was sure would genuinely be happy for her was Sandra.

Karen felt like doing something special. She wanted to hang out and have girl talk with someone who wouldn't judge her or look down at her. She wanted to eat out and pig out and she didn't want to feel stupid or inadequate or out of place or unwanted. She wanted to feel needed and loved. So as soon as it was time for her to leave work she started to feel the excitement build inside of her. She knew exactly what she was going to do, exactly who she was going to share it with and planned on having a wonderful evening.

At five she said her goodbyes for the night and made a special trip to the other side of the office to tell Terra goodbye. She really appreciated her concern and sincerity and she wanted her to know she appreciated it, but Terra seemed to have already left for the day. That seemed strange to her but she brushed it off and went on her way.

Outside she lifted her head towards the sky and took a deep breath. It was a cool day in Manhattan in the busy Wall Street area. Karen turned her head towards the skyline where you would usually have been able to see the World Trade Center or the Twin Towers as it was most commonly called and a tinge of sadness over came her as she thought about how cruel and sometimes naively destructive people could be. She still couldn't get use to the emptiness she saw in the sky from the terrorism that totally annihilated the Twin Towers. They were two powerful symbols of strength and perseverance by America that has now been destroyed. She remembered how the country was pulled together in loving support of each other, how everything and everyone was affected even today. This was partially the reason why she couldn't find a job, partially the reason why she had been working for an agency for the past six months. The September 11th destruction would live on forever and it would always affect us all, especially all the survivors of men, women and children who died either as unsuspecting victims or all the police officers, firemen, emergency aide and others who died trying to rescue them from the fiery furnace. No one will ever forget the horror of that day, how the towers exploded and terrorism took the United States by storm.

She felt herself being pulled into the sadness and shook it off. Today was a good day. No more job-hunting, at least not for a while. No more assignment to assignment thanks to Terra and from the looks of things, she finally found someone who might need and appreciate her friendship. This brought her back to what she was doing in the first place. It brought her back to her celebration. She got to the train station as fast as she could and hopped on the train. As the train went by the stop that old lady got off last week, she couldn't help straining a little to see if she could get a glimpse to see if she was still there, but she wasn't. Just the empty box she had seen her crawl into.

She decided she wasn't going to let anything bring her down and felt that even that homeless lady would have wanted her to be happy today. So she perked up and looked forward to her stop. Outside the train and walking distance from Sandra's apartment building she stopped at a Chinese restaurant to order food for five people. Then she stopped at the grocery store and bought essentials like milk and eggs and juices for the kids. Nothing could ruin Karen's mood today.

When she got to Sandra's building gloom set in again. That same stench from before like urine and vomit invaded her nostrils and nauseated her. The garbage scattered around what was meant to be a kid's playground, and graffiti on the   walls with the added touch of bullet holes to complete the picture. This, was not where she wanted to be and she wished there was some way for her to help her friend. She wished that there were something more she could do.

She brushed off the overwhelming feeling that threatened to dampen her day and jogged up the stairs as fast as she could go with the groceries in her hands.

When she got to Sandra's door she heard Anthony with a

cry in his voice, "get up mommy. Please get up." He pleaded but Sandra could not hear him. Karen pushed the door open and dropped her load to the floor when she saw Anthony next to his mother crying, begging her to wake up and nothing.

"Tony, what's wrong?" Karen asked trying not to panic and rushing to sit by his side.

"Where is Suzette?" She whispered as though Sandra would wake if she spoke too loudly. Tony started to cry freely as he pointed his finger to the pillows on the floor where the sleeping baby lay.

"Don't worry sweetheart. Mommy is going to be okay." She tried to reassure him as she herself started to feel worry taking over her.

She felt Sandra's pulse and felt the faint throbbing under her thumb. She breathed a sigh of relief at that moment knowing that she was still alive but she wasn't sure what Sandra needed. She couldn't force feed her pills and give her the wrong ones and she couldn't just stand there and wait for her to wake up. She didn't know what to do. She knew how Sandra was always afraid of her kids being taken away and not wanting to go to the hospital, but she had to do something.

Reluctantly, Karen made her decision and ran to the phone.

"This is the 911 emergency operator, how may I help you?" Came the calm voice over the phone that make Karen feel even more panicky.

"Yes, I would like an ambulance please." Karen spoke as calmly as she could.

"What's your emergency mam?" Came the voice again, annoyingly calm and condescending.

"My friend seemed to have fainted on the floor. She's not moving and I don't know what to do."

"Did you check her pulse?" Asked the operator.

"Yes, she is alive."

"Well listen to me and stay calm ma'am," she cautioned Karen. "What is your name?"

"Karen."

"Well Karen, I am going to be asking you a few questions and I want you to stay on the line with me okay?" She asked. This time concern and empathy reverberated in her voice. "There is an emergency vehicle on the way and it should be at your location in about ten minutes. What is your friend's full name?"

"Her name is Sandra. Sandra Gabardine." She told the operator and suddenly tears began to well in her eyes.

"It's okay Karen, you are doing great. Just stay calm with me okay? This is the only way you will be able to help your friend."

Karen's answer was barely audible but she answered and brushed her hand against Sandra's hair as if to soothe her.

"Now Karen, do you know if Sandra is on any medication." Karen heard the clicking in the background and knew the operator was typing every word she said. She didn't want to do or say anything that would be detrimental to Sandra later, but she didn't want her to die and she knew that Sandra was not healthy.

The operator heard her hesitation and stopped to urge Karen.

"I know it is hard to be in a situation like this Karen, but your friend can be in very bad trouble. How much information we can get from you will determine how quickly we can have her stabilized and back on her feet again. Sandra need your help Karen, so just answer as honestly as you can to the best of your knowledge, okay? That's really all you can do now until the ambulance arrives."

"She is HIV positive. She takes a lot of pills a day but I don't know which ones are which. I don't know what happened or whether or not she took any medication today. I just got here

and saw her on the floor and her seven year old son over her."
Karen told her openly crying now. At that moment she heard the
sirens and the footsteps running from the elevator and down the
hallway. She felt ashamed and embarrassed that she would be
there and that her friend was there in that hellhole of an apartment and she couldn't do anything to help her.

"It's okay Karen, the technicians will take over now. Just
put them on the phone when they get in." Karen put the phone
down and sat next to a bewildered Tony who knew that something was wrong but had no idea just how serious things were.
Since Karen had left the door open and her groceries were scattered across the floor the technicians just walked in and immediately began tending to Sandra. Karen motioned to one of them
to get on the phone with the operator. With all the noise and commotion Suzette woke and started wailing when she saw her
mother on the floor and strangers peering over her.

Karen rushed to her and huddled the baby close to her
bosom. She rocked her from side to side but more to soothe her
nerves than to soothe the baby's. She watched as the EMT's put
an oxygen mask over Sandra's mouth and nose and hooked her
up to IV's right before they rushed her out the door. Karen stared
after them in disbelief that all her plans for a wonderful evening
had suddenly come to a complete stop. She still stood there staring as they informed her that they were taking Sandra to Interfaith
Hospital and closed the door behind them.

It wasn't until Suzette started bawling again that she
regained conscious composure and started packing over night
stuff for the baby and Anthony and gathering as much necessities
as possible before walking out of Sandra's unkempt apartment.

Chapter 12

That Monday, following her unpleasant acquaintance with Delia and plotting what was to be the beginning of her boss's downfall, Sasha went into her office at the firm as if nothing had happened. Except today, she wore a body microphone recorder attached between her protruding bust line and well-enhanced cleavage. She didn't want to leave anything to chance even though that was not a part of the plan. She wanted to out do Delia's plan and get some incriminating evidence on Michael so she could have something tangible if this ever went to court.

As she walked in she felt all eyes on her as though she was caught in the act and didn't know about it. She felt confident that she just looked that good in her short knee length Gucci business suit and her coach pumps that accentuated her legs. She wore her hair in a bun and somehow felt over dressed. She reveled in the admiration of her co-workers and had no clue about the bombshell waiting for her as she entered her office.

"Sasha could you come into my office please." Came the authoritative presence of Mr. Branson over the intercom.

"I will be right in sir." She responded cautiously, her heart suddenly picking up pace and her palms becoming sweaty. She checked herself and her make-up inside her personal restroom located inside her spacious office and took a deep breath. *Okay, I am being paranoid.*

Everything is not about this blackmail and Michael would-
n't risk his job by telling anyone about this yet. He promised he
would give me some time to make my decision and I think I have
about a week left to get some dibs on him. So girlfriend, just relax
and go *work what yo' mama gave you*. She told herself with a
snicker and with one final touch of her hair she walked out of her
door with an air of confidence that could cut through glass. As an
added bonus she allowed her buttocks to sway by putting on a
killer swing of her hips that had everyone drooling over the way
her thighs went up and down taking her skirt with her and adding
to her already over boosted ego.

"Sasha, please sit down." Mr. Branson offered pointing to
the chair directly facing his desk and politely picked up a Cuban
cigar and slowly lit it as she sat.

"Mr. Branson, all this time I have worked here and I had
no idea that you were a cigar man."

"Yes I know. It is a rare occasion we get to sit like this."
Shifting in his chair Mr. Branson turned to face Sasha, "I have
watched and noticed how you have grown in this firm Sasha.
From the moment you came here fresh out of Law School I knew
you had the killer instinct it took to be one of the best and you
have made it, and proven your worth here." He told her with a
wiry smile.

"Yes sir. I have worked hard and put in all the time
required at the sacrifice of a social life. I really enjoy being a
member of this firm sir and I am glad that my services and my
hard work are appreciated." Sasha said proudly, her ego swelling
and her heart racing. Mr. Branson was senior partner at the firm
and it was a rare day that someone got to see him around or even
get to sit with him in his office. This was definitely a treat and
Sasha's heart started to race as she contemplated various reasons why he would be calling her into his office. The conversation was pleasant enough so she put Michael Brendan out of her

thoughts for the moment.

"I have been thinking about adding a new partner to our firm and we thought having a woman would be a great addition." He continued and paused to see Sasha's reaction.

As ecstatic as she was she remained calm and professional and waited for him to continue. I was wondering if you could give me some thoughts as to how you think this transition would benefit the firm?" Sasha was beside herself. She couldn't speak. She wanted him to just come out and tell her that they were considering her for the position. For that time all of her worries and problems with the other partner Michael Brendan escaped her and suddenly all she could see were the numbers and the prestige that would follow her name.

"Well Sir, I think that is an excellent idea. Adding a woman partner to the firm would market us to the female population and offer a softer side to the firm without sacrificing quality or our reputation of winning and getting the job done." She was tempted to ask whom they were considering but if there was anything she learned, as a lawyer was that patience was everything. You set the bait and wait for the victim to fall in.

"I am glad to hear that Sasha. As you know we highly value your opinion so I hope you don't mind me pulling you away from your busy schedule to chat a bit."

"Of course not, sir. I am in your employ and you can use my professional intellect in whatever facet you please."

As she pulled herself together to leave Mr. Brendan spun his chair toward his vast window over looking the city from his ten-story office. He listened as Sasha walked toward his closed office door before turning around.

"Michael Brendan and I have been doing a lot of talking about you." Sasha's heart stopped and she was planted to the spot where she stood. It was too good to be true, he did say something and they are toying with her. She told herself to stay calm until he has given her proof. She must stay in control.

"Is that so sir?" she replied as calmly as she could without turning around.

"Of course he is the other partner of the firm and the decisions that are made regarding this firm are joint, you understand?"

"But certainly." She replied, waiting for him to say the inevitable.

"Well, that's all for now Sasha. Thanks for you time and I hope to chat with you again soon."

"Thank you sir." Sasha said and quickly walked out the door. Outside his door she stopped and waited a second for her heart to stop pounding. She felt like it was about to jump from her chest. She couldn't understand what just happened. Was that a test? Was he waiting for her to come out and say something to test her integrity? Did Michael Brendan spill his guts that piece of chicken shit? She wondered. Suddenly she felt weak and nauseated. She walked back to her office as quickly as she could and grabbed her things. She didn't feel up to meeting with Michael today. Sitting with one partner was enough. She didn't want to be frazzled and nervous. She would have to do this at another time.

As quickly as she could, she made her way toward the elevator and to the first floor. She didn't answer the doorman when he gestured to her to have a good day. She just made a beeline to her car and sped away.

As soon as she got home she dialed Charmaine's number to cry on her reliable friend's shoulder. The phone rang and on the forth ring it picked up.

"Hello." Came the soft but firm voice over the phone. Sasha paused because she didn't recognize the voice and for a moment she thought she might have dialed the wrong number.

"Hello is this 961-3?" Sasha began to ask hesitantly still

not certain as to whether or not she had dialed the correct number, but before she could complete the phone digits Delia asked again.

"Hello may I help you?" Came the voice again.

"This is Charmaine's private number and I don't recognize your voice. Is this Charmaine's number?" Sasha demanded, more irritated now than ever.

"Yes, this is Charmaine's number. How may I help you?" Delia asked knowing full well from the arrogance blaring at her from the other end of the line that is was Sasha on the phone.

"Well is Charmaine indisposed?" Sasha asked, not wanting to get into it with Delia at that moment. She realized that Delia held her at no reverence and she could not intimidate her.
"No, actually she is not. Would you like to speak to Charmaine?" she asked.

"Yes, that would be nice." Sasha snapped. Delia handed off the phone to Charmaine without saying another word. She had not identified herself over the phone but she was certain of who the caller on the other end was. She rolled her eyes and went back to looking at the cards in her hand when Charmaine went off to take the call.

"Hello Charmaine speaking," she announced jubilantly.

"Who the hell just answered your phone? I thought you had gotten a private line?" Sasha demanded.

"First of all heffa, who the hell do you think you are talking to?" Charmaine's disposition changed in a snap when she heard the tone of Sasha's voice. "I am not fucking you and I am not one of the fools whose heads you've got turned. So why are you calling my house with an attitude and inquiring about my guest when I don't do that shit to you?" Charmaine questioned bafflingly.

"Well I called to talk to you and some other woman is answering your phone so why can't I ask? I thought I was your friend?" Sasha asked. Charmaine almost burst out laughing when she realized she detected a tone of jealously in her friend's voice. She decided she was going to let that one slide as she also knew that the only time Sasha came off so ignorant and annoying was when she was desperate and in trouble and needed her.

"Okay, just let go of it okay? I am your friend and I am here for you. You said you called for me and here I am so talk to me Sis?" Charmaine consoled her and urged her to change the subject to whatever she wanted to talk about.

"Charmaine, I think we are going to have to move up with the plan.   I think that son-of-a-bitch is spilling. I got called into the other partner's office today and he was talking about wanting to add a female partner to the firm." Sasha rambled on.

"So what does that have to do with Michael Brendan rambling? The man was talking to you about work and you freak out?" Charmaine teased.

"No I am serious," Sasha almost yelled, "he was hinting and trying to test me to see if I would say anything. He wanted to let me know that they were in control and to put me in my proper place. I am a lawyer trust me. I know these things." She sobbed.

"Well did you say anything Sasha? I know you know better than to show your hand when someone may be bluffing?" Charmaine asked her.

"Of course I didn't say anything, but trust me, I know when someone is bluffing and this is not one of those times. I work with these people remember? And they taught me every trick I know. So I know that something is about to go down and it is not making me partner that I am worried about." She spilled. Charmaine knew Sasha had a dramatic flare and was use to exaggerating the facts and sensationalizing situations, but she got the feeling this was not one of those times. Sasha sounded scared.

"Okay Sis, let me go see what I can cook up. Are you

home?" Charmaine asked half distracted. Sasha was interrupting her card game with Delia. She hadn't seen Delia since the last time Sasha and Kayla came over her house and she wanted to spend some quality time with Delia. She wanted Delia to get to know her so she could get an opportunity to make her move.

Charmaine turned to look where Delia had bent over on all fours to reach for her pocketbook. Charmaine's heart sped up and Sasha was not on her mind. All she could think was how perfectly rounded Delia's derriere was and how inviting. Sometimes she felt almost sure that Delia knew she was gay and was teasing her and playing hard to get, and at other times it seemsed like she didn't have a clue. She got really excited and suddenly frustrated about how to approach a situation like this. Usually the women she courted knew exactly who she was or what they were getting into. Delia was different. She felt different about Delia, like she could love her and she didn't want to ruin it.

"I am really going to have to call you back Sis." Charmaine told Sasha before hanging up abruptly. Sasha turned to look at the phone stunned. Out of all her girlfriends Charmaine was the one that started it all, there with her from the beginning through all her antics and misbehaving. Charmaine knew her and knew her well. Better than Kayla or the other bitches. Why was she getting put on the back burner? Sasha held the phone like that for maybe five minutes contemplating Charmaine's rudeness and her dire situation before she hung up and rushed upstairs to her elaborate bedroom she shared with no one and drifted off to sleep.

Once off the phone Charmaine sat back in her position and waited for Delia to finish doing what she was doing, pretending not to watch her every twitch and turn and pretended to be deeply fascinated with the cards in her hands. Once Delia returned she put one her most serious face on and stared at Delia.

"Is she always that unbearable?" Delia asked Charmaine once she realized she had her attention.

"Unfortunately, yes. I have known that girl since high school and she has always gotten what she wanted and I guess she has just grown use to it. She lives a very high maintenance lifestyle and people especially men cater to that." Charmaine explained to Delia. "That's why I don't deal with men. Never have and never will, because they are idiots and I have always known that I didn't want to waste any of my time on them." She took the opportunity to plug some information about herself. She wanted her sexuality to be out in the open, she didn't want to deceive or confuse Delia and if something was to happen between them she didn't want Delia to say that she didn't know and that she was tricked. Yet she didn't want to scare her with too much information, she wanted to do things gradually. She knew Delia wasn't a child and she definitely did not strike her as the naïve type, but she didn't want any mistakes. Not this time and not with this one.

"I don't know how you could be friends with someone that insufferable?" Delia stated and looked at Charmaine as though she expected more or better from her. She didn't understand how she could be so attracted and drawn to Charmaine's strength and clarity of mind yet was so confused about her choice in friendships.

She wasn't stupid; she knew that Charmaine was gay and had been trying to tell her. She just preferred to ignore the signs for now. Since what happened to her back four years ago, forced to have an abortion, used and discarded by a man she fell in love with, who told her he loved her too. Since then she hadn't had a man. As a matter of fact she had spent her time using and hurting them where it really mattered, in their pockets. She had never really thought of going gay even though she had become some-what of a feminist, but she was really sexually frustrated. The only true relationship she really was her closest and trusted confidant Chyna, who had stood by her through thick and thin for the long haul.

　　　　She didn't know what it was about Charmaine that intrigued her so, but she was physically attracted to her sleek long frame and dark complexion. She dreamt of running her fingers along that smooth cocoa colored skin from the moment she met her but wasn't sure how to go about approaching her. Her feelings confused her and caught her totally off guard, so she planned on taking things slowly, no matter how badly Charmaine wanted her to admit realization, until she was ready and certain.

Chapter 13

Chyna decided to give Justin a call and hoped she would-
n't get a voicemail, or a nurse again. She really wanted to talk to
him and she was getting tired of hanging up. She decided finally that if she didn't get a hold of him this time she would leave a
message. Delia was spending a lot of time with Charmaine planning some big scheme she really didn't want to be a part of and
she was getting really very lonely.

"Hello, Dr. Etnas office." Came the nurses' voice over the
phone. Chyna wanted to hang up but this time, she decided to
bite the bullet and stick to her guns.

"Hello, good afternoon. May I speak to Dr. Justin Etnas
please?" She asked as politely as she could without showing the
frustration she felt boiling at the surface.

"Sure. Please hold." Came the perky response. She
could not believe her luck. He was actually there. So why didn't
he just answer the phone. Duh! She told herself, he's a doctor.
Helloooooooo, he is busy. Is there a brain in Chyna's head or is
all sanity lost in the wetness between your thighs? She scolded
herself in a childlike jovial manner.

"Yes, Justin Etnas here." Came the deep husky sweetness over the phone that she had so longed to hear again.

"Eh! Justin, you don't know my name but we met about a

week ago in the super market and you gave me your…"

"Number. Yes of course. How could I forget?" He teased and she could hear the smirk in his voice. "So what took you so long to call? I was waiting for you. Or didn't you know that?" He asked her and she could sense his arrogant confidence reverberating through the phone lines. Usually this would turn her off, but maybe it was the raging horny hormones and twitching battles in the slit of her crotch that were making her go mad. She couldn't help it, she wanted him and somehow found everything he did at that moment irresistible.

"Well, I am here now, and I was wondering when you would be able to schedule me in for a little private doctors' visit?" She flirted blatantly. She knew that she had changed. This was not the same timid naïve Chyna who waited by the phone for her first love to disappoint her. This was not the same Chyna who believed that there was value in virtue. *Piss it all off*, she thought. She would not be had and made a fool of like that again.

"Hum! Now that sounds like an appointment I would like on my agenda." He paused trying not to sound too eager, but unwilling to let this opportunity pass.

"Tell you what. I should be getting out of here in another hour or so, how about I meet you somewhere?" He suggested. Chyna was so pleasantly stunned she couldn't help the glee that came out of her voice.

"Well now that sounds like exactly what I had in mind. I would love that." She squealed. Thoughts of where she could meet with him quickly darted through her head and were thrown unfavorably into the 'no' pile. Then it hit her.

"I have an idea," she began hoping he would go for it. This would give her home base advantage.

"I am staying at the Radisson Hotel off of the Belt Parkway. Do you know how to get there?" She asked him, hoping he wouldn't think that was too intimate a place to meet someone for the first time.

"Of course. That sounds fine. So we can say around 2'ish then?" He concluded.

"Two will do just fine." Chyna cooed. After giving him her room number and last name she got off the phone and hugged herself.

"Chyna's gonna get some, Chyna's gonna get some," she cha cha'd across the street and sang the Chyna booty call song all the way back to her hotel room. "Chyna's gonna get some...Cha.Cha.Cha.Cha.Cha.Cha..."

When she got back to the hotel she told the desk clerk that she was expecting company and to let him right up. She took a quick shower and pulled on a short pair of denim shorts and a blue tank top. She turned on the thirty two inch television she had in her king sized suite and lay there blankly, crossing and crisscrossing her legs to ease and quell the quivering yearnings and desires that were building and ailing her. Her body on fire and a wet twat that seemed like it took on a shower all of its own, Chyna grew tired of the torment. Soon she fell asleep and dreamt fondly of Justin walking in through the hotel room door and just screwing her like a wild animal. No formalities necessary.

Justin was all too happy to hear from her. He had been waiting for her call all week and when she didn't call he thought she wasn't interested, though to protect his fragile male ego, he much preferred to think that she had lost his number and was trying desperately to contact him and couldn't.

He chuckled to himself as he got off the phone and checked his watch. It was barely twelve 0'clock.

"So what's the sudden anxiety doctor? I havn't seen you look at your watch all morning; until now." His nurse teased him playfully.

"Well, all work and no play makes this doctor a very naughty boy, and I am feeling extremely naughty right now." He chuckled and winked at her tellingly. His nurse who had been his assistant since he got transferred from Rochester to Interfaith Hospital in Brooklyn New York more than two years ago now, smiled. She resented the assignment at first. She thought that she being white and he being black was going to pose a problem. But she was wrong and she had enjoyed working with him thus far.

She knew how wound up he had been and in the entire time that she had known him, she had never seen him give the time of day to not one woman. He usually worked really hard and for very long hours. This was the first time a woman called for him that wasn't a patient and she was intrigued.

"Christina, do me a favor and double check to see what's on my agenda for the rest of the day. I would like to take off now if I can."

"No problem Justin, I will be back with that in a sec." She rushed out the door to check on that information before he could turn around. She never ceased to amaze him; it was as though she worked with Houdini on his disappearing acts. Justin liked her spunk, she wasn't lazy, and she showed initiative and was hard working.

While Christina was working on his agenda, he went into the locker room and freshened up. He needed to get out of there and there was only one hour holding him back. Someone else could cover for him. He thought as he quickly changed into his ragged old dirty jeans and a t-shirt. When he retuned to his office Christina signaled to him that he was clear and laughed heartily at his enthusiasm when he said, "YES!"

Justin's bachelor pad wasn't far from where the Radisson was in Queens. Matter of fact, he was right around the corner off of Rockaway Parkway and not too far from the Belt. He was not far at all. He pulled up in front of the house where he had rented the top loft There was no need to get anything bigger. Fact was that the two-bedroom loft was too big. He hated having to be there by himself with no one to share it with.

He parked his Z3 BMW in front of the house and ran up the stairs to take a shower and freshen up. He took care in spraying a tad bit of *Obsession for Men* strategically over his body and pulled a pair of casual baggy dress slacks over his throbbing hardness that he hoped would concede as he made his way to see Chyna. Since he wore no undergarments, he hoped his desires for her wouldn't be too readily evident.

He pulled on a muscle top to show the striking leanness of his muscular frame and took one last look in the mirror before he put on his wrist watch, his pinkie ring that his mother gave him after his father passed, and pulled his neat shoulder length locks into a ponytail. He grabbed his keys and sashayed to the door. The ego in him gave way and he took another step back to the mirror winked at himself and said; *well done Justin, well done,* and was out the door.

Justin was impressed with the preparations that Chyna had made. He eased himself into the elevator and headed to the seventh floor suite as the desk clerk had directed him. He had a guest key in hand and was ready to use it. Pushing the door slightly open he ogled to see if Chyna was decent and if she would respond. Hearing nothing, he pushed the door so much more open and peeked in.

"Hello. Chyna may I enter?" He asked in a gentlemanly fashion. Still no response, so he let himself in and heaved a sigh of disappointment. He couldn't believe he came all this way, sexual excitement and tension building inside of him only to find an empty hotel room. Nonetheless, he was impressed with the elegant taste of the big hotel suite. It seemed as though she had left the television on in the bedroom because he heard the distant sound of people laughing and talking. There was a kitchen area tucked neatly in the corner and facing a small study, which housed a desk, telephone, phone book and other office necessities. As he walked further in he noticed the comfortable lounge sofa, chairs, ottoman and a sixty-inch television in front of it. It was gracefully enhanced with a huge picture frame of a vase with roses and thick heavy lavender flowered drapes adorned the windows.

Since he was alone he decided to give himself the full tour and headed toward a foyer that seemed to lead to the bedroom suite. As he entered he saw the bathroom, which was quite large and sported bright, colorful towels and an assortment of feminine products for hair and personal hygiene. He knew those did not come with the suite. He chuckled softly to himself and gingerly walked farther and gasped slightly at the sight that bombarded his eyes. It wasn't just the Jacuzzi or the large king sized bed. It was the sight of barely clad Chyna laying all cavalier across the bed. Her long thin frame gracefully breathing softly invited him to her peaceful beauty. He walked towards her as stealthily as he could, he did not want to wake her. He was happy she hadn't left him to face her hotel room suite alone and his heart became filled with longing and anticipation.

He sat by her bedside and slowly inched as close to her as he could without waking her. He leaned in close to her and nestled his nose into the nape of her neck to breathe her perfume, *Tommy Girl* he thought. She's got taste.

Chyna felt the warm presence beside her and didn't move. She didn't want to startle him. She felt she was at an advantage to just lie there and see exactly what he would do. Justin took his fingers and gently traced the contours of her hand, with her back to him she smiled, *this is nice*, she thought to

herself as the warm tremors of desires began to come alive and
stir inside her again. She shifted a little as she felt his fully
aroused shaft press itself into the spine of her back. She could
feel him trying to will his sex mantle to ease, but it wouldn't listen.
She could visualize his frail attempt to not allow her to feel how
much turmoil she was causing in his groin when he stuck his bottom out, away from her, hoping to give his penis room to roam
without it having to touch her but was unsuccessful.

Chyna couldn't resist how adorable he made her feel.
Watched and admired like a precious porcelain China doll. He
took his nose and sniffed at her again, like a dog in heat that had
been drawn to the sexual smell and chemistry of its female counterpart. When she didn't wake he took his hands and brushed
against the small curls that lay relaxing on her face. Small beads
of sweat had arrived on Chyna's forehead as evidence that she
was awake, her breathing picked up pace even as she tried to
remain calm, to allow him to indulge in the sheer sin that had
washed over them. Desire stirred and fought to amalgamate like
two magnets being pulled apart with force knowing full well that
the strength of the attraction would be too hard to resist and soon
they would unite, joining as one in a connection that would be
hard to disengage.

He realized that he must have gotten too close, because
Chyna stirred and when she opened her eyes ever so slightly, a
smile crept across her face to show her total approval. She
couldn't resist any longer. The cat and mouse game of pretending that she didn't know he was there, pretending that she was-
n't being washed into some sea of erotic oblivion needed to end.

She didn't waste time, no hesitation, and no hello. She
just stretched her long, long arms around his neck and turned her
body so she could press herself as closely to him as possible.
She pulled on his neck to usher him down to come face to face
with her and in one final breath she plastered a kiss as tender

and wet and as inviting as he had ever felt. He did not resist her. He allowed himself to be swept away into the tidal wave of total erotic rush and delved into the sweet sexy taste of her fruity fresh mouth.

Not being able to control the raging passion that had been building inside of him from earlier that morning, he slipped off his shoes and allowed his body to indulge in the plush softness of the bed that seemed to blend as one with her. He pressed his hand under the perky tight package of her behind and squeezed as though he had never felt a grown woman's ass. As though every breath he took depended on it.

Chyna wasn't being coy. They both knew why he was there, there in her hotel room. Why they did not choose to rendezvous at a restaurant or movie, go on a sky trip or a get away weekend. No. They were there for one purpose and one purpose only, to satisfy the carnal cravings of raging sexual hunger and to quell the urges of passions long deferred.

Justin pulled back and took quick rash breaths, his eyes surveying her face for answers to questions he hoped he didn't have to ask. He looked deeply into her eyes and Chyna released her arms from around his neck and sat up, she knew the questions he sought and felt irritation. She couldn't believe he was stopping her.

"Hello Chyna, I am Justin. It's so nice to finally have you to myself." He started in the most nonchalant manner. He knew that this wouldn't be the most popular response for the average guy, to put a halt on what was obviously a win-win situation. But he wanted this encounter to be more than just wham bam thank you ma'am. If that was all he wanted, he wouldn't have waited so long for the woman he wanted to re-invite him into the world of intimate pleasure. He was sure that woman was Chyna. He couldn't quite put his finger on it, but there was something there. Something special about her that drew him to her. He couldn't remember the last time he just handed his card out, just for the pleasure of it. He had gotten rusty and out of the game.

Chyna looked at him in utter disbelief and was relieved to see the smile that mockingly appeared on his beautifully dimpled cheeks. It told her that he was not stopping maliciously. It was a smile that told her that there was more to this man and that the mystery that his dimples hid would be worth unraveling. Just in that moment, Chyna panted at the breathtaking effect his deep, adorable dimples had on her, how they were able to bring a fresh burst of sultry sex stains to mark her panties.

"Well, hello there Justin," she wheezed in pretence nobility. She lifted her hand as royally as she could and presented him with the back of her hand to kiss. Without removing the sexy as hell smile from his face, he took her hand and gently pressed his full soft lips to it. She found this whole thing to be sweet, but she wasn't in the mood to be sweet. She wanted to get fucked like there was no tomorrow, as if being enraptured with him was the alpha and the omega. She wanted to feel like a woman in all the ways that God intended and he was the chosen one.

"Justin, I don't mean to be blunt, but I must be honest with you. I have wanted you from the moment I laid eyes on you and I take it that you wouldn't be here if you didn't feel the same." She stated in a rushed quick sentence and waited for his response.

"Chyna, of course I want you. Look at you girl, you are scrumptious." He responded, and again his eyes danced as he took a quick once over of her elongated frame, and Chyna hung her head. She didn't like it but she felt a BUT coming on.

"But…" he began again. "I really want you to know that this is not just another fling for me. There is something special about you that I want to get to know and I don't want to ruin it."

Special? Ruin it? Chyna asked herself. What is going on? Is this guy for real? I just want to get laid by a fine brother and this dude is acting like he's looking for love.

"You are not going to ruin anything Justin. I really like you. I want you. I want to be intimate with you." She paused. "Can you handle that? Can we get past that threshold first and then take it from there?" She asked, taking his hands and squeezing them gently, urgently. She didn't want him to back out on her now by misconstruing what she had said. Not when they were so close.

"Chyna?" Justin cooed her name in the sexiest way she had ever heard, it made her pulse stop and she couldn't respond. He realized that at that moment if he kept talking, he might chase her away, so he decided to give her what she wanted and keep his fingers crossed that she would allow him to see her again.

"Can I be intimate with you…right now?" He asked, wanting to make the interaction as proper and decent as possible.

"Justin, after today if you pass this test, you can make whoopi, sex, anything you want to call it with me anytime you want." She said with as much emphasis and meaning that she could muster in her vulnerable needy sexual state, and winked at him with laughter and mirth dancing in her eyes.

"Well then…" he said and pressed his lips firmly to hers without another word. He stuck his tongue deep within her throat and gave her a taste of the full length of his other sexual organ, one of soft unobtrusive heat that would taste Chyna in the most unbelievable ways.

Justin unbuttoned his pants and dropped them to the floor without releasing Chynas' lips from his captivity while Chyna yanked at her shorts. They had surprisingly quick snap buttons at the sides and just fell easily between her legs. She felt for his manhood and was pleasantly greeted by the well-endowed length and thickness of his love making shaft and a new explosion of heat permeated her body.

Reaching for a condom in the night stand beside her bed she had to lay on her tummy and stretch her hands to get across the king sized bed. Grabbing a condom she handed it to Justin who ripped at the wrapping and gently slide it onto his ever-ready penis. He pressed Chyna into the bed with his hands and forced her to stay on her tummy, kneading his free hand into her ass and spreading her cheeks to give him full view of her clean-shaven lips.

Positioning himself over her backside, he lowered himself into her and she squealed and the throbbing hardness that had just re-christened her born again virginity because it had been so long and the tightness of her warm meaty insides caused him to plunge deeply within her. He felt his earnest need and wanted to stop the orgasm that was threatening to embarrass him and felt that the condom break so he pulled out.

"What are you doing?" Chyna asked slightly perturbed, her needs unfulfilled and frustration beckoning at her door to do a dance with anger.

"I am sorry, I think the condom broke and you feel so good, I just didn't want to..."

"No it's okay. I understand. I think I have more." Chyna reached for the night stand again to find that there was nothing there. In his earnestness Justin grabbed his pants and slipped it over his thighs. He hadn't removed his shirt and was as eager as a schoolboy at his first time to get back to the task at hand.

"Is there a machine or something in the hallway or in the gift store downstairs that might carry condoms?" He asked her hurriedly.

"Yes. I think the gift store in the lobby might have condoms. As Justin ran toward the door, Chyna inserted her fingers inside of the burning heat in her vagina and screamed Justin's name as the orgasm rocked her body in an unrelenting and powerful way. She laid there, the thought of Justin building and new desire within her and she waited impatiently for him to return.

****

Justin ran to the lobby and to the elevator. He waited impatiently and pressed the lobby button when the doors finally opened for him. He made a mad dash as calmly as he could to the gift store in the lobby and searched frantically for whatever condom they may carry. Just as he made his choice from the minor selection they had and was walking toward the sales lady to pay for his purchase, the security guard walked toward him and tapped him indiscreetly on his shoulder.

"Excuse me sir. I think you may have dropped something." He snickered in an attempt to hide the sheer amusement of the situation. Justin turned to look at him and curiously wondered what this big goofy looking guy was smirking at.

"I am sorry, what do you mean?" he asked him in an annoyed uppity tone that the security guard didn't like. Justin reminded him of those uppity, snobby black people who wanted or thought they were better than the average black folk and it made him want to embarrass Justin all the more.

"Well, I was trying to be inconspicuous, but since you are having an attitude *sir*, I think you just dropped your used condom on the hotel stores' floor."

Justin's mouth dropped open and embarrassment and humiliation caused him to hang his head in shame. How is it that he didn't feel the slime of the rubbery fabric as it slid from his shaft and to the floor from under his pant leg? How he didn't feel the drip of excitement and premature ejaculation as it streamed down his thighs to alert him that something like this was about to happen? The sales lady stretched herself over the counter to look at where the condom that was still oozing cum had settled on the floor. The few shoppers in the store turned to look at the used condom with the evidence of his sexual encounter and started laughing. The security guard laughed so hard that people walking by stopped to see what the commotion was. The sales lady couldn't stop laughing and could barely see to give Justin his change for the fresh pack of condom he just bought.

Justin hung his head in total awkwardness and walked as briskly as he could back to the elevator and back to Chyna's suite where she waited for him fervently.

Chapter 14

Karen jumped on the train, with Suzette in hand, bags over her shoulders and Anthony walking close beside her. She had tears welling in her eyes as thoughts of what was going to happen next bombarded her brain and she tried hard to be strong for the two babies that now depended on her. She took the train straight back to her small apartment and wondered what she would do next. She had no inkling how to raise children and Sandra's situation didn't look good. As she dragged herself, the bags, and the two kids back to her apartment, she secretly hoped that Shawn wouldn't be there waiting for some ass as usual. She didn't want to deal with him right now.

Slowly she eased herself and the kids up the stairs and into her small two-bedroom apartment. She was not surprised to see Shawn sprawled out on her sofa with a bag of potato chips in one hand and the remote control in the other.

"Well lookie here," he greeted her in a matter of fact tone. "We done got us a family I didn't even know about."

Karen ignored him and moved quickly, walking into the extra room she used mainly for storage and where Shawn would sleep if he were there and in the doghouse and refused to leave. She threw the bags on the floor and gently placed Suzette on the floor next to them.

She ran to the phone to dial Kayla's number to see if she was home and got the voicemail. She tried again, hoping that Kayla would pick up the phone.

"Hello Kay, this is Karen. Could you please pick up the phone if you're there? It's an emergency." She pleaded after the beep, but still no answer. She decided to ring again. As she waited for the answering machine to pick up again, Shawn came up behind her and pulled her behind into his groin so she could feel his throbbing hard on.

"What are you doing Shawn? Can't you see I am on the phone?" She couldn't hide the annoyance in her voice that was easily detectable, and her confusion and fear for Sandra and her children building.

"Kayla, please pick up the phone…" and before she could continue Michael picked up more drunk than before and continued on his rampage.

"Every fucking thing is an emergency for you bitches. All day long you people call this house; First that other half dead one Sandra, and now you. Don't you sluts have a life? Why don't you go be like your friend Sasha and fuck somebody else's man?" He suggested and slammed down the phone in Karen's ear.

Before Karen could think about what he said or erase the question mark off of her face from the conversation that just happened on the phone, Shawn started in on her.

"What is this? You prefer to talk to everybody else except me." He whined and grabbed Karen's small breasts to emphasize what he needed from her just in case she didn't quite get it.

"Listen you prick, there are some things that are more important than sex, and even more things than are more important than you." As the last word filtered out of her mouth a slap hit her across her face and sent her flying to the floor. Anthony ran and grabbed on to Shawn's foot and started biting him and

Suzette started to cry. Before Karen could grab Anthony away from Shawn's angry outbursts he grabbed Anthony and threw him into the wall across the living room and moved in again on Karen.

"What the hell did you just do you stupid piece of worthless shit?" She asked totally flabbergasted and ran to Anthony who just lay there almost unconscious.

"Oh my God, Shawn what did you do?" she asked rhetorically not really expecting an answer as fresh tears ran down her face. She couldn't believe that this was happening again. Happening now.

Shawn didn't answer her. He unzipped his fly and pulled on her leg to pull her skirt up so he could access the object of his insanity. But this time Karen was not going to let him get away with it. She crawled as quickly as she could to the night stand and pulled on the lamp until it fell to the floor. With all her strength she picked it up and threw it hitting him in the side of his head. While he stopped to examine the damage that she had done, Karen ran to the phone and dialed 911.

"Hello this is the operator. What's your emergency?" Before Karen could answer Shawn was back at her again.

"Why do you even bother?" He snickered condescendingly. "Its not as if you are really going to do anything about it anyway." He told her arrogantly and the anger that boiled in her abdomen was like nothing she had ever felt.

"Helppppppppp!" She yelled as loudly as she could, hoping the operator didn't hang up. Shawn drew nearer and nearer to her and grabbed her by her neat white shirt and raised his hands to assault her again.

"Somebody please help me!" She yelped again as loudly as she could before his hands came crashing down into her mouth and loosening one of her teeth. She took a few beatings from him like this for an amount of time of which she had no idea. Anthony still lay there semi-conscious and Suzette's wails could wake the dead. Soon she heard sirens and police officers knocking at her door.

They grabbed Shawn and cuffed him.

"Would you like to press charges ma'am?" One officer asked her as the other read him his rights.

"Yes! I would like to press charges," she told them looking directly into Shawn's eyes. She didn't flinch or flutter her eyelids.

"I would like to press charges for battery and physical child abuse. He tried to rape me in front of the children I am babysitting and wouldn't take no for an answer. I want a permanent restraining order against that man." She could barely muster the words but she knew she had to say it. She had to put an end to the madness that had cornered her life and held her hostage for so many years. She had to say enough was enough.

After they carted him away they advised Karen that she had to come to the police station and file a formal report. She told them she had to get the kids together and that she would be right there.

She didn't want Shawn to get away with this again. She wanted to put him away for a while and let him pay for what he had been doing to her for so long. So she got herself together, went to the bathroom and washed out her blood stained mouth. She picked up Anthony and placed an iced pack on his head and calmed Suzette's crying.

There was still another important matter here at hand and she could not slow down now. She had to find a way to get to the hospital and she had to let the others know what was going on with Sandra.

Her nosy neighbor Debbie, the one that was always in her business came knocking on the door. She never really talked to Debbie, but every time she was in an argument with Shawn or getting a good old' fashion whooping from him, she would be there refereeing. Memories of the last and one of the worst fights she had with Shawn on the street while waiting for Kayla to come pick her up to go to Sasha's house came crashing back to her. She didn't remember everything the way Charmaine and Kayla explained it to her, but she remembered hearing Debbie's familiar ghetto fabulous behind admonishing her to run away from Shawn.

"Yes, what is it Debbie?" Karen yelled at the intruding knock at the door. She didn't feel like moving away from Anthony's bruised head. She just wanted Debbie to go away.

"You okay in there Karen? It's just that I heard the whole commotion and then I saw the police dragging your man away..."

"...And is there something else I can do for you?" Karen responded, her pride wounded from all the shame he had brought her and getting fed up with Debbie's annoying mannerisms.

"Well I was just concerned for you Ms. Thing, I thought you might like some company or something, somebody to talk to or a shoulder to cry on. But if you are going to get all uppity on me then I will just go back to my corner and leave you alone."

Karen listened to hear if she had left, but she heard no retreating footsteps. She waited another minute or two and listened into the silence and still nothing. She must have gone, she thought to herself and sighed. Suddenly she thought that maybe she could ask Debbie to watch the kids for her so she could contact Kayla and get to the hospital. Slowly she released Anthony from the security of her arms and ran to the door to see if she could catch her before she made other plans to stick her nose into another neighbors business. Just as Karen opened the door, she saw Debbie slowly creeping away and making her way up the hallway stairs.

"I guess you were really concerned about me eh?" Karen asked her sarcastically and waited for lies that she could contrive to cover her sneaky behavior.

"I was you know, whether you believe it or not. I just did-n't want to leave until I was sure you were okay." She smiled as she descended the few stairs she had taken to return to Karen.

"So, are you really okay? I know it must have been really hard for you to just lock him up and send him off like that. But you should be really proud for standing up to yourself." With all the sincerity she could muster.

"Debbie, if you are not busy, maybe there is something really important you could do for me." She asked and hoped that she wouldn't say no. She was her only option besides getting the kids all packed up again and dragging them on the train with her, and she really didn't want to take them to the hospital. She was-n't even sure what kind of state their mother was in.

"Sure I will help you Karen. What is it?"

"Could you watch these kids for me until later on tonight? I am not sure how long I am going to be gone or what to expect to happen, but their mother is in the hospital and I have to go see her. Do you think you can do it for me? I will pay you."

"Oh hum bug," she giggled and straddled her huge Jennifer Lopez behind into Karen's apartment. If only the rest of her looked like Jennifer Lopez, she might actually be pretty. But she was one of those women who had a body a man could work with, but a face fit for a paper bag.

Karen was surprised that she accepted the offer so easi-ly, she was sure she would embarrass her and talk her into relin-quishing some ego damaging details before accepting.

"Thank you Debbie, this is very decent of you."

"Now what's that supposed to mean?" Debbie turned to look at her defensively.

"I didn't mean anything by it Debbie, I just think it's a nice thing that you are doing and I appreciate it." Karen told her, she didn't feel like getting into it with *yet* another person for the day.

"Okay, no problem, I am sure if I had my girlfriend's kids

that my boyfriend didn't want around you would watch them for me too. Right?" she asked as serious as a heart attack. It was as though she didn't realize the lack of scruples she displayed by showing Karen just how insensitive she really was.

"I would definitely do the same thing for you Debbie." Karen rolled her eyes and walked as fast as she could to her bedroom to freshen up and whispered *bitch*, under her breath.

Within minutes, Karen was ready to go. She picked up the phone and dialed Kayla's cell phone number and asked her to alert every one else. She didn't bother to mention Michael's attitude on the phone with her earlier. Anthony and Suzette had fallen asleep right where they were and she instructed Debbie not to move or wake them.

Chapter 15

Justin was paged to the emergency room and rushed over there as fast as he could. He didn't know what the circumstances were, but apparently they needed all of their resident physicians on staff. When he arrived he was briefed on two incidents. A boy, at about eight years old had been rushed to the hospital from school because of a massive seizure, and a woman, HIV positive and apparently on the verge of death from improper care and administering of her medication.

He decided he would check on the boy since Dr. Walker and Dr. Hudson were already catering to the adult, which was appropriately so since she was in their specialty area. He rushed into the boy's room where he had been stabilized.

"Hello, my name is Dr. Etnas. I will be the attending physician to your son until we can find out what his problem is and then get a specialist in here to administer to him." He introduced himself to the worried elderly lady who sat fixated by the boy's side holding his limp hand.

"I am sorry doctor but he is not my son, he is my foster child." She corrected and wiped away a tear that slipped from her concerned eyes.

"Okay, I need to you fill out this form as thoroughly as you can. I will go check his chart and get back to you in a few m inutes." He informed her as he walked out the door. Justin reviewed the boy's chart and found that his name was also Justin, and he smiled as a tinge of sadness crossed over him. He had always wanted to have his own child, and to have a patient with his name hit close to home.

As he re-entered the boy's room he saw that he was awake and was happy he would be able to speak with him.

"Hello Justin, how are you?" He said as chipper as he could.

"I am fine. Am I going to die?" The boy's question was direct and took him off guard, but he knew he had to be honest and tactful in his communication with the boy.

"I don't think so Justin, but I am going to need your help to make sure that you get better as fast as possible. Okay?"

"You know, Justin plays pee-wee football, and he is an A student in his elementary school." His foster mother glowed with pride.

"Yeah is that true? What position do you play?" Justin asked as he pulled up a chair by the boy's bedside.

"I play full back," the boy said with a struggled dry cough. "But I haven't been able to play since last season because of my illness. I had to stop last year when they found out I had cancer. They said if I had a bone marrow transplant from a parent, I would have a better chance and that maybe one day I would be able to play ball again. But I don't have any parents." The boy said and sadly looked away.

"Hey guess what?" Dr. Etnas asked Justin, "My name is Justin too." He smiled widely at him. "Do you think we could be related?" He asked the boy who laughed boldly.

"No, I don't think so. You don't look like the type who would abandon your family. Especially not a child." Justin told his doctor with a mature acceptance.

"Okay Justin, just rest now for awhile. I am going to take

your foster mother out for a few minutes and fill out some paper work okay? Then we will be right back." Justin nodded his head in approval as Dr. Etnas and his foster mother left his room.

"I am sorry ma'am, what's your name?" Dr. Etnas asked her politely. She looked to be somewhere between fifty-five or sixty years old, definitely his senior and he wanted to be respectful.

"My name is Edna, Edna Barker." She told him. "I know what you are going to ask me next. No, as far as I know he has no next of kin. He was given up for adoption at birth and his adopted mother was killed in a car accident five years ago. The adoptive father felt like he couldn't raise him on his own, so he put him in an orphanage. Two months after he was placed there, he had a seizure and was brought to the hospital where I work. That's when he was first diagnosed with cancer. I asked to take him in and was able to have him placed with me as his foster mother and he has been with me since."

"Do you have anymore foster children?"

"No, just him. I have never had a child, and he just seemed like a blessing. I don't have much but I was blessed with a nice home and a good job since I have been a nursing assistant for fifteen years at Bellevue Hospital. Last year when we found out about his illness we tried everything we could to find his biological parents, but we turned up nothing. At that moment we were told that we would be placed on a waiting list for a bone marrow match, but nothing has turned up." She told Dr. Etnas sadly. "His best hope is to find a parent who can donate, other wise we wait and watch him get worse or eventually die.

"Do you have all his documents? Birth certificate. Birthplace? Do they make any mention of the maternal parent?" Dr. Etnas quizzed.

"No, we went through all this already when we first started searching. We turned up nothing. All we know about his maternal parent is that she was in a psyche ward in Rochester New York where she gave birth and gave him up for adoption. No one knew her real name. She was known only as Jane Doe." As Justin heard this information he was floored. The shock and surprise of hearing this was evident on his face and left Edna Barker puzzled as to why he was reacting that way. "Are you okay Doctor?" She asked him with genuine concern.

"No ma'am, it's nothing. Please excuse me I have to make a quick phone call and I will be right back." He didn't wait to hear her response. He took off down the hall and around the corridor where she could not see him.

The memory of Jane Doe saturated his mind. He remembered how long it took for him to get past the feelings he had developed for her. Could this have been the same person, the same baby boy he watched her give a way? Could this be the child he was willing to father? The questions came and flooded his mind and heart. He ran to his office and remained there paralyzed for an unknown amount of time, wondering if the irony of the story was purely coincidental.

Justin Etnas knew that he had to go make a few phone calls to get a specialist in on the boy's case. However he wanted to be sure to stay close by. He wanted to see what developed with this child. If he was right, this is the child he delivered into the world.

****

"Karen, what happened?" I asked as I rushed up to Karen happy to see her. At that same moment, Sasha and Charmaine also arrived, each bombarding Karen with questions about what happened to Sandra.

"I don't know okay? She called me at work and asked me

to come over and when I got there she was passed out.

"Yeah, I got a message from her at my house. It's like she started to leave a message and then she stopped. The message got cut off."

"Well Kayla, Sandra said she called you and asked you to come by and you just ignored her like she meant nothing to you." Karen told her.

"Oh come on, so now it's my fault that she is in here?"

"Possibly," Karen spat and everyone looked at her in awe. Karen has spoken up. I looked at her in bewilderment and walked away. I couldn't believe that Karen would even insinuate what we thought she was trying to say.

"Okay enough, what's going on?" Charmaine asked Karen, hoping that she would give her a little bit more information.

"Sandra called me and asked me to stop by, she said she wasn't feeling well and when I got there she was passed out. I called 911 and here we are." Karen told them just as the doctors walked over to them.

"Hello, who's next of kin?"

"We all are." I decided to speak up. Karen did not say anything. "How is she? Can we see her?" I asked the doctor, and watched Karen from the corner of my eyes to see if she was going to say anything.

"Well, she is not awake now, but she should be in a few minutes." Informed Dr. Walker. "Did you all know that she was this sick?" He continued before they had a chance to ask more questions. They all turned to look at each other and none of them knew quite what to say.

"No, I don't think any of us knew exactly how sick she was." Karen told them. "I know that she didn't want us to worry about her because she was very independent. But I think I began to have some idea of how serious her illness was a few weeks ago when she called me over for some help." Karen continued.

"Well what do you know about her illness?" Dr. Hudson jumped in to follow up on what Karen had told them.

"Well, we all know that she is HIV positive." Karen answered.

"Could you all just take a seat please?" Dr. Walker requested and both doctors pulled up chairs and sat adjacent from them.

"First of all, your friend is not HIV positive, she has AIDS. It seems that she was either not taking her medications as prescribed or she wasn't able to afford the recommended pharmaceuticals. We took a look at what she had in her possession at home from what the paramedics brought in and these are not the appropriate medication for AIDS. We are sorry to tell you that the virus has now spread and she has full blown AIDS. You cannot get it by touching her, there has to be an exchange of bodily fluids like blood, saliva, semen etc." Dr. Hudson told them.

"So what are you saying? Is she going to die?" Sasha asked. Hesitantly, Dr. Hudson looked at them solemnly and answered shaking his head in a solemn yes.

"The virus has progressed too far too fast without proper supervision and now it's too late to even try and slow down the deterioration process. I am sorry." He told them.

"You can go in and see her now if you like. We will release her later on today. Will there be someone to take care of her." Every one turned to look at the other at the on set of the question but no one had an answer.

"Yes, I will take care of her. She can come stay with me." Karen told them and everyone again, shocked at her newly found voice, strength, independence and outspokenness.

"Karen are you crazy? What are you doing?" Sasha asked her.

"I hate to admit this Karen, but Sasha's got a point. This is going to be a lot of responsibility."

"Listen to me the whole bunch of you. You are all a set of non-caring backstabbers. We are all supposed to be a friend to Sandra; she has done nothing to us. Yet when she turned to us we found it too much trouble to be there. Right now she is dying. There is not much left of her life so I want to be the friend I say I am now before she is gone. If you are going to criticize me and judge me then I don't need your friendship either." She said and walked towards Sandra's room.

They were all stunned and stood there without moving and watched as Karen walked away. After a couple minutes they followed her to Sandra's room where she was awake. There they found her with two social workers that quizzed her on the kids. Karen was able to speak up and update them on her decision to take the family in and be responsible for them.

After they left, the group sat by Sandra's bedside and talked about the events leading up to her hospitalization.

"Kayla, you said you would stop by and you didn't? What happened?" I felt guilty, but I had to turn and look at Sasha, who was to blame for keeping me too long. I wanted to go see Sandra but no, she had to have my full and undivided attention. Again Sasha was too concerned and preoccupied with herself and about her own problems to care about anyone but herself.

"Why are you looking at me? You are your own adult and nobody forced you to stay out with me. If you had other things to do then you could have just said so." Sasha spat defensively at me.

"Do you hear yourself Sasha?" Sandra turned to ask her. " Here I am, in the hospital dying and all you can think about as usual is yourself." Sandra barely managed to say.

"Listen, you have no idea what I am going through okay. No idea what so ever."

"What you are going through?" Sandra mimicked with a snicker. "You selfish bitch. Are you dying right now? Do you live in pain and fear everyday? Do you have children and have no idea how they will eat or get along if you were no longer around? No! Yet here you are talking about what you are going through."

Everyone was shocked when Sasha raised her hand and slapped Sandra straight across her face. No one could believe she would be this callous, heartless and cold.

Sandra reached deep within herself and with every ounce of her body she reached up and scratched Sasha along her arm, leaving fingernail makes and slight bleeding.

"You ignorant self-righteous obnoxious bitch. Since you want to know what an emergency is, what a crisis is. Now there! Deal with that." Sandra laughed.

Sasha freaked out and ran to the table that the nurse had just brought with Sandra's meal on it. She grabbed the dinner knife and rushed at Sandra. Charmaine jumped up and pulled her out of Sandra's room.

"Are you loosing your cotton picking mind?" You just hit a dying woman. Now what do you think you were going to do with that dinner knife? Are you stupid?" Charmaine yelled.

"Did you hear the way she talked to me just now. What? Did you just expect me to sit there and take that? I don't care if she is dying. That's not my damn problem." Sasha yelled and the commotion caused a stir in the hospital and security as well as the nurses walked towards them asking them to hush or take it outside. "Do you see what she did to me? That bitch gave me AIDS."

Justin also heard the commotion and walked outside his office to see what was going on. He walked towards the nurses who were trying to convince a most unreasonable Sasha to leave the ward and take the argument outside.

Justin recognized Charmaine and walked towards her to find out what the situation was.

"Hey, remember me? He asked Charmaine." The look of

confusion on her face told him that she didn't so he thought he would jog her memory. "Well, we didn't officially meet but I was at the supermarket when you were there with two other young lady, Chyna was one of them." He told her and at that moment Charmaine smiled.

"Yes of course I remember you. How are you?"

"I am doing fine thanks. But I have to ask you what the problem is here? You are causing quite a scene at the hospital."

"That bitch in there scratched me and she is dying of AIDS. Am I going to get it doctor?" She screeched, panic and concern grabbing her.

"Are you sure the person who scratched you has AIDS?" He asked, a bit concerned.

"Nurse," he called to the first attendant that passed, "take this lady and disinfect these scratches and put some bandages on her for me please." He ordered.

"I am sorry I didn't get your names."

"My name Charmaine and this is Sasha."

"Well ladies, please return to my office when the nurse is finished. Let's clear this whole thing up." He told them, giving them a card directing them to his office where they should meet him. In all the commotion, neither Justin nor Sasha recognized each other. Sasha went off with the nurse to get cleaned up and Justin returned to his young patient who he had left abruptly more than an hour ago.

Karen and Kayla remained in Sandra's room trying to calm her laughing cough.
"You really have to calm down if you want to live to see your children tonight Sandra. You are acting way out of control and allowing Sasha to take you down to her level.

"Why did you bring that woman here? She is absolute poison. Nothing or no one matters but herself. She is like a snake,

a poisonous snake and I don't want her anywhere around me."
Sandra fumed.

"Okay, why don't you have some juice?" Karen suggested
and moved towards the same cart that the nurse had left with her
meal and retrieved her juice. While they sat and watched Sandra
drink her juice, Kayla noticed the scratches and bruises on
Karen's face.

"Hey Karen, what happened to you? You've got bruises all
over you."

"It's along story. Nothing I can go into right now."

"Now wait a minute. Karen, you have been the only person I have been able to count on. As far as I know, I might not
even live through the night. Confide in me please. What happened to you?" Sandra asked her, reaching out and gently placing her hand on Karen's arm.

Karen sighed. "After the paramedics took you away, I
took Anthony and Suzette back to my place to get some rest. As
usual Shawn was there waiting and we got into a big fight." I sat
there speechless alongside Sandra, as Karen told us about her
fight and how she finally got the nerves to press charges and put
his butt in jail.

"Well, it's about time." I finally found the words to say.

"Yeah Karen, you have put up with a lot of crap from that
guy. I am glad you are finally rid of him." Sandra told her and
pulled her closer to give her a hug.

Chapter 16

"Hey girlfriend," Delia greeted as she walked toward Chyna.

"Hey woman, what'cha been up to these days eh?" Chyna asked her as she jumped from the park bench she was sitting on and threw her arms around Delia. "I was just sitting here trying to catch up on some reading waiting for your late butt." Chyna joked as they walked back to the bench and seated themselves in the shade of an oak tree.

"Nothing much girl, just trying to hook up with this sista' and finally pay Michael Brendan back for what he put me through."

"So you guys are really going to go through with that eh? I cannot believe it. After all these years of moving on and trying to put all this stuff behind us, you are going to go digging it back up." Chyna shook her head in disbelief. She wanted to spend time with her friend and have fun, which was the reason they were there, not to go looking for a fight and digging up old coffins.

"Chyna, I cannot believe that you of all people are saying that. You know what I went through, you saw me go through it. How could you expect me to pass up an opportunity like this?" Delia asked her. But she didn't have to. She knew that Chyna spoke the truth, she knew that if there was anyone who wouldn't want to see her hurt again would be Chyna, but the anger and rage that grew inside her again when she heard Brendan's name couldn't be contained. She needed to hurt him.

"Okay, how about we agree to disagree right now, and you tell me what you've been up to while I am away plotting evil and vengeance." Delia laughed, making a sinister sound like Dr. Jekyll and Mr. Hyde.

"Oh you need to quit." Chyna laughed, elbowing Delia in the ribs and then hugging her tightly to prevent her from hitting back. Once the laughter subsided, they sat back and sighed.

"Remember that doctor guy we met at the supermarket a few weeks ago?" Chyna broke the silence.

"Yeah of course I remember. You couldn't take your eyes off of him and for days he was all you spoke about." Delia teased.

"Well, we hooked up the other day." Chyna squealed like a lovesick teenager. "And girl, he was good." She bragged. "You would not believe what a great lover this guy is. Not only is he tall, dark and handsome, but also he's got grooves, moves and talent. I don't know where this guy got his lessons in love but I am glad I am now his willing student." Chyna rambled on.

"Hold up. You mean to tell me you slept with him *already*?" Delia asked surprised. The look on Chyna's face told her the answer to her question. "I cannot believe you Chyna. This is not like you. You never give it up that easily." Delia stated completely flabbergasted.

"Well, that's what I've been trying to tell you Dee, I am not the same Chyna. I don't want to be the good little girl, sitting by the phone waiting for no man to call me, use me, then put me away like some book they already read, leaving me on some shelf to build dust. I want to get something out of it too. I want what I want and this time, I will not be the one left holding the telephone.

"So are you saying this guy is just a fling?"

"I didn't say anything like that. All I am saying is, if he plays around and tries to screw with my head, I am going to drop him like a hot potato, because this time I am not staying around to get hurt.

"Chyna, please be careful. I don't want you to harden your heart and then possibly lose love just because of one bad experience." Delia pleaded.

"Naw. It's nothing like that. This heart is far from hardened Delia. I am open to whatever comes what may. Honestly, this guy could be something special. I am keeping my eyes open but keeping the door to my heart closely guarded. That's all."

"Okay well it seems like you have got it handled, so how was he?" Delia asked as she giggled childishly ready to hear some juicy gossip. Chyna began to outline for her the beginnings of their encounter. How Justin showed himself into her hotel suite, how he made love to her and had to go to the store to pick up more condoms because she ran out.

"When he returned, he came back with a vengeance." Chyna continued her story, "I don't know what got into him, but when he returned he wasn't all gentleman like, childish and innocent. He returned with a passion and hunger to meet the yearnings that I needed to be quenched. I waited for him on the bed naked. Touching myself so that I wouldn't lose the desire. I couldn't believe it. He just walked up to me, dropped his clothes and all I could do was stare in disbelief that his huge dick was going to come jabbing inside of me. Just seeing it standing there and drooling ooze turned me on. It was as though he wanted me to see it, wanted me to look at him. Because he just stood there for what seemed like forever before he pressed forward and began crawling towards me."

"No way. Weren't you nervous, scared, worried he might damage you? Nothing?" Delia asked jokingly.

"Of course not, I had already felt him inside of me and girl all I know was that I couldn't wait. I was a little sore, but it was worth it. All those years of waiting and being afraid just because of my experience with Miguel and what he could have done to me almost ruined my life. I am now ready to move on and I am okay" Chyna reassured her. They looked at each other and shared a reflective smile.

"I don't know if I could handle all of that girlfriend. But don't stop now. What happened?" Delia urged her to continue, allowing the conversation regarding the past to drop and pick up on the here and now where Chyna is happy.

Chyna smiled brightly before continuing, as the memory of her day with Justin came flooding back.

"Well, he reached for my leg and pulled me toward the edge of the foot of the bed bringing me directly beneath him. His big ass dick was right over my mouth. For one second I contemplated whether or not to taste him, but before I could decide he decided for me. Next thing I know he was riding my mouth in a sexy sensual way that made my pussy jealous. He was all over me and every part of my body was on fire.

"Damn girl," Delia exclaimed. "You sound like you hit the jackpot."

"Well, something funny did happen," Chyna told her in a tone of confession. "I don't even know if I should tell you this." She laughed.

"Oh you see now, you cannot do that. You started something heffa you better finish it." Delia demanded.

"Well okay, but while he was riding my mouth, I heard this farting sound," Chyna began and couldn't contain her laughter. "Delia I didn't want to believe that in this great erotic experience that this dude is farting in my mouth. So we just kept going and I kept moaning and sucking, until I smelt it."

"Oh you are nasty!" Delia exclaimed.

"Delia, I couldn't believe it. It wasn't one of those loud

obnoxious farts, it was one of those quiet, sneaky ones he was hoping I wouldn't notice slipped out." Chyna threw her arms around Delia hysterically. She couldn't contain herself or the embarrassment she felt for Justin.

"So what did you do?"

"Chile please, I sucked it up and pretended nothing happened. I was not about to allow anything to get in the way of me having some of that dick." Chyna told her in a more serious voice. She wanted Delia to know she was not kidding.

"Oh my!" was all Delia could say as she fanned her face with her hand and exhaled slowly as some elderly women walked by slowly as though they intended to hear Chyna's recap of her first intercourse experience in four years.

Delia had seen Chyna date men and go out, but she would barely so much as kiss them. There were a few special ones that she had allowed to go down on her and make out, but she couldn't understand why the hold out on penetration.

For Chyna however, what happened to her with Miguel was like being raped all over again. She couldn't stop the violation she felt. He had sex with her, put her at risk with a life or death disease and then she had to find out the way that she did. She just wasn't ready to move on that way. She knew her friend couldn't quite grasp her feelings on this, but it was okay. She knew that Delia cared for her and that was enough.

Chyna waited a few extra minutes out of respect for the two elderly white ladies to ease their way out of earshot and then continued her story.

"Just when I thought his penis was going to rupture my brain he pulled out and kissed me deep and passionately as though he was trying to let his tongue compete for space in my mouth, but all I could think was, *you better put that long ass tongue in my pussy*," she chuckled.

"Oh no you didn't?"

"Oh yes I did. Why waste it in my mouth?" Chyna asked "Put it where it could really be appreciated." She laughed out loud and slapped her bare naked leg that was exposed under her skimpy white shorts.

Delia was laughing so hard that she squirmed off of the park bench and almost hit the ground, balancing herself with her hands to prevent herself from falling.

"Shoot, that's what I'm talking about." Delia approved. "Now you are talking my language." She told her as she pulled herself back up and replaced herself next to Chyna. "So what happened? Did you have to pass out instructions or what?"

"No I tell you, it was like brotha' was reading my mind. He licked and sucked his way right down between my legs and his tongue was like a ladder leading down into my birth canal. I swear it could have knocked one of my eggs loose as he used the tip of his tongue to guide it though my fallopian tube." She continued barely able to contain her laughter.

This time two women overheard this snippet and were unable to contain the humor they found in that statement and started laughing so hard, that Chyna and Delia turned around only to find that their mirth was shared and they all laughed together. As that shared moment passed, Chyna got closer to Delia and began to talk about the way Justin penetrated her. She moved closer to Delia's ear not wanting to be overheard again.

"Delia, before he entered me he laid on top of me and kissed me like he had just proposed and I said yes. There was a strange connection between us as he looked into my eyes. It was as though he wanted to wait and make sure that there were no objections. And it seemed as though he waited for an eternity, just lying on top of me with that huge penis between my legs teasing me and drooling pre-ejaculation all over my legs. I was so wet I couldn't believe it. I don't remember if I had ever felt that tantalized. Next thing I knew he was kissing me and I felt the tip of him pierce me again as though he was entering me for the first time. He was so gentle that I felt every inch of him glide its way through me. I felt every muscle, every vein in his seemingly expert penis because by the time he was halfway inside of me, I felt myself almost go into a spasm of the most eruptible, explosive orgasm I had ever felt. I swore if he had asked me to have his baby at that moment, I would have said yes!"

This time, Delia was so caught up in the story of Chynas experience that she couldn't help feeling her own excitement flood her thighs. There was no laughter now. It was as though the realization of Chyna's words were as big as God saying 'let there be light', this was the kind of experience that a woman can pay homage to, light candles and thank God for creating a creature such as man. But a man was not on Delia's mind. Charmaine was. It was Charmaine's tongue that she envisioned, but that thought, she kept to herself.

Chapter 17

"Well Ms. Alberdine," Dr. Hudson announced as he walked into Sandra's hospital room and waited for Karen to pull out of Sandra's embrace. "You already know the nature of your situation." He said with his eyes locking into Sandra's and speaking directly to her. It was though Karen and I were not there even though we sat close by. "The good news is that you can go home today." He said, managing a reassured smile.

"Great, can we get ready to go now?" Karen asked. Her thoughts of this moment bitter sweet as they both knew that it was only a matter of time before Sandra would die.

"Yes, that's exactly what that means." He confirmed and stood to leave.

"Doctor, can I have a moment please?" I asked and rushed out behind him as he exited Sandra's room. "Are you sure she will be okay at home, with her children?" Dr. Hudson looked at me and remained quiet for a brief moment.

"I understand your concern Ms...."

"Kayla..." I offered him my name

"Ms. Kayla. Your friend Karen seems to have no concerns for this. Will you be living at the same residence?"

"No, I will not. It's just that everything seems so delicate, and Karen is frail and emotional. I know she really wants to help but I am just concerned."

"Well, as long as all open wounds are taken care of by a medical professional, it should be okay. Be careful how you touch her because her body is deteriorating and she can get scratches and bruises easily. She won' be able to fully interact with her children of course. That was the concern that child protective services had, but as long as the children are supervised they should be okay. The hospital has no way of housing a patient like this until their demise. Your friend is really a special person. You are all lucky to have her." He finished and took a long breath and smiled at me. "I have to go now, will you excuse me?" he asked.

I couldn't believe how abrupt he was with me. As if I was the worst person in the world for asking the questions I did. All I could do was just stand there and watch as his white coat disappeared down the hall. I couldn't help the tears that rolled down my face and I remained there, paralyzed, face in my hands unable to move from the spot where the doctor left me to feel empty and cruel.

"I am sorry miss are you okay?" Came the concerned male voice that walked over to me. But I could only shake my head. "What's wrong? Why are you crying?" I heard him asked, but the tears just kept coming and I sobbed harder and the tears flowed faster. "Why don't you come sit over here?" He offered and he took my hand and led me to some chairs in the adjoining waiting area.

"I'm sorry. I am okay." I finally managed to say, and the stranger's gentle hand reached to me and handed me a hanky to wipe my tears.

"Well, okay then. Why don't you just stay here until you have composed yourself?" He offered, but the tears just came faster and I didn't want him to leave just yet. I didn't feel like being alone right now, being with a stranger was better than being with my own friends who thought I would just leave some-one to die on purpose. So I reached to him for support and held him closely so he wouldn't leave just yet.

"A friend of mine is dying. It's all my fault, she needed me and asked me for help and I wasn't there. Now she is dying and I feel so guilty. I know everyone thinks it's my fault." The more I thought about it, the worse I felt.

"I am sorry about your friend, but don't you think it's a lit-tle too much to think her situation is your fault?"

"No," I told him and kept my face buried in the arms of the stranger whose face I had yet to look at. He felt safe.

We sat there for a few minutes until I could pull myself together and cease the crying. Finally, I pulled myself away from this stranger's comforting embrace and carefully wiped my eyes and face before I raised my head to look upon the man who was so kind to sit there with me.

"Thank you," I told him as I finally got the nerve to look upon his face and smile. But suddenly there was a strange look on his face as though I had offended him.

Justin looked at her and a puzzled look appeared on his face. "What, is something wrong?" I asked him, because his entire disposition changed from the kind gentle stranger to some-thing else. Distant maybe, it was just strange. I couldn't help feeling as though I knew this man, I felt a strange connection once I looked into his eyes, but I couldn't quite place him at that moment.

Justin pulled himself away putting a few more inches between them while his brain tried to register what he was see-ing.

"Kay? Kay is that you?" He asked, the puzzled look turned to pure confusion and then annoyance.

"Okay, how do you know my name?" I asked him, wonder-ing how on earth this stranger found out my name. First he was comforting me and now he was treating me as though he had known me for a lifetime and I had offended him somehow.

"Oh, so you don't even remember me? Doesn't my voice sound even slightly familiar to you?" Justin asked, offended that after all they shared, he didn't even seem remotely familiar to her.

"I am sorry; I don't even know your name." I admitted, despite the fact that he seemed like someone I might know, I was still so caught up in my own sadness and confusion that I wasn't even sure if I really cared at that moment to know who he was, whether or not I knew him from another time or place. I just wanted to be left alone. Granted he was fine, tall, dark and handsome, but that was the last thing on my mind and I really don't feel like having someone hitting on me while I feel so vulnerable. Not while I am a complete mess. I thought to myself.

"Kayla, it's me, Justin. It's just like you, selfish and self absorbed. After everything I did for you, after everything we went through together, you just took off and left me."

All I could do was sit there mortified. I couldn't believe that this was the man he was revealing himself to be.

"Justin wow!" I exclaimed and threw my arms around his neck in sheer glee and surprise. How great could this be? Justin of all people, I thought.

Justin thought she must have lost her mind greeting him like they were good old friends. Slowly, he removed himself from her embrace.

"Kayla, you left me because I wanted to be a better man for you, because the money wasn't coming quick enough. Remember that? Remember all the nights you would cause me to lose sleep, waking me in the middle of the night to create arguments when you knew I would have a final the next day. Medical school was no joke. It was hard work."

"Justin, you have it all wrong. I did believe in you, that's not why I left." I started to explain. I wanted to explain but he stopped me. He didn't want to hear what I had to say.

"I thought being ambitious would have made me an asset but to you I was worthless. You wanted fast men with fast cars and quick money. You did anything and everything you wanted to do and it didn't matter to you how I felt. You walked over my heart whenever you could, going out to clubs and hanging with your girls were more important to you than I was. Does any of this jog your memory?" He asked her, the anger building in him. Anger that he thought he had put behind him.

I stared at him and I am sure my eyes must have been as wide as the equator and I could feel my mouth hanging open. I couldn't believe my luck. Here I am at a time in my life where I am different, I have changed and right about now, I am about to lose one of my closest friends, only to find the one man that I truly regretted hurting the way I did so long ago. But it was a long time ago. And I had hoped that if chance or fate brought me back to Justin, that he would forgive me, that I would be able to explain and that he would understand. But I was wrong...again.

"Well? Aren't you going to say anything?" He asked her, appalled at her audacity. He waited almost eight years to see her again. It took him eight years to get over the idea that he would ever be able to see her and ask why she hurt him so much. How he loved her. Withdrew every dime he had in the bank and bought her the diamond of her dreams. He proposed to her, only to find her gone, his ring left in the small loft they shared. The loft he promised her would one day be a house with all the trimmings. But she just couldn't wait.

"Justin, you don't,"

"It's Dr. Justin to you. Don't ever address me by my first name again. You don't deserve to. You are below me." He fumed.

"Doctor? Wow. So you made it? Your dreams came true." I told him, not the slightest bit surprised. Justin was always the go-getter, the over achiever. He never failed at anything. That's one of the reasons I had to leave. I couldn't measure up. I was nothing like him and I felt as though I didn't deserve him. I was not good enough for him. And that night when I slept with his roommate, I knew I would never be able to face him again. So that one night turned into many nights as I fought with myself for Justin's attention. I wanted and craved excitement. I needed something. I felt empty, and even though I knew it was wrong, one thing led to another and I couldn't stop myself. I knew how Justin felt about white men taking black women away. It would kill him to know that I was with a white man. Not just any white man, but Joshua his roommate of over two years while I was his woman. It would make him feel like less of a man. It would damage his friendship with Joshua. It would hurt him and make him feel betrayed and inadequate. I had to go. It was the only way.

"Yes, and with no help from you." He retorted.

"Justin, you don't understand. That was a long time ago. I am not the same person you knew."

"And thanks to you, I will never be the same again. You left me afraid to love and let someone in. You destroyed the best of me. You destroyed the trusting, loving part of me that could make a woman happy. You have left me neutered."

"I never meant to do any of those things Justin. I loved you. You know I did. I was scared, young and foolish. I made a lot of mistakes that cost me you and I have had to live with that. Please let it go, let's not be this way." I pleaded with him for understanding, but I knew my words fell on deaf ears.

"It's too late Kay. I would never be able to forgive you. I am happy to see you again. You look good." He pulled himself together and tried to remain calm and composed. It took all the training he had to quench the anger that was rising inside him like a volcano about to erupt.

"Justin…"

"Kayla, I have to go. I have patients to attend to." He told her and got up to leave.

****

I decided that I had a full day and wanted to go back home. I already felt like my entire world was crashing down on me. First finding out that Sandra was going to die and then the doctor basically telling me that I am a selfish bitch for asking a simple question out of concern for my friends. And then out of the blue was Justin. I am just batting a thousand today. What else can go wrong in my life today?

I hopped into my old Volkswagen vehicle and drove the long way back to Starrett City. I really just hoped that Michael wouldn't be there because I just didn't feel like dealing with him and his cheating. As the thought escaped my mind I couldn't help but laugh at myself; look at me? I just ran into the one man, besides Michael that was good for me, and I screwed it up and here I am giving Michael a hard time for doing the same thing to me. It was so ironic, that the laughter just came harder and harder. A classic example of what comes around goes around. I wasn't sure how I was going to handle knowing that Michael had the smell of Sasha's perfume all over him. Maybe the best thing to do right now was to let it go, forgive him and move on, especially after my trip down memory lane with Justin. I really had changed a lot; but I wish I could change the past. I cannot believe that I hurt him so bad.

I pulled into my assigned parking spot in the apartment building, and looked to my window on the Far East side of the complex. I could see my brand new lavender curtains flow out the open window in response to a light breeze that came on suddenly. I couldn't help wondering if he was waiting for me there.

Minutes later when I walked into my small but perfectly immaculate apartment, I was stunned to find my love sitting there in his favorite chair which I loved so much because it smelled like him. He was dressed only from the waist down and slumped down in a stoop. He was obviously drunk. I decided not to wake him and just get in bed for a nap. The strain of today was too much to bear and I could really use some peace.

Just as I crawled into bed with just some silky boy boxers and tunic top the phone rang. I didn't want it to wake Michael so I moved to turn it off and Michael shifted. He seemed to move in a timely manner as though aware of me but still had his eyes closed. The answering machine picked up and I heard Justin's voice came through the device.

"Kayla, I am sorry I was so rude to you today. I got your number from Karen your friend. I hope you don't mind. I just wanted to call and say goodbye, seeing you today has finally given me the closure I need to move on. Thank you."

When it sounded as though he was about to hang up I grabbed for the phone in hopes of talking to Justin again without waking Michael but he grabbed my hand.

"So that's what you are doing when you hang out with your girlfriends eh?" he asked me in the most disrespectful way. I am not used to Michael raising this tone of voice too often unless out of extreme anger for which I have never been the focus, and I have never seen him that drunk. It's as though he had been sitting there for days, just stewing and waiting for me to return.

"Okay Mikey, don't get carried away okay? That's just an old friend whom I hadn't seen in years that I ran into today." I tried to explain to him.

"Well the way you were just grabbing for the phone just now, didn't seem that old to me. What did you do, go out and get a fuck for old time sake and then come dragging yourself back to me for me to take you back, again? Put up with your shit, again?" he fumed and I couldn't understand why he was so mad when all I did was leave a note to let him know that I realized something was up and that I was not that stupid.

"Sweetheart, you are drunk and you are getting carried away. Nothing is wrong okay? Everything is fine between us and all is forgiven."

"Why is all forgiven? Is it because you said so? I don't care what I have done recently, after all the crap I put up with you, you should be begging me to forgive you and stay even if I went out and got myself laid for a change. It's not like you have been giving it up that easy these days, like you have been saving it for somebody else." He spat and the words hit me in the worst possible way.

Ever since I decided years ago to change my life when Michael decided to love me, all I had done was to love him the best way I knew how. Granted we have had our problems, but I stayed true and made sure that I dotted all my I's and crossed all my T's.

"What are you saying? Do you really believe that I cheated on you? When only last night you came dragging yourself in here with the smell of Sasha's favorite perfume on? Do you think I am that stupid to know that you are not screwing my best friend behind my back and that she is laughing in my face and calling me an idiot because she thinks that I don't know?"

I couldn't help the anger that came spilling out of me. It wasn't fair. All I have tried to do was be a good friend to everyone and a good woman for my man. This must be payback for my past because I cannot think of any other reason why I should be going through something like this right now.

Michael got up from his chair and walked towards me, never in a million years would I have imagined what happened next, his anger exploded in a way I had never dreamed possible.

In one swift motion he grabbed me and flung me halfway across the room. I could feel the rip in my tongue and the blood dripping from my mouth. In total shock and disbelief I asked in a child like timid voice that I didn't even recognize, "why did you do that?" and the tears came running down my face.

"I don't want you anymore Kayla. Yes! I fucked your smutty whoring friend Sasha, if you can call her that." He slurred. "So what? Every man in this damn neighborhood has fucked her, including Shawn and even your new lover here calling you at my damn house." He stammered on and on and I couldn't believe that he was actually saying what I heard.

He walked towards me and I ran into the closet. I heard him throw something and breaking it on the door.

"I am so tired of you rationing the pussy as though you are saving it for God and then have the nerve to act all high and mighty as though you are fucking perfect." He yelled at the door. Suddenly the room got quiet and a few minutes later, I heard him walk out and slam the door.

The weight and pressure of the day's events just crashed in on me with and the realization that my life was falling apart literally before my eyes and I sincerely didn't have a clue what I did today to take such a tragic turn. I just stooped in the corner of the closet on top of a pile of shoes, dresses and pants hanging from the rack and onto my hunched shoulders, and cried.

Chapter 18

Delia had been trying to reach Charmaine all day after her talk with Chyna, she wanted to see her and soon. She needed to know just how much she was feeling and the only way she was going to do that was by having a candid talk with Charmaine. Either that or just allowing Charmaine to follow through with one of her antics that she usually used to flirt with her when they were hanging out plotting to bring down Brendan and Branson Law firm for Sasha. However, she was unable to reach her. She left numerous messages on her private line and even dared to call Charmaine's mother once just because she was unable to reach Charmaine within an hour, which was very unusual. So she decided to go back to the hotel with Chyna and they went to their own private rooms to relax and shower.

Chyna dreamed of Justin and when she would see him again. She didn't want a relationship and wasn't looking for one, but she liked him so much that she decided to remain open. She pulled on a long pink cotton pajama bottom and an over sized tee shirt and threw herself in bed. She felt good about the way things were going at the moment. She was not quite sure what was happening but she liked it and would just let it flow. She reached to the side of her huge bed to the night table and turned on the radio to CD 101.9 FM to listen to some smooth jazz, and pulled the covers over her head hoping she would dream of Justin.

Delia worried herself half to death, that just when she had decided that she wanted to see if what Charmaine had to offer could be so much better than a man, she was no where to be found. She feared that she might have taken too long and had lost her opportunity. So she showered and threw herself into her king sized bed, wondering if she should go and bother Chyna and tell her the truth of how she had been feeling about Charmaine.

Delia felt the heat between her legs grow as she thought about Chyna's passionate sexual adventure with Justin, she wanted to feel good too and she was growing increasingly agitated not knowing where Charmaine could be or how to reach her. She didn't even know for sure whether or not Charmaine had a cell phone. Finally not being able to stand the frustration that refused to allow her to sleep, she decided to slip into Chyna's room and talk to her. Maybe she could shed some light on the situation and put some sense into her head. She found herself to be acting very irrational which was quite unlike her and she didn't like the feeling at all.

Knocking on the adjoining door to Chyna's room she waited for her friend's usually excited and chipper voice to respond, but heard nothing. She listened closely and heard the barely audible music coming through the door. Turning the knob she peeked into Chyna's room and noticed her friend curled into the fetal position with the blankets draped over her head. Delia felt her heart drop. Nobody was available to her right now. Deciding that she still didn't want to be alone, she crawled into bed beside her friend, pulled the blankets off of her and snuggled into Chyna's tall slender frame.

Chyna threw her arm over Delia's petite voluptuous body and pressed her nose into the top of her head. They had done that a million times before, being each other's confidant and comforter, but this time was different for Delia. Her entire body was on fire. She couldn't help that every move she or Chyna made brought butterflies and tingles all over her. Her thighs began to soak with desire and she carefully placed her fingers inside her panties in hopes of alleviating some of the excitement that was growing more and more uncontrollable. As she inserted her finger into her vagina she felt an overwhelming power over come her, she didn't want to wake Chyna but she was so excited that she just wanted to get laid. Removing her finger she turned slightly to see if Chyna was fully asleep and then she took Chynas hand and placed it between her thighs and inserted Chynas long fingers inside her.

She had never thought of her friend this way, but to feel her inside of her forced her to release a slight scream that was building in her abdomen. Suddenly feeling the tension and stress from wanting Charmaine build into something else and leave her body, she moved faster and gained momentum.

Moving Chyna's hand back and forth inside of her she could feel her climax mounting. She pulled at Chynas pajamas and inserted her finger between Chyna's legs. To her surprise, Chyna shifted from her fetal position, to lay semi flat on her back and her legs slightly parted. Delia took advantage of the opportunity plunging her fingers into Chyna and felt the heat between her friend's legs grew. She couldn't believe how excited she was.

Slightly she felt Chyna moan and move her hips slowly to meet her thrust. The movement from Chyna's body caused a catastrophic chain reaction and she felt her orgasm rise from her vagina to the pit of her stomach and through her entire body. She moved Chyna's hand harder and pressed her fingers deeper within her soft moist flesh as the fire burned inside her vagina and her clit felt like it was about to split open. Just when she felt her orgasm about to explode, she felt Chyna gyrate her hips to meet her thrust, her moans and groans growing louder and her heart beating faster.

Chyna started to move her fingers on her own; her eyes still squeezed shut and her legs opened. Delia pulled down Chyna's flannel pajamas below her buttocks so that the fresh air could cool the fire that they were both feeling, the blanket now resting on the floor and the both of them masturbating and fondling each other into an uncontrollable passionate climax. Their screams synchronized and the room shook with the erotic sensuality they released into the hotel suite.

Fatigue and disbelief came over them and they lay there, shocked by the experience they both shared. Chynas eyes remained shut with Delias now relax fingers still inside her vagina, and Chyna's fingers flooded with Delias juices still resting on her thighs. Soon they slept, still surprised and without saying a word. Both of them making a silent vow not to ever make mention of what happened between them on that day.

Chapter 19

Sasha went straight home after having her hands bandaged by the triage nurse who Justin recommended to her. She was furious at the nerve of Sandra for scratching her and laughing in her face with absolutely no respect and she just knew she had to get her back, show her who is boss. She knew that Sandra felt that she had the upper hand on her since she knew a lot about her past. But she was not going to let that get in her way. She was going to show everyone who underestimated her that she was not to be messed with.

However, she had to get back to the most important situation at hand, Michael Brandon. When she awoke the next morning, she noticed her voicemail box light blinking that she had messages. There were almost twenty messages recorded. When she listened, he had left almost fifteen messages for her. Since her meeting with the senior partner she was starting to get the feeling that something was up. She didn't return any of his calls because she knew they were for one reason and one reason only, sex. She would not be forced into prostitution. She did that before as a dancer and it almost cost her her life.

She could feel the rage build inside her as she pressed the delete button to erase the last message. Anger bubbled inside her like boiling water and she knew she was on the verge of losing control.

As she grabbed her towels to take a quick shower to calm herself down, the phone rang.

"Hey Sasha, are you there girl?" She listened to Charmaine's concerned voice over the answering machine. "Okay, when you get a chance give me a call okay? We need to talk." She finished. Charmaine hung up the phone before Sasha could answer it, but Sasha needed to talk to Charmaine. She was so happy to see that the one person she could depend on didn't abandon her. Happy that the new bitch in her life didn't steal their friendship away. Sasha dropped her towel on the floor and quickly pressed the automatic dial for Charmaine's number on her phone and listened while it rang.

"Hello," Charmaine answered.

"Hey Charmaine, it's me, Sasha. You just called."

"Hey girlfriend, I was just wondering how you were doing. I know you were really upset at the hospital and with everything that happened. No one saw you after you left with the nurse so I was a bit concerned. Is everything okay?" Charmaine quizzed. She knew that Sasha's temper would eventually get the better of her if somebody didn't intervene. No one knew Sasha like she did so she knew the person to prevent something tragic from happening would have to be her.

"What do you mean if I am okay Charmaine? What kind of dumb question is that?" Sasha stammered through the phone lines. "Of course I am not okay. Do I look okay to you?" She asked rhetorically.

"Okay Sasha, no need to blow this whole thing through the roof okay? I knew you would be upset that's why I am calling you. You are my best friend and I care about you." Charmaine soothed. She knew that Sasha was due for some ego stroking. "How is your arm?" She continued when Sasha didn't respond.

"It's okay I think. The nurse said that I shouldn't become

infected just from those scratches, but she said to be safe than sorry I have to go get tested in a couple months. I am furious. After everything that I have gone through in my life to get where I am today, for her to come and do this to me." Sasha argued. "She is going to pay for this you hear me?" She fumed.

"Sasha, Sandra is sick. She didn't know what she was doing. She might die any day now and she has no one."

"I am so sick and tired of everyone drooling over her as though she is the only one with problems. You all just forgot all about me and the fact that my life is going to be shot to shit if I don't take care of my boss, and for some reason, suddenly all everyone can think about is Sandra, Sandra, Sandra. She is going to die already. There is nothing that can be done about it. But my life goes on and I need help more than she does." She flared.

Charmaine knew that Sasha had always been selfish and self absorbed, but to hear her talk like this was shocking. She couldn't believe that this was the same Sasha who stood up for her so many times, could be so cold and heartless.

"Sasha, don't worry okay. It's all going to work out. Delia and I have some ideas we want to run by you."

"Delia? Who the fuck is Delia and why all of a sudden is she all up in the mix? We don't know her from Adam."

"Listen Sasha, I know that you are upset but now you are getting way out of hand. I am trying to be patient and understanding here and you are not making it easy at all." Charmaine scolded her, trying hard to keep her voice on an even tone so that the anger that was rising inside her didn't show.

"Are you defending her? What, she gave you some pussy and suddenly you are seeing stars?" Sasha snickered. She couldn't understand why she was taking her anger out on Charmaine, but she couldn't stop. It was as though all her frustrations from the day events came pouring out and she could not control the flow. She could feel tears burn her eyes as she fought for them not to come up. But she kept hurling insults at her truest friend.

"If all you wanted was some ass to stay focused on helping me Charmaine, I could have given you that." She spilled and before she could say another word, Charmaine hung up the phone. She couldn't take another word from Sasha. Sasha had lost her mind and Charmaine could not help Sasha while she was attacking her.

Charmaine got off the phone and sat in her sofa with the phone still in her hand and starring at it after pressing the off button disconnecting her from the assault Sasha hurled at her. She still couldn't believe her ears. As the words repeated and played themselves over and over in her mind she became furious with Sasha. If that's the way she wanted to be then that's the way it's going to be. She will be on her own from now on. Charmaines thoughts broke her heart. She thought she would be the last person on earth Sasha would speak hate to like that. She had always known her friends true nature but a scorpion cannot help but sting…it's just in its nature.

Sasha was enraged that Charmaine dared to hang up the phone on her. She couldn't believe it. She said hello into the phone a few times before realizing that she had really hung up.

"That bitch," she screamed and flung the phone to the ground. She grabbed her towel and headed to the shower. She needed to focus on her own problems and today she had to go into the office. She was tired of hanging around her friends making her situation worse instead of helping her. She didn't stay long in the shower before she was dressed and out the door.

****

Justin slept in his office on the small pull out cot he kept there just in case he couldn't get home. He was glad he had it there because he felt not only physically drained, but also emotionally and psychologically. He was not prepared for the surprises that he encountered, like the phenomenon of finding and being the doctor of Jane Doe's son. Son of the same Jane Doe who stirred a fire within him and made his body feel again after his devastating loss of his first love. Jane Doe, whose son was now sick and whose life he must now try and save, just like he saved his mother's life almost eight years before. And just like the first time, he couldn't do it without her and needed her if Justin was to survive.

He was happy he had called in Dr. Calvin McKinley who was a cancer specialist for the boy, a specialist who wouldn't mind Justin assisting him. He wanted to stay close to this patient.

Then to make matters worse, on top of that, running into and finding Kayla again. After all those years of waiting for her, she just came bamboozling herself right back into his life without permission. It wasn't fair. Not now when there might actually be someone capable and worthy of unlocking his heart...he smiled when he thought of Chyna.

After he walked away from Kayla he felt guilty about the way he spoke to her. About the way he ended it. That's not the way he had imagined it all those years. He wanted to let her go, let go of the memory so that he could move on, and now more than ever, because of Chyna, he had a reason to. As the darkness of the small office space curled around him, he thought back to what Kayla had said about her friend dying and feeling guilty, so he went back to where he found her crying and did some investigation and found out about Sandra. Since she was the only patient admitted at that time that was diagnosed as terminal, he took a chance that she might be the one Kayla was talking about. While Sandra was packing to get checked out with Karen and Charmaine, he decided to approach her friends.

He tossed and turned as he remembered his conversation with them, how they told him how Kayla was sensitive and always there for them. He was amazed by the revelation of hearing that she was a good friend and truly torn up by the circumstances surrounding her friends. He told them how she was crying and felt responsible for Sandra's worsened illness. That's when they told him about the strain she had been carrying about Sasha's extenuating circumstances with blackmail. He had at that time felt that maybe Kayla had indeed changed and wanted to call her. He didn't tell them his true purpose for calling Kayla, and disguised his purpose with a medical excuse.

He was sorry that he didn't get a chance to talk to Kayla personally. Maybe she hadn't arrived home yet when he called and he told himself that he would call again in the morning. Even this admission and consolation didn't appease him and he tossed and turned the whole night through waiting for morning to come, or an emergency that would draw him to a patient's side.

As if he dreamt the *code red* into reality, his young patient Justin had a lapse. His pager went off and the sound of his name reverberating over the intercom shot him straight out of his restless slumber. He got up and ran to the young boys' side where his foster mother wailed loudly over the boy's bed.

"Ms. Barker, it's okay. I will take care of him, but I am going to need you to step outside for me right now. While he ushered her out the door he motioned to the nurses to get the equipment together to stabilize him.

"Nurse, please page Dr. McKinley, stat!" He said almost in a whisper to one of the emergency nurses as he turned and focused his attention on the boys' foster mother.

Edna Barker went outside and moaned the possibility of losing the only child she had ever had. She prayed that God would find a way to help the doctors save young Justin's life. After what seemed like hours, Dr. Etnas appeared in front of the weary eyed foster mother and nodded slowly allowing a sigh of relief to escape him as Ms. Barker jumped into his arms panting how grateful and thankful she was to him for saving her son.

"He is okay for now, but he is going to need a transplant soon in order to put him into a better situation. His chances of survival now are very slim. We need to find a blood relative or a donor match." Dr. McKinley explained to her, while Justin stood by his side sadly and watched as the woman went into another fit of wails. He felt helpless and out of control, and he knew the only reason his emotions were getting the best of him, was because he was almost certain that this was Jane Doe's son. There must be a way to find her or someone close to her who could lead them to her.

Justin convinced Edna Barker that she needed to go home and get some rest. She wouldn't listen to the specialist for some reason and it was obvious that a bond had been forged between her and their young patient.

It was almost four in the morning and if she didn't get home and rest a bit she wouldn't be strong enough to be there for the boy if he needed her. After she left, he pulled up a chair, and just like he had done with his mother before him, he rested by his side waiting for the boy to wake.

Chapter 20

Sasha pulled into the law firms' parking lot at about 11am. She was running late and she knew that Michael wanted to see her in a meeting at 10:30 a.m. She was intentionally delayed because she wasn't ready to see him again. But she couldn't refuse to see him if work was involved. She made her familiar trek to her office and then to her private bathroom where before each case, she would give herself that final pep talk and ready herself for battle.

Even though Michael Brendan said this meeting was a case he wanted her to take on, she didn't feel comfortable going in without having all of her grounds covered. She had to be prepared for the advances she was sure he would make. She might be asked about a dinner date or he might make a pass at her. He loved to fondle her breasts and brush his hands against her ass during case briefings making them all together look accident. But most of their colleagues she suspected was on some level suspicious that there might be something more than just a working relationship between them, but none would be so dumb as to mess with one of the most powerful criminal attorneys in the country. He was not a man to be reckoned with. Unless you were as brave as the male black widow that took a chance for procreation but knew there would be sudden death afterwards.

No, she must be prepared. She would not be the one to be a victim this time, not by him, not by anyone and not anymore.

As she rushed down the hall towards the high priority section of the firm she took in the feel of the plush beige carpeting under her heels making her feel like she was floating on air. She could smell the fresh clean of furniture and oak wood as she reminisced back to the time when she first stepped foot inside the large conference room for attorney's with high profile cases. She felt awed by the cathedral high ceiling and huge stained glass windows adorned by damask draperies of the most tasteful and simplistic nature. This was a place that echoed success and power. The conference room leading and veering off into the offices of the partners and senior partners of the firm showed how much respect and power was given to each on the ladder on the supremacy food chain as their names were carefully engraved on their respective doors. It was really a lavishly beautiful place and she knew that she was blessed to have been offered a position there. She was not at the top yet but she was getting there, and she knew that any kind of scandal could cause her all that she worked for to create an air of confidence and success around her. Any tarnishing would destroy her clients' confidence in her abilities even though it had nothing to do with it. Everything was about image and one thing could cause a catastrophic effect and topple over the entire card deck.

She stood outside the glass door that led into the conference room. The glass on each door was as thick as the bullet proof glass you see at the post offices but beautifully stained and could be seen through from one side of the mirrored illusion. As she stood there steadying her breath and pleading with her heart to stop racing, she could feel Michael Brendan's stare penetrating her, like he wished he was still doing in an intimate way. She envisioned the growing bulge in his crotch that she knew all too well and the desire that she stirred in him. There was a time when it made her feel sexy and powerful to have him succumb to her that way, but now she found it revolting and she wanted the thoughts to be erased from her memory. Just scrubbed clean the way her grandmother back in Panama would take the Ajax, scrub brush and wash basin and forcefully erase the dirt from their clothing.

Slowly she pushed open the heavy doors and glided into his presence. She knew he was surveying her every move so she moved carefully, calculated and sat at the opposite head of the conference red oak table and sat down.

"Good Afternoon Mr. Brendan." She greeted him after taking one quick glance at the large early 1900 grandfather clock that showed that it was already past noon.

"You are late Ms. Henderson."

"I apologize sir." Sasha said dryly but offered no explanation. She didn't think she had to. She was on vacation and he had called her in on her time to take on some dumb pro-bono case that the firm must sometimes do to maintain integrity and look good in the eyes of the *poor* community. She hated these cases. They tended to be boring, time consuming and have absolutely no value whatsoever to her.

"Well?" Mr. Brendan Esq. asked appalled at her superciliousness.

"Well we can get started now sir." She responded, opening the folder filled with filed documentations regarding the case that was placed carefully on her desk previous to her arrival.

"We are in the office now Ms. Henderson, and I expect you to regard me with the respect and authority that I hold in this firm. Are we clear?" He stated firmly, but still Sasha neither budged nor looked up. She just carefully scanned through the folder to gather her thoughts on the case to be discussed. He knew arguing with Sasha would be futile at that point there was something more important at hand. It was *State vs. Edna Barker*, and of course, they must represent the underdog. It looked better on their records.

"Basically everything you need is in that file. Visit that address listed there for Ms. Barker first thing in the morning. She will be expecting you. She wants to adopt the child she has been a foster mother to since he was three years old and the state wants to take him away from her because they feel that he has health concerns that she can not financially handle or emotionally since she has no one to help her and it would cause her to lose her job if she were to put in the time he needed for proper nursing and care."

"Well it says here that Ms. Barker is a nurse. It doesn't make sense. He would be better off with her since she has expertise in the health field and she loves him like her own. Isn't that what's best for the child who has lost parents twice?" She quizzed brashly.

"Great. As usual you have got the case pegged. This should be an easy one for you Sasha... Umm, Ms. Henderson." He corrected himself when he used her name informally and cleared his throat.

"You should be able to walk in and out with this one in five minutes." He told her smugly and a strange eerie feeling flooded over her. Why did she feel as though he was toying with her? The complacent look on his face and his coolness as if there was and is nothing going on between them.

"Thank you sir, I will get on this right away." She told him and hoisted herself up from the comfy recliner business chair to make her exit.

"Thanks for taking this case on your vacation and on such short notice Ms. Henderson. I am fully aware that you have your hands full these days and I want you to know that we at Brendan and Branson law firm appreciate your commitment and loyalty." He continued as she waltzed towards the large doors to exit down the hallway back to her office.

As she stepped into her large immaculate office she flung herself into her lounge chair by the door, as it slammed shut behind her. She couldn't help feeling like that man was toying with her, as though he felt like he had her right where he wanted her. She was proud of the way she handled the meeting that was shared only between the two of them. This was the first time since their dispute between each other that they had met privately without anyone else present, for work or otherwise.

Taking a deep breath she stood up and gathered her things. She threw the file into her briefcase and closed it. She would go though it more thoroughly at home over a glass of gin while listening to some Mozart over her pristine Bose sound system. She rushed back to her car so fast she almost tripped. Opening the door to her red mustang she ripped the Perry Ellis blazer from her shoulders and threw it nonchalantly in the back seat revealing her heaving bosom that felt relief from the presence of Brendan's scrutinizing stare that still managed to make her hot. One final look into her rear view mirror and fastening her seat belts and she was off.

Chapter 21

"Karen could you come into my office please?" Came Tarra's voice over her phone line.

"Okay I am on my way." Karen told her and hung up. She didn't need to ask questions. Tarra had become a trusted friend and a good employer. She felt blessed finding the confidence she had found in her despite the rumors and the hearsay that said she was a hard up butch who hated anyone straight.

"How are you today Karen? How's Sandra" Tarra asked.

"She is doing good Tarra. She is stable and seems to be improving now that she has the care she needs that she wasn't getting before. And rest.

"You are a good friend Karen. She is blessed to have you. I am blessed to have you here working with me as well. Tarra said and rest her hand slightly on Karen's before getting back to the business at hand.

"I need your help. I am going to be taking a few days off and I need someone to oversee things here while I am gone. I know you might not be able to take that responsibility since your friend is at home and you might have to go at a moment's notice, but I want you to tell me if there is anyone else here that you would trust to help you share that responsibility while I am gone." She asked Karen, her eyes pleading and soft.

"That should be no problem Tarra. Mitisuru has been a doll and she knows her job. She is hard working, dedicated and loyal and one of the only other people besides me who does not engage in damaging character attacks like the rest of the office. Yes, she is quiet and laid back, but she gets things done and she is respected around here.

"Okay, Mitisuru is it then. I will be leaving here in a few minutes. I am flying out of town. My best friend's son has died and I must go help take care of his funeral and put him to rest." She confided in Karen. "We have been friends for many years and he was her only child. This is not something a friend should have to do alone. I know you understand." She continued quickly.

"I am sorry to hear that Tarra. What happened if you don't mind me asking?"

"He was shot and killed senselessly by a drug addict. He was walking down a street and someone asked him for some money. When he refused and kept walking they just walked up behind him and shot him dead. All they got was five dollars. That's all he had on him." As she related the story to Karen the tears that she tried to hold back flooded down her face and her neatly made up mascara now stained her pink cheeks.

Karen moved around her desk and comforted her. She felt deeply for Tarra especially having to take care of Sandra for the past two weeks. It was hard, but a friend had to do what a friend had to do.

"It will be okay Tarra. God has a plan, I know he does." Karen soothed her.

Pulling herself together, Tarra stood up and smoothed out her clothes and grabbed her purse to leave.

"Here are the keys. Please take care and I will see you next week." Karen took the keys from her and watched as Tarra walked out the door. She could say nothing more to help her grieving friend. As soon as Tarra was out of sight she took up the phone and dialed Mitisuru's extension. She relayed the information to her and sat down to breathe after hanging up the phone.

As she approached her desk the phone began to ring so she rushed and grabbed the handset before her voicemail picked up.

"DMac, Inc. Karen Grace speaking how may I help you." She asked.

"Yes, this is Dr. Etnas from the hospital where your friend was admitted. I got your work number from hospital records. I hope you don't mind." He continued.

"Dr. Etnas, what a surprise. Of course I don't mind. Is there something wrong with Sandra?" Karen whispered, fear rising in her voice that if she said that out loud it might actually happen.

"No, nothing like that." Justin rushed to quell her fears. I was calling for another purpose. I was hoping I could get a minute to sit down and speak with you. I know this all seem so weird but I need to talk to you about Kayla."

"Kayla? Did something happen to Kayla? Is she in the hospital?" Karen asked, a new rush of fear curdling in her throat and tears began building in her eyes before she could hear any of the answers to the questions she just posed to Justin. Just the thought of something happening to one more of her friends freaked her out, and she had to sit down from the weakness that had started to buckle her knees.

"Karen please? Calm down and hear me out. I am not calling on hospital business. This is personal. I realize that the two of you are close and I was just hoping for a minute where I could sit down and talk to you. Please? If that's not too much to ask." He reassured her rushing his words out in almost one blurb so that he wouldn't frighten her much more.

"One moment please." Karen excused herself and put the receiver of the phone on her desk in order to compose herself. So much was already happening. She could feel the tension that was rising between herself, Sasha and Sandra. Her boss had just lost her godson, she had the love of her life put in prison and God only knows what else. She just couldn't handle another tragedy. She was starting to feel worn and emotionally fragile. Some days she felt as though she would lose her mind. Her instincts told her to lash out, but her gentle disposition and cool temperament wouldn't let her. On the inside however, she felt as though she was on the brink of a nervous breakdown.

"Dr. Etnas, I apologize for the wait. Now you said you would like to talk about Kayla?" she reiterated to be sure she heard right.

"Yes. I knew her a very long time ago. She was a different person then. That's why I need to talk to you. I need to understand something. Now I know this is a lot to ask being that you are friends. So if you feel that this is not a good idea, then I would understand." He told her, making sure she knew that this was not something she had to do under any circumstance.

"Well, can I get back to you on that? I need to think about this. Is there a way for me to reach you?"

"Just have me paged at the hospital. If I am there I will respond. If I'm not there have them page me at home on my pager. Leave your name and number for me to call you back and I will."

"Okay, that sounds good. I will get back to you in a couple days."

"Sounds good. Nice talking to you again Karen."

"No problem. Thanks for calling. Goodbye." Karen said and hung up the phone as quickly as she could. *What is going on?* She asked herself as she decided to remain seated at her desk a few moments longer. She dropped her head into her hands and buried her face in her sweat-drenched palms. She was losing it and she just didn't know how to stop herself from feeling like something terrible was going to happen to her. This was just too much for her to handle, especially the whole thing with Sasha. She didn't know how much more she could deal with.

****

The phone rang again and Karen jumped. The phone startled her as though hearing it ring was a strange and unexpected thing. She stared at it for a few rings and then decided to pick it up. It was Sandra.

"Hey Sandra, how are you feeling. Is everything okay?" Karen quizzed in one rush of breath all the while thinking, *please God please don't let anything happen to her now. I just cannot take it, I cannot.* She said a silent prayer to herself.

"Karen sweetie, slow down. Everything is wonderful. This is the best I have felt since I gave birth to Anthony." She chuckled a peaceful sweet kind of chuckle that slowly drew a smile on Karen's face. "I just wanted to give you a call. Your place is so peaceful and homey Karen. Different from when you were with Shawn. The vibe here is tranquil and I can feel the positive energy from all the beautifully pastel colors used in your decorations and the flowers you bought for me just lift my spirits and my heart. You are a true friend Karen. I just wanted to say that." Sandra sighed.

"I just want you to be comfortable Sandra. I am sorry we were not there for you before. If I had known…"

"That's enough girl. You are ruining the moment." Sandra cut her off deliberately. Just smile, say thank you, whatever. So please, I just don't have time for what ifs and I wish I should have known. I have today and I have you." Sandra told her and before Karen had a moment to respond she continued. "Besides, I know you have work to do so I am gonna go now. See you later Karen." Sandra told her and hung up the phone.

Karen felt a little better from Sandra's phone call and smiled at the message she sent her. She needed it right at that moment. Realizing it was almost quitting time she gathered up some papers and called Mitisuru. They spilt the office responsibilities and broke the employees up into two response teams. Tarra was only going to be gone a few days, a week at the most. It didn't take long to brief each team on what was going on, and by quarter to five, Karen was walking out the office door and into the busy Manhattan streets.

She was happy when she walked in through her apartment door. She closed it and pressed her back to the door for a minute and breathed in the essence of the room. She was happy when she heard Suzettes giggle coming from the spare bedroom where Sandra now stayed and Anthony telling his mother what he did in school. She was happy Debbie had decided to help them out for a minimal fee to take the kids to school and pick them up.

She snuck up to Sandra's room to listen in on her conversation with the little ones. A flood of sadness washed over her to know that Sandra would die soon and these last moments with her children were all she had. She would never see them grow up, marry or have children. All she had was today. And here she was feeling sorry for herself.

Chapter 22

I was shocked and remained locked in my apartment for days hoping that Michael would come back. But he didn't. I couldn't understand what just happened. It seemed as though I woke up and the world just turned against me. I had decided not to go to my little café where I usually found refuge in my books, the smell of fresh French roasted coffee brewing and the sound of African drums playing softly throughout the small, quaintly decorated café I had always dreamt of having. Just the smell of Egyptian musk incense and a nice hot cup of rich ginger and caramel tea would temper my soul, but not this time. This time, I feel so lost and confused. *I thought if I changed, if I did everything right, that life would be good to me. But instead, I have to deal with old wounds, old troubles that must first be confronted. I thought my past was behind me. But I was wrong.*

Finally dragging myself out of bed, I decided to take a shower and go right back in. *What's the point in waking up?* I asked myself as I yanked the plush down comforter from over my head I could smell Michael as a whiff of our mutual lovemaking a few days ago still lingered in the sheets and the smell bombarded my senses and almost brought a fresh burst of tears to my already red tear stained eyes. I didn't feel like covering myself, as I already felt naked to the world, so I decided to walk stark naked from the bedroom to the bathroom fighting off the strong emotion of defeat that had overcome me.

As I stepped into the off white tiled bathroom that was adorned around the edges with my favorite pink and green flowered border, I surveyed how hard I had tried to create a home for Michael and myself. No, it wasn't big and extravagant like Sasha's place, but it was warm, and loved, and lived in.

I took up a bar of soap from the soap dish and allowed the almost hot water to beat against my senses when suddenly I heard the phone ran.

My heart stopped and renewed hope that it might be Michael swelled from deep within me. I don't know why I was hoping. He had never been gone so long, never spent the night out. *He is not coming back*, I told myself, but my heart didn't stop racing. I dropped the bar of soap I had picked up in my hands and ran to the phone. The number wouldn't register on the caller ID so I knew it was from out of town.

"Hello." I answered, trying my best to sound upbeat and nonchalant as though it was just another day for me. My voice was strained and I hoped that the party on the other end of the line did not notice the distress in my voice.

"Hello, may I speak to Kayla McIntosh please?" came the voice on the other end of the phone line. It was a voice I didn't recognize and my first instinct was to hang up because it might be some telemarketer or worse, a bill collector. But something told me to stand it out and listen to what she had to say before freaking out and hanging up the phone like I usually did. The disappointment of it not being Michael hit me like a ton of bricks and almost made me lose my balance, but I stood my ground firmly.

"This is she. May I help you?" I asked her cautiously, wondering what would come out of her mouth next.

"Well." The stranger on the other end of my phone line began, and without knowing why panic suddenly began to rise from the pit of my abdomen. "Ms. McIntosh, you don't know me, but I am Eleanor Sekowsky, and I was asked to call everyone whose name and contact information I found." As she kept speaking the name did not ring a bell to me so I just kept listening keenly to understand why I was being contacted by someone that I didn't know and who didn't know me.

"Okay, so how can I help you?" I asked again, hoping that the proper speaking lady with the accent that sounded European on the other end of the line would just spit out what she had to say and get it over with.

"I was calling because Mr. Sekowsky Jr. has met his demise and I was to inform all those that he had listed in his personal contact information. You were one of them Ms. McIntosh." She concluded slowly as though she didn't want me to miss one word she was saying. My mind being totally shattered I still didn't understand what she was saying and just preceded to follow her directions and take down the information she insisted on giving to me.

"Okay, I am ready." I told her after grabbing a pen and paper as she had instructed. Hastily I wrote down the address that she gave me with the proper spelling and pronunciation. I was about to hang up when she unexpectedly blurted through the phone line.

"How did you know Joshua?" she asked me quite daintily as though I was in her home in an attempt to prove why I was worthy of her son's hand in marriage.

"Excuse me?" I asked her, not quite sure what I had just heard.

"I just asked if you would mind sharing with me how you met my nephew Joshua?" She repeated but the words just kind of floated through one ear and out the other. *Did she just say Joshua? I only knew one Joshua and that was Justin's roommate while he was in medical school.*

"Do you mean, Joshua who studied internal medicine? White Joshua?" I blurted out, after which I realized I sounded quite ignorant.

"Yes, I assume you can describe him that way as well. Did you go to medical school with him?" She continued without much more contemplation on my words. *She probably wrote me off as stupid.*

"No, actually I didn't. If." I stopped for a moment. *Isn't life some weird shit? A few days ago running into Justin in my freaking back yard, and now some woman calling about Joshua, his roommate.* "If we are speaking about the same Joshua, then he was my boyfriends' roommate while they were both in medical school." I told her without much hesitation once it dawned on me what she was trying to say. "Is he dead? Joshua, is gone?" I asked her repeatedly.

"Yes, I suppose he is." She answered, still sounding daintily obnoxious but now with obvious tears in her voice that she had been trying to camouflage

"Oh my gosh, I am so sorry. Joshua was a really good person, and a good friend. What happened to him?" I wanted to ask her more questions, like how it was that he had my correct address, since I had moved several times since I left Justin so many years ago and why she was calling me? But before my next question left my lips I heard the click on the other end of the line disconnecting me from her. And all I had was a piece of paper with an address and phone number of the funeral home and burial site in upstate New York where I had once shared Justin and Joshua's bed.

Suddenly, I found my legs and ran to the shower, all the images of Joshua barraged my mind and senses. Unexpectedly I felt his touch, as his hands had at one time been the cloth to wash the lukewarm water and suds from my smooth caramel chestnut almost orange skin. Joshua had started to hold me and caress my trembling arm one day after a long heart to heart we about one of my latest escapes after he had discovered a month earlier that I was cheating on Justin. I was so sacred that he would tell Justin and I had begged him not to. We had struck a deal where he would joke about me cooking and cleaning for him.

While Justin was the workaholic over achiever Joshua just did his dues and that was that. One day, as I cooked for him he teased that I should dance as well while flipping on the stereo to house Techno music and my hands started flying everywhere. My skimpy top that was cut just below my small perky boobs left nothing to the imagination as I started bopping around acting crazy.

That was the day that it first happened. When Joshua decided to dance with me as the music drenched our bodies with sweat and our clothes began to cling to us as we gyrated against each other's bodies. I hadn't realized at that point that Joshua had a thing for me, and it was in that heat filled moment that he told me so. Not withstanding the shock of the information he had placed his lips to mine and devoured my mouth.

I didn't stop him.

He was a great kisser and led me to the shower where he had washed my body clean with his hands, mouth and body. Something that Justin had never done. He had parted my legs until both my thighs were around his neck, my back pressed up against the wall and Joshua's head sucking the heat from my needy, sexually heightened clitoris. He ate me as though he was a hungry man with his last plate of food and felt my orgasm coming when he removed his mouth and replaced it with his throbbing and amazingly decent sized dick. My moan was one of not only pleasure but also a pleasant surprise that he was well endowed.

It was on since then. And though Joshua put an end to my countless one-night stands, he replaced my indiscretions with himself, it didn't break my trust in him because I was all too okay with that.

I laughed as I remembered those memories. Joshua was a good man.

I remembered as if it was yesterday how it all started. How he was the listening ear and shoulder I cried on when I wouldn't see Justin for days, and when he was home, he would sleep for a few hours and be gone again. It was Joshua that held my confidence about the many one-night stands I had to try and forget the need for Justin's love, to replace it. He was the one who understood how much I loved Justin and how badly I wanted to be the right woman for him.

All those years and he died with our secret. I must pay my respects.

****

Sasha checked her voicemail on her way home from her tense meeting with Brendan. She couldn't believe that Michael still had such a hold on her. Even after all the blackmailing she still found him irresistible. She wanted him while they went over the brief of the new pro-bono case they had dropped in her lap and she couldn't explain the joint yearning and the revulsion she felt simultaneously.

She pressed through the intro on her voicemail to hear that she had an urgent message and pressed one to listen.

"Hey ma, it's me lover boy." Came Shawn's voice over the phone line. "I didn't want to call you seeing that you all busy and all, but a brotha need some assistance if you get my drift. I can't stay long but that bitch Karen got me locked up. I been in this prison cell now and she wont drop the charges and they say I need a lawyer and some bond shit I don't understand. So check it. Can you come get me? I'll give you some real good loving tonight. And I know how you like that ice thing." He said before the phone went dead.

Great she thought.   The asshole didn't even leave a phone number or the name of the jailhouse where he was being held.

Being the high-powered lawyer that she was Sasha made a few phone calls and found Shawn's location. He was going to have to make up for this big time.

Making an immediate U turn, Sasha sped to where Shawn was and rescued him. On their way back to her place, he explained to her what went down the night Karen wanted to go hang out with the girls and Sasha realized that Karen had chosen her over Shawn. Not that it really touched her emotionally or anything. She just thought Karen was too naive for this world and would get screwed. She wasn't all too happy that he had chosen Karen over her but right now he had some making up to do and she was hot as hell. Just having him in her car was making her panties drenched. Not because there was anything particular appealing about him. He was Karen's man, and she was all about control and power. *To the victor go the spoils.* It was really just all a game.

It was late as Sasha pulled into her parking garage. She had grown weary of listening to Shawn's ignorant chatter and just wanted to get a shower and have him fuck her brains out so she could toss his ass to the curb. She walked into her immaculate bedroom and Shawn followed her. She was so tired when she arrived that she didn't notice that she had a houseguest. Michael had decided to pay her a visit since he knew where her spare key was. She had offered it to him when she first tried to seduce him away from Kayla, and when she couldn't; she committed the unforgivable sin in the *playas'* handbook. She disclosed the location of her spare key and offered him shelter whenever he wanted.

Michael slept naked in Sasha's bed even though there were more than enough room in the house to choose from, and waited patiently for her to return. He had been there all afternoon and had showered and gotten comfortable. He knew that Sasha had a thing for him beyond sex. He was special and he wanted to take full advantage of it.

He didn't hear the commotion as they walked into the bedroom, with Shawn winding on Sasha's tail and Sasha warding him off like an annoying fly. He was sleeping peacefully and comfortably for the first time in days. Hanging out with the boys was no longer what it was cracked up to be. He missed the sweet smelling comfort of a woman and missed Kayla, but couldn't go back to her. His ego and his pride were hurt. He couldn't believe that he hit Kayla, *what had gotten into him?* It was like suddenly in the past month or so things just got heated with her and her friends.

He didn't know where the anger came from, probably some of it was guilt but he shouldn't be feeling guilty from a couple of escapades with Sasha. It wasn't as though he had been running around cheating on Kayla with every Sasha that crossed his path, he had been faithful to her. She was the one that he found kissing his basketball buddy not months after they started dating. She was the one who he found out had been going to the movies and entertaining with *his* friends at *Nutria Café* that he had helped her financially to obtain. Technically it was half his and he could fight her on that.

What about when he found out that even though they had been together for years she still didn't have him in her heart. He was sure she still didn't realize it and it happened over a year ago now. But it still stuck heavily on him, that as he came home one night and snuggled up to a perfectly long lean Kayla who he had missed all day, called out the name of a man named Justin, who until a couple days ago he thought was just a dream. He would have done anything to stay and love her, until a couple days ago when the same named man called *his* house and left a message on *his* voice mail for *his* woman. It was all too much for him and he had to getaway. He needed to recuperate.

Sasha turned on the water in the tub to let it fill so she could take a bath. There was a full adjoining shower so she shoved Shawn off away from her to go and grab one himself before he was allowed to touch her. She watched as he dropped his filthy clothes to the ground and jumped behind the almost see through glass doors that separated him from her sight. She sighed a breath of peaceful relief as he turned on the shower and started to bathe.

Before stepping into the tub that she had now bubbling with jasmine, vanilla and jade scents, she walked over to her shower stereo and popped in her Waiting to Exhale CD for some relaxing. She needed to hear some sistahs singing about *letting go*, and how *sometimes it hurts so badly*. She dimmed the lights, which had a three-way switch that could change the bulb color, and now it illuminated a soft hue of dark red where you can barely see your toes unless you looked really hard. Satisfied with the ambiance, Sasha slipped into the tub with a loud murmur and dipped all the way down almost covering her head. She felt as though she had been *Waiting to Exhale* all day.

Shawn peeked out from behind his caged shower and saw that Sasha had immersed herself in complete tranquility and all that was on his mind was to taste her. He had been in prison long enough to have all of his senses heightened and his cravings intensified. He stepped out of the shower, dripping wet and didn't even attempt to dry the suds from his slender body. He walked lightly; almost tip toeing as not to startle her and was soon kneeling on the floor next to her.

Sasha felt his presence but didn't move. He placed his

hand in the tub and slowly began to drip water onto her body with his palms, then taking his index finger, tracing the moisture that had gathered on her arms and then washing them gently away. Slowly, as he felt the intensity of his manhood become gorged with excitement, he took his hand and gently palmed her breasts, then kneaded them until a moan escaped Sasha's feisty lips.

Taking her cue he let his hands drop down into the bubbly foam that hid the rest of her body. As he went he allowed his hands to caress the silky smoothness of her skin until he reached the hidden fruit of her womanhood. Finding her center he slipped his finger deep within her vagina and felt her muscles clench his hands and her legs became filled with tension.

Michael stirred, and was jolted from his sleep by the radiance of the light and music coming from Sasha's bathroom. He hadn't used music when he had showered, and the light was a bright yellow hue not red. Curiosity got the best of him and he sat up straight in Sashas king sized bed of satiny softness. It was completely dark in the bedroom because Sasha hadn't bothered to turn on the lights when she came in. Michael slid himself down towards the edge of the foot of the bed and strained his ear to hear if there were any sounds besides the CD that was softly playing in the backdrop.

The dim lighting and soft music sent an immediate cannibalistic urge through him. His hormones raged and his desire ripped at his skin as though it was trying to gash through it. Michael stood up and was guided by the urgency of his fervor towards the bathroom door that was ajar.

As he approached he took his member into his hand and felt the throbbing hardness of his erect penis and gently guided his hands back and forth over the delicate skin that now strained to contain his excitement. As he moved toward the door he heard Sasha moan and the sound of her voice sent waves of goose bumps down his spine, all the way to his toes, and a new gush of excitement through his aroused organ.

He still couldn't see anything, so he pushed through the door quietly to enjoy the vision of Sasha in the bath. He was sure she was masturbating and didn't want to interrupt. This was something Kayla didn't do, and it was a rare treat for him to observe a woman in the total acceptance of her desires and appreciation for her body.

The music filled his senses and his hands took on a rhythm of their own as he massaged and propelled his penis back and forth through his enclosed palms, his desires growing ever so intensely and bringing him to the verge of orgasm.

As his eyes became more and more adjusted to the dim red tint of the bathroom lighting he started to make out that there were two figures in the bathroom. His passion had grown and he could feel the eruption at the tip of his hands ready to explode at the sight of Sasha's hands fervently pushing in and out of her hot twat.

They did not see him. Sasha had lifted her body above the water, her legs and arms straddled the bathtub and she looked almost like a spider perched on its web. Shawn was center focused with his face buried deep between Sasha's clean-shaven pussy. His fingers moving rhythmically to Sashas grinding hips as she fervently met his mouth and tongue and fingers and sighs of soft passion and desire melted from her lips.

Michael eyes saw red at first. Anger drenched his ego and his excitement, but not enough to stop his unrest desires. He couldn't believe the sight before him. Sasha and another man, But who was he?

The idea of it burned through him and excited him. The conflicting stimulation he felt almost made him explode and the passion escaped from his lips at the thought of what he had just encountered. Watching Sasha being pleasured that way

harnessed above a tub of scented water enticed him and ground-
ed him to where he stood. He wasn't sure what to do next; a
threesome is something he thought was long in his past. A pleasure he hadn't participated in since he turned his life over to Kayla.

Sasha heard Michael's moan and turned to look at him.
Shawn stopped momentarily and looked from Sasha to
Michaels's naked body with questioning eyes, but said nothing.
When Sasha did not seem alarmed and made no effort to move,
Shawn returned to the duty at hand and probed Sasha's clit and
heated volcano with his tongue and fingers. The thought of being
watched adding new exhilaration to his actions and he wanted to
make her scream his name.

Sasha smiled weakly at Michael at first. Not expecting his
presence and not alarmed. She found herself reaching out her
hands to him to join them. But Michael remained rooted to the
spot on the cool Italian tiled bathroom floor. He was so wound
up, one move and he would come to full orgasm.

"Michael?" She whispered almost as if she was asking if
that was really him and at the same time sounded as though she
was calling him to her. He shook his head in a definable yes but
said nothing.

"Michael, it's okay sweetheart. Why don't you come over
here and let me help you with that." She urged him with a smile
sweet and inviting that gave his feet strength to uproot from their
position and march forward toward her.

He stood next to the tub and could now see clearly that it
was Shawn who had stopped sucking and licking between
Sasha's thighs and had now stepped into the tub, positioning
himself between her legs and prepared to enter her as she
moved and wriggled her hips.

"Get in the tub Michael, and stand above me so that I can
taste that beautiful throbbing dick of yours." She bid him to her
service and this time he wasted no time. The way she laid there

with ease as though the water beneath her was a solid bed, impressed Michael. Her time at the gym was well spent.

He got into the tub and harnessed her face, pounding his love stick into her open mouth and watched as she closed her full luscious lips around his cock. Still riddled from the event that was unfolding with him now apart of it, his body became flushed with desire and passion oozed through him as the heat from her throat gorged at the base of his member and he felt her tongue licking at his balls. Already so close to rapture he was unable to contain his thrusts and forced himself deep within her mouth.

Sasha moaned, feeling the jabs of pleasure between her legs, as Shawn nailed her in and out with all his strength. Having another man there brought out territorial urges in him and he wanted to make her explode all over him. Watching the expressions of enjoyment on Sasha's face sent a stream of uncontrollable tremor through Michael and he discharged all of his tensions, worries and stress into Sasha's welcoming month and watched as the warmth of her tongue, licked every drop of ooze from him as though she was bathing his manhood with warm soft kisses and caress.

As silent tremors rocked through Shawn, Michael sank into the water next to Sasha giving her support to handle the animalistic thrusts that Shawn administered to Sasha, kissing her softly and massaging her breasts helping to bring her to full peak. He ran the tepid water over her belly and stroked her abdomen gently as orgasmic pleasure took over. It rocked Sasha so hard that her legs became weak and her body gave.

The strength she used to maneuver herself above the tub drained from her and she sank below the water, Michael catched her and cradled her as though he had just delivered his first-born child. He saw Sasha as an unwavering vessel of pleasure and kissed her hair, forehead and eyes as Shawn washed her legs, thighs and buttocks with the lukewarm water that cradled them.

Sasha wasn't finished with them. She wanted more. The newness of this experience excited her beyond belief and the urges that barraged her senses and her loins couldn't be contained. She reached her hands up around Michael's neck and began to kiss him. Sasha kissed him softly at first, then delved hungrily into him. Pressing her tongue deep towards his tonsils and nibbling sensuously on his lips. He did not resist her, and as she kissed and ran her fingernails across his strong back, he felt his urges return, giving new life to his earlier deflated manhood. She writhed her thighs and pressed them against Shawn as in a challenge.

Shawn wasted no time taking her up on her obvious offer and dropped his head between her legs once more to soothe and heighten the heat that was calling all the emotion and lust in him. This was better than a dream.

Stopping, Sasha untangled herself from the men's embrace and found the vigor to rise from the water that was now dirty with the essence of three full grown bodies. She stepped out of the tub and water ran down her beautifully sculptured body. Michael and Shawn watched in the dimmed redness of the bathroom light that cast a shadow that transformed Sasha into a miraculous Goddess in the night. She removed the Waiting to Exhale CD that had stopped playing hours ago and replaced it with R. Kelly's 12 Play. That was more appropriate for what she was experiencing right at that moment.

She walked or waltzed into the bedroom, leaving a trail of sensuality and freaky enticements inviting the two men to follow her. They did. There were no words uttered so they were not sure what Sasha's intentions were. She was as temperamental as a black widow spider, mate them then go for the kill. They were sure she was about to kick them out, send them on their merry way now they had served their purpose and she had her way with them. They watched as Sasha moved with stealth and womanly wiles toward the far corner of the room. She looked behind her briefly and smiled broadly before kneeling to the ground with her ass posturing for effect. She looked at them once more to be sure that they were watching as she opened the very bottom drawer of her bedroom chest and pulled out a mangled glob of materials that they could not decipher.

She sat and untangled them one by one in the dark room with expertise and precision. Shawn and Michael looked at each other with curiosity and questions tumbling through their minds. *What was she doing?*

Sasha slowly walked to the bed with an amount of effects in her hands and they were still undecipherable. She lay down and began getting dressed. She easily slipped into what seemed in the dark to be a black overall, body-fitting suit. She seemed comfortably experienced as she moved swiftly as Shawn and Michael's eyes followed her. She pulled at her nightstand and pulled out some wrappings and called the men over. She motioned to them with her hands that she was ready to move on to the next step. As they got closer, she handed them each a piece of candy and they uneasily popped it in their mouths.

"Menthol," Michael chimed in realization. "Is there something wrong with my breath?" he asked half jokingly as he sucked slowly on its icy cool cherry flower and breathed deeply to feel it surge through his head and heaved through his nose and sinus.

Once the menthol was in their mouths Sasha reacted quickly, moving towards her mini bedroom bar and retrieved a glass of ice and returning as quickly as she had left. She took her original spot on the bed, flat on her back and began to masturbate. Moving her right hand tauntingly above the surface of her clit and then allowing her index finger to slip into the taut heat and wetness of her burning appetite.

Shawn was intrigued but made faces as the coolness of the candy messed with his senses. He was trying to concentrate on getting his grove on and the candy was distracting him. He didn't like the taste at all. Michael turned to look at Shawn who was visibly dismayed and didn't like the taste either, but took it anyway as Sasha grabbed the renewed erection of the two men standing next to her by the bed and began stroking the length of their shaft and watching their excitement heighten.

Sasha didn't respond to Michael's comment she just gestured, telling Michael to move forward. He wasn't sure what she wanted him to do so he sat awkwardly next to her on the side of the bed. She was impatient and shifted her body to help him with coordination. When that didn't work, she became annoyed and raised up on her elbows.

"Michael. Hun, I know we haven't done this before, but my pussy is hot and wet and I just want you to kiss and caress my pussy with that cool menthol in your mouth and then using your teeth, I want you to nibble on my clit. Can you do that for me?" She asked as sexily as she could. Pouting her lips slightly and running her tongue over her teeth in what seemed like a teasing gesture.

Michael positioned himself between her legs and found that the tight fitting overall she wore was crotch less and leather. This realization sent a new rush of desire through him causing his manhood to throb in anticipation. He decided to stop playing the fool and get down to business. Sasha was not one to ask twice.

As he tasted her slowly, the feel of his tongue sent a wave of shivers through Sasha's body and she could feel the cool icy flavor of the mint in Michael's mouth. It almost felt like she was on fire and she couldn't help wrapping her legs around Michael's head and pressing her thighs together across his temple tightly, causing Michael to lift his head slightly to take a breath. He gently used his hands to pry her legs from against his face and encouraged them to relax. But he wouldn't take any chances.

He held her legs apart with his strong arms as he used his

tongue to part the outer lips of her abyss and placed the menthol deep within her. The sensation caused her to tremble, and the hand that held Shawn's throbbing stimulation tightened, causing him to grab at her, urging her to release the pressure she was administering to his hot rod. She did and then pushing Michael away, she urgently ushered Shawn between her legs and inserted his penis inside of her before he was ready. The heat, or icy coolness of the menthol bombarded the senses on his penis and he immediately went limp. The unusual sensation taking away all the heat and excitement he was feeling.

Sasha squirmed, her body feeling like it was on fire and she needed to be soothed. She looked to Michael who replaced Shawn, pulling her down toward to foot edge of the bed so that her buttocks were directly at the edge about to fall off. He placed her legs over his shoulders and entered her. He felt her shudder and screamed out. The sound of her voice gave him renewed vigor and energy. He pounded himself into her quickly, riding the wave of moist flow that welcomed him. She moved briskly, raising her hips to reach his with each stroke. Goosebumps covered her and the hair on her body stood on edge as the feeling of the menthol's frosty coolness mingled with the heat that she was exerting and joining with Michael as he met her every thrust, and every inch of him blended into her and she took it all.

Sitting there watching Michael reap the fringe benefits of his hard work, Shawn became angry and excited. His anger melted with passion sending a surge of heat through his body and to his dick that immediately got as hard as a rock. He tapped Michael on his shoulder and indicated that he was ready but Michael didn't want to move. She saw an argument coming on and she didn't want them to ruin her experience.

She slowly pushed Michael up from her and told him to lie down on his back, and then she climbed on top of him. She laid down with her ass sticking out inviting Shawn to join in. He mounted her, licking the entrance of her anus first then slipping his fingers in and out to lubricate the entrance. Sasha started moaning, the sounds of passion competing with the music that ignited their lust. He dipped his penis in, slowly at first, but the rhythm of Michael and her gyrating antagonized him, taunted him, teased him, so he didn't hold back, he plunged himself deep into her causing a scream of pain to bellow from her.

Her screams excited him and he didn't hold back. He jammed himself into her hard and deep so she would scream and she did. With Shawn behind her back molesting her from her behind and Michael beneath her, tormenting her pussy she felt sandwiched like a meal and she was happy she was being enjoyed.

Their orgasms grew quickly, and Sasha Henderson experienced an arctic fiery explosion that shook her entire body, the bed and forced Michael into an automatic release. His body complied. He couldn't withstand the furnace that was wrapped around him, she burned him almost and he couldn't distinguish the heat of her vagina from the cold of the menthol that was inserted deep within her.

Michael felt Sasha flop on top of him. Exhausted. Their bodies still shuddering and trembling. Sweat drenched Michael's body and Sasha's outfit clung to her adding another skin in addition to her own that she was already grabbing at, ready to rip it from her body.

Chapter 23

Edna Barker left her son in the care of the competent physician Dr. Calvin McKinley after Dr. Justin Etnas reassured her that he would be right there by her little boy's side. She returned to the house that his presence had made a home for her. His toys, his room and school artwork projects all brought a sense of purpose and fulfillment to her home. Plaques on the wall from his baseball achievements and the refrigerator stocked with child like desires and treats. Her home, like her body, was barren before the young boy came along. She couldn't believe that she could just as easily lose him.

She shuffled through the house, quickly grabbing a bite to eat and taking a shower. She took care to pack more of Justin's toys and his favorite books to take to his already over crowded hospital room. She wanted to make sure he was comfortable.

When she was all done, she made herself a cup of tea and sat on the porch in her front yard, watching the empty swing sway to the cool summer breeze, listening to the rustle of the leaves of a tree that was shared abundantly between her and her adjoining neighbors house in Elmont Queens New York. This was a nice home for a child, and she was saddened again at the memory that she couldn't have any. It was too late for her now to even try any invasive surgical procedures and she didn't know what she would do without Justin.

As her thoughts drifted, she looked up to see a red Mustang drive by a couple times as though lost. The lady seemed confused and annoyed. Edna Barker watched as she pulled up aside her.

Edna Barker watched closely and silently as the lady with the briefcase stepped out of the car and closed the door. She surveyed her cool and calm disposition and the way her Ann Taylor suit clung to her was enough to cause a stir yet look stunningly professional. As if in slow motion the lady adjusted a pin in her stylish up do and looked down again at a piece of paper she had in her hand.

Rising from her seat on the porch she walked to her front gate and addressed the lady, she wanted to know if she was lost.

"Hello there young lady. Nice afternoon for a drive eh?" She asked nonchalantly trying to stir conversation with the flustered looking woman.

"Hello," Sasha responded imperturbably, throwing her hand in the air as though the woman was a bug or fly about to annoy her.

"Seems to me like you're lost," Edna Barker continued, not too much interested in the woman's disinterest.

"No, just trying to find an address." Sasha told her, turning to address the elderly woman for the first time since Ms. Barker approached her. Swiftly tugging at her mid length blazer top that was buttoned double breasted in front of her to ensure a neat appearance, she walked up to the woman's gate and with outstretched arms, extended the piece of paper she held in her hand with the address on it.

"I can never understand why it's so difficult to find an address in the borough of Queens." Sasha laughed with a strain. She didn't feel like participating in small talk with this woman who seemed old and lonely. "Listen, can you help me? I have a very important appointment and I must get to this address." She asked attempting to hide now that she had grown perturbed.

"Well, as a matter of fact, since you asked, you are at the address Miss. This here is my home and this is the address you are looking for." Edna Barker reassured her and smiled kindly at the young woman who seemed anxious and annoyed. She watched as the expression on Sasha's face changed from anxious to attempting to seem pleasant and wondered what was on her mind. "Is everything okay Miss?" Edna Barker asked again, "Would you like a glass of water?" She offered sweetly, the inflection in her voice of a worried woman who anything sad would bring her to tears.

"No, I am fine thanks." Sasha told her, again waving her hand as though she was brushing away someone whispering gallingly in her ear.

"Well then, can I help you? This is the address you are looking for and this is my home." Edna Barker told her again growing impatient at the young woman's reluctance to relax and just get to business. She didn't have time for this.

"I apologize. My name is Sasha Henderson. I am looking for Ms. Edna Barker. Do you know who she is?" Sasha asked, quickly composing herself and gathering her wits about her. She was here to do business and that's what she was going to do. Never mind that after reviewing the case that the similarity of her own past hit close to home. There was no way she was going to go there. Her past was her past and she was going to get this child away from this old woman who seemed to think she could handle a child under such severe circumstances. If she couldn't do it, no one could. Sasha thought harshly.

Sasha's maternal instinct never kicked in. She never felt the bond of love grow inside for her child. The few thoughts she had on the situation was good-bye and good riddance of the child she felt held her back tremendously. She wanted as far away from this case as possible and had called Michael asking him if he could get another attorney on the case. But he had emphatically told her no. This was something she had to deal with, a revisiting of her past that her mind and conscience must face.

"I am Ms. Edna Barker." Justin's foster mother responded to her question jolting her from her thoughts.

"Oh that's wonderful," Sasha jumped naturally into her work mode, focusing on the target at hand. She couldn't come out and be obvious about the fact that she wanted no part of the case that she read over. Couldn't be open that she had contacted the state legal defense team and told them that though she was responsible for appearing to be on Ms. Barker's side, that she would lose this case on purpose. The State didn't want to spend the thousands of dollars it would cost to have Edna Barker be the permanent foster mother of Justin Barker, as she had dropped the child's adoptive parent's name of Stephenson. They would have to compensate her taking care of Justin and would rather keep him in the foster homes where he would be given minimal care according to state standards.

Sasha didn't think twice about the fact that winning this pro-bono case would help jolt her career forward. Her despise for Sandra and her kids and their recent confrontation fueled her anger and she wanted nothing to do with this child. He could die for all she cared.

"May I come in?" Sasha asked politely, smiling brilliantly at the elderly woman in front of her. She observed that Edna Barker must have been a beauty in her time. Beautiful long salt and pepper Native American curly lock cascaded pleasingly down her shoulders. She was stocky, but wore her clothes immaculately. Her full figured body sported full DD breasts that seemed full and firm. It was obvious that not only did this woman have no kids; she must have been an athlete in her time. Her long shapely legs were obvious through her jeans. Though looking tired, with bags under her teary eyes, she looked clean, like a step above the average New York City resident. This woman was no fool. She seemed educated and well spoken. Sasha admired her enviously. *A woman of Edna Barker's age had no right to look that good. She thought maliciously.*

After taking Sasha inside and making sure that they were comfortably seated, Edna Barker handed Sasha a glass of ice and some bottled water. She could tell that this woman was not very pleasant at all. She smiled nicely, but it didn't cover the ugliness that Ms. Barker felt exuding from Sasha's pleasant exterior.

"I take it that you are the lawyer to represent me?" Edna Barker asked rhetorically. She didn't need an answer; she just wanted to know how such a spiffy looking attorney would come to represent her in such a menial case.

"Yes, I will be representing your case against the state for custody of Justin Stephenson whom you have illegally renamed, Justin Barker. At the very least, you are asking to be his permanent foster guardian is what I understand from my briefing." Sasha rambled quickly, then reached into her attaché case and placed the file neatly on her lap.

"If you don't mind me asking, how is it that a big time lawyer like you come to represent someone like me in a case where there is obviously no money?" Edna Barker asked her pointedly. She didn't have time for games and she wanted to know if she could trust the woman in front of her.

"Well," Sasha began clearing her throat. "This is what is called a pro-bono case at my firm. Sometimes prestigious law firms take on notable cases that might set a record or change a law. This would benefit the lawyer and the law firm immensely if it's handled properly and the case is won. For you Ms. Barker, this is extremely good news. You get the best of the best and one of the top lawyers in the state of New York to represent you, almost guaranteeing victory. I will get a notch on my belt and everyone will be happy." She responded, not holding her tongue or being tactful in any way while explaining to Ms. Barker why she was representing her. She wanted to get this done and over with.

Edna Barker, having been born and raised in New York, knew what seemed like a stroke of luck. Yet, she didn't like the tone of this young woman's voice and she didn't like the way she stiffly and without feeling discuss *her son* with her. Sasha didn't look at her during her explanation of why she was represented her. She just sifted through her files to pull out the appropriate documents to be signed. Despite all this, Edna Barker was more concerned about making Justin Stephenson *Barker's* stay with her permanent, and if this arrogant attorney sitting there looking aloof could get her there, she would work with her.

"Okay so what do you need me to do?" Edna Barker finally said with a deep sigh. "I have to get back to the hospital to Justin. I only left to take a bath and get a change of clothes. I need to get back as soon as possible." She reiterated so that there would be a clear understanding that she needed to get back to her child.

"Well, in that case Ms. Barker I am going to have to meet up with you another time, or if you don't mind, give you a lift to the hospital where you can reminisce and tell me what's so special about this boy Justin and why you want so badly to keep him." As the words trailed from her mouth Edna Barker looked at her incredulously. This woman was just talking as though Justin was an inanimate object or something. Not at all as though she is talking about a child.

"I guess that would be okay." Edna Barker agreed still stupefied by Sasha's indifference.

"What would be okay Ms. Barker? Do you wish for us to set another date or would you like for me to give you a ride to the hospital where the boy is so that I can meet him?" Sasha asked again coldly.

"I guess a ride would be appreciated. Taking the subway

will only take that much longer to get me there." She settled and got up to get her things that she had already prepared. As she moved briskly from room to room of her modestly decorated but clean and comfortable home, Sasha talked at her, as she too gathered her things and replaced the documents in her attaché case until needed again.

"The more I know about you and your emotional attachment to Mr. Stephenson, the better I am to epitomize your case for the judge. Meeting him should help with that and I will have an opportunity to see his response to you and what kind of relationship the two of you share." Sasha continued. This time, she walked to the door to signify that she was ready to go. Ms. Edna Barker walked past her and out the door, leaving it ajar for Sasha to follow suit then close it.

As Sasha popped the doors open and threw her brief case into the back seat, she stopped for a moment and placed her dark sunglasses cavalierly over her eyes.

"Hum." She mused, and glanced at Ms. Barker from the brim of her glasses and smiled before sliding comfortably into the drivers seat.

"Yes, what is it?" Edna Barker asked, confusion drawn across her face.

"No husband eh?" Sasha commented rhetorically, and without giving Ms. Barker a chance to respond, she took off and pressed the CD player in the car to play Mozart. I hate pro-bono, she thought disgracefully, untouched by the woman's obvious pain.

****

Dr. Justin Etnas sat with the young boy watching him sleep in his hospital bed. Justin's hospital stay was getting worse. His condition dropped and picked up at intervals and the situation was beginning to seem too gloomy for words. Dr. Etnas couldn't believe that there was no one who knew who this boy was. Given up at birth by a parent that was in a psychiatric hospital, it would be almost impossible to track down any blood relatives. He felt himself tearing up, watching the boy in a fitful restless sleep.

Justin jumped as Dr. McKinley entered the room to check on Justin Barker and smiled wearily at Dr. Etnas.

"Why don't you go home Justin, or tend to your own patients? There is nothing more you can do here for the boy. He needs family right now." Dr. McKinley advised and tapped Dr. Etnas on his shoulders in friendly sympathy. Mr. McKinley had noticed the attachment that Dr. Etnas has with the boy and was curious as to why. He looked furtively at Dr. Justin Etnas, the young gynecologist who insisted on assisting him with Justin Barkers care and wondered what the connection was as he flipped through the boy's medical charts.

"Justin?" Dr. Calvin McKinley turned and looked at Dr. Etnas. "Why are you so concerned about the boy? Besides the fact that he bears your name?" Dr. McKinley asked, looking at Dr. Etnas from the brim of his glasses.

"Calvin, I delivered a baby boy eight years ago by a woman with the exact description of this boy's circumstances. I cannot help but think this is that same boy, and if it is, I have unfinished business with his mother." Dr. McKinley looked at the young doctor suspiciously. He thought how kind hearted and wonderful this young man was, and how lucky the medical profession was to have him in that career field.

"Justin, it's very good that you are not the boy's attending physician." He said with a chuckle, "matter of fact, you are lucky that you are in an entirely different field of study. If there is anything personal at all between you and this boy, it would be totally unethical and inappropriate for you to be anywhere near this case." Dr. McKinley concluded. Justin looked at him, visibly rattled and unable to hide just how distraught he was.

"I know. That's my only consolation and I am grateful that you have allowed me to work with you on this case." Justin mumbled. Feeling himself shaking deep from inside, he knew he had to leave the presence of this doctor who seemed to be reading deep within him and he wasn't ready to share with anyone the deep love he harbored for this boy's mother. The more he thought about it, the more certain he became that this Justin Barker was the same boy he delivered eight years earlier.

"Thanks Dr. McKinley. I will go to my office and check in with my patients now that he is in your capable hands. Please page me if you need a break, a fill in or to give me any update or information you find."

"That sounds like a wonderful idea Justin. Go take a break and check in with all those new mothers and the beautiful babies you delivered. I will be in touch with you doctor. You are an invaluable assistant." Dr. Calvin McKinley told Dr. Justin Etnas as he placed his arm in fatherly affection around Justin's shoulders and they walked toward the entrance of the boy's room. Turning to look at the boy one last time before leaving, Justin walked away, closing the door behind him.

Justin stopped in the quaint waiting area of the small private Interfaith Hospital. He had to get something from the candy machine to boost his energy levels. This was really starting to get to him. He dug deep within his pockets gouging for change and found fifty cents jingling around, just enough to get him a Hershey bar.

Voices suddenly came into hearing distance and grew nearer and he turned to look in that direction. He saw Ms. Edna Barker descending on him with a stunning beauty beside her.

She turned and his face lit up as they approached him, they were absorbed in chatter and didn't see him standing there waiting for them to notice him.

As they drew closer, Ms. Barker recognized Justin's familiar face and smiled widely with relief.

"Dr. Etnas, how good to see you again." She said with out stretched arms and a warm smile. "Is Justin okay? Is he asleep?" She quizzed eagerly with sparkling eyes at the mention of the boy's name.

"Not to worry Ms. Barker. Your son is doing fine. When I left he was asleep. I stepped out to grab a quick energy boost, as you can see, nothing healthy." He chuckled embarrassingly.

"If I had known, I would have brought you some nice home made cheese cake and iced tea," she offered. "Maybe next time." She smiled and shook his hand.

"Hey there," Sasha interjected when she realized that Ms. Barker wasn't introducing her fast enough for her liking. "Remember me?" She asked, wondering if the handsome doctor remembered her from their earlier encounter when she had rushed out of Sandra's room freaking out that she had been scratched. She hoped he would say no.

"As a matter of fact I do. Weren't you the one who not two weeks ago was here with your sick friend? The one who had AIDS and scratched you? You thought you were going to die." He reminisced in mock humor. He wanted to laugh but thought it not polite since the expression on the woman's face in front of him turned grim. "I'm sorry, it wasn't that funny. I needed a good laugh." He told her still smiling from ear to ear and not being able to contain the mirth of the situation now as he remembered it.

"Yes okay, well I am happy you remember me." Sasha told him lightening her disposition to a somewhat more pleasant tone and stretched her hand out to him. "My name is Sasha," she introduced herself, "Sasha Henderson. How are you?" she asked him pleasantly.

"I'm sorry. My name is Justin Etnas. It's nice to meet you." Justin shook her dainty but firm hands and smiled brightly at her.

"Dr. Etnas, Ms. Henderson is my lawyer. She is going to help me fight for permanent custody of Justin Bark...Stephenson." She corrected herself. The confusion on Justin's face was obvious and his expression quizzed with numerous questions that he didn't voice. Noticing this change, Sasha volunteered to explain.

"The boy's adopted name is Stephenson. Ms. Barker illegally changed it to her last name when she took charge of the care of the boy."

"Oh," Justin said, understanding caressing his once confused disposition. "Well, in any case, I will refer to him as Justin Barker while he is here if you don't mind." He told them and again, Ms. Barker's face became illuminated with pure joy.

"Thank you doctor. You are such a sweet young man." Then pausing, she stole a glance at Sasha and turned back to Justin. "Can I see him now?"

"Oh, of course. Dr. McKinley was in there with him a few moments ago, I am not sure if he is still there. But you are free to go in and check on your son." He re-affirmed and she reached up to him and planted a sweet polite peck on his cheek making Justin blush. Sasha steamed, taking a hard look at Ms. Barker and then at Justin who simply shrugged his shoulders and smiled broadly as he watched Edna Barker saunter away to the boy's room. He sheepishly tugged at the wrapping of his Hershey bar and tried to open it.

"What was that about?" Sasha asked him hastily as soon as Edna Barker was out of earshot. "Didn't you just hear me say that the boy did not belong to her? He was simply in her care for a time and she had illegally claimed him as her own." She stammered without taking a breath."

"Okay, so?" Justin asked a bit puzzled. "She has not harmed the boy in any way and you are speaking about him as if he is some sort of inanimate object. He is a child Ms. Henderson, and Ms. Barker has probably saved his life, giving him the love of a real mother. He is lucky to have found her." Justin continued, still half smiling as he munched on his chocolate bar and wondering what was eating this young lady in front of him. Had it not been for her superiority complex and bad attitude to the situation, she might appear pretty. Then as an after thought he added. "Aren't you supposed to be on her side anyway?" The question was off handed, but Sasha fumed.

"Listen, I am an attorney at law. My job is to uphold the jurisdiction of the courts. I don't make the laws or the decisions." She spilled angrily.

"Whoa, okay. I was only asking. Nothing personal." Justin mumbled, swallowing hard so that he could speak clearly to her. As he looked at the determination in Sasha's brow and the darkness that over shadowed her once gleaming brown eyes, she seemed vaguely familiar to him. The familiarity seemed stronger, beyond the scratching episode at Interfaith Hospital two weeks before. He looked closely at her and mused over why this woman seemed so intimately familiar to him, and then it hit him.

"Can I ask you something?" He asked, suddenly appearing serious, the smug mirthful look disappearing from his clean-shaven handsome face. The rusty colored red hue of his shoulder length dreadlocks pulled back from his dark chocolate brown face and his mustache trimmed neatly above his full tantalizing lips. He studied Sasha closely and placed the empty chocolate wrapper in his white coat pocket.

Sasha was growing impatient, watching him survey her. It's not as though she didn't like having a handsome man look at her, she craved it, but he wasn't looking at her "that" way. Not like he wanted her, or was admiring the way her curves prominently displayed themselves through her suit. Not like he couldn't wait to have her number. The look he gave her made her uneasy, like he was judging her.

Justin suddenly felt urges for this woman before him and became perturbed. Why would he be feeling sexually attracted to this woman, who was undoubtedly beautiful but not on his mind in any sexual way what so ever. Why was he drawn to her? Shaking the discomfort that had come over him, he focused on his original thoughts.

"By any chance, do you know Kayla McIntosh? She was also here that day when you got scratched, crying over a friend with AIDS that was about to die. Do you two share the same friend?" Justin Etnas rambled off questions, trying to make the connection with his past love Kayla and this woman standing so boldly before him, poised and temperamental. He wouldn't want to get on her bad side. He thought jadedly.

"Yes, Sandra. She's a mutual friend of both Kayla and I. Why do you ask?" Sasha asked baffled by this abrupt question.

"No particular reason I supposed. It's just that you and Kayla displayed two distinctly different reactions to this friend Sandra." He mused pensively. "You were really angry and from the looks of things must have fought with your friend to have received a scratch. But Kayla was sad, regretful and blamed her-self for the situation. And then there was Karen, the one who did-n't say much." He ruminated, masticating over his words and mulling over them carefully before saying anything.

"Don't you think you are getting way too involved in some-thing that does not even in the slightest concern you?" Sasha asked him straight faced, her eyes dark and serious and a smile that was out of place from the lines of anger drawn against her cheeks. Sasha's question stumped Dr. Justin Etnas and halted his tongue for a few minutes. The feisty no nonsense woman in front of him held such a close resemblance to someone else, someone he knew. But Dr. Etnas could not put his finger on the familiarity that was forcing him to the place where he stood and compelling him to condone the rudeness of this lawyer.

Sasha had placed her briefcase at her right ankle and had her arms folded. Perturbed and wondering why this man was so knowledgeable about her and her friends. Curiosity and suspicion gnawed at her thoughts and the thought of so many unknown people, people out of her circle that she did not choose to inform or be familiar with, people like Delia who were just popping up into her life and ruining her friendships. This did not make her happy.

Dr. Etnas decided to shake clarity with words back to his tongue when he shook his head from side to side with mock laughter, and a few loose strands from his locs fell across his face and down his cheeks.

Sasha stepped back. A surge of awareness about him swept over her body. She did not know. She had been losing control of everything around her. Flustered and angered all the time and all too easily. The people she thought she had at her whim had basically abandoned her, her job was about to be lost, her hard work down the drain; her emotional out bursts and sexual escapades. Sasha could feel that she was on edge. Everything and everyone was her enemy and no one understood her. After all that she had been through. She needed to slow down. She looked at the uneasy man before her who was about to speak and then his pager went off.

Dr. Etnas looked down on his waist to the device attached to his pants belt. The word read urgent on it. He pressed the button to make it stop. He looked up at Sasha and smiled.

"I am sorry. I have to go." He said simply. And in that same instant, turned and walked away from Sasha. She was furious, her deep dark tree bark brown complexion turning raspberry red as a black over-ripened plum. She hated the feeling of everyone walking away from her, everyone with the last word. She felt like screaming, her once folded arms now hung to her sides and dropped down past her thighs. Her fists were balled so tight the veins popped from her knuckles.

Chapter 24

Charmaine sat at her phone starring at it and willing it to ring. She wanted Delia to call her. All the time she spent with her and she did not bother to find out her hotel name, room number or location. Delia had spent most of her time with Charmaine since their meeting and there was no need to. Now, she wished she could call her.

The phone rang a few times and it was not Delia. She wondered if she had decided to return home back to Jamaica or if she was simply mad at her and refused to call. Either way, how could she blame her?

Charmaine's heart was full for Delia; she was falling in love with her. She wasn't sure if what she had done was cheating. After all, she and Delia never made a commitment to each other; they had not so much as kissed. Yet there it was as clear as day. She was feeling guilty and was saddened by her actions. It had been two weeks since she last saw or spoke to Delia. She needed to get in touch with her.

Charmaine sat like that for hours, waiting by the phone. She hadn't had breakfast and was starting to feel fatigued from hunger. She had begun to nod off when the phone rang. Groggy with sleep she grabbed for the phone.

"Hello," she asked wearily, wanting it to be Delia but not really expecting it. Her mother had told her that Delia had tried to call her when she was away. Delia had left three messages on her voice mail and she was not there to answer or return the call.

"Yes, hello Charmarine. I see that you are alive." Delia stated sarcastically. Realizing that it was Delia on the phone, Charmaine jumped to her feet and a big grin came over her face.

"Delia, how are you?" Charmaine asked, knowing she must choose her words carefully if she wanted to see this luscious diva again.

"I have been fine. If anything, I should ask you that question. You seemed to have fallen from the face of the earth." Delia commented with a smile in her voice but as serious as a heart attack. She wanted to know why she couldn't reach her. Anyone interested in someone does not just disappear like that without reason.

Charmaine's grin subsided. She knew she must give Delia an explanation but what? Should she tell the truth and take a risk at losing her. Or should she lie, giving them both the opportunity to get to know each other on *that* level?

"Delia," she started. "Remember me telling you about a friend of ours, Sandra? The one who is HIV positive and lived out in Brownsville area?" She said and waited for a response, buying herself time to get her story together, which was in fact, half-truth.

Delia being the kind hearted person she was, took the bait and wondered what that had to do with anything.

"Yes Charmaine, I remember. Is she okay?"

"Well, she is dying. She was rushed to the emergency room a couple weeks ago and everyone had to basically drop everything and go. It's been a really long worrisome time for us all. She really has no family or friends to speak of besides us, and we had to prepare and make plans for her just in case. She has a little boy and girl." She concluded, rushing the words out of her mouth before Delia could say something else.

"Listen Delia, I need to see you. I really really need to talk to you very badly." She begged, dropping her voice into a girlish octave and whimpering like a pouting child, while adding a tint of seduction and sensuality. Delia laughed, and Charmaine knew that she had won her over.

Charmaine did not go straight home that day from the hospital when Sandra got admitted and then released. She had to go check on school registration for the fall. She had taken last semester off after only just returning to school from years of a sabbatical and still she, as old as she was getting, could not find it in herself to settle down and do something with her life.

She thought the rejection she felt from Delia had something to do with that. The fact that she was closer to thirty than twenty and living with her mother didn't help. She wanted to try and get her life back together.

Walking from the registrar's office to bursar's office she ran into an old friend. An ex-girlfriend. It was good to see Amanda again. Amanda, her first love. Charmaine felt so laden with the burden of Sasha, her desires for Delia and her home life situation that she needed someone to talk to. Someone who would listen to her and never judged or condemned her. It had all happened so quickly.

"Amanda, what are you doing here?" She had asked her as they rushed to embrace each other. Amanda was half white and had a Turkish mother and an African father. She was a military brat, born in Turkey and relocated to the United States with her parents at a young age. Charmaine could never understand how she was able to understand her. Between the two accents of her parents tongue, Amanda sounded like a British Creole Caribbean.

"Hey Charmaine. What a pleasure to see you. Where have you been hiding?" Amanda asked her. Charmaine had broken up with her almost one year earlier and Amanda was heart broken. She couldn't bear to see Amanda that way, so she severed all ties and just allowed time to separate them.

"I have been around. Still here I guess." Charmaine told her, guilt from their relationship skewered her thoughts. Amanda was a beautiful woman. Long thick curly hair like Diana Ross, but it burnt fiery red with hues of copper and brown. Her eyes were so hazel they were almost not there, blending into her eye socket and her dark pupil protruding out. Even Amanda's eyelashes were as an albino sort of red.

"But enough about me. What are you doing here *Kine*?" Charmaine found herself referring to Amanda by the pet name that she used to call her once Amanda had explained to her that the European word *Kine* was an endearing term, meaning little one or my sweet one.

"Oh, I have decided that I wanted to go back to school. You know how bored I get?" Amanda giggled. That was another thing about Amanda; she was a forever student, having never had to work a day in her life. Her father being from a rich tribe in Ghana and after serving his time in the military became an African trader. Her mother was an Opera singer and insisted that Amanda studied the arts.

They wanted her to be a ballerina, but Amanda's black girl posterior and voluptuous curves did not offer the kind of physical build that she needed to be dainty and light enough to fly across a stage. At twenty-eight she already had two degrees and now she wanted to get a third. She was extremely disciplined and held degrees in Philosophy and Anthropology. She was completely opposite from Charmaine, who was flighty, unfocused and did any and everything that caught her fancy at any given moment. That was the reason she couldn't find something that she was good at or wanted to do. She didn't like studying and was horrible at the English language and was well versed in Ebonics. She failed anything that had to do with writing or reading. But she loved technology. Even trying to go back to school now, she still was uncertain as to what she would attempt to get a degree in.

"Wow, that's awesome Amanda, I know that whatever you set your mind to, you will achieve." Charmaine told her.

"Except you Charmaine. I couldn't achieve you." Already frustrated with her present life situation, she didn't want to become confused by dredging up the past. She had to break up with Amanda even though she offered her everything that a woman could want from a lover. Amanda pampered her, took care of her, provided her with a gorgeous apartment that was lavishly furnished. She didn't need a thing, because on top of it all, Amanda was a great lover, striving to pleasure Charmaine in every way possible. Always coming up with new ideas to try in bed. But she made Charmaine feel insecure. Charmaine's low self esteem and lack of achievements of her own propelled her to fight with Amanda, chastising her for the life that she was born in. She couldn't understand why Amanda loved her so much, she could do no wrong in Amanda's eyes and that just made her feel worst, blazing the jealousy that was ignited in her and caused her to walk away from one of the best things that ever happened to her.

"Hey Charmaine, I am having a party tonight. I would love it if you came." Amanda said changing the subject quickly. She knew she was treading on dangerous waters and she was too happy to see Charmaine again. Her first and only lover, and she wanted to keep it that way.

"I don't know Kine," she told her hesitantly, drawing out the word pronouncing it Kin-a the way Amanda had taught it to her. "I have a million things I need to get done today."

"Oh com'on Charmaine, please. I haven't seen you in so long." Amanda looked at Charmaine charismatically, batting her long eyelashes and hoping that Charmaine would remember just a little about how much she loved her. Charmaine just couldn't see the beauty in herself. Amanda couldn't help but love her.

Charmaine reminded Amanda of her father, tall statuesque and graceful. She was almost midnight black just like her father with light brown eyes that didn't match. Wearing her hair cropped closely to her oval shaped head, Charmaine was everything physically that her mother would have wanted. Charmaine would have made a great ballerina. But she wanted to model and Amanda had used her mother's contact and gotten Charmaine into Ford Model and Talent, which was one of the biggest and most renowned agencies across the world. But when Charmaine broke up with her, she also disconnected herself from all ties with her modeling and anything that Amanda helped her with.

Taking a deep breath, Charmaine decided that she could use the break and looking back up into Amanda's beautiful eyes and warm smile, she knew that she could make her feel better.

"Okay Kine, it sounds good." Charmaine submitted and they both laughed again and hugged each other. They decided that they would take the bus and walk through the park the way they use to as lovers.

It was there that everything got confused. There in the park, Amanda confessed to Charmaine that she still had not been with anyone. That their two year relationship was all that she wanted even if that's all she would ever have in her life. That she couldn't move on. So right there in Prospect Park, at barely six o'clock in the summer evening, that Charmaine reached her hand up and touched Amanda's bouncy bountiful hair. Amanda had stretched her five feet seven inch frame to reach Charmaine's mouth six feet high and kissed her like only a well-acquainted old lover could.

It played out like a wet dream, where Charmaine found Amanda's full bosom and nestled her face in the sweet fragrance of butterscotch and powder, overwhelming her senses and drenching her panties like only Amanda could. Just knowing that Amanda had been faithful to her all this time, her sweet Amanda who wouldn't know how to tell a lie to save her life. Amanda who walking down the street could cause a traffic jam with her white girl hair, eyes and color and black girl mannerism and a Jennifer Lopez body that she rocked with ease.

She had turned Amanda against the tree that shaded them and fell to her knees, savoring the sweet taste of Amanda's essence. Amanda wrapped her legs around Charmaine's shoulders and balanced herself with her hands digging into the tree bark for support. She did not disappoint Charmaine. She moaned and sighed and screamed. Each lick and thrust of Charmaine's tongue elicited a stronger conviction from Amanda, voicing her emotions with her eyes closed to the world. It was only she and Charmaine, no one else and she didn't care if anyone saw or heard.

"Ah, Charmaine I missed you." She wiggled, bouncing her bottom into her lovers face and pulling her into her crotch with her feet. "Eat that pussy bitch. Its all yours and only yours." Amanda screamed, and tears ran down Charmaine's face. How could she have walked away from this? She loved Amanda's vocal expression of passion, so unlike her other experiences where they would experience quietly their own selfish pleasure and then roll away distant from each other.

It was there, in Prospect Park, only minutes from Amanda's apartment in the Jewish area of Eastern Parkway where she kept the apartment that Charmaine no longer wanted to share with her, that they made love, kissing and pleasing each other for more than an hour, before continuing on to Amanda's apartment where they showered, partied and spent the night and the next two weeks together.

Charmaine jumped from where she was sitting after

making arrangement to meet with Delia. She had to find a way to win her over. She was now confused, her old emotions clouding this new feeling growing deep within her for Delia. How would she explain Amanda? Did she want Delia or Amanda?

Delia got herself together and dressed to go to see Charmaine. Excitement rising in her abdomen and butterflies fluttered in her stomach at the thought of seeing Charmaine. She missed her. Her crude and erotic sense of humor, her deep belly hollowing laughter that could bring about your own happiness unconsciously. Her desires had grown for Charmaine and now she was no longer on testing grounds. She wanted to go all the way.

"Hey what are you up to Delia?" Chyna asked nonchalantly flopping herself down on Delia's sea green down blanket that decorated her bed. Delia liked that ugly color for some reason that Chyna didn't question. She loved this girl dearer than a sister.

"Oh nothing much." Delia lied, she wasn't ready to go there with Chyna, to explain her sudden change of heart, especially what happened between them two weeks ago, an experience that they had both buried and not one word was uttered about it. "Just going to hook up with Charmaine and the rest of her crazy friends again I guess. You know? Plotting." Delia said with a snicker. Stopping what she was doing to point her fingers like claws and made a sinister face as she prowled towards Chyna, who squirmed and ran away pretending to be afraid.

Delia returned, quickly stuffing a change of clothes into her backpack before Chyna saw, she didn't plan on coming home tonight. She had things to take care of.

"What are you going to do with your day Chyna? Are you planning on going to see your precious doctor friend today?" She asked. "Hasn't it been like two weeks since your escapade together?" Delia rambled on, trying to distract the attention from herself.

"Yes, yes," Chyna said, pouting with disappointment. "He is busy at the hospital. He had gotten paged and ran off like a bat out of hell the other day." She informed Chyna.

"Really?" Delia mused, wondering what was the deal with people in the hospital lately. "That's the same thing Charmaine told me. That her friend Sandra was in the hospital two weeks ago."

"Well, I really don't know. When I spoke with him the last time, which was a couple days ago, he was assisting with a young boy who was dying of cancer. Didn't know anything about him or his family since he was given up at birth and then ended up in foster care. Poor thing." Chyna said shaking her head.

"That's life Chyna, there are tons of situations out there like that and their voices will never be heard." She said, zipping the pack and looking around for her keys.

"Delia, I don't mean to change the conversation, but I am getting bored here. Something has got to give or I am ready to go back home." This stopped Delia in her tracks. She was not ready to go home. True they were there on an extended vacation. They built their own business and had been quite successful. Delia's masters in business economics and Chyna's knack for marketing, organization and building clientele, they plummeted into a high profile real estate business, forming alliances with American Banks and recruiting and assisting talented real estate brokers with their licenses. They were able to become Jamaica's number one buying firm for tourists, actors and rap stars that wanted to build exotic homes in the islands. They had just started expansion in St. Kitts and Trinidad and Tobago, and after four years felt it was time to revisit the past, take a vacation and relax.

Delia wanted to know where her and Charmaine's relationship would lead and it wasn't time for her to leave.

"Chyna, why now? I thought you were having a good time

with Justin? I thought you wanted to feel it out, see where it would lead?" She asked, wondering if Chyna was serious or just feeling lonely.

"I do, I am just starting to feel a little unproductive, stagnant." She chuckled.

"Okay, I tell you what. Why don't we make a date to have a little BBQ party or something. Maybe you can invite your doctor and I can ask Charmaine if we could have it in her back yard. Then you can meet all her crazy friends. What do you think?" Delia asked. Suddenly thrilled about the idea.

"Hum, let me think about it. I guess it does sound like a good idea. I will let you know how I feel when you get back." Chyna assured her, and lay back on her bed and waved bye to her friend who gathered her things to go.

Picking up her keys, Delia blew Chyna a kiss and walked out the hotel suite to meet Charmaine.

Pulling up to Charmaine's front door in her 2003 black Acura rental, Delia was surprised to see balloons in black and gold adorning the outside entrance to the house the woman of her affections shared with her mother. She wondered if there was a party of some sort that Charmaine failed to mention.

Delia got out of her car and moved towards the door that was slightly ajar. The butterflies that were there earlier batted their wings furiously. Excitement crawled up her legs like spiders and put the hairs on her body on edge. She saw no one and proceeded in. Delia knew Charmaine's house well, and moved toward the downstairs area where Charmaine had her own little loft decked out for privacy.

As she moved closer, she noticed the dimmed lights and the music blaring in the background, Daniel Bedingfield crooning the love song that had made him famous. Hearing the words lightened her heart and she could feel her heart rate race, *"if you're not the one then why does my soul feel glad today, if you're not the one they why does my hand fit yours this way..."* This is a song that Delia had grown increasingly fond of from the moment she first heard it. And for the first time in a really long time, it fit. It fit the way she felt about Charmaine.

The stairs were lined with rose petals and the room from the stairs down was filled with balloons of all colors, strings dangling from their hanging positions, filled with helium and guiding her to the bedroom. Still no sign of Charmaine she skipped, spinning around now in Charmaine's living room where she had sat many times before. Smelling the scented candles Delia was flabbergasted. Not even a man had done that for her. She spun around and around happily like a little girl in a candy factory. She couldn't remember the last time she felt so free, so special. She dropped her bag to the floor and moved daintily towards the bedroom where she was sure Charmaine was waiting for her. Yes, today she would allow Charmaine to have her way with her all discussions aside; this was indeed a special occasion.

As Delia approached the door she peeked in, wanting to sneak up on Charmaine and surprise her with a deep long kiss, she envisioned her tongue seeking out the concaves of Charmaine's mouth. Charmaine's hands molesting her clothes and freeing her to be submitted to her every whim. Delia was on fire, panties drenched with love juices waiting to be released. Her nipples perked and aroused at the thought of having Charmaine's tongue bathe her clit.

She stuck her head in and was totally surprised at what she saw. In total shock she backed away, bouncing into the cabinet behind her and knocking one of the candles over putting out its flames instantaneously. The candle's flame died with Delia's as she covered her mouth to stop herself from screaming. Frightened and disoriented, tears stung at her eyes and blinded her. She ran, grabbing her bag as she left out the door leaving it the same way she found it. Delia jumped into her car and sped off.

   With tears in her eyes she replayed the image like a video in her mind. Charmaine straddled between the thighs of a beautiful white looking woman. Their bodies naked, drenched in sweat and love juices as they made love to a song that she believed Charmaine was playing for her. The video reel did not stop. Delia kept squinting and closing her eyes to top the images from raping her mind, suffocating her senses and showing thoughts with pain. She did it again. She got burnt, this time by an unknown fire of passion. Women were no different from men, she thought as she sped back to the hotel, speeding to tell Chyna that they could go now, that she was ready to return home. The pain didn't go away and the video was set on auto replay. She heard their moans and groans in slow motion, each sigh stinging at her heart.

   Delia laughed psychotically to herself and mumbled under her breath, *stupid, stupid, STUPID*. She couldn't help going back so long ago to Michael, couldn't help reliving the pain of abortion, her child being ripped from its life sources. She thought to turn back and confront Charmaine, but why? What could she do? They had no relationship except the promise of some potential desire. There was nothing between them. She thought and laughed sarcastically to herself. She was going crazy over someone who never even touched her or kissed her. Was she crazy?

   Delia returned to the apartment but Chyna was gone, and was nowhere to be found. She tried calling her cell phone, but Chyna had it off during her encounter with Justin and Karen. Delia had no one to turn to, nowhere to go. She had to wait until her friend returned to the hotel. So she waited, crying into her pillow until dusk covered her like a blanket and hid her pain. She stayed in the dark, feeling humiliated. Her pride once again violated. Her emotions tampered with, she didn't know what to do so she curled herself into her pillow and swallowed her tears.

****

Chyna decided that she didn't want to stay in the hotel room all by herself. She didn't feel like being alone. She went back to her suite and found something cool and relaxing to slip into. A sun dress, skimpy short and flowing, not clinging to her giving her room for the cool summer breeze to fondle her skin.

Since Delia started frequenting her new found friends, the car they had rented to share was no longer adequate for their stay, so Chyna had rented something of her own, a brand new sporty jeep wrangler. She was not big on air conditioning so it was perfect, built to be open and free after taking down its plastic soft top, Chyna hopped in bare footed throwing her sandals in the back seat and allowed her long chestnut sun baked legs to dangle free. She was off to the mall, hair flowing behind her, dark sunglasses protected her eyes, and Bob Marley the Jamaican reggae legend blaring through the CD player, *"no woman no cry..."*

Chapter 25

Dr. Justin Etnas was happy that Karen was willing to meet with him. He didn't know why he chose her, but she seemed nice enough, genuine. When his pager went off in the hospital waiting area he was glad for the interruption that prevented him form losing his temper with Ms. Fine Almighty Sasha Henderson. He didn't like her, but her name stuck with him. She was definitely an unforgettable woman. He couldn't figure out why she seemed so familiar to him, so he chalked it up as simply deja vu.

He asked Karen to meet him at Green Acres mall, it was someplace that they both knew, and Karen wanted to meet him somewhere public, out in the open. The mall was on the border of Queens and Long Island and close to where Justin lived. It was Tuesday and Justin was happy he could rearrange his schedule to meet with Karen. It was Karen's day off.

He secured a place in the food court and had himself a slurpy while waiting for Karen to arrive.

Karen took the LIRR to Valley Stream and arrived at the mall promptly. She was curious why this doctor must speak to her about Kayla. She walked to the food court where they had agreed to meet and recognized him from what he said he would be wearing. She approached the handsome dark skinned doctor with his locs pulled back from his face into a ponytail, a single streak dangling by his ear. She noticed he had his hair tinted at the ends in a rusty mud red hue that highlighted his high cheek-bones and dimples that dug into his face as he sipped on his drink. He was dressed casually in jeans, sneakers and white cotton dress shirt that he had hanging open with a white cotton undershirt underneath, clinging to his chest. She sighed and wondered if there was something going on between him and Kayla. She couldn't imagine Kayla cheating on Michael, but she assumed she would know soon enough.

"Hey Dr. Etnas. How are you?" Karen greeted as she approached him. Noticing her advance, Justin stood to shake her hand.

"Hello Karen, I am really happy you could join me. Thank you." He told her as he tugged at a plastic chair from the table, pulling it out to help Karen seat herself. "And please call me Justin." He requested with a smile that caused his eyes to light up and his dimples to excavate deep into his cheeks.

"Okay," Karen smiled and blushed slightly as Justin took his seat.

"Would you like something?" He asked. "Maybe some-thing to drink? Some pizza? Anything. My treat." He told her again. Flashing beautifully outlined white teeth that sparkled.

"Okay, I could use something to drink. But you wait here. I will get it and come right back." She told him, pushing herself away from the table and retreating into the food area to get some-thing to munch on. Justin looked on, noticing that she was con-siderably smaller in height and body frame than Kayla who was almost six feet tall, and her other friend Sasha, who stood some-where between five foot eight or nine inches. Instead, Karen appeared to be a petite five foot two, probably weighing a measly ninety-eight pounds and very muscular and athletically built. She was pretty, with her light marmalade complexion and even skin tone. Her hair cropped short to a bob that reached the length of her ear and cut low, faded in the back. She seemed so fragile, vulnerable. Karen seemed like the kind of woman that made a man feel as though he should sweep her up and protect her like a porcelain doll.

Justin watched as she made her way briskly back to their table. She carried herself confidently. Walking with pride and an aura that forced you to pay attention. But that was a far cry from the way Karen really felt. As an only child she frequently felt alone, an easy target to be taken advantage of, and was often sad. She needed to feel that her friends cared for her as much as she cared for them but it typically didn't happen that way.

"Sorry, I couldn't decide what I wanted." She told him, and they both smiled feeling awkward and not really sure what would come out of their meeting.

"I know this is awkward," Justin started, "but I really appreciate you coming all the way out here to talk to me."

"That's okay Justin, anything concerning my friends I am willing to help out. You want to tell me what's wrong with Kayla?" She asked not wanting to drag out the inevitable. This man before her seemed decent and kind, but she didn't want them to become blind sighted by the awkwardness.

"Well, yes. I was wondering if you could tell me what you know about Kayla?" As the words escaped his lips, Karen stopped eating in mid bite and became suspicious. "No please, hear me out. It's not what you think." He jumped in to soothe her hesitation before she got up and walked away. "I am an old friend of hers. And I was surprised to have run into her two weeks ago when you came in with your other friend Sandra. We had a falling out eight years ago, and she said she is different. I just wanted to know if it's true." He laid his feelings on the table.

He didn't want this amicable woman before him to mistrust him and lose his only connection to Kayla. This was the only person he had ever known connected to Kayla whether it was friend or family. She kept those secret inside her, and despite it all, he loved her and wanted to marry her.

Karen took a bite of her cheeseburger and placed it back on the plate. She masticated slowly, chewing on her thoughts and absorbing his words.

"I have known Kayla since we were kids. Her mom and my mom were good friends. We sort of grew up together and then she moved away after high school. We ran into each other again through mutual friends." She told him in a matter of fact tone, still not sure what that had to do with anything.

"See, I met Kayla about nine years ago. She was working in a coffee shop next to my college campus where I was in medical school. We fell in love. She never mentioned any family or friends." Justin told her puzzled. "Why wouldn't she want me to know her family," He blurted out, not speaking to anyone in particular but thinking out loud.

"Well, we had a rough time growing up." Karen said. "I am not sure what happened to Kayla, I think you really need to ask her that." Karen told him adamantly.

"Can you tell me about the Kayla you know now?" Justin asked in a quiet murmur. Hands folded on the table and his body pressed forward. Karen laughed out loud, her eyes slanted downward like a crescent moon, but wide and bright like the sun. Her oval shaped face rounded out flashing her teeth and releasing a pleasant sound that almost sounded musical. She stopped and looked directly at Justin.

"Kayla is one of my most trusted friends. I don't ask her certain things because I think if I needed to know she would tell me. The same thing goes for all my other friends. Friendships are very fragile. You don't ruin what you have by trying to insinuate yourself into a part of a friend's life where you don't belong. Each of us serve a purpose in the others life. Do all of your friends know the same things about you Dr. Etnas?" She looked at him and saw the concern in his face; facial stubble threatening to overtake his cheeks and chin.

"I have very few friends Karen. I spent my life trying to make something special out of myself so that I could have more than just words and my heart to offer a special woman. Kayla was that woman at one time for me." His voice dropped two decibels lower, the inevitable sound of heartbreak quivering in his voice.

"You must have really loved her?" Karen reached across the table and touched his hand, the warmth of her long frail fingers sent a tremor through him and he struggled to keep himself together. They would have had a wonderful life together if she had opened up to him. "Do you have friends Justin?" Karen almost whispered, not wanting to disturb the moment. Justin laughed.

"Yes, my parents. Also one guy who is very special to me. His name is Joshua." He chuckled again at the mention of his name. "Life can get so busy and confused that it takes you away from what's important. This guy is a very special friend. I haven't spoken to him in months." It dawned on him and his expression changed.

"You know, he was the only friend that Kayla and I shared. He was truly there for her, and for me." He confessed.

"He sounds wonderful," Karen remarked removing her hand from his and reaching to take another bite of her almost cold cheeseburger. In that instant she looked up and noticed a tall, statuesque, almost Asian looking woman standing within harms length of Justin. She wondered if she knew the woman. She could pass for Kayla's fraternal twin, except she might be a inch or so taller than Kayla. Wearing a sundress that hung slightly below her thighs revealing long shapely legs, urging you to look upward, to follow them to their destination below her skirt tail.

Justin noticing Karen's prolonged stare, turned to look

behind him. He smiled brightly, his eyes gave her a once over and a new feeling came over him. Excitement. *What a beautiful specimen of a woman, he thought.* He watched her eyes move from him, to Karen who sat mesmerized opposite him, and realized the thought that might have crossed her mind.

He started to push his chair away to go to her, but she turned and began walking away. Not running or acting out. Just as though she was on a runway, clairvoyant and nonchalant. She just turned, her sundress turning with her, giving one a sneak peak glimpse of her enticing posterior.

Justin quickly excused himself from Karen, and ran to her. Gently taking her by the hand. Karen watched on. She turned and politely smiled at him. She had no words. Karen watched as he tried to explain something to her. This woman whose hair flowed to her shoulders, its black curly waves identifying her African Ancestry. Her high cheek bones almost Indian. She was exotic. Breathaking. Karen couldn't help staring; watching the nuances between them. Then the woman smiled, and threw her arms around Justin's neck.

They walked back to the table together, holding hands, and Justin reached over to another table and got a chair so that she could join them.

"Karen, this is Chyna. Chyna, Karen." He introduced them and Karen sweetly outstretched her arm and took Chyna's.

"It's really nice to meet you Chyna." Karen smiled, "you are very beautiful." She complimented.

"Oh thank you, that is very sweet of you." Chyna told her. "I hope I am not interrupting anything?" Chyna said knowing full well she wasn't, but didn't want to insult Karen.

"Of course not. We were just talking." Karen told her.

"I ran into an old friend about two weeks ago, and Karen is a very good friend of hers. We were just playing catch up." He told Chyna honestly. The terms *old friend* and *of hers* didn't sit well with Chyna, she felt the pangs of jealously churn in her stomach. She and Justin had no commitment towards one another. There were no plans made or profession of love. Just sex. She needed to get a grip.

"Oh really, is everything okay?" Chyna refused to be made a fool of again, and she was going out on top this time.

"Oh yes, everything is okay. Kayla and I have been friends since we were kids. But lately, we have all been going through some things. Mainly Sasha and Sandra, two other friends of ours." Karen explained.

Chyna's eyes narrowed almost disappearing and her mouth frowned.

"What do you mean Sasha and Sandra? Those names are familiar to me." Chyna quizzed, anxiety growing in her voice and she couldn't contain her excitement of the strangeness of the situation.

"Darling, you know these people?" Justin turned and took her hands, clasping them between his larger ones.

"Well, not directly. But my best friend Delia met someone over a month or so ago now, this girl happens to be friends with these people. What was her name again?" Chyna squinted her eyes, trying to remember. "Charmaine." She blurted in recollection, "Her name is Charmaine. And Delia has especially told me much about this Sasha person. She doesn't seem like a nice person at all." Chyna concluded. Now both Justin and Karen stared at her, their eyes filled with questions and speculations. She came out of nowhere and threw a wrench into the whole conversation.

"You know about Sasha?" Karen asked bewildered.

"Yes, she is being blackmailed by her boss. She's a lawyer right?" Chyna asked before continuing, wondering if she did in fact have the right Sasha. But how many people could have the same friends with the same exact names. The puzzle was obvious.

"Chyna, did your friend Delia, ever mention the name Kayla to you?" Again jealously reared its ugly head in Chyna, but she obliged Justin. Giving him the benefit of the doubt. The way he said Kayla's name as though it was sacred with his voice filled with emotion and longing, bothered Chyna, even hurt her.

"Yes, she has mentioned that name off handedly. Apparently she and this Sasha person are very close.

"Well, we all are. Sasha does have her ways, but she is our friend." Karen jumped in not wanting this new addition to their table to overshadow the value of her friendship with people she had known forever.

"Oh, so you are Karen." Chyna announced, realization captivating her. "I am so sorry to hear about what Sasha has been doing to you. I hope you are doing something about that boyfriend of yours. You seem so sweet, my gosh, now I under-stand." Chyna divulged this information innocently, but the memory of how Sasha had been treating her, the way Kayla had been wavering, the whole situation with Shawn physically abusing and hurting her. It all came back rushing in like a flooded dam.

Anger ripped through her and she struggled to contain the hurt that a stranger knew so much about her.

"What do you know about Shawn?" Karen asked irritated, not trying to hide the annoyance in her voice. "Just what Sasha has told my friend Delia. See, Delia used to work for Sasha's boss and went through almost the same situation of being seduced. She didn't fight back like your friend Sasha is." Chyna told her sadly, the memory of what happened over four years ago now, plummeting back to her thoughts. "Delia is trying to help your friend, but from what I understand, she is very obnoxious and wicked. She thinks that she does not need anyone."

Karen realized that Chyna wasn't trying to demean her. She had just shared painful information about her best friend, and in light of the situation, she should at least be grateful and think of this woman as a blessing in disguise.

"Sasha said she could have anyone she wanted, and that no man was immune to her." Chyna said and furtively glanced up at Karen. Karen knew that look. That secret look but it was as though Chyna was her friend, looking out for her. Not wanting to say what Karen saw in her yes.

"Yes, that sounds like something Sasha would say." Karen hung her head, shame and anger rising in her simultaneously. Her heart ached and her brain was like an open faucet leaking and filling with thoughts, making connections, pulling together a puzzle where all the pieces didn't quite fit, but she forced them together anyway. A single tear escaped her right eye and she brushed it away bashfully.

"Yes, our friendship has been tested lately. All of us." Karen told her with a smile, now making eye contact. Then her eyes gleamed, and familiarity like a storm rose within Karen. She began to shake and point at Chyna.

"You, it's you." Justin jumped to his feet concerned. Suddenly Karen had started to shudder as though she was going to have a seizure. She pushed him away and reached into her purse. There it was, that piece of paper she had walked around with for years, the newspaper clipping of four years before that had touched her heart. The article about a woman who lost her lover in a car accident, the memory that kept her together every time she had a nervous breakdown, every time she needed to be reminded how precious life was, how short it was, every time she reached out for *one of her friends*, and they were no where to be found. This was the woman before her, who had helped her to live and survive over the turbulent few years of her life.

"What are you talking about?" Chyna reached for her, got to her feet and moved around the table towards Karen, who Justin was lowering to the floor, a crowd of onlookers, started to gather.

Chyna took the paper from Karen's iron grasp almost ripping the old frail article from her hands. She looked on to see a small thumb print picture of Miguel's mangled car, a vague image of his body caught in the photographer's image of the accident. And a younger Chyna that the press had caught off guard as she tried to come to terms with information she learned about the man she loved on the five o'clock news. Her short hair at that time, matted to her head and her tear streaked face.

Karen couldn't explain what was happening to her. She had never felt this much pain. She was filled with hatred now that ran through the line of people she loved. Kayla, Charmaine, and Sasha. Especially Sasha. She knew it was her that Shawn kept boasting about. How he had a woman who was better than her, who had everything and that he didn't need her.

The way Sasha treated her, looked at her. Hatred, like a venomous poison surged through her and she pulled herself together. Suddenly she stopped shaking and an eerie smile crept to her face.

"I am okay." She told Justin, allowing him to pull her to her feet.

"Are you sure?" Chyna asked, now trying to contain her own tears. Holding back the memories that still hurt so badly. She had destroyed any physical evidence of Miguel in her life. Newspaper articles and even left behind people who knew her then.

"I am so sorry," Karen reached for her and hugged her. Chyna was almost kneeling to allow the petite little woman to embrace her around her neck, and grabbed onto her as though she was an old friend.

"I am sorry too Karen." She sniffled a tear and choked out her words. Justin was flabbergasted at the revelations that were made, shocked to paralysis at how life's coincidences could take you in directions that you didn't expect. He watched as the two women embraced like old estranged friends. He was touched. But he knew Karen was not okay. Something changed in her eyes. They were different, lifeless, over cast. She was going to need psychological help to get through this, her frailty and vulnerability showed, her trust and innocence stolen from her.

He looked on; curiosity about Chyna's past getting the better of him. He wanted to know what suddenly drew them so close together. What was it that Chyna now concealed? The piece of paper that looked almost muddy brown from age, wrinkled from multiple folding.

"Would you like a ride back to Brooklyn Karen?" Justin asked approaching their union. He waited not wanting to push, and watched as the ladies reluctantly released each other. They made eye contact and Chyna smiled at Karen warmly.

"Thank you." Karen mouthed without words and Chyna returned the sentiment. Karen waited while Justin spoke on the side with Chyna.

"Can I see you later?" He asked her gently taking her hands and kissing the back of it. He pulled her close to him so she could feel his desire for her had not changed. His erection surprised him; she looked so feminine, so sensuously attractive when she seemed weak. "I need to hold you." He told her and understanding that what he said had a double meaning, she nodded. He took her face in the palm of his hands and forced her chin upward, bringing his lips to hers tenderly. "Later then." He told her, and released her.

Chapter 26

Karen was quiet on the way home in Justin's BMW. She had never before been in such a luxurious car. Under other circumstances, she might have enjoyed the sleek feel and comfortable ride as Justin zoomed through traffic on the Belt Parkway, his doctor license plate giving him edge with the officers and boyish passion for speed showing itself as he maneuvered the enchanting vehicle.

He glanced occasionally at Karen to see her face mangled with the pain of whatever she was thinking and feeling. She was almost in a trance and he became increasingly concerned for her. He had suggested once that he take her directly to the hospital and without saying a word, she looked at him in a way that petrified him. Almost had him frozen to his seat and he feared for what she was pondering and going over in her head. So he drove in silence, not even bothering to put on some of his favorite driving music, Latin Music. Instead, he focused on the road, feeling the gravity force him to his black leather seat and feeling the magic of the car as it cut through the wind.

He arrived at Karen's apartment building and offered to walk her up. She obdurately said no thanks. No smile on her face, no sparkles in her round eyes. Just placid.

"Karen, thanks for coming out and meeting with me today. Your insight and thoughts on Kayla really helped me. I loved her once, and in a way, I suppose I always will." He told her with a wide smile hoping to loosen her disposition. She didn't respond, she just looked at him with the same disinterest that captivated her the entire ride.

"Hey Karen," Debbie yelled from the apartment building window. "Who's the hottie with the fly car?" she inquired, but Karen just slightly turned her head to look at her and turned back, now with a sense of annoyance on her face.

"Karen," Justin called after her, "I will give Kayla a call and let her know the situation okay? I will tell her that I solicited you and that you did not betray her trust or friendship in anyway." She smiled warily at him then, and turned to walk away.

He waited until she disappeared into the apartment building, a wave that he almost missed before she closed the door behind her. Justin felt that something bad was about to happen, but it was out of his hands.

Karen went upstairs and Suzette ran to her excitedly. Anthony was taking a nap and she didn't realize that seemed unusually late for him to be napping when it was almost bedtime. She didn't grasp that it was already almost seven at night. The day had passed with her mind. She moved robotically, kissing the baby girl on her forehead and hugging her then walking past to her bedroom.

"Karen," Sandra called, excited to tell her some good news and discovery that her visiting nurse told her only minutes before. "Karen come in here sweetie, I'm going to make it just a little longer. I am going to live longer." She shouted, but Karen didn't hear her. Sandra, wanted to show Karen the improvement that she had made, and the experimental drugs she had tried had given her new hope, she was not going to die in a few weeks as they thought. She might actually have years.

Something clicked inside Karen and for a second, the bubble of hatred that boiled in her ear subsided and she heard

Sandra's joy. Karen stopped and turned to Sandra. That was
indeed great news, because when she was done with Sasha,
Sandra was going to need to be around to take care of her children. She was tired and fed up with life and the backstabbing
betrayal of people she trusted.

"That's great Sandra," she said with a semi-smile still
walking toward her bedroom. Sandra hobbled as best she could
standing before her and stopped her dead in her tracks.

"Karen, are you okay. What's wrong? You are not acting
like yourself today." Sandra insisted planted to the spot that led to
Karen's private domain.

"I am okay Sandra, really." She tried to convince her, but
her eyes and heart were focused on the growing hatred she harbored for Sasha.

"Okay, now I know something is wrong. Come sit here
with me for a second." Sandra coerced her and reluctantly, Karen
followed.

"I know that there has been a lot of pressure on you lately Karen. Is it me? I am sorry." Sandra told her apologetically.
She knew she was a lot of work for Karen, especially with two
young kids and her working a full time job. Sandra felt useless
and sad that she had placed such burden on her friend. If she
had a choice she would have chosen differently. Even Seth, the
man she chose to be with since he too was afflicted with the virus
that had no cure. Even he cheated on her and left her when she
needed him most. Where he was, she didn't know, and at this
point didn't care. She was so grateful for Karen.

"It's not you Sandra, it's okay. You are fine in my book."
She whispered so low that Sandra almost missed what she said.

"Then what is it?"

"I don't know okay. I just don't know"

"But Karen, this is not like you. You seem out of it. I love
you and I know I cannot do much, but please don't shut me out.

I want to help."

"You don't understand Sandra, I am just tired of everyone running over me like some sort of doormat. I don't understand what I did to cause this kind of attack on me." Karen opened up to her and left open a way for a whole on slew of questions.

"Is it me? Something I did?"

"No, and to tell you the truth, this really does not concern you. Just leave it alone." Sandra was taken aback and stood shocked with her mouth hanging open in mock offense.

"My, my aren't we testy today?" she responded with a snicker trying to lighten the dense atmosphere that had grown thicker and more heavy by the minute. "I was just trying to let you know that if you need your space, I might be living long enough to give it to you that's all." Sandra turned the conversation back around to her, hoping that it might strike a cord to force Karen into speaking to her.

"It's just something I found out about Sasha today that's all. She's apparently been telling the world how irresistible she is to my man as well as everyone else's. Apparently, she didn't think there was anything we could do about it, I guess." Karen whispered aching at her own words as they said things she didn't want to hear all over again.

"Why is it that Sasha is the way she is Sandra? I just don't get it. Why does she do the things she does and behave as though the universe revolves around her?"

"Karen I don't think you should worry about Sasha. She is the way she is and nothing is going to change that."

"Why hurt the people who go so far out of their way to love you, to protect you and be there for you?" Karen intoned, questions bombarding her mind.

"Because some people are just sick Karen. Some people have so many issues and are so unhappy with their own lives that they cannot stand to see others, not even their friends happy.

There are some people who need reassurance and reaffirmation everyday to feel alive, Sasha is all of those people in one. She does not know how to create her own happiness so she steals others; unfortunately, it's easier to do when she destroys her friends because she knows our secrets, our pains and our shame. That's the power we give to people we chose to share our lives with and sometimes we just choose wrong." Sandra tried to console her. But the more Karen heard, the angrier she became.

She started to shake her head and closed her eyes squeezing them shut to block out what Sandra was saying.

"No, no, no these are not acceptable reasons for this behavior. This does not justify the way she has hurt me over and over, time and time again." Karen said firmly, struggling to maintain her tone of voice as not to alarm the children who shared her home.

"Okay listen," Sandra started and took a deep breath. She wanted to calm Karen down. She knew that Karen was a sensitive reasonable lady, so maybe if she shared with Karen what she knew that would help to soothe her anger. She had never told any of her friends Sasha's secrets, the ones from college, the rumors. But maybe telling Karen would help her to understand, and maybe even sympathize with Sasha.

"Listen to me Karen, I am going to share something with you that has never left my heart or my lips for years. But I think you will understand Sasha more when I do."

"There is nothing you can tell me to make me like, forgive or even want anything to do with that cock sucker again." Karen spoke between clenched teeth.

"I know you Karen, this is not like you and you will understand."

"Don't you see that is the problem? Everyone thinking they know me and that nothing bothers or hurt me? Everyone dumping on me like some garbage disposal that you can just

leave your unattended shit?" She looked at Sandra with eyes that
fought building tears and refused to let them fall.

"Karen, Sasha has a child. A son."

"What do you mean?"

"We met in college and the rumor is that she got knocked
up stripping and drugging up with some high rolling pimp that
thought she had the making of his number one whore sidekick.
She freaked out and tried over dosing on drugs when she found
out she was pregnant and he wanted nothing to do with her. She
ran away and was picked up on the streets upstate, admitted to
a psyche hospital and the rest is history." Sandra paraphrased in
a nutshell.

"You mean that piece of shit had a child? How could God
be so cruel?" Karen thought, the thought of a child devastating
and tugging at her already fragile heart. "You know, a couple
months back she called an urgent meeting talking about being
blackmailed by her boss that she's been boning. She never mentioned anything like this." Karen told her, shaking her head wildly
and irritably. "This is not a good person Sandra. How was this
supposed to make me feel sorry for her or understand her? I
loathe her! She is not fit to be in her profession deciding people's
fate or even walk the face of this earth." She intoned.

Karen suddenly stopped shaking and the tears stopped
and dried almost immediately from her cheeks as though they
were never there. She smiled a sinister eerie kind of smile that
scared Sandra. She became almost tranquilized.

"Karen, are you okay now? You do understand don't
you?" Sandra asked, shaking off the peculiar vibe that held her
only moments before.

"Yes Sandra. Thank you. I understand exactly who this
she-devil is who has disguised herself as our friend." She said
quietly, almost in a hushed whisper, with that same smile on her
face.

Karen stood and walked to her bedroom, which was not too far from the sofa where they sat speaking for what seemed like forever to Karen.

"Where are you going?" Sandra asked.

"What does it look like Sandra? You are dying I didn't know that you were blind too." She spat viciously, annoyed that Sandra wouldn't leave her alone."

Sandra stood this time almost paralyzed to the place she sat on the sofa, shock and hurt flooded her heart and pinched at her soul. She knew that Karen didn't mean it; she knew that she was upset, but the poison of her words didn't hurt any less. She allowed Karen to walk away, in almost zombie-like movements to her room.

Sandra peered into Karen's room. The door was ajar and she saw Karen on the phone, speaking quietly, but she couldn't hear the words of anger that exploded from her mouth.

"Sasha you good for nothing fucking bitch. You are nothing but an undercover slut. What are you? You call yourself a friend. You are a backstabbing freak who cannot find a man of her own. I hate you. You are a fucking whore, streetwalkers are above you. I hope this Brendan guy fuck the shit out of you. I hope everything comes out in the open and you get exactly what you deserve. I don't want anything to do with you ever again you asshole." And she quietly replaced the phone on its cradle.

Sandra had never seen Karen like this, the usually optimistic pleasant friend that she could count on. But within seconds of her hanging up the phone, Karen came to life again. She turned and saw Sandra and she ran to her.

"Hey Sandy, how's it going?" She said cheerfully. Sandra looked at her perplexed, she wasn't sure what was going on with her friend but she didn't seem the same.

"Karen, what's going on? You look different." She told her,

choosing her words carefully. "Yes Sandra, I am different. I feel good. Liberated." She told her emphatically, almost wheezing. Her heart beating fast, she wanted to kill Sasha, the thoughts that went through her head, imagining Sasha laughing at her all that time. The betrayal.

"I am okay Sandra. But look at you, you are out of bed, walking." Karen noticed, but her exaggerated jubilance scared Sandra.

"Let's go sit down Karen." Sandra suggested again to her, but Karen ignored her. She had seen things like this happen to people before, people in the projects of East New York, right before they snap. Something got to them, the realization that they may never make it out of that lifestyle. Home and family riddled with drugs and booze with no future. Some of them snapped, taking their own lives and sometimes the lives of others with them. Maybe even the lives of their children, thinking that they were saving them from the same fate. Yes, Karen looked as though she was on the edge.

"Hello Francine, look at that. Sandra is moving about all on her own." Karen turned her attention to Sandra's nurse as though she had just noticed that she was standing behind Sandra the whole time.

"Yes Ms. Grace, she is doing wonderful. We spoke to Dr. Walker and Dr. Hudson today. They believe that Sandra is reacting to the experimental drugs and that she might have some more time with her children." Francine told her.

"This is great news." Karen said, "This is a reason to celebrate." And she ran to the kitchen looking for some wine or champagne.

"What are you looking for Karen?"

"Alcohol, we have to celebrate."

"But neither of us drink remember? You never keep alcohol in the house.

"Well then, it is time." Karen told her shrugging her shoulders, "I will go and get some." Before Sandra or Francine could talk her out of it, she had grabbed her purse and walked right back out the door.

Karen wasn't sure where she was going. She just walked, and walked and walked. Tears flowing freely down her soft cheeks and questions that she would never get the answers to surged through her mind. She wandered like that for over an hour before she remembered why she wanted to come outside. She went into a liquor store and asked for something; anything and they gave it to her, keeping the change from the twenty-dollor bill because she didn't bother to wait. She walked back the quarter mile distance to her house, still crying.

****

Sasha had a rough day on Tuesday, going over Ms. Barker's statement and documents regarding Justin Stephenson, the orphaned boy. She had met with the State's attorneys and attempted to propose a toast. They wanted the boy back. The funding they could get regarding his care could be split amongst other children.

Sasha left that meeting angry and frustrated. She wasn't getting anywhere and she didn't feel like failing. The firm would not take this lightly. Even though she didn't want this old woman Barker to get the boy, she didn't like the way the state attorneys wouldn't respond to her offer; they were hard and radical. They were not going to compromise or even work with her on her plan for them to get the boy; they wanted to win, all or nothing.

She dropped her briefcase at the entrance of her door and walked on the cool marble floors. She made herself a stiff brandy and plopped herself down on the sofa in the living room.

She reached for the remote control that put the manipulation of all her technological gadgets at her fingertips.

She pressed the button for phone and listened to the prompt that came over her loud speakers, *Phone is on.* Then she pressed play and waited for the recording to regurgitate whatever messages she had while she was out. She sipped on her brandy and almost choked when she heard Michael Brendan's message.

"Hello honey bun. How's it going? I could tell your panties had gotten all wet the other day at out meeting. Why not stop all this pretending and come over here so I can fuck you. You know you like the way I do it. We can put all this other stuff behind us." His voice crooned in an attempt at sensuousness.

"Bastard," she uttered and pressed next on the remote control to skip the rest of his message. *Next message received today at 7:15pm.* The machine told her. It was Karen this time. And when she heard this message her brandy fell from her hands and crashed to the floor. Her mouth fell open and if she was in the bunny rabbit cartoons, steam would come from her ears and the sound of a smoking train engine would toot from her brain. Sasha was pissed.

She didn't bother to turn off the voicemail so it kept running, but she didn't hear a thing after Karen's message ended. She grabbed her car keys and slipped on a pair of slippers. She didn't care that the brandy would stain her white carpet that she was so protective of, nor did she care that she hadn't changed. She still sportedher red short skirt suit that was almost too tight but enhanced all of her physical attributes. Sasha believed in using everything she had to her advantage in a case. Everything.

She got into her car and sped to Karen's house. Someone had just walked out of the building so she took the liberty of catching the door and letting herself in. It was 9 o'clock when she got to Karen's door.

"Karen, Karen you bitch you better open this fucking door right now." She screamed. "Karen you little mouthy twat, why don't you come say it to my face you bitch." She yelled, waking up the neighbors and Sandra's children who had already turned in for the night.

Francine could not wait for Karen to return, so she had left over thirty minutes before. Sasha had walked up the steps right past Karen, who sat under the stairway in solitude, not ready to go back inside.

Sandra heard the noise and raised herself up out of the bed. Debbie, Karen's nosy neighbor, already had her ear pressed to her apartment door listening for every juicy detail.

"Karen, you South Africa starving looking scrawny bitch, you…" and Sandra opened to door just as Sasha was going to bang on it again.

"What are you doing here Sasha? Don't you have more important things to do than assault people at night." Sandra spat sarcastically.

"You watch your mouth you welfare dying heffa, before I do you a favor and help you to your grave." Sasha told her as she roamed about Karen's apartment looking for her.

"Sasha, you don't belong here. Leave." Sandra told her. But Sasha didn't intend on going anywhere.

"Listen Sandra, I am not here for you, but I will deal with you later since we have unfinished business from two weeks ago." Sasha stared at Sandra up and down; she knew she couldn't take her. But Sandra was not going to be intimidated.

"All the pretending you want to do with the others you are free to do Sasha, but I know who you really are. The drug addicted whore who got knocked up and got thrown into a psychiatric hospital up North. I knew all along you piece of shit, and now Karen knows too. She knows everything now. And the others may not know the details, but they know that you are not the almighty class act that you are pretend to be." Sandra mused, almost spitting the words at her, throwing Sasha for a second. She wasn't aware that Sandra knew all this about her.

"You bitch," Sasha whispered almost, and sent Sandra crashing to the floor, her crutch flying to the side and knocked the crawling baby who was attempting to get to her mother out. Suzette didn't even make a sound. She was knocked out cold.

Karen crept up the stairs, following the noise that was coming from her apartment. She prowled, almost like a predator on the hunt. She salivated and licked her lips; she was hungry to cause Sasha pain. She walked in behind Sasha who didn't see her; she was too busy punching the living daylight out of Sandra who lay defenseless beneath her, but Sandra wasn't afraid. There was nothing Sasha could do to her that AIDS hadn't already done.

Karen walked into the open door of her apartment and walked directly into the kitchen. She went through her cutlery drawer and sought out the biggest sharpest butcher knife she could find. She held it carefully at an angle that she thought would cause the most damage. She walked up behind Sasha and climbed on her back with one spring, angling the knife at her throat. Sasha stopped mid punch, and Sandra smiled.

"You were looking for her, so now you have found her." Sandra told her weakly chuckling. Sasha was not afraid of Karen; she felt no need to be. Even now with a knife at her jugular she felt that Karen would do nothing.

"So what are you going to do now?" Sasha snickered, turning to see a highly disgruntled Karen behind her. She looked wild, and animalistic. But that did not deter Sasha in any way.

"Kill me." She laughed. "Bitch, you don't have a vindictive bone in you. You are a weak bitch. You couldn't do it if your life depended on i…" Before she completed her sentence, Karen slit her throat wide open; putting all the strength of her five foot two body into the one solid movement that almost took Sasha's head off.

Blood gushed everywhere, splattering over Sandra's face and body as Sasha's dead weight fell on top of her, Sasha's head falling to the side hanging only by her neck bone and a few pieces of flesh. Karen was still sitting on her back.

Sandra started to choke and puke, vomiting up everything she ate that day. Panic in her eyes as she watched the rage seep from Karen while a wicked grin plastered itself on her face. Karen was not in the least bit moved or swayed, she felt she had just done the world justice by ridding it of Sasha.

She got up from Sasha's back and moved swiftly to the kitchen. She pulled out some utility rope and returned to Sasha's dead body, blood still spewing from her neck and mouth.

"You are not talking anymore shit now are you?" She asked Sasha's dead body and got no response. Her eyes still wide open in shock. Her last thoughts were evident on her face. She couldn't believe it.

Karen rolled Sasha' body from on top of Sandra and tied the rope around her body, then finding strength in her petite frame, she dragged it to the window, tied the rope to the sofa and lifted Sasha's body, throwing it out the window for all to see. Then she went and picked up little Suzette who was still breathing, just knocked out.

Sandra watched the whole thing, petrified and started to choke on her own vomit. The smell of excretion came from her. The smell of her own defecation suffocating her, she coughed and vomited and shock took over her. Her eyes rolled back into her head, and she went into a seizure. She couldn't stop herself from shaking and the image of Sasha's lifeless eyes imprinted themselves into her mind's eyes. She tried to speak but nothing came out, she vomited again. She reached for Karen and tried to call her name, but Karen had left this dimension, eyes focused on the baby in her arms, brushing invisible hair from her face and kissing her forehead. Sandra reached again, grabbing at air. She tried to speak, but this time blood came out of her mouth, and then silence. Sandra died and Karen didn't even notice.

Debbie stood outside Karen's door and watched the whole thing, horrified. She couldn't even move. The neighbors all stood outside, spectators to a gruesome crime of passion, betrayal and anger. The building was eerily silenced by the picture of Sandra's dead body on the floor, blood, vomit and secretions all over the floor. And Karen, loss in the embrace of a baby who opened her eyes now but did not move. Anthony, still sleeping soundly in the spare bedroom his mother had previously occupied.

Chapter 27

Justin received the message about Joshua's passing on his voicemail when he awoke Wednesday morning, Chyna still sleeping soundly next to him. He couldn't wait to see her again.

He rushed home after dropping Karen off in Brooklyn and headed back to his apartment, asking her to meet him there and giving her directions. She wasn't staying too far away from him since her hotel was only minutes away.

As he drove he thought about the day's events and the coincidence of Chyna showing up and adding new light to him meeting up with Karen. As he thought of Karen he worried that she would be okay. He wasn't sure if he did the right thing leaving her behind like that but he knew better than to force someone into talking when they didn't want to. He pulled over to the side of the road and searched through his address book for Kayla's newly added phone number and dialed it. He wanted to let someone know that Karen was in trouble, someone close who could go to her and talk to her about what's been going on. He dialed Kayla's number and left a message on the voicemail.

Thoughts of the previous day drained from his mind as he sat and looked at Chyna's naked body, his erection coming to life again as he remembered how he made love to her the night before.

"Are you okay?" he had asked her as she took the steps to meet him at his door way.

"Yes I am fine. Thanks for asking." She told him sheepishly. She knew she would have to explain the paper, the connection to Karen.

"Come on, let's get inside. The air is chilly outside tonight." He explained and they entered his immaculate apartment loft. "Have a seat sweetheart. Would you like something to drink?" he asked her, already pouring two glasses of dry white wine to help smother both their nerves.

Chyna didn't feel like explaining the whole situation to Justin about her past, so instead, she carried with her the article that she had confiscated from Karen and showed it to him. He had read it silently and slowly placed it back in the palm of her hands. He understood now, and there was no need for more talking.

Justin had swooped her up in his arms as though she was feather light and held her close to him. He didn't want to let her go. So he didn't. He held her all through the night and made love to her until she asked him to stop. He recited words to her of long ago, words he didn't have voice to say before, words of promises for tomorrows and protection from future pain. He wasn't sure if she heard a word he said. And even as he sat now, looking at her lying naked next to him, almost ten o'clock on a beautiful Wednesday morning, he made those promises again, and spoke those words into her ear with a kiss.

He stood up and walked to his kitchen bar and started putting together a simple scavenger hunt for breakfast. He wasn't much of a breakfast person, so he placed a cereal bar on a tray and filled a glass with water. He pulled on pajama pants and went into his landlord's garden for some simple wild flowers that he gently placed in the glass of water that he poured. Placing a glass of orange juice next to it, he moved towards his bedroom and sat next to Chyna, shaking her gently.

Chyna turned around and smiled at him sweetly.

"Good morning." She whispered, wiping sleep from her eyes and attempting to cover her face with his sheets.

"Oh no you don't." He told her laughing adoringly at her childlike nuances. I want to see all that sunshine that is radiating from your beauty." He told her making her blush.

"Hey, look what I've got for you." He told her and she looked at his attempt and smiled brightly.

"I see you're not much of a breakfast person." She teased. "Well, lucky for you, neither am I." They giggled and Chyna threw her arms around Justin's neck, then slowly kissed his cheeks, his collarbone, his Adams apple and then full and passionately on the lips.

Justin released her and sat her back on the bed.

"Here, I want you to eat up. Then we'll go for a walk. I want to spend a few more hours with you before I have to go to the hospital." He instructed her and walked out of the bedroom, back into the kitchen. He noticed that the flashing light on his phone indicated he had voicemail so he pressed the button to listen.

Justin held on to the bar, suddenly feeling weak. He almost passed out. The voicemail of a woman's voice he recognized, a woman he had visited and shared meals with on many nights as a broke medical student intern where she saved their lives. It was Joshua's aunt. He listened, the recording fading into the background and his memories of Joshua cascading through his mind.

Joshua, the only person he considered a true friend. He felt everyone else wanting to be associated with him for status, not for friendship. He couldn't believe Joshua was gone. He had spoken to him only a few weeks prior. He had wanted to tell Justin something important. A secret it seemed. He wanted

Justin to fly to Rochester that weekend, but that was the week-end he spent with Chyna the first time. He thought he had time to talk to his old friend. As he remembered it now, it seemed so urgent. Joshua wanted to clear the air. *But of what?*

Silent tears flooded his face, as the next message came through it was Kayla.

"Justin, I hope you don't mind but I had the hospital patch me through to your home phone. They wouldn't give me the number. I don't know if you have heard, but Joshua." Her voice trailed off and he knew she was crying. She couldn't finish, she didn't have to, someone special they both knew was gone, life cut short by circumstances, wrong place at the wrong time.

Chyna walked into the kitchen a smile on her face and still as naked as the day she was born. Her smile died with the meet-ing of Justin's eyes. His tears caused a strange new wave of emotions through her that she couldn't understand.

"Justin," she called out to him, quickly placing the tray on the bar end and grabbing onto his arms that were so strong ear-lier, protecting her and giving her strength. Now he hung from the bar, barely holding on.

She supported him and they moved to the living room and sat on the sofa. Chyna found a spot on his thigh to sit and placed her legs between his opened ones.

"What is it my love? Why are you upset?" She asked soft-ly. Justin shook his head and tried to speak, but it just came out the sound of a choked sob and he wept in Chyna's arms. She sat there on his lap; his head buried in her chest and allowed silent tears to seal the intimacy and confidence between them.

****

I waited in the hospital waiting room all day on Wednesday waiting for Justin to come in. He had asked to have his patients covered and would not be in until early afternoon. It was now after one and there was still no word from him. I couldn't tell whether or not he had gotten my message, but I must talk to him.

If he doesn't show up by two I will have him paged again. I just need to let him know what had happened to Joshua.

I decided to check my messages to see if anyone had called. I felt so frustrated and helpless. I didn't know where Michael was but from the perfume on his clothes the last time, he might be with Sasha. She was the only person we knew that had enough space to put him up because I knew he didn't want to go to his family.

I listened quietly as my messages were played back; I hadn't checked it in days so I was surprised to hear Justin's voice.

"*Listen Kayla, I know that there are some things we still need to talk about but there is something more important that you need to do right now. I just dropped your friend Karen off at home. She didn't seem well and I was very worried. I just thought it would be nice if you or someone would check on her.*" She hung up the phone after the beep and checked her watch. It was already almost one in the afternoon.

He was right, since Michael left I hadn't spoken to anyone, not Charmaine, not Sandra, Sasha or Karen. I must have been really out of it until I received that message from Joshua's aunt. Oh my goodness, maybe I should call Karen at work and see what's up while I wait.

"DMac, Inc. Maybe I help you," came the voice on the other end of the line.

"Yes, may I speak with Karen Grace please?"

"She is not in today, may I take a message?" Came the

polite voice from Karen's job.

"Well actually, do you know when she will be in? It's kind of urgent and I am her sister," I lied, heaviness and anxiety building in my bosom. There is definitely something wrong. It's not like Karen to ever be irresponsible to miss a day of work if there was not some emergency.

"Well actually, we haven't heard from her all day. We have been trying to reach her at home but there has been no answer." The lady informed Kayla.

Panic came over me and I decided to leave another message for Justin after the nurse patched me through to his voicemail again.

"Justin, it's urgent and we need to talk. Please contact me as soon as you can." I paused before letting the last few words leave my lips. "I am happy to have you back into my life." I said. I knew it was a lot and it was not like I wanted to be his lover again or anything, okay, maybe I am hoping, but I really just want him to forgive me.

I ran to my car and out of the hospital parking lot to Karen's apartment. My heart started pounding as though it was about to jump from my chest as I approached and saw the crowd. It was barely visible because there was such a commotion around Karen's apartment building. As I neared I slowed down because there was nowhere to drive, cars stacked as though on top of each other and radio and TV vans with anchormen and women setting up their scenes for the evening news.

I couldn't believe my eyes. As I approached I had to fight my way through to onlookers who had their hands covered over their eyes, nose and some of them their mouth. I saw some people regurgitating in side corners from the stench that invaded my senses as I approached. I saw a figure hanging from the window that seemed to be from Karen's apartment but I was still too far away and buried deep into the crowd to tell. As I neared, the disgusting odor became more saturated and I too found myself holding my nose and mouth shut to prevent from losing my breakfast. As I slid through the audience I overheard a conversation between a man and a woman.

"I don't know, heard she just snapped." The woman said shaking her head sadly.

"I thought they said she was just protecting her newborn baby?" The man asked.

"No such thing," another jumped in. "She has no children, she is a sweet quiet girl. Good, never any problems." Another mumbled.

Hearing these things rattled me and I began to shake. I was able to peer above some heads and saw a whole set of police squad cars and flashing lights. There were no sirens but some were hidden behind car doors with guns drawn, while others crawled towards the door and up the stairway.

"What do they intend to do, kill everyone in the building?" One onlooker whispered.

"I just cannot believe this is happening. I have to get myself and my five kids out of this crazy ass neighborhood that's all I know." One woman whimpered.

I kept walking, fighting to get closer to see what or who was hanging from the window. It seemed that the head was falling off and flies and birds swarmed around the dead thing that was blood stained and smelly.

"I cannot believe she threw the dead body out the window. She lost her mind." One stranger said and other started laughing.

"That's right, why would you allow someone to come into your house and attack you. Kill her yes!" The person praised with a Trinidadian accent throwing his hands in the air-making gun shot sounds. There was a police barrier blocking the crowd from going too close to the apartment as the police swat team flashed

their guns and waved sign languages at each other. I was stupefied as the figure hanging from the window became recognizable.
It looked like Sasha. Her long beautiful bouncing hair hanging
down her arm now drenched in blood and clumped together in
glued blood. I choked on the scent and the image of my friend
hanging dead from the apartment of another friend. I wanted to
faint and dropped my hands to my side, my mouth hanging open
in disbelief. I couldn't get any closer and everything around me
became silent. I couldn't hear or see anything but Sasha's dead
body as my scream became lodged in my throat and tears took
on a life of their own washing my face in an attempt to soothe a
pain so powerful that words or tears or time would never erase.

"Put the knife down." Came the warning from the doorway
of Karen's apartment. She had sat in the same position all night
holding the baby Suzette in her arm, rocking her and Suzette did-
n't move. The commotion petrified her and the baby lay traumatized in Karen's arms, looking at the lifeless body of her mother
who defecated on herself.

"Ma'am, please place the knife down on the floor and
release the child." Came the command of the hostage negotiator
they had brought in to reason with Karen who they thought had
taken the baby hostage. But Karen didn't hear them. She was
lost in a world of peaceful tranquility. She just needed to be rid
of Sasha and she too was traumatized, still unaware that Sandra
was dead.

"Listen to me, if you don't put the baby down, they are
going to think you want to hurt her. You really don't want to hurt
the baby do you?" The female negotiator asked, reasoning to the
female maternal drive and instinct she was taught as one means
of connecting with the emotion of a person in a hostage situation.
"The baby might be hurt," the negotiatior whimpered trying to surface emotions of empathy in her voice. "We have a doctor right

here who could take care of her." She said as she waved her hand furiously behind her requesting the man in white coat and a stetescope around his neck to appear for Karen to see. But Karen didn't see, she was lost in thoughts of childhood, walking through a field of roses. She smiled then and the female negotiator thought she was getting through to Karen.

"Yeah, that's it. Everything is okay now. We will just come and take the baby, she is such a beautiful baby." She crooned in mock adoration. Her only focus was on keeping the Special Forces on standb. They were there with guns ready to take this woman down. She tried to crawl to Karen who seemed cognizant, ready to relinquish the child, but the male negotiator pulled her back. He wanted to go. They had worked as partners for years and he knew he was more skilled in getting in and out of a situation where there was this much firepower and anything could happen and go down at any second.

As he crawled towards Karen, she envisioned spiders crawling around and over her. She started to sweep frantically at them. The negotiator jumped, alarmed at her sudden movements and stopped mid way across the floor where he could almost touch Suzette's feet.

"Listen to me, it's okay." The negotiator consoled in an attempt to calm her again. But all Karen heard was Shawn's voice, mocking her. His laugh. She started to laugh too, and gently eased herself away from the baby.

"Yes that's it." The female negotiator instigated. "It's okay, we are going to take very good care of you and your little girl." She reassured.

Karen's hands found the knife sitting next to her and she eased herself from her sitting position to her knees. She could still hear Shawn's voice calling her. She had visuals of him kissing and penetrating Sasha's fornicating flesh, the memory of his hands as it stung across her face and body. She smirked and drool ran down the sides of her mouth like a rabbit dog.

"It's okay Karen, please don't do this." The female nego-tiator begged, still keeping her voice firm and calm, trying not to sound alarmed or to alarm this small woman who didn't seem to hear a word she had said. The police got in fighting stances and shooting positions. They hoisted their guns as she rose to her knees.

"It's safer to stay sitting Karen. I won't come any closer okay. I will stay right here." The male negotiator tried to convince her, but all she heard again was Shawn condescending her. Telling her she didn't have it in her to be strong, that she should just sit by like she had done for years. But she couldn't do that this time. She was strong and she could do anything she want-ed to do.

"Target is on the move, prepare for stand off." Came one swat member's voice over their shared speaker for communica-tion.

More target swat members surrounded the apartment building on the outside and inside at Karen's door, watching in slow motion as she moved slowly in an attempt to stand taking the bloodied butcher's knife with her, angling it dangerously to finally teach Shawn a lesson about women.

"Release the knife ma'am or we will have to shoot." Came another warning and Karen slumped down, fatigue and depres-sion surging through her. She couldn't understand why there were so many voices in her head, so many people yelling at her. *Why was Shawn there? Wasn't he supposed to be in prison?* She wondered while looking around her, trying to comprehend the commotion that was making her head pound. The noises and voices she couldn't decipher.

"Good, that's it Karen," consoled the female negotiator, "just relax, it's going to be alright now. It's all going to be alright." She smiled and the male negotiator kept crawling closer to

Karen, closer to the baby who only looked on in terror, no sound escaping her lips.

The male negotiator reached up, and Karen saw what she thought was Shawn's arm ready to smack her down again. Karen found renewed strength and vigor and before anyone realized what she was about to do, she raised the knife high above her head and an ear-piercing shriek like a banshee forced everyone to cover their ears from the inside of the apartment to outside where the police squads were on stand by to raid the apartment at any given moment.

Her scream brought her strength and she lunged at the male negotiator getting the knife split center in the palm of his hands and in the very same instant, the order to fire upon the target was given. The swat team opened fire and released uncountable rounds of ammunition into Karen's midsection, chest and abdomen sending her flying out of the window on top of the surrounding cop cars that were parked in front of the apartment building.

I was fixated by the image of Sasha hanging from Karen's window and a million questions went through my mind, shock and fear caused me to panic and I knew I had to call somebody. I pressed the automatic dial on my phone for Charmaine's number.

"What's wrong Kayla, what is it?" Charmaine asked me sounding a bit annoyed that I just kept crying and breathing on the phone.

"Kayla, listen. I cannot help you if you don't talk to me." She sounded exasperated but I couldn't help the emptiness that I felt inside of me.

"Its Sasha, she's, she's. Oh my God." I yelled in the phone and doubled over as the thoughts reverberated though my mind and I couldn't get myself to say the words.

"She's WHAT?" Charmaine squealed. "Would you just

spit it out already?" She demanded. I couldn't stop crying now that the tears were coming, "She's dead, oh God she's dead Charmaine, she hanging out of Karen's window…police, my God, I don't know." I wailed into the phone before it dropped to the floor and I fainted.

"Hello? Kayla are you there" Charmaine wailed as the sting of tears blinded her eyes. She grabbed her purse and headed to Karen's apartment.

Chapter 28

After calling Joshua's family and talking to them, Justin kissed a distraught Chyna and told her that he would see her soon, that he loved her and that he was happy to have her in his life. She had parked right outside and he was already late for work. He had to check in on Justin Stevenson, the young boy who was left fighting for his life.

Justin got in his car and headed for the hospital wearily, he didn't want to go in today, but he needed to clear his desk for a couple weeks bereavement and get to Joshua's funeral. On his way to the office the triage nurse stopped him to pass a note to him that Dr. Calvin McKinley had left asking for his immediate response and attention. His heart found wings and flew at his chest like a ton of bricks. He needed to get to the boy but he had been moved. He rushed back to the triage nurse desk.

"Cathy, where did they move the boy to?" He asked hurriedly in a tone that the nurses were not used to. They all lifted their heads flabbergast at his disposition.

"Oh, they moved him to recovery."

"Recovery, what do you mean recovery?" The annoyance and irritation in his voice evident and threw the new nurse Cathy aback.

"I'm sorry Dr. Etnas, they found a match and wanted to act quickly, he had an emergency bone marrow transplant last night and he and his donor are doing really great." She told him offsetting the concern he exudes for the boy's life. The smile that broke out on Justin Etnas's face was that of a father for a son. He harbored feelings for this boy beyond his comprehension.

He took the stairs in twos to the West Wing building where the cancer research and operations were administered and rushed to the recovery ward; Dr. Calvin McKinley who met him greeted him with a fatherly embrace.

"I tried to reach you Justin, but you were indisposed eh?" He winked knowingly. "Sorry your personal assistant Christina filled me in on your new recreation. Which is truly overdue. It's good to have a woman in your life. Sometimes they cause unnecessary distraction, and sometimes the distraction they are from life's pains are what makes them perfect." He said and landed his right arm on Justin Etnas's shoulder as they walked to the room where Justin Stevenson-Barker lay side by side with his mother in every way that was important, Edna Barker. Dr. Justin Etnas lost all composure at the sight and pulled Dr. McKinley next to him, embracing him thankfully for helping him to save the boy. This was definitely news he needed, something positive to uplift the cloud of sadness of losing his friend.

"This is great news. How did it happen?"

"The boy went into cardiac arrest and it was starting to look gleam that we would ever find someone that we knew for sure would be an identical match. His foster mother wouldn't have it. She demanded that she tried, that she be tested."

"What? How? That's almost impossible."

"Yes, but I guess with faith and love, anything is possible. She couldn't stand to see this boy die. He gave her new life and everything about her was because he lived. She wanted to be sure that she did everything she could. We were also shocked and pleasantly amazed when the match came back. Once we had the boy stabilized we performed the surgery and from all likely prospective, see to be a success." Dr. McKinley brought Dr. Etnas up to speed on the miraculous story of a mother's love that came from the heart and not from genetics.

"Thanks Calvin. Thank you." Justin told him in a steadfast handshake as the gloom of his friend returned.

"Calvin, I must take some time off. I lost a dear friend and I must go see to his family."

"I am truly sorry to hear that Justin. Take care of yourself and not to worry about the boy. He is in good hands and I will keep you posted on his progress."

"That's all I ask Sir, I will be in touch frequently and will stop in from time to time as well." Justin told him and took one more look at the pair laying peacefully at rest as their bodies acclimated themselves to the new life that they would both live together.

Justin walked away with mixed feelings of sadness and joy in his heart. So ironic that the boy's foster mother was right under their nose all this time and was a perfect match and no one thought to test her. *Why was it so important to find a biological parent?* Justin thought to himself but brushed it off. If he were to start thinking that he was being so unprofessional that he lost sight of medical procedure, he would also have to admit that his presence did nothing but aided in the boy almost losing his life. He brushed the thought away and rejoiced in the good that had now come to light, he must get to his office.

Closing the door behind him, Justin sat at his office desk and flicked on the lamp. He didn't bother to turn on the illuminated office overhead light, as he wanted it to remain semi dark. He placed his hands to cover his face and then rubbed his eyes that were filled with fatigue and grief. Taking a deep sigh, he looked at his desk and saw that there was a bundle of mail in his inbox.

He flipped through the regular stuff about conferences, insurance mumbo jumbo and follow-up charts for patients who were coming due on their pregnancy terms.

There amongst them was a package from Joshua's aunt. He picked it up sheepishly and examined the package. It didn't feel fragile or too heavy, felt more like a book. He tentatively ripped the package opened that was overnight delivered to his office. *It must have arrived this morning*, he thought as the shedding came undone and the interior was revealed. It was a nicely embossed gold book with a clasp on it. The engraving was raised from the surfaced and titled **JOSHUA'S JOSHED** in bold letters. Justin shook his head and snickered, running his fingers over the words one letter at a time as though it would breathe life into it.

"Joshua's joshed." He snickered again and then started to laugh. This was his sacred tease journal that he wouldn't let him see all those years. What his friend called a dangerous combination of his little black book and his practical jokes and thoughts combined. He couldn't believe he had finally gotten his hands on it.

Justin hung his head again as the thoughts of the circumstances again overwhelmed him. He would have liked to go through this with his friend. He laughed at what Joshua considered opportunity to josh. But he knew had Joshua been alive he would live his days wondering what was in that book. Joshua swore that no one would see the contents except him and God.

Justin placed the book on his desk and fondled the note that was attached to it. It was Joshua's mother's penmanship.

Justin, my son adored you. In his entire life I have never known him to relish in the joy of anyone's friendship as he did with you. I was going to read this book, but as I opened it the first inscription was that if he was not the one reading those pages, it should be read through the eyes of his only brother...it was your name signed next to this. I thought if my son felt so strongly about this in life, then in death, he would want you to have it. Please carry my son's soul with you and let his eyes see through your life.

Justin began to cry then. Tears rolling like water balls down his cheeks and onto the note that was so carefully penned. He stood up and penetrated the wall with his fists. His punch left the imprint of his hand in the sheet rock wall and blood flowed from his knuckles, but he did not feel or see it. He banged on the wall and threw himself in the corner of the office, falling to his buttocks with his face covered by his hands as the pain and reality of death of his friend seeped into his mind.

He stayed there for a good half hour before getting up and pulling himself together. Gathering his things he changed the message on his voicemail, Justin dumped the journal into his backpack with all his other important documents and files to be reviewed while he was gone and walked out of the office. As he scantily waved goodbye to the triage nurses and followed the path to the exit where he was parked he was stopped by the news report that mentioned what he thought was Karen's name. He stopped briefly to see the image of the woman who introduced herself to him only days ago as an attorney hanging from the building where he dropped Karen home. His heart stopped and his eyes squeezed shut in hopes of blocking out the image of what he saw. He turned and walked away. This was all surreal. All this was not happening, just a really bad nightmare he needed to be awake from.

****

When Chyna walked into her hotel suite she knew something was wrong. It was getting late in the afternoon and there was music coming from Delia's adjoining suite next door. Last she saw Delia she was packed to be gone for a while. Delia didn't think she noticed, but she didn't want to spoil her friend's fun.

She dropped her purse on the bed and walked to the adjoining door, which was slightly opened and saw Delia lying on her bed. Her body heaving as she cried deeply and took breaths that caught in her nasal making her wheeze.

Chyna walked towards the bed and sat down. When Delia felt the pressure of her friend next to her, a fresh burst of tears enveloped her and she moved closer to Chyna, placing her head in her lap and allowing the tears to just flow.

"Oh Delia what happened? Why are you crying?" Chyna asked brushing her friends full head of hair from her face what was sweat drenched and teary.

"Chyna." She whispered her friends name and said nothing more; the memory of the humiliation she felt came to her mind with renewed life.

"Delia please talk to me, what happened." Chyna couldn't imagine why her friend could be crying like this. Lying there in solitude, her face drained of life and glow, her voiced mimed to being barely audible. She was beginning to feel anxious and frustrated with her thoughts and attempts to guess what was going on in Delia's head and being unsuccessful.

"Listen, sit up and tell me what happened. I cannot just sit here and watch you bawl your eyes out and you not say anything." She demanded pushing Delia into a sitting position and brushing away her hair and tears from her eyes so she could look upon her friends' face.

Delia shook her head remorsefully.

"I am ready to go home now Chyna. Can we leave right now?" Delia managed to say. The surprised look on Chyna's face brought her eyebrows together into a uni-brow and she wrinkled her nose as she broke out into nervous laughter.

"What do you mean go home? Only yesterday you were begging me to say." She reminded Delia but she didn't want to hear that.

"I want to go home Chyna and I am going with or without you." She whimpered.

"Delia you can't be serious. You asked me to stay when I wanted to go and I did because you are my friend and we came here together. But you cannot just demand that I up and leave now that I want to stay without even offering me an explanation." Chyna was standing now, pacing the floor as she spoke, her hands flying every which way and thoughts of Justin running through her head. No, she didn't mean to fall in love, but here she was, happy. Finally happy with someone who felt exactly the same way about her, and Delia wanted to selfishly take that away from her.

"Why does this have to be about you? We are best friends and we have suffered and survived through thick and thin. Why do you need a reason to be there for me?" Delia bellowed, anger replacing the humiliation that held her captive for hours since the vivid replay of a love scene that should have terrorized her mind and her senses.

"I don't need a reason to be there for you Delia."

"Then why don't you just go pack your stuff and we will clear our tab and go?"

"Because it's not that easy Delia. There is something more for me here. I need to stay and see it through. And from what I remember, so do you."

"There is nothing for me here Chyna. Absolutely nothing."

"Well that's new because yesterday you were packing your hoogie-boodie call bag and I was nowhere on your mind." Chyna cursed.

"Oh so it's like that now? You are calling me a whore?"

"Delia it's nothing like that and you know it. I am just try-ing to say that we were both happy with possible prospects that might convince us that remaining here in the States and conducting our business from here would be ideal. What about that house we were looking at near that girl you don't like, that lawyer girl? You liked the Hampton." Chyna tried to remind her but it only infuriated Delia."

"Don't talk to me about that bitch okay. This is about you and me and if you are trying to tell me that you don't want to be my friend anymore then fine, and if you want to stay here and fuck up your life then fine. It's amazing how some people get some dick and suddenly they lose their fucking minds." Delia attached and stormed into her bathroom slamming the door behind her.

"Don't you go walking away from me Delia, because last I checked you were looking to get laid too, and don't think I don't know you wanted to fuck that dike." Chyna fumed.

Delia did not respond. She sat quietly on the floor crying.

"Listen Dee, this is ridiculous. Why are we fighting? You are my best friend and I love you."

"You don't love me Chyna, you don't need me anymore." Chyna listened to Delia and realized that her friend must be in some deep pain. She allowed her body to fall against the bathroom door and sitting back to back with Delia and hung her head between her knees.

"I do need you Delia."

"No you don't, because I need you now and you would prefer to just ignore me."

"I know you know that's not true. Delia you are closer to me than a sister. I would do almost anything for you. But be fair. You just demanded that I get up and leave and offered me no explanation whatsoever. What kind of way is that to treat a friend?" Chyna asked her meekly, trying to speak to her friend without upsetting her.

"You shouldn't need a reason Chyna." Delia moaned.

"Yes I do need a reason. You need to tell my why you are behaving this way and attacking me when I did nothing to you."

"See that's what I mean. We have been here only a couple months already and you have changed Chyna. You just don't need me anymore."

"I do need you Delia. I need your friendship and lifelong companionship. I need you to be the maid of honor at my wedding and the godmother to my babies. I need you to cry with me as I have cried with you. But you cannot expect me not to change. We both have changed and for the better. I love you and the woman you are and will continue to evolve into. We have shared things that only you and I will ever know."

Delia stopped sniffling and allowed her head to fall against the door. Slipping back into the recent past of the memory of her taking advantage of her friend's availability to her. How she was so horny that she had pressed her body and her fingers into Chyna's vagina bringing them both carnal pleasures that they had yet to speak of. She knew that's why her friend hinted to but would not say.

Slowly, Delia opened the door and allowed Chyna to go in. They sat there embracing each other for a while until Delia's tears subsided. It was then that Delia confided in Chyna the pain that had caused her to want to escape home to Jamaica once again.

"No Delia. Not this time." Chyna said. "I won't run away again and I wont allow you to either. This time when we return it should be on our terms, just like we came here on our own teams. I will not let anyone, for love or other wise chase us from a place that we love and want to be.

"I thought I was strong. I thought I could do this but I cannot."

"Yes you can. You can and you will. She cannot be another Michael Branson. This time you must confront the situation head on and deal with it. Don't let this be a secret that eats your heart out forever, taking your life sources with it. You have to fight. You cannot let these people control your life and I cannot walk away before seeing this through.

"I know Chyna. You are right."

"Of course I am right."

"Who got your back?" Chyna asked

"My girl Chyna…." Delia sang

"And who's got your back?" Delia echoed

"My sister Delia…." Chyna sang and they hugged again. Laughing. Lighting up the bathroom with their smiles and pulling each other to a standing position.

****

Justin got into his car and sped away from the hospital and to Karen's apartment where he found Charmaine and Kayla. Although it was already almost eight in the evening the sun had not yet set in the hot August day. Sasha's body was no longer there hanging from the window and the crowd had diminished. Blood stains still tarnished the window walls and grounds in the surrounding area from where Sasha hung.

The police car that Karen fell on as she dropped from the same window was smashed in and the windshield window was shattered as well. Blood splattered everywhere and ran down the sides of the police car in little trails to the street asphalt.

The media was clustered in around someone like fiends for information and details on the killings. They had trucks, microphones and antennas everywhere. He couldn't hear any response from whomever they were blaring questions at. He searched to see if he could find Karen or anyone of her friends, but didn't.

Justin decided to walk over to the crowd and peer in at who was giving the interview. When he noticed a distraught Kayla sitting on the street floor with her hands over her head and Charmaine hovering over her, protecting her from the vultures that wouldn't leave them alone, he forced his way through to them.

"Can't you people see that they are in no shape to answer any of your questions?" He blurted out.

"Sir, are you familiar with these people?"

"Do you know why Karen Grace went ballistic and murdered her best friend?" Came another question.

That question took him off guard. Karen's name again. Murdered! The thought almost paralyzed him.

"This is not the time. Excuse me." He told them.

When I realized who it was, I ran to and threw my arms around Justin's neck. I knew he would be there. Justin was always there when I needed him the most.

"Come on, let's get out of here." He ushered them through the crowd and to their cars.

"Hey are you okay?" He asked Charmaine and she waved, quietly standing by her car not yet finding the strength to leave.

"Wait a minute, you were the one with Chyna and her friend the day we met." He recollected and Charmaine shook her head up and down in confirmation, while Kayla buried her face into his chest and clung to him as closely as possible, all three of them filled with anguish and pain.

"I am really sorry about your friends."

"They are gone Justin. All three of them were taken out of here and to the morgue. The department of social services took Sandra's children away. They wouldn't even let us look at them or talk to them." I told him, my voiced caught in my throat and I couldn't say anything else.

"Oh my God, I am so sorry Kayla." Justin told her. His own pain still clung to his mind and heart. "Is there anything that I can do? Anything at all." He looked at Charmaine but she didn't respond or look at him. She remained sedated, almost tranquilized and fixated to the spot she stood when she shook his hand.

"Listen, you guys have to get out of here or they are going to come at you again with questions." He warned them, prying Kayla from him and ushering her into her car. He watched as they pulled off slowly and the media that tried to follow them. When they realized that they were gone they turned to Justin. He ignored them and walked briskly back to his car and sped away.

Justin drove to his apartment and sat at the doorway quietly, contemplating the catastrophe of the day's events. He dropped his backpack to the floor at the foyer and allowed sleep to take him over, but sleep offered him no solace as he dreamed heavily about Joshua and why he wanted to meet with him a couple weeks earlier, that Joshua was handing him his journal. Guilt riddled his subconscious with images of Karen walking away into her apartment building. Thoughts that maybe he shouldn't have left her. He knew something was wrong, that she needed help. He sensed it, but his own desires pressed him forward and now lives were lost because of it.

It was midnight when he awoke, his shirt ripped to pieces and he was sprawled out on the wooden floor in front of his doorway.

Justin stood up and grabbed his bag. He pulled Joshua's journal from the pack and walked to his sofa. He turned on the lamp on the night stand to illuminate the dark room and sat down, once again tracing the embossed titled signature on the front cover. He opened it, and it was dawn when he was finished reading. Justin read the journal from cover to cover. There were things he remembered as those memories were

shared with him, and things that made him laugh and cry. When
he read about the affair between his best friend and Kayla, he
was already numb. He didn't know what to feel, and in light of all
that had happened, he didn't know if it mattered anymore. It had
hurt him deeply that Kayla had left, and it has been eight years.
He didn't expect to see her again and he had and was now able
to put it all behind him. The possibilities of the love he had now
found with Chyna brought him healing power to help him let go.

He put the book back in his bag and was finally able to
sleep, but before he did, there was something he had to do. He
waited for the phone to ring and no one answered. When the
voicemail picked up he swallowed hard and left a message.

"Hey Kay, it's me Justin. I am really sorry about what happened with your friend. I am also calling because I got something
in the mail that Joshua's mother sent to me. You remember that
lady? She is truly and wonderful woman. Anyway, not to ramble
but I wanted you to have it now. So whenever you get a chance,
please give me a call or stop by the hospital. Thanks, goodnight."

With that, sleep came easily and Justin slept until one in
the afternoon on Thursday waking only to go and use the bathroom and returning back to bed and staying there the entire
weekend. He shut off his phones, turned out the lights, closed
the blinds and pulled the covers over his head and let depression
seep into his soul.

Chapter 29

That Monday the Hospital was a buzz with the news of the story of the triple killing. They couldn't believe that the sweet girl who took in her friend with AIDS and her children could have killed anyone. They speculated that something must have happened to push her over the edge.

Everyone gathered around Francine, the visiting nurse who was taking care of Sandra when she found out that she had been granted an extension on life.

"You are so lucky you left when you did." The nurses told her as they sat back and listened to her gossiping stories about the conversation she overheard. How Karen was upset when she came home that night. How Sandra tried to talk to her and told her secret things about Sasha.

"Nooooo!" whispered one of the nurses who listened, while everyone remained captivated by a now popular Francine whom everyone hated before because of her gossiping. Now they rallied around her as her stories told more than the news did.

"Yes," she reassured, "Sandra, the one with the kids told Karen that Sasha got knocked up by some drug lord or the mafia or something. That she got admitted to some psychiatric center and never told anybody that she had a son." She told them as they encouraged her to press on.

Dr. McKinley was walking by and over heard the story as Francine spoke of a child that was born under the same circumstances that was in the records of his young patient.

"Excuse me. Pardon me." He told them as he entered the center of the crowd where Francine was being pampered hand and foot for dishing out the juicy details.

"Francine may I see you in my office please." He told her and was almost down the hall before he turned around. "Don't you all have work to do?" He asked and they all scrambled back to their assigned and designated areas in the hospital. "As for you Francine. I meant right now." He commanded and continued down the corridor to his office.

"Yes sir." She responded and hopped to her feet and followed suit. Closing the door behind her he motioned for her to take a seat at his desk and he went and lounged in the lavish recliner on the opposing end.

"Francine, do you realize that you can be fired for what you just did?"

"I am sorry Dr. McKinley, it's just that I feel like I narrowly escaped with my life. I have done over night visits there before. What if that had been one of those nights?" she exclaimed.

"Granted, but this is a police matter. Have you been questioned by the police yet?" He quizzed.

"Yes doctor."

"Good, now why don't you tell me everything you know, then I want you to pack your bags and leave. Take a month vacation, half with pay and keep your trap shut." He told her.

When Francine left his office he was stumped and at a loss for words, everything that she said, if there was any true merit to it, could cause problems for the hospital, endorsing a sick patient to go home with a friend and the department of child protective services allowed the children to go based on the hospital's recommendation. This could cause some irreparable damages for the hospital and he needed to get this under wraps soon.

But there was something about the story of the lawyer friend that ticked off Karen. That's the same lawyer representing Edna Barker and her foster son. And then the child's record, this couldn't be possible.

"Police department."

"Hello, my name is Dr. McKinley here at Interfaith Hospital. I am calling about a Ms. Sasha Henderson who was killed last week."

"Yes Doctor what can we do for you?"

"I have a patient here, a young boy who was given up for adoption at birth that I have reason to believe is her son. I would like to know where I would have to go to get permission for a DNA test?"

"That's not a problem sir. I will patch you through to the appropriate office and they will give you details on the procedure."

"Thanks." Dr. McKinley told him and waited to be transferred. When he hung up the phone he was so excited he could barely sit still.

Delia decided she should go back and confront Charmaine, let her know that she was there and what she saw, so when Charmaine called her to find out why she didn't show up she was happy.

"How about I come over and discuss that with you Charmaine?" She suggested, and Charmaine was more than happy to accommodate her. She would try and use this opportunity to seduce Delia and make her the woman of her dreams.

"Okay Delia, I will be waiting for you."

"Yes Charmaine, I am sure you will." Delia uttered sarcastically and hung up the phone. Charmaine had never heard that tone in her voice before so she was uncertain as to what was going on.

Delia pulled up to the front door with Chyna in the driver's seat of the Acura, she didn't feel like driving. She hopped out of the car and rang Charmaine's doorbell.

"Delia I am so happy to see you." Charmaine grabbed Delia, pulling her to her body and squeezing her tightly. "You have no idea what I have been through these past days.

Feeling Charmaine against her body brought back a familiar heat between Delia's thighs that made her want to melt in Charmaine's arms. But she couldn't. The pain in her heart ached and tripled over as she thought of the lies that Charmaine would tell. Delia wasn't going to ask her what she'd been through, she didn't want to know, she came there for one purpose and one purpose only.

"Listen Charmaine, about the other day when we had plans. I am sorry I didn't show up." Delia lied, she wanted to know if she would tell her.

"You didn't, why?" Charmaine inquired.

"Why don't you tell me Charmaine?" Delia solicited.

"Listen Delia, there is something I have to tell you. About that day, I really put a lot into your visit. I had planned a really special evening for us."

Before the words were finished from Charmaine's mouth Delia slapped her. She couldn't help the rage that she felt after what she saw transpired between Charmaine and some white woman on her so called special plans for them.

"Why did you do that?" Charmaine asked, shocked and bewildered

"Because you are a liar Charmaine. You are a liar and a cheat and a fucking whore." Delia told her calmly between clenched teeth.

"I saw you here, that day that you begged me to come over. I came here like a fool ready to give you my heart and my body, and what did you do, you fucked some woman right under my nose, to my favorite song. How could you Charmaine? And then have the nerve to act as though you have been missing me." Delia spat.

Charmaine didn't know what to say, tears stung her eyes and she held her cheek with Delia's fingers still imprinted on it.

"Well aren't you going to say something?" Delia asked, but Charmaine just stared at her. Longing and disappointment swelled her heart. She had lost her.

When Charmaine said nothing, Delia turned to walk away.

"Delia wait. I don't blame you for being mad at me. But something has happened."

"I know something happened Charmaine."

"Not that's not what I meant. I mean something really horrible happened." And Charmaine's voice began to tremble; the confidence and arrogance that would make Delia shudder with desire now drained from it.

"Do you think that what happened was just a walk in the park for me? That my heart does not feel as though it has been ripped from my ribs and thrown to the dogs?" Delia fumed, the persistence of Charmaine trying to annoy her fanning the flames of her broken heart.

"You see Delia, my friends. Sasha, she's dead. Its, its really bad Delia, it gets so much worst. These things really horrible Delia, I just need you right now. Please Delia."

"Charmaine, you see, you don't understand." Delia began with her voice as calm as a steady wind and as powerful as surfing wave. "Your somethings are no longer my business." She differed without turning around, and walked back to the car wear Chyna waited. A sense of victory surged through her giving her momentary relief from the hurt she had witnessed when she walked in on Charmaine and the other woman.

"You okay?" Came the question with the turning of the key firing up the engine and the changing of gear as Chyna pulled off slowly allowing Charmaine to absorb the vision of Delia's tail moving away.

"I am okay Chyna." Was all she responded and said nothing more until they were safely back in their hotel suite, quietly contemplating the day's events and their next move. While Chyna gorged her body with steamy hot water from the shower, wondering how she could tell her friend that she was not ready to return home to Jamaica, tears of joy mixed with sorrow found way to her heart and blended with the water that cleansed and washed her clean.

She didn't hear when Delia opened the door that was already partially ajar and sat on the toilet seat. The sliding glass door that separated them was frosted with steam from the shower and Chyna's head was saturated with water as it dripped down her smooth skin, over her perky palm sized mounds and down her back, posterior and into the tub where it drained away the dirt and pain from her.

"Chyna, I have come to a decision." Chyna's heart stopped because when Delia had come to a decision it was done. There would be neither discussions nor negotiations. So she stood still, her arms wrapped around her thin frame holding her shoulders as she waited for Delia to continue.

"That house we talked about, the one in the Hamptons. I am going out now to purchase it so I will not be here when you get done with your shower. I will stay here with you and you can stay with me as long as you want to. I am ready to spread my wings and not be afraid anymore. We have worked hard to reclaim ourselves from years ago when we were young and easily manipulated. We are not those people anymore." She continued almost as though she was just echoing her thoughts, releasing them out into the world so they could take root.

"What changed your mind?"

"We are best friends Chyna. You know things about me that I wouldn't dare utter and still you love me. You deserve to find happiness and explore the possibilities that you have found here. It's what I would have done. I don't want to leave you and have you make rushed and hurried decisions based on circum-stances. We are by far not needy. If things work out with you and your doctor friend, I want to be there for you, and I will be happy for you."

Chyna's mind reeled from this and she was so happily stunned, the two remained without words until Chyna broke the silence.

"What about Jamaica, our business?" Delia laughed then, her voice reverberating through the bathroom walls and bouncing through Chyna's suite.

"You are kidding right?" came the rhetorical question to Chyna.

"Oh come on Dee, you know what I mean." The glee in Chyna's voice evident.

"We have employers, accountants, secretaries, executive staff members. We don't need to be there. And the same way we managed and ran our business from Jamaica, we can do the same thing from here, or anywhere else in the world if we so choose."

"Is this really your final decision Delia?" Chyna asked again, not believing her ears or her luck and blessings. "You would do this for me?"

"In a heartbeat." Was Delia's response and then she was out the door to put their discussions into action.

****

"Dr. McKinley, the DNA test results for Justin Stevenson-Barker and Sasha Henderson have returned," said the voice on the telephone intercom as Dr. McKinley sat patiently Wednesday morning waiting, trying to kill time as to not allow his nerves to kill him.

"Thank you Christina. Did you contact Dr. Justin Etnas regarding this matter yet?"

"Sir you did not ask me to."

"No, no, that's fine Christina. I didn't want you to. Thank you. Could you please bring it to my office in the cancer research wing?"

"Okay Doctor." She told him and disconnected their conversation. Doctor Calvin McKinley couldn't contain his excitement. He didn't want to alarm Dr. Etnas needlessly knowing how much he had invested in this child. Why? He didn't know, but he was drawn to help him. Dr. Etnas reminded him of himself when he was younger, before the passion for medicine and the love for what he did got stolen from him through the medical bureaucratic crap and ungrateful medical recipients. He didn't want this doctor's love to die. He wanted to nurture whatever it was that gave life to him and his passion for helping people.

He tapped his fingers, toes, threw paper balls at his garbage pail during what seemed like an eternal wait while Christina hand delivered the document to him. The rapping at his office door startled him momentarily as he composed himself to review the paperwork.

"Doctor, I have brought you those results." Christina announced.

"Come in Christina." He welcomed her. Dr. McKinley liked Christina, her enthusiasm and vigor energized him. Nurses' assistants were as vital to a good doctor as his stethoscope. He could tell that she was a small town girl who may have had some hang-ups working with a black superior, but he knew that if anyone could make her snap out of it, it would be Dr. Etnas. He being an elderly white doctor he knew what it felt like to be god-fathered into certain situations where a black equally qualified doctor would not. He was happy he was called in on this case and had met the people who gave it a heartbeat.

"Sit down Christina. I am going to need your assistance if this is what I think it is." He told her with a smile, and then pro-ceeded to open the package. His hands trembled as he read the positive results. There was 99.999999 percent accuracy that the deceased lawyer, Sasha Henderson was in fact the mother of this boy.

"Christina," Dr. McKinley said her name deliberately and slowly, "I need you to get Dr. Etnas on the phone immediately. This concerns him." He told her, and she jumped from his pres-ence and left the office. Dr. McKinley's curiosity as to why Justin Etnas was so consumed with the boy had gotten the better of him. He tracked the child's record as far back as it could go and also tracked Justin Etna's rise as one of Interfaith Hospitals lead-ing gynecologists. What the papers didn't say he put together. He knew that this was going to be a lot for the young doctor hav-ing just lost a friend recently. But this was not the kind of situa-tion you could sit on until later, sensitive yes, but he had to move right away.

Justin sat on his sofa that Wednesday morning with the blinds still closed, still in his pajamas and feeling a little groggy. He knew he couldn't stay in bed forever, Chyna had probably been waiting to hear from him and he needed to still take care of some unfinished business with Kayla so he could move on.

He saw that the voicemail on his phone was blinking furi-ously. The fact that he turned off his phones disabled it from ring-ing, giving him peace. Anita Baker's soulful voice filled him and gave him focus.

Suddenly realizing that life was passing him by and there were things to do, Justin shook his head and stretched out his muscular frame. Jumping to his feet, he walked briskly to the windows and started to open all the blinds and drapes, allowing life to seep into him with the sunshine.

He walked to his kitchen bar table and plugged everything back in, turning up the volume and flipping the television on to CNN, while simultaneously turning off the CD. He pressed the voicemail button and heard that Kayla had called, so did Chyna, Joshua's mother wanted to know if he had received the package and finally, Christina, whom he had told not to call or page him unless it was an emergency. He decided he wouldn't bother returning the hospital's call because he would be going in to check on his patients and the doctor that was covering for him while he took his leave.

He couldn't imagine why his assistant would call but he figured he would find that out sooner or later. He picked up the phone and left a message asking Kayla to meet him for lunch at the hospital so she can pick up the package and then he dialed Chyna's number.

"Hello," Chyna answered exuberantly.

"Hello sweetheart, how are you?"

"Justin!" She squealed. "Where have you been? Is everything okay?" She asked him excitedly. Hearing his voice was just icing on the cake after her conversation with Delia earlier.

"I am better now my love. Now that I have heard your voice." There was a pause and Justin's voice trailed off.

"Chyna, remember Karen? The girl I had lunch with at the mall?"

"Yes, of course I do, she was a wonderful person."

"Chyna, something horrible has happened."

"Okay Justin, you are starting to really scare me now. What is it?"

"I really don't want to be the one to be telling you this, and I was hoping that by now you would have seen or heard something on the news or maybe from your friend, but you don't seem to know." He delayed telling her, trying to find the words and wondering if he should or even if he should be the one giving her this information.

"Love, I really wish you would just tell me. I haven't seen the news or watched television at all. I have been preoccupied with my friend among other things. Please tell me what's going on Justin."

"Well, that young lady Karen died last week."

"I don't believe it. Are you sure?" Chyna asked gasping with her right palm over her mouth as if to stop the news from entering her psyche.

"Chyna are you okay?" Do you need me to come over there?"

"No I am okay Justin, what happened to her?"

"Well, I am still not sure of all the details. I am really just re-entering the world of the living right now so I haven't been caught up to speed yet. However, the most horrific thing about this is, remember that girl everyone was talking about? The lawyer Sasha?"

"Yes I remember, what does she have to do with this?"

"Well, they say that Karen killed her."

"You have got to be kidding me. Karen? That girl we met, she could not hurt a fly."

"Well, that's what I said, but that's where the story seems to be going. I am not sure how the whole thing is playing out but this is what I have so far." He told her, the painful memories of the past few days taking a hold of him once more and choking him up.

"Justin, can I see you today?" Chyna asked, concern and worry plummeting through her. Delia was okay and the decision had been made. She needed to be with Justin.

"Well, I am supposed to go check in at the hospital and meet up with someone, but..."

"Forget it Justin, I am sorry, I didn't mean to pry or let you feel like was imposing myself on you." Chyna told him knowing full well that jealously and the thought of being rejected by him was manipulating her ego and that she was acting irrational.

"Chyna no, it's not what you are thinking. I would love to see you. I just didn't want to drag you through my day. Listen, why don't you meet me at the hospital? I am heading out in a few minutes and when you get there, we will maneuver though my mundane duties and errands together. How does that sound?" Clearly cheered up and appreciative of Justin's intuition and sensitivity to her, she blew him a big kiss over the phone.

"That sounds absolutely wonderful to me." The smile on her face stretched from ear to ear and the bubbling joy in her voice energized Justin through the receiver and making him look forward to the day.

"Great. So let me get going and I will see you soon then."

"Okay Justin, I will see you at the hospital."

"I love you Chyna." Justin's words caught her off guard and stunned her for a moment. Her fist held on to the receiver and her knuckles turned white from holding it so tight. Justin was also taken by surprise as the words escaped his lips and it was too late for him to stop them. But once they were out he smiled. His heart was filled with new promise and hope and he waited for Chyna to respond. He wasn't afraid of love this time and he knew this love, this woman was different. He knew that Chyna was the right one.

She tried to get the loud banging in her chest to quiet so she could hear herself breathe. She couldn't believe what she heard. Could it be that love had finally come to her?

"What was it that you just said?"

"I-love-you Chyna." He told her slowly, dropping his voice a couple of octaves and romantically saying her name so she knew that what he said was no mistake and that he was by no means ashamed of it or wanted to take it back."

"Really?" She asked

"Yes Chyna, I am in love with you. I just have a few loose ends to tie up now so I can show you." He told her.

"I love you as well Dr. Justin Etnas." She said slowly at first. But once the words were out of her mouth they sounded so beautiful, like music.

"Yes, yes, yes, yes!" She screamed removing the phone from her ear and spinning around in a girl like fashion. "I LOVE YOU." She said again out loud and this time, Justin laughed. For the first time in days he heard his voice rise up from the bottom of his toes to his abdomen, he felt it marinated and surge through his vocal cords, ripping at his heart and mind and resounding through his home. It was a powerful happy laugh that only Chyna could invoke.

"Okay, so let's get moving. We have a lot to do." Justin reminded her.

"Okay then, I will see you soon." She told him and hung up the phone.

As Justin walked into the hospital, he saw an impatient Dr. Calvin McKinley walking back and forth pacing the hallway in anticipation of Justin's arrival.

"Justin, what took you so long? Didn't you get the page from the hospital?"

"Yes I did, but I knew I was on my way in so I waited. What's wrong? Is there one of my patients in labor that hasn't gone full term?"

"No, it's nothing like that."

"What is it McKinley, is it the boy? Ms. Barker? Are they

okay?" Justin rattled off questions in deep concern for what may have happened while he was away.

"Let's go into your office Justin, I have some news." Dr. McKinley told him and led him by the elbow to Justin nearby office.

"Justin, a couple days ago something hit me, information about this murder drama that's all over the media waves right now and the connection to the boy Justin Stevenson who is fostered by Edna Barker. Now I don't want you to get upset because I did some prying. I found the mother of your young patient."

"What are you saying? Is she here I want to see her." Justin jumped to his feet and moved towards the door.

"No it's not that simple. You see, the mother of that boy is dead, and you knew who she was." Dr. McKinley told him. He wanted to just blurt the whole thing out but he wanted to give Justin time to absorb the information one piece at a time.

"What do you mean I knew her, if I knew who she was we would have saved the boy from all the unnecessary pain he endured." Justin snapped, the thought that this doctor was implying that he did nothing when he could have done something all along.

"Sit down Justin, that's not what I mean. You knew her but you did not know that she was the boy's mother. Do you remember, Sasha Henderson Esq.? The lawyer handling the State vs. Barker case?"

"That doesn't make sense. That woman had no children." Justin bellowed

"Yes she did. She is the Jane Doe from your first year at Rochester Psyche ward as a gynecologist. She was the one who gave birth to the boy and gave him up for adoption. It was her all along, right under our nose." The excitement and adrenaline rush that Dr. McKinley got from finally being able to share this news was phenomenal. He was drenched in perspiration and his nerves were sensitive to every touch.

"You cannot be serious." Was all Justin could say, the memory of that day he met her. Their conversation, the feelings of closeness he had with her, the intimacy his body felt and reacted to from his groin up. It was her?

"Wait a minute, how can you be sure of all this?" Skepticism still vibrated through Justin Etnas, the awareness of the news throwing him off guard.

"I knew you would ask that, that's why I had the morgue do a DNA test report on Sasha Henderson and the boy, I wanted to be sure before I said anything to you."

"You what? I don't believe this bullshit. You mean to tell me that woman has fucked me up for years, the same bitch that gave away her son was going to give him away to the state, befriended my ex-lover from eight years before and hurt all her friends was the same woman, Jane Doe, who left my hospital years ago? That makes no damn sense."

This information broke Justin. He was trying to be strong, holding it together as not to fall apart from the loss of his friend, finding out that Joshua was the one Kayla was fucking all along right under his nose, that the parent of a dying boy was right in front of him. To make matters worse, the only one of their friends that he met and liked was gone, dead; all because of Sasha. This whole thing was because of and revolved around her. Even in death she was still fucking everybody up.

Justin banged at his office wall and sent his desk chair flying out the window.

"This is ridiculous. Do you know how unbelievable all this is?" He turned to Dr. McKinley who expected Dr. Etnas to react somehow.

"I didn't even know her name." Justin said before he put his hands over his face to hold back the anger and devastation that was threatening to over take him.

"This is not your fault Justin. Sometimes the world works in mysterious ways and we can never control how the cards of our life will play out. All we can do is do our best to be good and prepare for whatever comes." Dr. McKinley told him, moving slowly towards the grieving young doctor who seemed to have finally allowed the past week to sink in and feel the pain of the situation.

"Don't touch me." Justin didn't want Calvin to comfort him, but Dr. McKinley pursued anyway. He pulled Justin into his fatherly embrace and held him.

"It's okay my young doctor friend. It's okay. Let it all out. That chapter of your life has come to a close and you can let it go now. Let it go." Dr. McKinley whispered in Justin's ears. He held on tight to Justin who tried to push him away and resist the consolation, but this Dr. McKinley, a father of four grown boys and getting up in age in his mid sixties, had seen many cases of sadness and grief as a doctor, as a man and as a father. He had to hold on to this one. He couldn't let Justin handle this one on his own.

"Please doctor, please let me be alone for a moment." Justin pleaded, "I need to clear my head." He told him in resignation.

"Justin…" Dr. McKinley started, as they were both startled by the knock at Justin's office door. Before they could answer, Kayla had turned the handle and slightly stuck her head in.

"I'm sorry, I didn't mean to disturb anything." I didn't expect there to be anyone with Justin. When I got his message about coming by it was the best news I had in months. I felt like my entire life was falling apart and having to tell Karen's mom that her only child was gone and to deal with how my friends died have really freaked me out, bringing me face to face with my own mortality.

I was hoping that this could be the day of new beginning

for us. A day when I could sit down with Justin and put an end to the gap that the years had brought between us. Being able to see him again like this gave me enough of a thrill to get out of bed this morning and I couldn't wait to see him. I really hoped this third wheel would be leaving soon.

"I am really sorry for barging in Justin, I got your message about the package you wanted me to pick up. I hope you don't mind that I stopped by today." I said hoping to remind him that he had invited me.

Dr. McKinley looked at Justin with curiosity on his face. He looked at Kayla closely and ushered her in. Then he turned once again and absorbed Justin's disposition to see if he was okay.

Justin was flustered; this was all happening too fast. He felt overwhelmed by the information of Sasha that had been dropped in his lap, as though he had no feelings. He felt like a fool and a complete idiot. How was he to live with himself now knowing all that had transpired right before his very eyes and hadn't seen it?

He looked toward Kayla who stood there with a big smile on her face. He looked into her eyes and was transported back to a time when he could almost see her pain, desires and joys. At this moment, he saw it again. He felt her energy as though it was only yesterday that he last saw her. He knew she wanted to reunite and he felt a familiar urge to take her into his arms. But he couldn't. Whatever he felt for her she killed and took them away herself. Leaving was her choice and she left him to deal with the repercussions of it. Now she must face up to the consequences of her own actions because he has finally moved on.

Justin cleared his throat and ran his hands through his dreadlocks before speaking. He was looking for a headband to pull it into a ponytail but found none.

"Dr. Calvin McKinley, this is Kayla McIntosh." Justin

introduced and watched as they shook hands. "It *is* still McIntosh, isn't it?" Justin asked sarcastically.

"Yes Justin, my name is still the same." My heart jumped in anticipation. Maybe he just wanted to make sure it was safe for him to make a move. I really hoped we were still connected the way we use to be. There use to be a time when we could almost read each other.

"Kayla was a friend of the deceased." He informed his elder colleague.

"Ms. McIntosh I am very sorry to hear about your loss."

"No it's fine, thanks for your condolences." I told him, as thoughts of how much this older gentleman knew barraged my mind.

"Kayla was also very special to me when we were younger. We dated while I was in medical school and she also knew my best friend Joshua who I told you was killed recently." Justin informed. He wanted to let Kayla know that there were no more secrets for him. Everything was out now as it should be because he was moving on.

"Yes, Justin and I had only recently been reunited. I am hoping that this time we will stay in each others lives." I said to no in particular. I looked at Justin as I said those words hoping he could see that the love I held for him all those years never diminished and that I wanted and was open to a relationship once again. I wanted Justin to know that I was there for him and this time there would be no running away.

"Wow, there is quite some history here then." Dr. McKinley acknowledged and then turned to Justin. He could feel the tension raise and see the dismay on his younger counterpart's face. He did not look pleased.

"Should I go then?" Dr. McKinley asked. But before he could make his exit the door was tapped softly. Justin shook his head clear of the confusion he felt for a second and then it hit him who it might be that was tapping so gently at his office door this time. It had to be Chyna. Her presence always seemed to clear things up. The thought of Kayla meeting Chyna amused him and a smirk appeared on his face that was so noticeable that Dr. McKinley sat down and raised his eyebrows curiously.

Justin excused himself and walked toward the door. He slowly opened it to an illuminated Chyna. She threw her arms around him and kissed him on his forehead, nose, cheeks, eyes, ears and lips, whispering she loved him with each tenderly placed affection.

"Chyna, sweetheart, we have company." Justin whispered with a smog look of satisfaction on his face. He could feel Kayla's eyes burning in his back.

"Oops, I am so sorry." Chyna said quickly composing herself and blushing from ear to ear.

"Dr. Calvin McKinley. Kayla" Justin grinned, taking Chyna by the hand and placing her securely in front of him. "This," he said, turning to look at her with pride and hope in his eyes. Then looking back at Kayla and Dr. McKinley he took a deep breath. "This is Chyna Campuzano, the woman who is soon to be my wife." He exhaled, as though the words had been kept hostage in his heart and were finally freed.

Chyna gasped and turned to look at him.

"Yes Chyna. I heard what I said. I know I don't have a ring, with all that has been happening I didn't have time. But I hope you will complete my life by saying yes."

"Yes Justin, I want to complete my life with you."

"Congratulations," Dr. McKinley jumped from his seat in front of Justin's desk and shook Justin's hands firmly. "What a beautiful woman Justin, I think she loves you the way you deserve." Dr. Calvin McKinley said with a broad smile, everyone almost forgetting that I was present.

I couldn't take it anymore, watching them smooch and

cuddle with their wonderful news right in front of me. It was like seeing Sasha hanging from that window all over again, but this time, it was me who was hanging there dying. I had to get out of there. The air suddenly became dense and heavy and the walls were closing in on me.

"I am sorry, I have to go." I told them making my way around Chyna and Justin to the door.

"Kayla wait." Chyna stopped her holding on to her hands lightly stopping her from leaving. "I am really sorry about your friends. Justin told me what happened and I cannot tell you how much I wish that things were different. I met Karen an she was so wonderful." Chyna tried to express her sympathies to Kayla, but Kayla was in no mood to be nice to the woman who took her last chance at making things right with Justin.

"Yes, I supposed that she was. Excuse me." I told her, pulling my arm from her grasp and reached for the door.

"Kayla wait. The package." She was stopped again and watched as Justin released Chyna from his embrace and moved toward his desk where his backpack rested on the floor. He reached inside and pulled out the beautifully embossed journal with Joshua's name on it.

"I would like you to have this."

"Justin, that's Joshua's journal. Where did you get it?" I asked, alarm struck me and I knew that there was something more to this.

"Joshua's mother sent it to me as a gift. She said that Joshua would have liked for me to have it. I read it from cover to cover, and now I would like to pass it to you."

"But, I don't know what to say." I told him, not wanting to take it. I just had this eerie feeling that this book would end something very precious to me.

"Justin I am so sorry." I said, as I realized what Justin must have read, must know by now why he appeared so cold and distanced from me.

"Don't be sorry Kayla. It took all these years and all of this pain for the truth to surface. There is nothing left between us now, except that we both obviously had special experiences with Joshua. He would have taken your secret to the grave had he not written it down." Justin told her calmly. He felt strangely free and light.

"Okay." It was all I could say. I had lost everything at that moment. No friends, no man since Michael left and who I had yet to hear from since that day, and now, no more Justin. My past had gone full circle. I hung my head and walked out the door.

"Justin, you have been blessed with many things. You are a good man and from what I have witnessed, without much explanation, you have a good heart. I hope you will be able to move on now from all of this and blossom into the great doctor you are and will continue to be. It has been my pleasure to be assigned here at this hospital for this case and to have met you." Dr. McKinley said finally bringing himself to his feet as he studied the joy that beamed from both Chyna and Justin's face.

"I think my job here is done. So I might be gone when you return from your bereavement leave."

"Doctor," Justin sighed and moved to stand before him. "Thank you."

"This has been the reason I first became a doctor Justin. You have managed to remind of the flame that gave me peace and inspiration." Justin embraced him and held onto him firmly then pulled away.

"I will expect you to be at our wedding then." Justin said with a smile, reaching for Chyna who moved and stood beside him in agreement.

"I wouldn't miss it for the world." Dr. Calvin McKinley said and headed out of Justin's office.

THE END